Praise for *Betrayed*

"Unforgettable characters, taut action—Bell nails every page. Each time I thought I had it figured out, I was wrong. I loved that."
—*Amy Atwell, Amazon/B&N Bestselling Author of* Ambersley

"Betrayed is a tightly-plotted, edge-of-your-seat ride with fresh, vivid characters. I could not put this book down."
—*Susan M. Boyer, Agatha winning author of the* Liz Talbot Mystery Series

"Five stars ***** Two thumbs up!!

Absorbing and fast-paced from the chilling opening chapters to the shocking denouement, Donnell Ann Bell proves once again to be a master of suspense with Betrayed, a tale of consequences from a Colorado woman's long-ago indiscretion that domino into a nightmare of deception, bitterness, greed, and murder. A compelling must-read!"
—*Rochelle Staab, bestselling author of the* Mind for Murder Mysteries

Other Donnell Ann Bell Titles from Bell Bridge Books

Deadly Recall

The Past Came Hunting

Buried Agendas

Black Pearl

Betrayed

by

Donnell Ann Bell

Bell Bridge Books

This is a work of fiction. Names, characters, places and incidents are either the products of the author's imagination or are used fictitiously. Any resemblance to actual persons (living or dead), events or locations is entirely coincidental.

Bell Bridge Books
PO BOX 300921
Memphis, TN 38116
Print ISBN: 978-1-61194-372-6

Bell Bridge Books is an Imprint of BelleBooks, Inc.

We at BelleBooks enjoy hearing from readers.
Visit our websites – www.BelleBooks.com and www.BellBridgeBooks.com.

10 9 8 7 6 5 4 3 2 1

Cover design: Debra Dixon
Interior design: Hank Smith
Photo/Art credits:
Shattered glass (manipulated) © Randy Mckown | Dreamstime.com

:Lvbn:01:

Dedication

To Mo,

My heroines are fictional. You're the real deal.

Chapter One

Oklahoma City, Oklahoma

IF WEBB JENKINS winked and said, "Good luck, little lady," one more time, Irene Turner would be hard pressed not to look over her shoulder—the one with the 12-gauge shotgun nestled beneath it—and quip, "Thank you, little fella." That, or maybe she'd just tell Webb's wife about all that winking the next time she and Stephen got together with the couple.

To call Irene "little" made about as much sense as her calling Webb, a lumberjack-in-disguise, "tiny." Irene stood five-foot-eight inches tall.

Besides, there was no luck involved in this charity exhibition to aid tornado disaster relief. At one time or another, both she and Webb had been trap shooting champions.

Thankfully, her ear protection muffled any other comments he made to the range safety operators. She resisted an eye roll behind her amber shooting glasses and ignored the overgrown oaf who sported a fine-looking over/under trap gun. Better shooters than Webb had tried to mess with her head. Well, this event proved she was back, so let him try.

The operators stood by. The smell of spent gun powder filled the air. Irene took her place at the designated station. Inside the trap house several feet in front of her, an oscillating machine sat loaded and ready to do its job.

She snapped the gun to her shoulder and hollered, "Pull." A clay bird flew from the trap house. She led the target, tracked it, and squeezed the trigger. The bird exploded into a puff of black dust.

But darned if old Webb didn't hit his targets, too. The match continued; neither missed. People on the sidelines cheered; onlookers in the stands came to their feet.

It was seventy degrees on this clear blue day. At one-hundred-forty pounds, Irene dripped with sweat, and her gun grew heavy from so many fires. She could just imagine at two-hundred-forty something what Webb must have been going through. But at least he'd tired of all that winking. Nor, come to think of it, was he wishing her luck anymore. As a matter of fact, with every clay pigeon she brought down, he gave her a look that said *this is war.*

While Irene tried for an expression that said, *oh, don't be a bad sport.*

Finally, after decimating one hundred clay birds, the two tied. Their vests lighter from spent ammo, Irene and Webb headed to the 27-yard line for a sudden-death shoot off.

The crowd joined in a collective groan when she missed the last target. While in truth, it left her ready to jump up and down. Her imperfect score had saved Webb's manhood and raised money for a worthy cause. Most importantly, this tourney had restored her confidence. As Webb sauntered off with his back-slapping cronies, he was either so generous or so relieved not to have been bested by a woman he doubled his contribution to the charity.

Afterward, her shotgun unloaded and secured in her trunk, she sat in the clubhouse with friends. The waiter delivered their entrées, but with Irene's, he included a note. Assuming it was from her husband who said he'd be in meetings all day, she tore through the seal.

But Stephen hadn't left her a message. As unobtrusively as possible, she made her excuses and left the table. Alone in the parking lot, Irene reread the letter, trembling.

Mrs. Turner, urgent I speak with you. It concerns the death of your child. ~ Mrs. Norma Mitchell

"YOU'VE GONE PALE, Mrs. Turner. Do you understand what I'm saying to you?"

Irene stared back at the elderly woman seated across from her. The students and faculty in the crowded Oklahoma University café all but disappeared. Dizzy from the sudden roaring in her ears, the smell of pastry and coffee made her gag.

Torn between outrage and being sick, Irene said, "No, Mrs. Mitchell, I don't understand. I'm not sure you know what you're saying. How can my little girl be alive, particularly, when I was told I delivered a stillborn?"

Tears welled in the old woman's eyes.

Irene had never treated a senior citizen so rudely in her life, yet this was too much. The only reason she'd agreed to meet Norma Mitchell was because Irene thought the author of the note had information on Danny's bus accident. But the meeting had nothing to do with her teenaged son's death. The woman wanted to meet Irene concerning a costly mistake she'd made twenty-eight years ago.

"Forget falling off the turnip truck yesterday, lady, I've never been on one." Irene clenched her jaw so hard she thought it might snap. "You were once Dr. Mitchell's nurse. All right, I get it. You later married him. I get that, too. What I don't get is why I'm here and what you hope to accomplish by bringing this up."

Mrs. Mitchell lowered her head. "Was, Mrs. Turner. *Was* married. Cliff died six weeks ago after a long struggle with Parkinson's. I finally had the strength to clean out his office. And what I'm saying to you is that you've been horribly duped." Reaching into an oversized handbag, the woman's arthritic fingers shook. She withdrew a file and slid it across the table. "I found a false drawer in his desk. I want you to know, I've instructed my attorney to do whatever it takes to make this right."

Make what right?

Studying the white-haired lady, Irene tried to rationalize the situation. Norma Mitchell had to be in her eighties. Was she senile? While going through the long-retired doctor's effects, had she stumbled upon information that confused Irene with one of his other patients?

Look at the file and be as kind as you can when you set her straight.

The file's contents, however, did nothing to settle Irene's stomach. The first pages contained patient history sheets. *Hers.* They listed her maiden name, age, weight, and pregnancy charts. After the history sheets, the file included a non-negotiable copy of a cashier's check. Her gaze honed in on a bank signature and an illegible scrawl made payable to the *Mitchell Medical Clinic* and the *Victoria Mitchell Memorial Home for Girls.* Nothing alarming there. Irene knew both places instantly.

Years ago, the Victoria Mitchell residence had been her home for the last three months of her pregnancy when she'd defied her parents and refused to give up her baby for adoption. It was the ungodly amount of eight hundred thousand dollars that stole her breath away.

The whirring in her ears growing louder, Irene moved on to an envelope marked simply "Kinsey." Inside were photographs, along with invoices bearing the letterhead of the Trevelle Detective Agency, labeled, "Yearly Observations." Photo number one, dated 1983, was of a smiling toddler pulling a sled on a snowy day. Her rosy cheeks matched the color of her snowsuit, and wisps of dark brown hair the color of Irene's peaked out from beneath her fur-lined hood.

In the second image, Kinsey looked to be about four or five. She and two playmates hung from the monkey bars. Whoever had taken the shot had used a black marker to draw a circle around Kinsey. Irene's heart twisted. With or without the marker, Irene would have known her. The child bore an uncanny resemblance to Danny at that age.

As surreal became real, she located a snapshot dated 1989. Decked out in an athletic uniform, Kinsey stood with her hands on her hips, one foot resting proudly on a soccer ball.

The timeline advanced, every picture depicting the girl's passion for the game of soccer.

In the last image dated 2001, there was nothing awkward or gangly about Kinsey. During what appeared to be the end of a championship match, she sat triumphant, hoisted on the shoulders of her teammates, while a banner in the background read, "We love you, Special K."

Irene pressed a shaking hand to her pounding heart and choked on her warring emotions. Special K was the nickname of a world-class athlete whose fame had crossed the line to celebrity, who up until this second had been no more than an interesting tidbit to Irene.

"You're too calm, Mrs. Turner," Mrs. Mitchell spoke at last. "You may be in shock. May I get you something?"

Shock? No. She'd simply regressed to the icy numbness that had claimed her when she'd learned about Danny's death. Damn it. Where were her tears? Today, after the shooting match, she'd thought she was back.

"I know it's no consolation, but whoever adopted your daughter seems to love her and has cared for her greatly."

Slowly, Irene lifted her head. The restaurant once more came into focus, and the events of the past twenty-eight years skidded into place. "You're right," she said. "That's no consolation." She rose from the table and commandeered the file. "Were you serious about making things right?"

Mrs. Mitchell stammered, "I—I have no choice. Cliff's daughter will fight me, of course. Would a monetary settlement help in any way?"

There was only one checking account Irene wanted to drain at the moment.

So much made sense now. Stephen's reappearance during her third trimester after his adamant rejection. Then, his performance in the delivery room. She'd awoken in a drugged stupor to find him holding her hand and sobbing, telling her she'd lost the baby.

Irene snapped back from the past. "I don't want money just yet. What I want is the use of a computer. Also, I won't be using my credit cards, so I could use a place to stay."

"Will my house do?" Mrs. Mitchell's voice quivered. "Now that Cliff's gone, I live alone. I have a computer. You can have complete run of the place. Won't you at least tell me what you're thinking?"

Irene knew better than to voice it out loud to a perfect stranger, no matter how sympathetic Norma Mitchell appeared. But for the first time in her forty-six years, she thought herself capable of using her sharpshooter skills on something other than a clay pigeon or a paper target. If she went home, she'd put a bullet through her husband's lying skull.

"I'm thinking my daughter's been raised by her biological father, and my husband of twenty-seven years helped him do it."

Norma Mitchell gasped.

"You claim I've been duped," Irene said. "That's too kind of a word. I've been *betrayed*."

Chapter Two

AT FIRST WHEN Irene vanished for several hours, Stephen Turner worried. His call to her mother netted him nothing—Vanessa hadn't heard from Irene. He was seconds from calling the police when the First National Bank president phoned and said she'd been in, emptied their joint checking account and most of their savings. Concerned, Wendell wanted to know if there was a problem with the bank's customer service.

Stephen glanced at Danny's picture over the fireplace and shook his head. He'd thought she'd been improving. He should have insisted Irene seek counseling. From here on out, no matter how much she fought him, she was going on meds.

"How much did she take, Wendell?"

"Twenty-six-thousand dollars," the bank official replied. "Of course, she didn't touch the other accounts. They're in your name only. But I got to thinking, maybe you were upset with us, too."

He'd been careless letting Irene keep so much money in their joint account. Stephen gripped the phone hard. "Nah, not upset. You know Irene. She's been through a lot since we lost Danny. Probably took something I said the wrong way. I'll clear this up when she gets home."

"Uh, that's the thing." Wendell cleared his throat. "When I said to give you my regards, she told me to tell you myself. Said the next time she saw you, it'd be in court. Then she walked out, pretty as you please, got into that slick black Mercedes you bought her—"

"Wendell," Stephen growled. "You repeat this to anyone, and I *will* take my money out of your bank. My wife's unstable. I'd ask you to show her a little kindness and not be a party to spreading gossip."

"You're the only person I've said a word to," Wendell backtracked. "Just thought you should know. We go back a long way."

Stephen sighed and raised his gaze to the ceiling. Third grade to be exact. The only reason this clown got to be a president of *any* bank was his granddaddy came from money.

Well, Stephen Turner was richer than most these days, thanks to a smart move that had set him up years ago. Not the proudest moment in his life. But damn Irene, she belonged to him. For years he'd taken precautions in case his accounts were frozen and the Feds showed up. When that didn't happen, and the years passed, it was as though the incident never occurred.

No. She couldn't possibly know. If she did, Irene wouldn't be saying, "See you in court," he'd be in handcuffs right now.

He said good-bye to Wendell and tossed the phone on his desk. Ungrateful bitch. She'd stepped out on him, and, still, he'd given her another chance. He paced over the antique carpet she was so proud of.

All right. She'd gotten a bee in her bonnet about something. He'd leave her a message. That way, when she cooled off and came to her senses, she'd know where he stood. He picked up the phone and punched in the number to her cell.

But in the next moment when Stephen listened to an automated recording stating, "The number you have reached is no longer in service," he stopped stomping all over Irene's rug. Suddenly, he had the damnedest notion he knew where she stood.

WEARING YESTERDAY'S clothes, Irene entered Norma Mitchell's elegant south side home and stood in the foyer. Irene should probably confront Stephen. Still, learning after all these years that Evan Masters had conspired with her husband to take her daughter did not put her in a conversational mood. She wanted to shoot first and talk later. Besides, if the man had any brains—he obviously didn't have a conscience—he'd figure out pretty quick that she was leaving him.

His constant calls had annoyed her. To put an end to that nonsense, she'd closed her cell phone account and bought a prepaid plan at the local Walmart.

Mrs. Mitchell, now Norma to Irene, had proven to be a godsend. She might have been married to a non-ethical, greedy louse, but she appeared to be a beacon of honesty.

How ironic that Irene was using Mitchell's office to research the crime the doctor had perpetrated. As for Kinsey's father, if anyone would have told Irene that Evan Masters was capable of such deceit, she would have called him a liar. But the fact that Kinsey had been ripped from Irene in such a cruel fashion showed she hadn't known him at all.

It had never entered her mind that Kinsey Masters was Evan's daughter when she scanned a newspaper article or watched TV footage. Masters was a common enough name, and the girl was the star, not her father. Still, Irene berated herself for not paying attention. If she had, perhaps she would have discovered the resemblance between Kinsey and Danny years ago. Her daughter would be with Irene now, and these bastards behind bars, or at the very least, penniless and disgraced.

Norma came downstairs as Irene hung up the older woman's blue jacket in the entryway closet. "Thanks for letting me borrow it. When I left my place on Wednesday, it never occurred to me I wouldn't be going back."

"Looks better on you, anyway," Norma said in a way Irene best described as genteel. "I've been thinking about what you said last night."

"Oh, what part?" Irene replied wryly. "I said quite a lot. I hope you'll forgive all my ranting and name calling."

Norma smiled. "After the shock I gave you, you're entitled. I've called Clifford a few names myself over the past few days. I can't for the life of me understand why he was a party to this. I know I sound like I'm defending him, but in twenty-four years of marriage, I never knew him to be less than ethical. Anyway, where was I? Oh, yes, your son's portrait. You said it's the one thing you hate to leave behind."

Could a heart actually rip in two? Irene spread her hands. "If I go home . . ." No, that wasn't right. The home she'd shared with her husband and son didn't exist anymore. ". . . back to the house, I'm likely to do something I'd enjoy in the heat of the moment, but pay for later. By the way, did you call your attorney? Is he willing to file divorce papers on my behalf?"

"He is." Norma straightened her shoulders and motioned Irene into the living room. "What if *I* go to the house? What if I get Danny's picture for you?"

In that moment, Irene wanted to hug the old woman. She and Norma were fast becoming friends. Dropping onto the couch, both from physical and mental exhaustion, Irene leaned against the headrest. "As much as I want to say yes, I can't let you do that."

"Doesn't Stephen work?"

"Does a porcupine have quills? All the time. Although thanks to my vanishing act, he may have changed his schedule. Plus, on more than one occasion, he's worked from home."

Norma joined Irene on the sofa. "Nevertheless, I'd like to try. I may be old, but I'm still spry. What does the wretch drive?"

Wretch? Irene resisted a sigh. During last night's tirade, she'd used much stronger language, but so far Norma hadn't been swayed by her bad examples. *Wretch.* Good word. Irene might use it the next time she wanted to impress somebody. "A Cadillac SUV, but my answer is still—"

"You have a garage door opener, right?"

She folded her arms. "I do."

Norma sat forward and clasped her hands. "It's simple then. If his car's there, I close the garage and drive off. Do you have an alarm?"

Her unlikely friend's excitement was contagious. The rest of the house could burn down as far as Irene was concerned, but when she left to meet Kinsey, she wanted the portrait she'd commissioned of her son. "Stephen never arms it."

"It's settled then. Think I'll take a drive," Norma said.

Irene rose from the couch. "Think I'll go with you."

A few hours later, seated in Norma's Lincoln, the two covert watchers sat at an adjacent park observing the comings and goings of the Turner residence. Her neighbors wouldn't question a Lincoln parked near her house; still Irene wasn't willing to risk it.

Near dusk, Stephen finally drove away. Pressing the button to the garage door opener, Irene instructed a protesting Norma to circle the area and wait for her call. Though Norma wanted to come with her, Irene didn't want her in jeopardy. Stephen had never been violent, but then she'd never left him before. Further, Irene was armed, Norma wasn't, and the old woman would just slow her down. Along with Danny's portrait, Irene would take this one-and-only opportunity to pack a few clothes.

After a harrowing thirty minutes, Irene called Norma and opened the garage door for her to drive in. Arms loaded, Irene barreled from the laundry room into the garage where Norma sat waiting. Tossing her suitcase into the backseat, Irene slid into the passenger side and laughed when her accomplice gave her a high-five.

As they sped toward I-40, away from her soon to be ex-property, Irene clutched Danny's likeness to her breast. She was still bitter, but smiling.

Chapter Three

AT FIVE THE NEXT morning, Irene was packed and ready to go. She'd just finished making the guest bed when Norma rapped lightly and asked from the other side of the door, "Are you decent, dear?"

"If you mean do I have clothes on," Irene drawled, "the answer is yes. As for decent, you might want to take that up with someone less biased." Dressed in black leggings and a marigold-colored sweater coat, Irene sat on the bed and zipped up her favorite black boots.

Norma entered, grasping a stack of papers held tight by a binder clip. "My, don't you look fetching. So, you're serious then; you're off to Colorado?"

"I don't see any other choice," Irene said.

"No matter how well intended, you're about to disrupt a young woman's life. Have you thought about that?"

"Only every second of every hour since you told me of her existence. You don't think she has a right to know?"

"She has every right to know." Norma held out the contents in her hand. "I have something for you."

Irene had already packed away Dr. Mitchell's incriminating evidence. She placed a hand to her breast. "If you've come to tell me I'm the mother of triplets—"

"Nothing that dramatic." Smiling, Norma moved farther into the room. "This is information from my attorney. Lyle emailed me last night. I printed it out. Kinsey's father is quite the success story now. Evan Masters is CEO of The Master Plan, a commercial real estate and holding company. His wife Gwyneth owns a gallery, called—wouldn't you know it—Masterpieces, and the two travel in very exclusive circles. Not only because of their financial success, but their daughter's popularity, they've become something of celebrities in their own right around Denver.

"In addition to Kinsey, the Masters have two other children. As a result, you might get where you're going only to face significant hurdles. Lyle suggested you might want to work this out through civil litigation."

"Oh, I don't know," Irene said, rising from the bed and taking the proffered information. "Seems to me I've been pretty doggone civil. Twenty-eight years' worth to let these people have sole, illegal custody of my daughter. The other kids, they're younger?"

"Lauren Masters is twenty-three. Her brother Jay is twenty-one."

"Anything else I should know?"

"Kinsey occasionally makes media appearances, but for the most part, she's retired. Her first love these days is teaching. Naturally, she coaches soccer. She's also involved with an older man."

Irene stiffened. "How much older?"

"Early forties. According to my attorney's report, he's never married."

"I guess that's something. Hopefully, she doesn't take after her mama. At least she's twenty-eight and not eighteen."

At her hostess's worried gaze, Irene hesitated. "I'm angry, Norma, not hurtful. I would never turn Kinsey's life into fodder for the tabloids."

"So, you have a plan?"

Irene held a finger to her temple. "Something's rolling around up here."

"This is none of my business. And I know I shouldn't ask, yet according to these papers, Evan and Gwyneth have been married more than thirty years. How . . ."

"Did I end up pregnant by a married man?" Irene knelt by her suitcase and tucked Norma's research inside an outer compartment. "I guess the plain old truth is I chased him."

Norma lifted an eyebrow. "Something tells me, Mr. Masters didn't work very hard to get away. Apparently this is something you'd prefer not to discuss."

"Another time when I don't have a ten-hour drive in front of me."

"I'll look forward to our talk then. In those papers you'll find my lawyer's contact information. When you're in need of funds, call Lyle. I've instructed him to wire money into your bank account."

"I think we should hash this all out when this nightmare is over."

"In any case, you'll have money if you need it."

In the driveway, Irene hugged Norma then slid behind the wheel of the Mercedes.

"Call when you get settled," Norma said.

"Will do." Danny's portrait sat on the seat beside Irene. Norma had secured it in mesh and bubble wrap. What a dear.

As for her vow to take care, Irene didn't know any other way. Inside her purse she'd tucked away her Smith and Wesson Bodyguard .38 snub-nosed revolver.

Irene headed for the open road and Denver. How appropriate. The challenges and obstacles she faced felt more than a mile high.

Chapter Four

Denver, Colorado

DETECTIVE NATE Paxton yanked open the doors to District Six's Metro Division, identifying with a lobster about to be boiled. His nine-month tar-heroin smuggling investigation had blown up in his face. Short version, he'd been made.

At the emergency summons to break protocol and return to headquarters, Nate had already spouted, in English and in Spanish, every expletive known to his vocabulary. His strides might be long as he raced toward the private conference room his LT had directed, but this was the last place Nate wanted to be.

Forget the illusion he could right a drug-crazed planet. He should have taken his brother's advice and gotten a job in the private sector. Unfortunately, Nate had his own drug of choice. It was called adrenaline, and he was hooked on the job. He and partner Sammy Lucero were good at undercover work—they were outstanding liars with an uncanny ability to get inside a bad guy's head.

Or so Nate had thought. He'd spoken with Guzmán that morning and believed the phony philanthropist was beginning to trust him. Nate had been *this* close to uncovering the source in a drug cartel—reprobates that used the I-25 corridor to hook junior and high school kids on some highly addictive *shit*.

To make matters worse, Nate couldn't get hold of Sammy, and who knew if whoever had fingered Nate had done the same to his partner? The henchman who ran the Denver op of the cartel played for keeps. If Guzmán and his goons had Sammy, and they knew Sam was a cop, he was already in little pieces.

And if Sammy were dead . . . Nate gnashed his teeth. He didn't care that the Feds said lay off Guzmán, the murdering thug was going down.

Nate rounded a wall of cubicles as hot as a Colorado wildfire, knocked once and stormed into the conference room. The air left his lungs. Two men sat at the long oval table, and as his brain kicked in as to who sat beside his commanding officer, Nate found he could breathe again.

Sammy.

Arms folded, slumped in the chair, his wise-cracking partner lifted his chin in a "whaz-up," kind of nod. "Ah, man, were you worried about me?" Sammy glanced toward their lieutenant. "LT, would you look at that? How touching is this? Nate was worried. "

Nate glanced around the cramped quarters. The only thing saving his partner from doing a nosedive through the window was the conference room didn't have one. In a voice threateningly low, Nate asked, "Why didn't you answer your cell?"

"And tip my hand to Guzmán? None of those DEA dudes were around, and one of the cartel's little snitches had laid the hammer down on you."

Lieutenant Art Shields pointed to the pitcher of water at the far end of the table. "All right, you two. Playtime's over. Help yourself, Paxton, then let's get down to business. As of now, the two of you are off Vice."

Nate had just gripped the handle of the pitcher. He turned. Sammy no longer wore that shit-eating grin, and as a matter of fact, he leaned forward.

"That's a mistake, LT," he said, his Hispanic accent more pronounced when he grew upset. "I understand Nate. Guzmán's been suspicious of a *gringo* in the operation. But I can still nail these *pendejos*."

"And maybe I can't be front and center," Nate stressed. "But I can provide backup."

The lieutenant shook his head. "Decision comes from upstairs. We don't know who tipped them off. If they made Paxton, odds are they know about you as well, Lucero. So this is how it's going to be. You'll brief a new team to work with the DEA and then be assigned to a parallel investigation with suspected ties to Guzmán. But until you're off these guys' radars, you're both being reassigned."

"We've got nearly a year invested in this operation. A new team begins at Square One," Nate said incredulously.

"And how do you explain *my* disappearance?" Sammy lurched from his chair, nearly toppling it. "We have to go home some time, LT. You might as well advertise Nate's and my association on the scoreboard at Rockies Stadium if I suddenly don't show up. I'm supposed to make a drop in two days. I'm carrying around Guzmán's bread."

Lieutenant Shields folded one massive arm over another. "Through with your tantrums, children? That money becomes police evidence now. Also, if I were you, I'd think about finding temporary places to live. And, yeah, my order may come from the top, but for the record, I agree with it. Your jobs are risky enough. If Guzmán and his asswipes know you're law enforcement, you might as well strap bullseyes to your foreheads. We're not sacrificial goats. So quit your bellyaching. You're both being reassigned to Major Crimes."

A bitter taste rose in Nate's mouth. Every second of every day, thanks to the war on drugs, atrocities were committed against innocents on both sides of the border. It did no good to concentrate on Guzmán and those at the local level. They needed to cut off the head of the major player behind the cartel. But the LT was right. Best to have one's skin attached while doing it.

Off Vice? Nate tamped down the roar that threatened to rise up from his chest. He'd been undercover so long he wasn't sure what to do with himself.

He ran a hand over a face he no longer shaved.

Nate glanced at Sammy. He gave a noncommittal shrug. True, they wouldn't be where the action was, but as liaisons they could still have a part in bringing these lowlifes down.

"Another thing," Shields said. "When we're through here, report to Personnel. Tomorrow when you transfer, the two of you come in looking like detectives and not impersonating meth addicts."

Dismissed, Nate walked with Sammy toward Human Resources. He gave Nate the once over and grumbled, "You may look like a meth addict, but I don't look like a meth addict."

Nate glared at his partner. "I really wanted that conference room to have a window."

TWO DAYS LATER, Nate stood at a four-by-six-foot corkboard displaying a North American map. He was clean-shaven, dressed in a shirt and tie, pissed, and on to something. The parallel investigation his former lieutenant had said Nate and Sammy would work was heading south. Literally.

Pinheads of red, blue, and yellow trailed down the map of Colorado, extending all the way to the New Mexico border and into Mexico beyond. Arrest records had revealed some of the mules used in transporting the deadly black tar heroin into the United States had been picked up in sting operations during chop shop raids.

Nate stared at the spread of color dotting the map. Red represented parties arrested for both drug possession and auto theft, blue simply for auto theft, yellow for heroin. Well, would you look at that? Red really was a primary color.

He reached for a new box of pins. Didn't any of these bangers do time? They were in and out of prison with the frequency of a revolving door. The dismal economy hadn't helped, either. Crooked Americans owning two-bit auto-part stores and disreputable car dealerships had gone into business with these thugs. Stolen or hijacked vehicles were disappearing from driveways, garages, and shopping malls at an alarming rate, and citizens were screaming for law enforcement to put an end to it.

Yeah, right. He was a cop not a miracle worker. A cartel had the legs of a centipede.

Nate slid a glance toward Sammy. His partner sat opposite Nate's desk, squinting and pressing a palm to the headphones that covered his ears. The last few weeks Sammy had gotten closer to Guzmán's goons, and he'd worn a wire. Little good that intel would do them now. Their new boss, Major Crimes supervisor Lieutenant George Montoya, had given Sammy forty-eight hours to compile a report and hand it off to their liaison replacements.

By the sneer on Sammy's face, he didn't like the new setup any better than Nate. Per their former lieutenant's directive, Sammy had traded in jeans and a T-shirt for a suit. Ever the rebel, however, the last thing Sam was giving up was his soul patch or his ponytail.

So much for playing a part in bringing down a cartel. Major Crimes was as overtaxed as Vice, and Montoya was anxious for Nate and Sammy to take on his department's assignments.

As for their partnership, who knew how long that would last?

Nate tried to refocus on the corkboard, when the new boss made an appearance, escorting a woman through the division as though she were made of glass. Nate hadn't yet decided what to make of the barrel-chested man with the slicked-back gray hair. So far, he found Lieutenant Montoya as standoffish as a Saguaro cactus and just as sharp.

Nate had long dismissed the lieutenant from his thoughts when twenty minutes later, he headed Nate's way. Noticeably free of the woman he'd come in with, he said under his breath, "Paxton. Any truth what I read in your file? You're some kind of psychology buff?"

"I completed my Masters. Never finished my PhD—"

"Did I ask for your curriculum vitae?" Montoya made a tugging motion for Sammy to lose the headphones. Including Sammy in their conversation, Montoya used the same hushed tone, "There's a woman in my office, an Irene Turner. Oklahoma City resident. She's either the most tragic victim I've ever met, or not all there, if you catch my drift."

"How's that?" Nate asked, aware that every detective in the vicinity had stopped work and was scoping them out.

"She claims Kinsey Masters is her daughter."

Nate leaned back in his chair.

Sammy let out a low whistle. "I've never heard Special K was adopted."

"According to the woman in my office, she wasn't. Irene Turner claims Kinsey was stolen at birth."

Nate's mind wound back to the sitcom-like family he'd known for years. Kins didn't resemble her mom, but there was no question she had her father's height and coloring. "I think the Masters might argue that point," Nate said.

"You know 'em?" Montoya asked.

Nate froze. *Way to go, Big Mouth.* He'd traveled in the same group with Kins during high school but hadn't seen her for years. He thought back to his one and only date with Kinsey Masters and fought back a cringe. "Used to. A long time ago."

Sammy spread his palms wide. "Three years. We've been partners for three years. How come you never mentioned you know Special K? You could have got us tickets or something."

Nate shifted his gaze and crossed his arms. "She retired. It didn't come up."

The lieutenant cut in, glowering. "You two want to get back on track? She's waiting. Lucero, get me what you can on this woman and join us in my office. Paxton. You. Come with me."

Outside his office's closed door, Montoya hesitated. "If there's any truth to her story, the FBI might have an interest. It's interstate, felony kidnapping across state lines. But for now, we'll investigate on our own."

"Does she have any proof?" Nate asked.

"Claims she left it at her hotel. Like I said, she seems paranoid."

Nate scoffed. "Paranoid or not, if she wants us to investigate further, we need to see some evidence. Could she be a scammer?"

"You know many scam artists who stay at The Brown Palace Hotel?"

"Only the good ones," Nate said.

Montoya put a hand on the doorknob. "She says she came to us because she's not interested in hurting Kinsey. She wants our help in keeping this quiet, but she wants the responsible parties prosecuted. Plus, she'd like an introduction to her daughter."

"If she's a scammer, I'll bet she does. Why not call her bluff and insist we get a DNA test before we pursue this further? If she balks, we have our answer."

"Good plan. Let's see how she reacts." Lieutenant Montoya opened the door.

Nate followed him in. A trim woman in a figure-hugging pantsuit stood, hands clasped behind her back. She peered over Montoya's credenza, her interest apparently in his prize-mounted rainbow trout.

When they entered, she pivoted. "What a beauty," she said, brown eyes twinkling, Oklahoma accent unmistakable.

Nate curbed his surprise. She'd taken the words right out of his mouth.

The lieutenant introduced Nate; he extended his hand. Too bad the courts deemed *eyesight* inadmissible for determining parentage, because in this case, Nate didn't need DNA. Although older, the woman standing before him was the mirror image of Kinsey Masters.

Chapter Five

PEOPLE SAID RODRIGO Guzmán had the patience of Mother Theresa, but tonight, his tolerance was down to a thread. Pressing his thumb and index finger to the bridge of his nose, he clenched his jaw and replied to the imbecile on the other end, "No, Rafa, I don't expect you to barge into police headquarters and kill him. I don't want you to kill him at all. What I expect you to do is watch him, follow him. And then, when there are no *witnesses,* bring him to me."

"Gladly," Rafa argued. "But how? Your rat's a cop. Cops can spot a tail."

Rodrigo closed his eyes and shook his head. At times, Rafa served his purpose. This wasn't one of them. For most of Rodrigo's life, he'd worked to stay out of the gangs and only associated with them on the fringes. Now, much to his disgust, he'd been recruited by a cartel. He'd done everything within his power to climb out of the Denver slums. The cartel's bosses, called *jefes,* however, recognizing Rodrigo's intelligence, had sent him to school and made him richer than he ever dreamed possible.

And condemned him to the life he'd tried to escape.

"You let me down, bringing this *cabrón* into our network. To let him live sends the wrong message," Rodrigo said. "Our honor is at stake. Do you want the *jefes* to think we are not up to the challenge?"

"I'll deliver Paxton to you, and soon," Rafa replied.

Paxton. Not Gilcrest. *Detective* Nate Paxton. Rodrigo clutched his antique pocket saint and inhaled the scent of the limo's fine leather. If the cop had gotten any closer, he might have derailed Rodrigo's entire life.

"Any news on Eduardo?"

"No," Rafa said. "Eduardo hooks up with his contacts by tending bar. He called in sick the last few days, so I wasn't worried. But he missed a drop this afternoon. He was carrying around some serious *dinero.*"

The *cartel's dinero.* Rodrigo's icon bit into his palm. The arrogant cockroach. "Tell me Eduardo wouldn't be foolish enough to take the *jefes'* money and run."

The normally talkative Rafa remained silent.

One of the risks of running drugs was you couldn't watch people twenty-four/seven. Rodrigo sighed. Maybe one of these days he'd install tracking devices as conditions of employment. "If he's not dead, he better be. Find out what happened to him, too. And Rafa?"

"Yes, *primo.*"

"Cousin or not, the next time you tell me you're not concerned, I'll cut out your tongue."

Rodrigo pushed "end" and said to his driver, "Seventeenth Street, the Grand Hyatt."

He adjusted the platinum cufflinks on his newest tuxedo. Twenty minutes later, the limo deposited him in front of the hotel's posh lobby. His *jefes* had directed him to make a sizeable contribution to the Griff Colburn congressional campaign. Though apolitical himself, the people he worked for were extremely interested in ensuring their products met as little interference at the border as possible. At one time when he still had scruples, Rodrigo might have balked at the chore. After all, he was about to do to Colburn what his *jefes* had done to him.

The man's hand he was required to shake, and whose palm he was about to grease, had promised to vote in a manner that would make that happen.

Rodrigo entered the ballroom hosting the candidate's fundraising activities, immediately connecting with the gazes of two blondes. Returning their smiles and admiring their plunging necklines, he considered stopping to learn their names. Another time. Paxton had to be dealt with before he could relax into more pleasurable pursuits.

Colburn's staffers approached him. The spokesman of the bunch stepped forward and extended his hand. "Mr. Guzmán, thanks for coming. Mr. Colburn's been looking forward to meeting you."

Rodrigo shook the subordinate's hand and located Colburn across the room where the former wide receiver mingled with his supporters. Rodrigo did his best not to frown. The dinner he had no intention of staying for cost five hundred dollars a plate. When he was a boy, five hundred dollars would have fed his family for months. Five hundred dollars might have provided five-year-old Miguel with a competent doctor who wouldn't shirk his oath because a family was too poor to pay. Rodrigo had learned to compartmentalize his grief. But he never forgot. Miguel, ever trusting, with his pain-filled brown eyes, had told anyone who would listen that his ten-year-old brother would save him.

Rodrigo swallowed his sorrow. He found the pain as acute today as it had been back then.

He also took comfort that five hundred dollars was a pittance these days, and that although Miguel had died, other children without resources and with terminal illnesses had lived, thanks to him.

"May I get you a glass of champagne, Mr. Guzmán?"

"I don't drink." Rodrigo checked his watch. "I also have another engagement. So, if you don't mind, I'd like to say hello and extend my support."

For all intents and purposes, the staffer might as well have snapped his fingers. A cocktail waitress disappeared and returned with a tray holding a glass and a bottle of Perrier.

"Right this way, sir."

He negotiated the crowd and sipped his water. Then a few feet away from his target, he made eye contact with Colburn. The politician smiled an expression doubtless practiced in the mirror daily. Tall, muscular, and a Robert Redford-look alike, he had an appeal that would melt glaciers. And, if the moneyed crowd surrounding Colburn was any indication of those backing him, Rodrigo was looking at a future US Congressman.

Colburn pumped Rodrigo's hand and motioned to his drink. "I see we've taken care of you. At last, I get to meet the chairman of Continental Miracles in person and not over the phone."

Rodrigo barely heard the *chulo*. A shapely brunette faced away from him, her backless shimmering red gown revealing strength as well as feminine curves. She turned at the moment Colburn made the statement.

"Continental Miracles? Griff?" She stepped close to the politician.

Finding her face as appealing as her body, Rodrigo felt a stab of envy.

"Rodrigo Guzmán," Colburn said. "I'd like you to meet your biggest fan. Just say the word, she'll go to work for you."

"For free," she said, laughing. "But I'll need to clear it with my students first. You're a legend, Mr. Guzmán. I don't know many who could start an organization at seventeen—"

"That seems like a lifetime ago." Rodrigo held on to her hand. "Although to have such a beautiful woman say such flattering things . . . why do I feel I should know you? If you're the future congressman's wife, he just lost my vote—and my campaign contribution."

"Damn, Kins," Colburn quipped. "I'll need that ring back."

Rodrigo frowned. "Kins?"

Wrapping a possessive arm around her, Griff Colburn said, "Rodrigo Guzmán, may I present the legendary Kinsey Masters. Some people know her better as Special K."

Chapter Six

THE DAY AFTER his introduction to Irene Turner, Nate drove through the old neighborhood toward Lamar Bryant High School to pay Kinsey a visit. Lieutenant Montoya had felt that because Nate had a semi-*almost* connection to her, he was the best man for the job.

As a cop, he wanted the assignment. For personal reasons, he balked.

Yesterday, he'd gone back to Irene's Brown Palace hotel room to review what she claimed was proof. What he'd read in the file locked in her hotel room safe confirmed that something had happened, most likely criminal. Still, evidence could be manufactured. But could it be altered to look *this* old? What's more, Irene remained adamant that until she had a chance to talk to Kinsey, she wanted the file's contents kept quiet. Nor was she anxious to approach the Feds with interstate kidnapping charges.

Crazy. That's what Stephen Turner had said about his wife when Sammy called to corroborate her story. She'd lost a child, all right. Recently. The Turners' son's bus had overturned on its way home from a high school athletic event. As for her claim that a baby had been stolen? Turner called that statement delusional. She'd delivered a stillborn. He knew because he'd been there to witness it.

So, if all that were true, what was with the file's contents: a high-priced cashier's check? And why had someone from a detective agency captured all those images of Kinsey growing up? Which, Sammy had reported was another dead end. The Trevelle agency had gone out of business years ago. And now, while Nate went off to talk with Kinsey, Sammy had a new project on his hands—tracking down the agency's past owners.

Preoccupied, Nate didn't see the high school until he spotted it through the passenger side window. He checked his rearview mirrors and made a correction.

A few seconds later, parked in the visitor section, he switched off the Crown Victoria his boss had ordered him to drive and stared as the damn thing continued to knock. Hoping the car wouldn't explode while he was gone, or worse, when he turned it on again, he climbed out and thought of his ride stashed at police headquarters. His 2004 Ford Explorer, getting up there in miles, had never let him down. Still, Montoya had been adamant. With Guzmán looking for Nate and Sammy, their personal vehicles were off limits.

Nate meandered around the school's aging gymnasium, ambled past the baseball field and athletic center, and closed in on the football stadium, which during the spring and off-season hosted field hockey and soccer.

He stopped on a hill overlooking the field to watch a group of high school girls run drills.

The team, clad in shorts, long socks, and shin guards, was quick, he'd give them that much. But not nearly as fast as one dynamo Nate remembered. Years ago, he'd stood here often after practice, along with every other boy in school, to watch Kinsey Masters head, shoot, and dribble. In essence, take on the world.

His gaze traveled to the sideline where nostalgia overtook him. Clipboard in hand, she moved alongside her players, directing them via verbal commands. Finally, when they weren't performing to her satisfaction, she handed off the clipboard to an observing player. Then, just like old times, Special K sprinted onto the field.

KINSEY LOVED coaching soccer. Truly she did. What she didn't love was a selfish player, and Cara Carmichael was as selfish as they came. "There's a reason we call it passing, Carmichael," Kinsey hollered. "Send me that ball."

The above-average player stopped, put her cleat on the ball, then rolling her eyes at Kinsey, did as she was told.

For the next fifteen minutes, Kinsey concentrated on proving her point. She gained control of the ball, maneuvered it downfield, passing to anyone other than Cara, even when the ponytailed blonde was wide open.

Hands on her hips, the defensive midfielder eventually threw them up in disgust. "All right, Coach, I get what you're saying."

"Not yet you don't." Kinsey glanced toward one of the players on the sideline who hadn't been in yet. "MJ, sub for Cara. You're the striker."

Escorting the sulking teenager off the field, Kinsey held back a smile. Soccer wasn't a "me" sport. You didn't win without intense cooperation and counting on every other player on the field. Early on, a wise coach had done Kinsey this same favor.

Now if she could get the girls' raging hormones under control, they might have a chance at the playoffs. While she'd been scrimmaging with her starting eleven, she'd spotted a stranger watching. Nothing disrupted a teenager's concentration like that of her latest crush or a potential prom date. Kinsey couldn't very well order students not to attend a school-sponsored event, nor would she want to. But she sure as heck could ban boyfriends from attending practice.

Most of the team respected Kinsey and wanted to play. And since she'd issued the unpopular decree, members of the male persuasion had tapered off. But Cara had one beau who was certified trouble. He was notorious for lurking in the distance. He showed up constantly, much like the tall dude in baseball cap and sunglasses on the hill.

"He one of yours?" Kinsey asked.

Cara shaded her eyes and stared off in his direction. *"I wish."*

Kinsey kicked Cara a practice ball. "Work on your dribbling. Be right back."

Trudging up the incline, prepared to set the kid straight, Kinsey stopped midway up the hill. This was no high school student she was about to face. This was an adult male watching her team. He was too young to be one of their parents, and at the thought of a potential predator scoping out her girls, she pulled out her cell phone and prepared to call security.

"This is a closed practice," she called moving upward. "My players are on my clock now, so you'll have to leave."

"What if I'm not interested in the players? What if I prefer the coach?" the wise guy asked.

Much like Cara had, Kinsey shaded her eyes against the afternoon sun. She squinted some nice features into focus and stopped walking. "Nate?"

"Hi ya, Kins."

She gulped in disbelief. She'd spent much of her high school career pining over this creep, and all he had to say to her was, "Hi ya, Kins?"

"I'm working. Is there something I can help you with?"

He pulled aside his hand, revealing a badge clipped to his belt. "Maybe. I'm here on police business."

An odd sense of disappointment clutched at her chest. Somewhere she'd heard Nate had become a cop. Of course he hadn't had a secret crush on her all these years, awoken this morning, and come to his senses.

Really, Kins, he can still get to you? She'd been tied to celebrities, a man running for Congress had proposed. Not that she'd accepted. She was still incensed about Griff's engagement ring comment in front of the Continental Miracles CEO.

Men.

Her inner lovesick teenager disappeared, and the unbendable coach returned. "Does it concern one of my players?"

"It concerns you, Kins." He waved an arm around LBHS's wide open space. There weren't a lot of students on campus after hours, but there were enough. "Out here probably isn't the best place to talk."

Kins. Like everybody else, he'd called her that when they were kids. Even so, Nate using her nickname like she meant something to him ticked her off.

Wow, why was she having such a strong reaction to him? She wasn't sure she liked what she saw. The images in her mind were of a cute lanky boy. Standing before her was a fine specimen of man. He'd grown into his body and more.

She glanced at the clock on her phone. "I'll meet you at the baseball field in twenty minutes."

She kept him waiting for thirty. As the sun set and the temperature dropped, early April took on the climate of February. Huddling inside her warm-up jacket, Kinsey climbed the bleachers to sit beside him. She could easily picture him on the pitcher's mound. Just like the boys she tried to keep from distracting her girls, she'd come here often to sneak a peek at Nate.

"You said you had police business that concerns *me*?"

He nodded. "How're your folks, Kins?"

Well, that was truly irritating. Claim to be on police business and start out with small talk? She shoved her freezing hands inside her pockets. "They're fine, Nate, and . . ." Oh, God, she'd been about to quip, "And yours?" But like the scuttlebutt of him becoming a cop, she'd heard that his mom had passed away.

Kinsey had been overseas at the time, consumed with the Women's World Cup, so the details had been sketchy. But Janet Paxton had been a junior high school guidance counselor and a wonderful lady. Kinsey had often sat in these very stands with her to watch her son play.

She'd liked Mrs. Paxton too much not to say so. "I was sorry to hear about your mom."

"Thanks." He stared out at the baseball diamond. "We miss her."

Kinsey could only imagine how it would feel to lose either of her parents. She held out a palm. "She read my fortune once." Tracing a finger over her lifeline, Kinsey glanced around the stands. "We were sitting around here somewhere."

Nate laughed and shook his head. "She told everyone their fortunes. She was like that. My mother was into New Age."

Typical. Don't let me believe I was special. Kinsey smirked. "So, I assume she told you yours?"

His arrogant smile faded. "Once."

"And?"

He turned his head to look at her. Kinsey couldn't see his dark eyes behind those mirrored lenses, but intuitively she knew she'd broached a painful issue. "She said she didn't see me living long unless I changed directions."

Kinsey blinked. "She told you that in high school?"

"She said that to me four years after I became a cop." He returned his gaze to the field. "Your turn. What'd she say to you?"

"Hmm." Kinsey screwed up her mouth and tried to recall. "Something like, 'Don't count on love until you know who you are.'"

The man next to her deflated as though someone had let the air out of him. He leaned forward and clasped his hands. Strong hands that no doubt knew their way around a gym and a woman. He barely looked at her when he said, "How certain are you that Gwyneth Masters is your birth mother?"

The question was so unexpected that Kinsey shifted so she could see him better on the bleachers. "This is your police business? Really, Nate?" She laughed. "You've known my parents for years."

"That's true. Answer my question?"

Wow, when had he turned into such a cop? "Am I certain that my mom's my real mom? *Yes.*"

"You have a birth certificate?"

Time to nip this craziness in the bud. "Two as a matter of fact," she said doling out sarcasm. "One is from the hospital. It has my two little footprints and everything. The other is certified by the state, and the one I use for my *passport*. Once upon a time, I traveled internationally. And in front of God and everybody, both pieces of paper state that Evan Michael Masters and Gwyneth Joan Barry are my parents. What's going on, Nate?"

"Have they ever been separated?"

Kinsey rose from the stands. "You get to ask all the questions, but I don't get to know where they're coming from? Is that how you work?"

He held out his hands then dropped them. "If this was about anybody but you."

"I'll make it easy on you then. Not only are your questions out of line, they're ridiculous. We're done here." She bounded from the bleachers.

He followed, and with no trouble at all, caught up to her. *Show off.* She'd always admired his speed. "Kins—"

She kept walking. "Don't call me that. My friends call me that, and you haven't earned the right."

"I am your friend. Always have been. Just not in the way you wanted. I met a woman who claims to be your birth mom. I've seen what I think is substantial proof. She looks just like you."

Kinsey increased her strides. She hated to pull the celebrity card, but she could see no other way. "There are a lot of bad people in this world, Nate. People who see opportunities and use others to extort money. Do you have any idea how many people have contacted me with the claim they're my long-lost relative?"

The corners of his mouth tugged upward. Was he *laughing* at her?

"About those bad people, thanks for the news flash." His cell phone rang. Nate let it ring. "Will you at least agree to meet her?"

His caller was unrelenting.

"You should get that," she said, folding her arms. "Could be a real emergency."

He set his jaw and studied the phone as though he might throw it. At last he answered, "Paxton."

She walked off. Now that she'd dismantled his theory and sprinkled it with a heavy dose of what she'd faced in her life, he seemed less sure of himself. But what he said next made her slow her pace.

"Was she hurt? . . . Where? . . . She moved?" His voice shook with frustration. "I know where it is. On my way."

Reluctantly, Kinsey turned in his direction.

Removing his sunglasses, Nate shook his head. He ran his hand through his short black hair and seemed to gather his nerve. "The woman who claims to be your birth mother is named Irene Turner. She's from Oklahoma City. She came to us without going to lawyers, without going to the Feds, hoping we'd investigate, but mostly she'd like an introduction. Without media, without fanfare. Does that sound like someone who's out to extort money?"

Kinsey closed her eyes. How could he believe this drivel?

"She surprised someone in her hotel room," Nate said, stepping toward her. "Whoever it was got rough. When she came to, she'd found that her room had been ransacked. He got away with a file that proved her relationship to you and brought her to Denver in the first place."

"How convenient," Kinsey said. "She's definitely a pro if she can convince you. Never mind what she's alleging about my mother and father, who as you well know, are honest and decent people."

His entire body went rigid. "Just trying to get at the truth. Will you come with me to meet her?"

Kinsey stared into Nate's determined brown eyes. Amazing. *He* was the expert at saying no, not her. But this time a court order couldn't sway her. "Absolutely not." Kinsey walked away. Fast.

Chapter Seven

NATE ENTERED Blue Star Executive Lodging, which though adequate, was a far cry from the Brown Palace Hotel. He strode past the front desk, then observing the single elevator was occupied, bolted for the stairs. A clerk resembling a gopher popping out of its burrow stretched over the counter. Nate flashed his badge. The curious gopher slid back in its hole.

Sammy had said Irene was in Room 621, and a stair climb was just what Nate needed to work out his frustration.

Kinsey hadn't changed. She was still the same headstrong kid who'd asked him out for Sadie Hawkins then acted like that was the most natural thing in the world. Her being recruited by every college on both sides of the Mississippi, him wondering if he'd even *go* to college. As if they had a debutante/working stiff's chance in hell of ending up together. He'd made the decision then, and he felt the same way now. Forget not being in her league, he wasn't even in her world.

He reached Irene's room and rapped twice on the door. Sammy opened it, left it ajar, and stepped out into the hall. His designer suit phase hadn't lasted long. He'd traded in the name brand for a sports coat and jeans.

"She okay?" Nate murmured.

"The paramedics didn't think so. They wanted to take her to the ER, but she refused transport."

"Figures. If she and Kinsey are related, stubbornness runs in their genes. Any word on Stephen Turner?" Nate asked.

"Called his office. Secretary said he'd been running his business from home the last few days."

"Can anyone substantiate that?"

"Working on it," Sammy said.

Nate entered the large suite to find Irene holding an icepack to the back of her head. Barefoot, wearing jeans and a sweater, she sat in a wing-backed chair, her legs propped on an ottoman. Struck by how much Kinsey looked like this woman, he forced his eyes from Irene and onto his surroundings.

Lingerie dangled from open drawers and clothes on hangers had been tossed from the closet. The bed had been stripped. Blankets and a comforter lay in a pile on the floor. Pictures on the wall hung off-kilter, and a table and chairs had been overturned.

"Damn. All this, and none of the guests reported anything?"

"I talked to the people on either side of Mrs. Turner and across the hall."

Sammy knocked on a paper-thin wall. "Must be a bunch of deaf people in the building."

"Professional?" Nate asked.

"Or desperate. Someone didn't want anything incriminating left behind."

Nate stole another glance at their victim, even as Kinsey's words came back to haunt him. *She's definitely a pro if she can convince you.* No doubt about it, for a woman attacked, Irene was one collected human being.

Nate walked toward her. Was Kins right? Were they being played? "When you entered your room, did you see anything . . . hear anything?"

"Nope. I used my pass key, moved toward the bed, felt someone behind me, and woke up with a goose egg for a present." She rolled her eyes. "And here it is not even Christmas."

The bathroom was between the door and the bed. Sammy signaled to the adjacent room. "Intruder must've been standing in here."

Nate turned toward the hotel room's main entrance. "Yeah. If he'd been behind the door when she entered, she would have seen him." He shook his head. "What happened to The Brown Palace?"

Irene lifted her gaze from Nate and gave a cool nod to Sammy. "After your partner called Stephen, I couldn't be sure he hadn't mentioned my hotel, so I moved here." Adjusting the icepack, she winced. "Made sense at the time. I do plan to reside in Denver indefinitely after all."

Sammy strode beside Nate. "The only problem with that explanation, Mrs. Turner, is I didn't tell Mr. Turner where you were staying."

"But you must've told him you were a *Denver* detective when you identified yourself, did you not? My husband may be despicable, but he's not stupid." She waved an arm around the mess someone had left her. "And he obviously knows people. Call me Irene, by the way. *Mrs. Turner* flew the coop."

"Mind if I look at your head?" Nate asked.

She gingerly lifted the ice bag. The skin was broken, and a golf ball-sized bump protruded on her skull. Someone had hit her hard enough to knock her out. Nate made a fist, wishing he could give her attacker a sample of his own violent medicine.

Nonetheless, a cop's suspicions grew with his pay grade, and Kinsey's comment had only fueled his unease. Even so, Irene was genuinely hurt and didn't appear to be the type who would take one for the team.

What was going on here? Nate walked away. He checked the lock. No signs that it had been jimmied. Whoever had entered had either coaxed a maid or bribed someone in the hotel. He made a mental note to talk to the clerk he'd passed on his way in. In the hallway, Nate had noted the surveillance cameras, but they were only stationed near the emergency exits. An intruder who knew what he was doing could have avoided being seen.

"They broke into the safe?" Nate continued.

Sammy opened the closet's double doors, revealing a large gap in the wall. "They *took* the safe."

Nate flashed his partner a look. Well, hell. Irene couldn't have done this, at least not by herself. He pivoted back to her. "What besides the file was in the safe?"

She lowered the icepack to her lap. "My wedding ring and a couple more pieces of jewelry."

"Purse, ID?" Nate asked.

Irene motioned beside her. A handbag sat on the floor next to a pair of high heels. "I had it with me when I left the hotel."

"They did all this but didn't take your purse?" Up until now, Sammy hadn't speculated. He obviously had his doubts, too.

"I had it strapped over my shoulder." Her gaze slid between both men. "Are you accusing me of staging this?"

"Just processing the scene." An idea came to Nate, which would more than likely prove her innocence. "Yesterday, you showed me a portrait of your son. Is it missing, too?"

Her expression took on one of relief. She placed a hand over her heart. "No, thank goodness. Danny's portrait wouldn't fit in the safe. I asked the hotel manager to store it in the vault downstairs."

Definitely swinging wide of the strike zone. Her explanation made sense but did nothing to prove she hadn't paid someone to toss her hotel room. From the limited time Nate had spent with her, he'd formed one certainty—her dead son's picture was the one thing she wouldn't do without.

"Why'd you go out?" he asked.

"I left all my clothes back home." She motioned to bags from Gap and the Banana Republic. "I took the RTD to the 16th Street Mall."

"Why not drive your car?" Nate continued.

She returned the icepack to the back of her head. "The manager said RTD stopped right outside the hotel. Lots of traffic, and I don't know the area. He recommended I take it."

Sammy's phone rang.

Nate temporarily staved off his next barrage of questions.

Ending the call, Sammy fingered his soul patch. "Had the Oklahoma City PD check on Stephen Turner. House is locked, and one of the neighbors said Turner asked him to pick up his mail."

Irene dropped the icepack. Her face registered alarm as she attempted to rise. But the second she did, she lost her balance and fell back to the chair.

Her already abnormal coloring growing paler, Nate moved to her side. "There's no way you don't have a concussion."

She buried her head in her hand. "I think you're a genius, Detective."

Sammy's phone beeped again. Rounding furniture and stepping over bedding, he crossed the room. Once again, he said little and listened more. Then, wearing a perplexed expression, he made his way back to Irene. "When was the last time you drove your Mercedes?"

She tilted her head. "This morning, when I left the Brown Palace and checked in here. Why?"

He pointed an index finger downward. "You parked it *here*, in underground parking?"

"Where the hotel management assigned me. Space 39, directly in front of the elevator doors." She folded her arms. "I repeat. Why?"

Sammy glanced at Nate and back to Irene. "Your Mercedes was found behind an abandoned warehouse."

"That isn't possible!" Irene did come to her feet then. She wobbled, but Nate stood close to steady her.

"There's more," Sammy said, frowning. "We can account for Stephen Turner's whereabouts now. You're not the only one with a headache, Mrs. Turner. You're husband's dead. Patrol found him inside your car on Federal and Evans. Gunshot wound to the head."

IRENE SUDDENLY knew how the peasants felt when the lord of the manor served them up before the king. The two detectives standing over her thought her capable of murder?

React damn it. Show some emotion. Say a prayer for Stephen's good-for-nothing soul. Stop looking so guilty. But whoever had killed him—and it hadn't been her—had sent her estranged husband to meet Dr. Mitchell in hell where they both belonged.

As always, she thought of Danny, and that made her tear up. How fortunate her son never knew this end. He'd loved his daddy. Why wouldn't he? Danny was the one thing Stephen completely and honestly adored.

Detective Lucero veered away from her again and was back on the phone.

"This doesn't look good, does it?" she whispered to Nate. "I swear I didn't kill him. I didn't even know Stephen was in Denver."

The man she'd thought she'd befriended lifted a skeptical brow. "You're a gun expert, right? You carry?"

She nodded.

"I'll need your gun."

She reached for her bag, and immediately missed the weight of her 38. Her stomach did several flip flops and then plummeted. Talk about the shit hitting the fan—someone had sealed the door to the outhouse with her in it. "I had my gun with me when I went to the mall. Whoever attacked me must've stolen it."

The robotic Detective Lucero signed off from yet another one of his blasted calls. Yesterday, she'd observed him clowning around with his partner. Today he acted like someone had shoved a poker up his butt. One thing for sure, she didn't want *him* sitting on *her* jury.

"Montoya wants you and me at the crime scene," he said to Nate. "As for Mrs. Turner, we have two choices. Escort her to the ER, where he'll have officers waiting to transfer custody, or to the jail so in-house docs can have a look at her."

Her being Mrs. Turner. Good heavens, they planned to take her to *jail?* She should have gone with the paramedics in the first place. "When can I make a phone call? You two obviously doubt my innocence."

"Soon," Nate said. "Let's go. I'm parked in the garage."

In the garage. Her mind conjured up the empty space that had held her Mercedes. A new rockslide of foreboding had her nearly doubling over. Well, shoot. Might as well tell them the rest of the grim news. "Nate . . . Detective Paxton. My shotgun was in the trunk of my car. I had it in its case, and it was unloaded, but . . ."

A what-else-isn't-she-telling-us look passed between partners, and Nate raised his gaze to the ceiling. "Any reason you felt the need to come to Denver with an arsenal, Irene?"

Okay, she didn't want *either* of them on her jury.

"All we can do is wait to see what we find on scene," Nate said. "The good news is, since Stephen was driving your car, you may have an alibi."

Her headache didn't give an inch, but her stomach eased up a bit. "If I do, I'd love to hear it."

"Your receipts," Nate explained. "They'll contain the date and the times you were at the mall. Along with those, if we can find witnesses who remember you, not only did you not have your car to get to the murder scene, you can't be in two places at once."

"I do. I talked to *several* sales clerks." Disregarding the spinning room, she stumbled to the department store bags, rummaged through them, and withdrew the evidence that might keep her out of prison. She shoved them at Nate and said, "Here. I think you should keep these. Things have a way of disappearing around me."

That earned her a nod from Nate and even a fraction of a smile from Detective Lucero. She slipped on her shoes, picked up her purse, and with no other choice, prepared to face whatever came next—which turned out to be an inhospitable ride down to the parking garage.

The car door opened directly in front of spot 39, the place she'd formerly parked her Mercedes. Finding it occupied, she took a step back and suddenly prayed these two were bad at their jobs.

That apparently wasn't the case as the detectives stepped forward.

Irene fought back bile. Gone was Detective Lucero's improved disposition. He walked straight to the parking space toward Stephen's Cadillac SUV, the one with the damning Oklahoma license plates.

Nate grabbed her arm and took hold of her handbag. Why, she wasn't sure. She no longer had a weapon, and she couldn't possibly hightail it and run. When he reached inside and came away with a set of keys, the whirling in her head took on a tornado-like vengeance and funneled its way to her intestines.

What were the chances when she left Oklahoma in such a rush she'd grabbed the extra set to the Mercedes? When the cop pressed down on the remote, the horn sounded and the taillights flashed on Stephen's SUV, Irene got her answer.

Not good.

Chapter Eight

A HALF-HOUR AFTER Kinsey left Nate, she cancelled her date with Griff, went home and showered, then headed for her mom's Cherry Creek art gallery.

How certain are you that Gwyneth Masters is your birth mother?

Seriously?

Kinsey was no stranger to trash talk. When you reached her level of play, getting inside someone's head was as important as agility or speed. An opponent's skill and reputation could intimidate. An "I'll take you on" look or a "You're mine" attitude could result in players' penalties or stupid mistakes on the field.

Behaviors like these held such power her coaches had actually hired psychologists to counsel the USA team. Even so, Kinsey had been able to shake off the most threatening intimidator.

Why then, couldn't she ignore Nate's absurd, utterly crazy comment the way she had professional soccer? Because, damn him, he hadn't referenced a game, he'd questioned her life.

Her face grew hot, and her pulse quickened the moment she walked through Masterpieces's glass doors. Surrounded by familiar chimes, she'd come to tell her mom about Nate's assertions.

Based on what, though? She was certainly no mistreated stepchild. Soccer required a helluva lot of time and involved a lot of travel. Kinsey's parents had dragged her younger sister and brother to every event. For years, Lauren and Jay had accused Kinsey of being the favorite. Still, her mom and dad had spared no expense for any of their children, and there wasn't a closer knit family.

At the end of the foyer, Kinsey found Ryan Stone and Michael Whitney manning the front desk. This was another successful idea her mother had implemented, making artists available to the public. A well-dressed couple stood talking to the men.

Dressed in his ever-present black, the enigmatic Michael stood by, while Ryan or RC or was it Stone this week?—boasted about his wildly popular stained glass collection.

Michael Whitney was certainly no slouch in the talent department. A former aerospace engineer, he'd left his profession to promote his Stardust series—paintings based on photographs taken by the Hubble telescope.

With no sign of her mom, Kinsey tried to ease toward the offices unseen. Unfortunately, Ryan saw her. Rail thin with flaming red hair, he'd been pestering her lately to attend his exhibits.

She'd flat out forgotten. When he'd berated her on her no show, she'd politely told him her focus was on soccer and teaching, in that order. Unlike the rest of her family, art wasn't her passion.

"Kinsey, Kinsey, Kinsey," Ryan chanted her name like a rap song. Rounding the counter, he came toward her. "Love the effect, girl. Kind of like a homeless person on a fashion runway."

Michael and their visitors pivoted to take in the scene.

"Everybody?" Ryan said. "Do you know who this is?"

Kinsey groaned inwardly. Usually when she came to the gallery, she dressed as a family representative. Tonight she'd planned to arrive near closing so she'd settled for her Stanford "Fear the Tree" T-shirt, ripped jeans, and flip flops.

Never mind that her mother would kill her dressed this way; Kinsey didn't appreciate the artist's shabby attempt at revenge.

She stepped forward to meet the onlookers and said between her teeth, "Hi, Ryan. I dropped by to see my mom. Do you know where she is?"

"How would I know? I was a measly ten minutes late, and Gwyneth acted like she might string me up. But then, she probably remembered what she earns off of me and let it slide."

Like many artists, Ryan complained about the amount of commissions the gallery took in. Many seemed to forget the money Gwyneth spent on marketing and launching their careers in the first place.

Michael folded his arms and shook his head. "I don't think she's here, Kinsey."

"Thank you, Michael." She chatted a moment longer with the gallery's patrons and moved away from the redheaded toad.

As Michael had indicated, her mom didn't appear to be in the building. Although on the way out of her office, Kinsey ran into Yasmine Takeri, her mother's longtime assistant.

"Kinsey. What a joy to see you." Yasmine looked her up and down. "What's wrong?"

"Why does something have to be wrong?" Kinsey said, attempting to swallow.

"It's Wednesday."

Yasmine proudly wore a *bindi*, which accented her enviable satin black hair. More than once she'd threatened to cut it. As children, Kinsey and her little sister Lauren had sobbed at the thought. So far, Kinsey and Lauren had won.

"You never stop by on a Wednesday. Did you and Griff Colburn have a fight?"

"Griff Colburn, as you insist on calling him, and I have nothing to fight about," Kinsey told the perpetual matchmaker. "We're not serious. And since you opened the door, might there be any truth to the rumor that you've moved in with the very handsome, very eligible Michael Whitney?"

"Maybe," Yasmine hedged. But her smitten look gave her away.

"Good for you, Auntie Yas," Kinsey said, hugging her. "Any idea where my mother got off to?"

Yasmine's black eyes twinkled. "Your father closed the hospital land deal. To celebrate, he took your mother out to dinner." She grinned. "But there's more."

"What? Tell me."

"He surprised her with a Hawaiian vacation. They leave tomorrow."

A knot of panic settled in Kinsey's stomach. "That soon?" Her parents' traveling was nothing new. Still, she wanted to address Nate's claim sooner than later. "They didn't mention which restaurant, did they?"

"Something is wrong." Yasmine narrowed her eyes and moved closer.

"Nothing that can't wait." Though patience had never been Kinsey's forte, neither was addressing a private matter in a public forum. Even so, she desperately needed to confide in someone. She couldn't talk to Jay. Her younger brother had taken off weeks before to New Zealand. But her sister was always willing to commiserate. "Is Lauren here?"

"In the warehouse." Yasmine wrapped her arms around Kinsey. "If your problem can't wait, my dear, you should call Gwyn on her cell. I'm about to close up. If you and your sister do stay, be sure to set the alarm when you go. And, please, remind Lauren the fire department was not amused the last time."

"Check." Kinsey returned the woman's embrace. "Set the alarm. Tell Lauren not to torch the place."

But as Yasmine pulled away, the knot in Kinsey's stomach grew. She blurted, "You were around when my mom was pregnant with me, weren't you?"

"Of course." Yasmine nailed Kinsey with her intense black-eyed gaze. "Why do you ask?"

"I attended a baby shower recently, and the women in attendance were comparing their pregnancies to their mothers'. Mom and I have never discussed what hers was like, so I thought I'd ask."

Yasmine folded her arms and responded with a dubious look. "You're a dreadful liar, Kinsey. Is that why you're here? You're pregnant?"

"What? No! Not even close. I'm genuinely curious about what kind of pregnancy Mom had, that's all."

"What do you want to know?"

Why, oh, why did I bring this up? "Oh, I don't know. Did she have a typical pregnancy? Did she have morning sickness, gain a lot of weight?"

"If you're asking if Gwyn became *ginormous*, as Jay likes to say, no. She got over morning sickness fairly quickly, but it's common knowledge she had cravings. The woman would have stood on a street corner and begged for ice cream if we'd allowed it." Yasmine's happy recollection weaved into a frown. "Kinsey. You're sure? That's the only reason you ask?"

"Enjoy your evening with Michael, Auntie Yas. I'm not pregnant."

Happy with the knowledge her mother had gone through morning sickness, Kinsey smiled. She strode through the museum on the way to the warehouse. Wherever Nate had come up with this bogus information, he hadn't a clue what he was talking about.

Every time she passed through the gallery, she saw something new and eclectic that her mother had purchased. Artists lobbied to get their work in front of Gwyneth Masters. If an artist commissioned a painting with Masterpieces Art Gallery, his repertoire grew, and he could demand top dollar when he placed his art in more prominent galleries throughout the world.

The same went for the pottery and sculptures Kinsey strode past. Positioned on black pedestals, surrounded by strategic lighting, these too went up in value simply by attracting Gwyneth's eye.

But the future stars of Masterpieces weren't the artists banging on the door. The future of the art gallery belonged to Kinsey's siblings.

She stepped outside into the alley behind the gallery. Even from ten feet away, Jethro Tull's *Aqualung* blared from the warehouse the family lovingly called *Lauren's lair*. Darkness had fallen, bathing the spring night in cold air and a sinister energy.

An occasional vagrant had been spotted back here as evidenced by the empty bottles lying around. Gooseflesh rose on her arms. Kinsey removed her keys and sprinted for the door beside the loading dock. She slid the keys into the lock, but there was no need. Lauren never bothered to lock it.

Annoyed, yet consumed with pride, Kinsey entered her sister's studio. Years ago, her parents had combined her father's commercial real estate firm with her mother's art gallery. From there, they'd moved it from a tiny strip mall on Colorado Boulevard to this high end property in Cherry Creek. Jay also used the warehouse, but not as much.

His passion was photography. As a child, while the family traveled to all of Kinsey's numerous tournaments and she ran up and down the soccer field, Jay had jogged beside her—a boy who captured shots more experienced photographers only dreamed of.

He'd moved on from soccer these days but still loved action photography and the great outdoors. At twenty-one, he'd already won awards and been published in major travel and photography magazines.

With Jethro Tull shaking the walls, Kinsey crossed to the center of the warehouse and stood a few feet away to avoid being hit by flying sparks. There on scaffolding, her baby sister stood blissfully unaware she had company. A welding cap covered her blonde hair, and with the UV shield that protected her eyes and face, she did a fine imitation of Darth Vader. Blue and orange burst from her welding torch, filling the huge warehouse with the smell of smoldering iron.

At twenty-three, Lauren Masters was already something of a clueless celebrity around Denver. She sold her monument-sized iron work sculptures to office parks and civic centers. But she did nothing to promote her work. Customers found out about Lauren thanks to Jay and their mom. Jay took pictures of her creations; Gwyneth posted them on the company website and in an exclusive corridor dedicated to the Masters children.

Knowing Lauren at least had the sense to wear ear protection and would never hear Kinsey if she yelled, she strode to the surround system unit blasting rock music. She found the power button and switched it off.

The studio flooded with the sound of magnificent silence.

Lauren shut off the welding iron, flipped up her face protection, and located the source of her interruption down below. "Hey, you."

"Hey, you back," Kinsey said. "Door was unlocked again."

"Really?" Lauren shook her head. "Could have sworn I locked it. What brings you by on a Wednesday?"

"I didn't know I couldn't come by on a weekday."

Lauren frowned. "You can, but you never do. What's wrong?"

"Something weird happened today. Need some advice."

"Come on up here."

Kinsey drew closer, wincing and estimating the distance of her sister's dare. "Up there?"

"Yes, chickee. Up here."

Chickee aka chicken was close to accurate. Kinsey didn't like heights, and her family, who held that she was fearless in every other regard, loved to hold it over her head. Flying had been an absolute chore for her. With every footfall, she counted the thirty-two metal steps necessary to join her sister. Once she reached the heavy steel grating and could still see the floor through it, she said, "Nice view. I'll give you twenty bucks if we can get down from here and stand on the floor."

When Lauren laughed at her, Kinsey stared at the mish-mash of bronze. "What is it?"

"What do you mean, 'what is it?' It's on its way to being a dragon."

"Ah, I can see that now. Can we get down, please?"

A few minutes later, safely situated on the warehouse cement with her brains still intact, Kinsey said, "Have a drink with me?"

"You're on. Give me ten minutes?"

Lauren disappeared into the bathroom across the warehouse, and Kinsey rehearsed how she would repeat Nate's claim and envisioned Lauren's reaction.

For the first time, Kinsey noticed the flat screen TV was on. Unable to compete with the legendary Jethro, Lauren must have muted the sound. A breaking news story flashed across the picture. Kinsey ambled closer.

She grabbed the remote and turned up the volume. A Nine News reporter spoke into her microphone, announcing that a man by the name of Stephen Turner had been shot to death behind a shopping center off of Federal.

Assuming the crime was a drug deal gone bad, Kinsey started to press off.

That was until the camera man zoomed in on a sweet black Mercedes with Oklahoma license plates.

Surrounded by crime scene tape and flashing lights, the reporter approached a detective on scene. It wasn't the cop she was talking to that flagged Kinsey's attention, however. Kinsey recognized Nate among other people in the background. She stood on tiptoe to get a closer look. But in the next second, as the reporter's cameraman panned in on the entire crime scene, he turned his back.

Frustrated, Kinsey continued to stare, willing him to face her again, but it was as though the tall, dark and photogenic Nate Paxton had suddenly become camera shy.

Lauren came out of the bathroom. "Ready when you are," she said.

But Kinsey held up a hand.

"Any suspects?" the reporter asked, unapologetically shoving a microphone in a plain-clothes detective's face.

"Not at this time."

"What about the owner of the vehicle?" the reporter persisted. "Turner's wife?"

"The victim's wife, an Irene Turner, also of Oklahoma City, is currently being taken to the ER for medical treatment. She has not been charged with a crime at this time."

At this time? What does that mean? Kinsey continued to grasp for information via their body language. And why couldn't they spell out which hospital? Hospitals in Denver and the surrounding burbs had to be in the double digits.

Glancing from the big screen to the woman who'd silenced her, Lauren folded her arms and shook her head.

Kinsey pinned her sister with a pleading expression. "Can we have that drink later?"

Lauren added a tapping foot to her frustration. "Sure, if you'll answer one question."

"Okay?"

"How come I'm known as the flake in the family?"

Chapter Nine

WHEN THINGS WERE going well, Rodrigo talked to his bosses once a week. But things weren't going well, and they were willing to risk exposure by calling as often as it took to get the situation under control.

He despised being micromanaged but also valued his head too much to challenge them. He'd witnessed firsthand a beheading south of the Mexican border when the cartel *recruited* him into coming on board. It was then that he decided to keep his own firmly attached.

A *jefe* known only as Sombra spoke first. "You did well, Rodrigo. Colburn has already deposited the money, with assurances he is sympathetic to our plight."

Holding a burn phone to his ear, Rodrigo stood transfixed by the city lights winking back at him through his Denver penthouse window. How dare they use the word plight instead of the word *business*? The cartel couldn't care less about the men and women who simply wished for a better life and who wanted to support their families above the poverty line.

Perhaps Colburn was an idealist who didn't anticipate what other obligations he'd encounter by accepting their money—the transportation and distribution of black tar heroin and other insidious drugs. Or maybe he wanted his political office so bad he'd knowingly climbed into bed with the devil.

Rodrigo had. Rather than go to the Feds, he'd enlisted into this sordid arena to keep Continental Miracles alive. There was good and bad in this world, and he was no longer naïve enough to think one could survive without the other. He'd also come to realize he had two sides, one benevolent that he showed to the world, the other sadistic—a personality he hated—but at times, served him well.

Oso, another code name the cartel used during conference calls spoke next. "Ah, yes," he said in elegant Spanish. "Rodrigo can schmooze the Americans with their hands out. But can he stop the ones who mean to do us harm?" Oso spoke of Paxton, of course.

Rodrigo burned at the insult.

It also hadn't escaped his notice that although he was required to use the cartel's aliases while addressing them, they offered him no such protection. It was a slap in the face and a reminder that no matter how educated he was, or how well he managed their business, he was merely their tool.

"My men know his every move," Rodrigo said, praying he spoke the truth. "When an opportunity arises, Paxton will be eliminated."

"How sure are you," Sombra said, "that he didn't access your records?"

"Very sure. Paxton played no role in my day-to-day affairs." Even as Rodrigo made this comment, sweat beaded his brow. There were times he'd opened up to Paxton, but in metaphors. "Paxton was my bodyguard, nothing more. He might have hoped to worm his way into Continental Miracles, but he hadn't yet earned my trust when we discovered who he was."

Another cell phone shimmied on a table across the room.

Rodrigo's pulse quickened. "If there's nothing else?"

"*Adios*," Sombra replied.

Oso hung up without a good-bye.

Rodrigo rushed toward the burn phone. He opened his mouth to ask for an update, but Rafa cut him off before Rodrigo could speak. "You near a TV, primo?"

"I can be," he said.

"Channel Nine," the excited gang member growled in a low voice. "I'm standing with a crowd on the outskirts of the parking lot watching the cops."

Rodrigo switched on the remote and watched a reporter give an account of a murder that had taken place in southwest Denver. He frowned. "What am I seeing, Rafa?"

"Paxton. That's him in the background."

Rodrigo picked up the remote. He reversed it and replayed the scene. "Good work, Rafa. We now know what he looks like without the long hair and the beard."

"There's more. Check out the man standing near him."

Rodrigo froze the frame. White hot fear shot through him. "*Eduardo.*"

"Makes sense why he booked at the same time we made Paxton."

Another cop? Rodrigo saw more than the proverbial red. He pictured his body left to rot, his blood staining the desert. If the cartel found out about this second lapse, he was through. "Is anyone with you?"

"They can be—within seconds," Rafa whispered into the phone. "One drive by, we cap these snitches and send them to hell where they belong."

"If you want to commit suicide, do so on your own time," Rodrigo snarled. "You grow rich being my eyes and ears, Rafa, nothing more. Eduardo knows you. You do nothing that connects me to you. Unless I tell you otherwise, we stick to the plan. Regarding Eduardo . . ."

"What about him?"

"Watch him. See where he goes and who he cares about."

"And if I can't get close enough?"

Would this fool never learn? Rodrigo held the phone away from him. He breathed deeply and counted to ten.

When he returned the phone to his ear, Rafa said, "What I meant is right away."

"When you kill cops, you leave no trace. We destroy them when we find their weak links. Stick with Paxton, Rafa, and put a tail on Eduardo in case they separate. Don't let them out of your sight."

Chapter Ten

AS SHE APPROACHED Lundgren Medical Center, Kinsey realized she'd probably wasted a thirty minute drive. Her sister was wrong. Kinsey wasn't flaky; she was certifiable. The detective spokesman hadn't said which hospital Irene Turner had been taken to, and the Nine News reporter hadn't asked. But Lundgren was closest to the Denver PD's District Six, and as a coach and a teacher, Kinsey had accompanied her injured players there numerous times. She'd been struck then that the ER had almost as many police officers as it had medical staff.

That didn't erase the main issue on her mind. Exactly what did she plan to say when she walked through those Emergency Department doors?

The new health care organization that stood here today wasn't the impoverished hospital of yesterday. This new medical upgrade was nationally recognized as a level one trauma center. Kinsey had witnessed firsthand the hospital's efficiency, its incorporation of procedures, regulations, and security. Plus, the other times Kinsey had stood on these grounds, she'd had her student's parents' permission and orders from their doctors to bring them here.

This time, the only authorization Kinsey had on her side was the need to get at the truth.

After ten on a weeknight, she entered a department that might as well have been a beehive. It swarmed with activity. Gathering her bearings, she bypassed signs that said Laboratory and X-ray and headed for ER Admission. To her right sat a receptionist behind protective glass. Rather than approach her just yet, Kinsey veered toward the waiting room. Feverish, glassy-eyed individuals awaited an available doctor. Many put their troubles on hold, focusing on TVs bracketed to the wall. One exhausted-looking mom with two active children nearby bounced a fretting toddler on her knee while a wincing man held his misshapen arm via a sorry excuse for a sling.

Yet, nowhere in the waiting room did she see a woman who looked like . . . well, Kinsey.

This left her with no choice but to talk to the receptionist. Currently, she was preoccupied with an elderly man who waved one arm and grasped his wife's elbow with the other.

Kinsey maintained a respectful distance, but when the two sidled off, she stepped forward. "I'm Kinsey Masters," she said, smiling.

The employee's blank stare indicated she either didn't care or she didn't follow women's soccer. With Plan A going nowhere, Kinsey switched to Plan B—to stretch the truth the way a child might poor Gumby. "Detective Nate Paxton asked me to join him here to meet a woman named Irene Turner who was transported earlier." Kinsey glanced around the ER and shrugged. "But I don't think he's arrived yet. Can you tell me if Mrs. Turner's still in the ER or if she's been admitted?"

A man in scrubs with a stethoscope around his neck must've been listening. He moved close to the receptionist where the two studied a computer screen. When he pointed to something Kinsey couldn't see, she resisted pumping a fist in the air.

The young woman lifted her head. "I'm sorry. We have no one listed by that name."

After a while, teachers developed an internal bullshit detector. And these two could grow mushrooms. "Okay," Kinsey said. "Thanks, anyway."

Mr. Stethoscope extended a hand toward the lobby. "You're welcome to wait for Detective Paxton if you like."

For a woman who isn't here? "You wouldn't mind?" Kinsey asked.

"Not at all," he replied.

At any other time, she would have admired the rule followers. Not tonight. All she wanted was *one look* at Irene Turner. One look to get Nate's ridiculous notion out of her head so she could dismiss the woman's allegation and reclaim her life. Kinsey eyed the lobby again.

At LMHS, she was exposed to sick kids on a daily basis. Rarely ill, she had an immune system on overdrive. That didn't mean she wanted to test the odds. She couldn't *catch* a broken arm, she supposed. She sat by the grimacing man clutching his elbow when two uniformed police officers walked through the Emergency Room doors. Their stop at the reception area met with far less resistance than she had. A three-second conversation later, they strode toward the double doors.

Kinsey stood and grabbed her purse. She was so close. She knew from her previous visits that beyond those swinging doors was a security checkpoint and then the exam rooms. Last time, a guard had merely x-rayed her purse, and she was in.

She joined the officers at the doors. The first man went through, but the one bringing up the rear, paused, and stared back at her. At the intensity in his gaze, Kinsey almost lost her nerve and backtracked the same way she'd come in.

But when he simply held open the door for her and she could breathe again, she smiled and said, "Thank you very much."

STUCK IN A flimsy hospital gown that *no one* should wear, Irene sat on the exam room table for what seemed an eternity, rather than the couple of hours she'd been here. Nate and his partner had dropped her at Lundgren Medical Center like she was Poison Ivy and they were susceptible to rashes.

In between her pounding head and vertigo, she wanted to lay back on the tissue-covered black vinyl and go to sleep. But the stodgy nurse who had taken Irene's blood pressure and checked her vital signs said, "Nothing doing, Mrs. Turner. We need you to stay awake."

What good would that do? By trying to keep her nefarious discovery a secret until she knew how to proceed, she'd somehow contributed to Stephen's death. Desperation clung to her. Nate had been so preoccupied processing the Blue Star crime scene, he hadn't mentioned whether or not he'd talked to Kinsey. Irene hoped he hadn't. She certainly didn't want to be introduced as the fruitcake up on murder charges claiming to be Kinsey's biological mother. Norma Mitchell had been right. *No matter how well intended, you're about to disrupt a young woman's life.*

Had Nate met with Kinsey? Irene pictured the effect this would have on the daughter she'd never known existed. Whatever else happened, she had to make sure the police didn't contact Kinsey until Irene was cleared of this awful mess.

A glimmer of hope spiked through her. Maybe it wasn't too late. She had yet to get to a phone. Still, Nurse Stodgy, bless her unfeeling heart, had taken Irene's personal effects and her clothes. She hopped off the table. Nearly collapsing, she reached for it again to regain her balance.

The police officer beyond her door—the one who'd ma'amed her to death—he certainly wouldn't allow her to use one. But what if she demanded to talk to a lawyer? He'd have to say yes to that, right?

Irene let go of the table. Ignoring her lack of equilibrium, she staggered across the tilting room. That's when she heard voices. Good. If her doctor had finally arrived, she'd persuade him to help her. But what she heard next didn't have her returning to the exam table. A woman's voice had her pressing her ear to the door.

"Is there a . . . Mrs. Turner inside? Detective Paxton asked me to meet him here, and, well, I'm turned around. My name's—"

"I know who you are, Ms. Masters. Sorry, I'm not at liberty to say."

Frustrated at the lack of clarity, Irene cupped a hand to her ear and shifted positions. Kinsey was here? Right outside the door? Obviously then, Nate had talked to her.

"I'm sure if you called Detective Paxton, he'd vouch for me," Kinsey said. "I have my orders, ma'am."

"I understand." Her voice went from coaxing to pleading. "But one phone call to Detective Paxton will clear all this up."

Irene gripped the knob.

"My orders are from Paxton's lieutenant, Ms. Masters," the officer countered. "I'm sorry."

"I know, I know," she said unhappily. "You're just doing your job."

"Yes, ma'am." The officer cleared his throat. "I bet you get this a lot. But I have a nine year old who plays soccer. If she knew I'd stood this close to

Special K without getting her autograph . . . Do you think—"

"Of course." Kinsey's tone lightened. "What's her name?"

"Alyssa. She spells it A-l-y . . ."

Irene's heart nearly burst from her daughter's show of kindness.

But then the conversation died down and faded altogether. With only a wall between her and the child she'd given birth to, Irene was set to pound on the door. What had happened? Was she too late? Had Kinsey signed the autograph and left?

For crying out loud, Irene was already in custody. What more could they do to her if she stepped outside this room?

Only one way to find out, she yanked open the door.

And there she was. Kinsey. The most stunning creature Irene had ever seen. Her throat clogged and her eyes welled.

Kinsey stood with the police officer a few feet away, her pen poised over an open notebook. But one look at Irene, Kinsey's mouth dropped open, the color drained from her face, and the pen and notebook slipped from her grasp.

The man in uniform became a brick wall. He moved between them, unyielding.

Humiliated to meet her daughter under such degrading circumstances, Irene nevertheless had to try. "Kinsey," she croaked.

Kinsey focused on Irene for all of two seconds, backed up a few steps, and then bolted.

Chapter Eleven

CRIME SCENES WERE unpredictable. They could take hours to several days to investigate. This one, Nate thought as he strode toward homicide detectives, appeared cut and dry. All external evidence outside the car had been collected. As Irene had mentioned, her 12-gauge shotgun had been found, by all appearances unfired, inside the trunk of her car.

The evidence indicated that Stephen Turner had been murdered by an assailant who fired point blank range into a lowered driver's side window.

Nate circled the crime scene. What was Turner doing in this neighborhood? His gaze scanned a long vacated retail store, its doors and window boarded up, to the crumbling parking lot where he stood. Weeds had taken over and had long ago won the war.

In this area, for an out-of-towner driving a Mercedes to lower his window to a stranger was nothing short of foolhardy. Irene had said it herself. *My husband may be despicable, but he's not stupid.* Nope, everything about this set-up said Turner knew his killer.

By one in the morning, even the hardcore curiosity seekers had given up and moved on. A chilly breeze had set in, and except for the yellow police tape, all other evidence would be transferred to the forensic automotive facility where techs would take apart that beautiful machine.

Currently, a tow truck operator stood by, ready to do just that. He backed his rig toward Irene's Mercedes, attached heavy-duty pulleys, and angled a flatbed to load her possession.

Running a hand over the back of his neck, Sammy whistled. "Wonder if Irene realizes she not only lost a husband, she's lost her car."

Nate had been thinking the same thing. Rarely did civilians understand that if a homicide was committed inside a vehicle, it, along with its contents, became police evidence indefinitely. "And her prized shotgun," Nate said. "But I'd say that's the least of her problems right now."

"No way could one person do all this," Sammy said.

"Not unless he wore an S on his chest," Nate agreed. "He'd have to be one methodical SOB to break into Irene's hotel room, knock her out, take her gun and the safe, travel to meet Turner, and park Turner's vehicle in Irene's space at the Blue Star. I'm betting Turner wanted that file, paid someone, and then was double-crossed."

Sammy pivoted and surveyed the scene. "Not someone. Someone he knew—and trusted. That'd explain the rolled-down window."

Gene Whitehead, District Four's lead detective came toward them and extended his hand. Nate and Sammy returned the man's handshake as Whitehead said, "Pleasure, boys. Just got off the phone with my LT. Brass says this case goes to District Six. You're up on the parties involved, and you have a potential suspect. Looks like you drew the shorter straw."

"Lucky us," Sammy said. "Say, any of your people videotape the crowd tonight?"

Whitehead nodded. "SOP. Tomorrow too soon to email you the video?"

Sammy replied with a thumb's up then joined Nate in crossing the parking lot.

Nate had traded in the missing, pinging Crown Vic and borrowed a Police Interceptor for transportation to tonight's grizzly spectacle. Enjoying how he and Sammy had raced to the crime scene in record time, he slid behind the wheel and placed the key in the ignition. "I could get used to this."

For sixteen hours, they'd been on the job. Sammy fastened his seat belt. "Maybe Montoya will put one on your tombstone. You crashing at your place again?"

"Did last night, and I'm still here."

"*Eres loco.*" Sammy closed his eyes. "You heard Shields. The brass wants us to lie low until this thing is over."

Nate grumbled, "And how long will that be? The department can recommend all it wants, but they sure as hell don't tell us how to pay for it. What about Liz? You take her up on her offer?"

Sammy rubbed his bloodshot eyes. "The last thing I want is to be responsible for Guzmán's *pendejos* shooting up her house. I'm living it up at the Econo Lodge."

"Bet she had a few choice words to say about that. She wants you with her, Sam."

"Yeah, well, we don't always get what we want. Don't worry, she's through with me this time. I did something that really pissed her off."

"What'd you do?"

"Called her dad. Two hours later, Liz took Elena out of preschool and headed for Texas."

Sammy may have talked smack, but concern emanated off of him. One of the things that made Sam a good cop was that he was all over taking risks to himself to put a lowlife away. Not so if it endangered his family. Nate had long suspected Sammy didn't divorce Liz because he'd fallen out of love. If anything, he'd fallen deeper and couldn't bear the thought of losing his wife or his daughter.

In this case, Nate had to agree his partner had reached the only reasonable solution. If Liz's father, a retired police chief, couldn't keep his daughter and granddaughter safe, no one could. Further, Sammy's ex had enough police officer relatives in El Paso to start their own force.

"I feel better with them gone. But damn these jitters. Guzmán's watching us, I know it." Sammy went ramrod straight. "Look, I'll ignore that you shake the friggin' walls when you snore, but we should stick together."

Nate fired up the Intreprid's high-performance engine. "All right. But I know what you're up to, you cheap son of a bitch. You're just after me to split the tab."

Sammy's cell phone chirped. He glanced at the caller ID and flashed Nate a WTF-look. "I can't believe this. Why does he always call me? What'd you do, convince Montoya you don't carry a cell phone?"

Nate grinned, ready with a comeback, until Sammy went from adversarial to ass-kisser faster than the Interceptor went from zero to sixty. Easing out of the parking lot, Nate headed north on Federal toward Colfax.

As Sammy's tone changed from yes-man to we-got-a-problem, Nate gripped the steering wheel and fought to decipher his partner's side of the conversation. All Nate could make out was that something had gone horribly wrong with Irene.

Sammy pushed end and squinted against the headlights of oncoming traffic. "Doctor admitted Irene Turner."

Nate sped through a yellow light. "She get worse?"

"You could say that. She suffered a meltdown after she met Kinsey Masters."

THE MOMENT Kinsey thought she had her emotions under control, new tears formed and leaked from her eyes. Ignoring the speed limit, she pressed down on the gas of her Audi A4 and drove toward her parents' estate. It wasn't possible. This had to be a mistake; there had to be some reasonable explanation. Her parents would never keep something this crucial, this *monumental* from her.

God help her, one look at Irene Turner and Kinsey had known. Nate's claim wasn't crazy. He'd been dead on. Well, of course, he'd been. Even when they were younger, he'd had an analytical brain. Now he had a cop's intuition.

And while he was all these things, *she* was a damn coward. Why had she run? Turned her back on that poor lady who showed such anguish and grief?

A new watershed of tears poured from her eyes.

Drawing close to the guard gate, Kinsey eased her foot off the gas. During the day, she keyed in a code. But at night, the residents of the gated community weren't as trusting and paid top dollar for additional security.

Mr. Mike, ordinarily one of her favorite night watchmen, left the guard house and walked briskly toward her car. Tonight, embarrassed, she swiped at her tears.

"Ms. Masters," he said. "You're here awfully late, aren't ya?"

She gulped and tried to focus on the blurred digital clock on her dash. One-thirty in the morning. "I know it's late, but I need to see my mom and dad."

"You want me to ring the house?"

"Not necessary," she choked, doing her best to hide her face. "They're up anyway, packing for a trip. They know I'm coming."

Mr. Mike' brows drew together. "Ya'll get bad news? I hate it when good folks get bad news."

"Thanks, Mr. Mike," Kinsey said. "Something like that. Will you open the gate, please."

"Yes, ma'am."

The wrought iron gates swung apart. Kinsey drove her car through, entering the pristine, manicured property she had so many times before. Only this time it felt unnatural, otherworldly.

She scanned the acres of upscale houses. She thought all this was hers, that someday she'd live here, raise her kids here, live on a property near her . . .

Kinsey gritted her teeth. What the hell were they?

She traveled along a winding path, parked in a red-bricked circular drive-way, and stared at the stately home she'd grown up in. She'd always known she was fortunate, more so than most. As a result, she tried to be as generous as possible.

But this. In a few hours' time, she no longer knew who she was.

With the exception of street lights and motion detectors, the property was cloaked in black. Kinsey stepped out of the Audi, careful not to slam the door. If Cordie, the Masters's black Labrador retriever had been awakened by Kinsey's arrival, she'd probably tipped off her owners by now.

Call Kinsey vindictive, but when she confronted them, she wanted to watch their reactions. To do that, she needed the element of surprise.

She walked around back, letting herself in through the mudroom's entrance. Immediately the burglar alarm beeped, and Kinsey keyed in the code to silence the alarm. Spying three large suitcases near the door, she was glad she hadn't waited until daylight to talk to her parents—she would have missed them. Her dad, the consummate planner, had probably already arranged for a cab to take them to DIA first thing.

Before Kinsey could leave the mudroom, she heard the click, click, click of Cordie's toenails on Gwyneth Masters's cherry wood floors. Cordie gave a gruff bark then danced around Kinsey, undoubtedly happy to see the woman who took her on weekly runs.

"Hey, girlie," Kinsey whispered and hugged the dog's neck. Funny how a lolling tongue and rapid pants seemed the only genuine thing right now. "I know you want to play, but not now, okay? I need you to be quiet, and you're not going to be too happy with me." Kinsey scratched the dog's ears. Then tearing up again, she kissed Cordie on the top of her soft, black head. "I'll make it up to you, girl. Promise."

Closing off the lab in the mud room, Kinsey blocked out the dog's scratches and whines. She strode through the gourmet kitchen, the breakfast nook, and into the hallway that led to the second floor.

Aided by the decorative nightlights her mom had placed throughout the house, Kinsey climbed the stairs.

She traversed the long hallway, passed a home office and the bedrooms where she, her sister, and brother had played. Kinsey endured a new wave of grief. Jay and Lauren couldn't be a party to this, could they?

Stop it, Kins. Now you're just being paranoid.

Shaking, she reached the master bedroom at the end of the hall. She opened the door, located the wall switch, and flipped it on. And as the large suite flooded with light, Kinsey honed in on the couple asleep in a king-sized bed.

Her dad, with his arm wrapped around her mom, was the first to stir. He covered his eyes with an arm. "Kinsey, what are you doing? What's going on?"

Mom rose up on her elbows. "Sweetheart? What's wrong? What's happened?"

"Irene Turner," Kinsey said, leaning against the door jamb.

Gwyneth's eyes went wide, but her dad, still disoriented, said, "Who? What?"

"Irene Turner, my birth mother," Kinsey said in the doorway, afraid of what she might do if she ventured farther inside.

Gwyneth shot her husband of thirty-two years a knowing look. "*Irene Turner*, Evan. She knows."

Kinsey's dad ran a hand through his uncombed hair. He looked at his wife then at Kinsey as understanding dawned. "Oh, for God's sake, Kins. How'd you find out about *that*?"

Outrage superseded her grief. She couldn't even reply to such a nonsensical statement.

Gwyneth appeared more annoyed with Kinsey's father than anything else. She glanced at the clock, rose, and reached for her robe at the foot of the bed. "You had to know this day was coming." She slipped into her robe and said in an accusatory tone, "I'll put on coffee while the two of you talk."

Wearing a sympathetic smile, she approached Kinsey as though she had every right to hide the truth for twenty-eight years. Gwyneth extended her arms, but Kinsey, unable to bear the hypocrisy, stepped aside.

How backasswards was this? Point all the fingers you want, Mom, but by keeping silent you're complicit as well.

Her mother's shoulders dropped, and she sighed. "Come downstairs when you're ready."

Chapter Twelve

DESPONDENT, IRENE sat with her chin in her hand while a nurse's aide wheeled her into her hospital room. After her hysterical reaction to Kinsey, she was amazed the ER staff hadn't restricted her to the psyche ward. Instead, her doctor arrived and calmly announced they were admitting her for an overnight observation, ordered laboratory work and a CT scan.

The good news—if you could call anything that had transpired over the last few days good news—was that the scan had revealed no hemorrhaging from her attacker's blow.

The aide assisted Irene into a hospital bed, explained the call device to page the nurse, and lowered the bed from sitting to a horizontal position. At least her doctor agreed she could sleep now, albeit in snatches. Prepared to do just that, she leaned back, closed her eyes, and was alone for all of sixty seconds when a soft knock on the door summoned her awake.

Expecting the nurse, and so very tired, she prepared to tell the hospital employee these constant interruptions were overkill. But a man clearing his throat had Irene sitting upright.

"Mrs. Turner?"

Lieutenant Montoya stood in the doorway.

"Lieutenant."

He eased farther into the room. "My men tell me you've been through the ringer in the last ten hours. I'm sorry about your husband."

"Thank you. But from our first meeting, I think you know there was no love lost between Stephen and me. We'd been living together yet separately for years."

The lieutenant held papers and a small package in his hand.

"What's that?"

"When was the last time you washed your hands?"

"The staff ordered me not to." Irene shuddered. "Rather odd request in a hospital, don't you think?"

His mouth curved upward. Not for the first time, she noticed his smile. Too bad he didn't do it often. "This is a gunshot residue kit, Mrs. Turner. Sorry to delay your personal hygiene, but I asked that you not wash your hands until I had time to execute a warrant."

She sucked in air.

"We've determined that the weapon used to kill Stephen Turner was a .38 projectile."

Her heart commenced beating like a war drum. Damn this fight or flight response handed down from our ancestors. "I did *not* kill my husband."

Lieutenant Montoya moved closer to the bed. "My detectives are inclined to believe you. Your department store receipts, that nasty blow to your head. The test I'd like to perform is one more test to prove your innocence. When was the last time you fired your .38?"

"Months," Irene said. "The last time I fired it was at the club during target practice." She swallowed, and her throat felt like sandpaper. "I have asked for and been denied a phone. I'm ready to call a lawyer."

"And that's your prerogative. But first, you should know we've already tested your clothes. We found zero traces of gun powder. In my opinion, whoever's doing this is an amateur." He held up a box. "One more test should prove it."

Her heart rate slightly decreased. "Is this where the bad cop pretends to be a good cop and takes the poor *innocent* suspect into his confidence?"

The lieutenant lifted a brow and gave her another one of those smiles. "Mind if I use your restroom, poor innocent suspect?"

Sucker. "Suit yourself."

"I won't be long. I'm just going to wash my hands."

She scowled at him.

A minute later, he returned and opened the kit. He snapped on disposable gloves, removed a small vial and two small disks. Hoping she wouldn't regret this later, she cooperated while he did his thing. Irene fought to even her breathing. She knew she hadn't fired her .38. But then, who had? And exactly how long had she been unconscious? She'd returned to her hotel room around four-thirty, came to, and called the police at ten after five. Securing the evidence, Lieutenant Montoya sealed the kit. "Ideally, we should have this back in a matter of hours. In the meantime, try to get some sleep."

Irene glanced at the phone by her bedside. "Is this thing plugged in? Am I free to call a lawyer?"

"You're free to call whomever you like. You're not under arrest. We're simply investigating this case."

"Is there still a police officer outside my door?"

"There is," Montoya said. "But he's not there to keep you from leaving."

Folding her arms, she eyed him warily. "Oh? You have him stationed out there for my health?"

"I don't think I could have said it better myself. That blow to the back of your head . . ."

"Yes?"

"Your doctor said whoever dealt it wasn't worried about the long term effects. An inch or two to the left, he might have killed you."

Chapter Thirteen

AFTER HER MOTHER left the room, Kinsey stared at her father, unmoving.

Lips drawn into a tight line, anger and indignation spiraled off of him. For all of one second, Kinsey wanted to retreat. This was the man who had held her, kicked a soccer ball to her when work had been kicking the daylights out of him.

Too damn bad. He'd kept secrets. Monstrous ones. Secrets she deserved to know.

Like her mom had moments before, her dad rose from the bed. Dressed in pajama bottoms, he grabbed his robe. For a man in his mid-fifties, he still had a great build and kept in shape. "Frankly, Kins, this is none of your business."

She blinked then, grinding her teeth, said, "My birth mother is none of my business?"

Wearing a look of shock, he pivoted. "What? What in the *hell* has gotten into you?"

Kinsey's heart tripped. What was she doing? She'd met plenty of people over the years who didn't look like their parents, so it hadn't bothered her that she didn't resemble her mother. But her dad—Kinsey's resemblance to Evan Masters was unmistakable. She bore his height, his coloring. But, dear God, she also looked like Irene Turner.

All Kinsey wanted were straight answers.

"I saw her, Dad. Irene Turner. She claims to be my birth mom."

His face reddened, and his hands curled into fists. "She *told* you that?"

Kinsey shook her head. "Nate Paxton did. He came to my school this afternoon." Kinsey's shoulders sagged. "Mrs. Turner went to the police with the allegation. Nate's a cop now."

"And one I'm about to sue," Evan said, for the first time raising his voice. "Why didn't you pick up the phone and call us the minute this happened? What were you thinking letting a stranger fill your mind with this *bunk?*"

She welcomed his outrage. Relief washed over her. "Really, Dad? You were there when I was born?"

"Right outside this room. You know how, after the way Grandpa died, your mom felt about hospitals. She hired a midwife."

His features softened. "You were the prettiest little baby I'd ever seen. Lots of dark hair, pink wrinkled skin. And your mom, well, she could barely talk she was so exhausted."

Kinsey's eyes filled. Of course her mother had shared these stories. But coming from her dad, Kinsey started to believe—wanted to believe. Even so, the seed had been planted. "So, why would Irene Turner say such a thing?"

Any remaining anger seeped out of him, replaced by something else. *Guilt?* He squeezed his eyes closed. "Sit with me, Kins."

She joined him on the edge of the bed.

Focusing on the ceiling, he blew out a breath. "I think I've shared with you kids that before I went into business for myself I did contract land management work."

She nodded.

"Many years ago, I had a six-week assignment in Oklahoma City. That's where I met Irene." He placed his hands on his knees and hung his head. "I was twenty-seven, she was barely eighteen. She worked for the same firm I did, saving for college by doing clerical jobs.

"I worked long hours back then, which suited me fine at the time, because your mom and I had separated."

Kinsey gasped. "Why?"

"Stuff most couples face, but our main reason was we'd been married for four years, and Mom had tried to get pregnant for most of it. With each passing day, she got more depressed and consumed that she couldn't. One day, she insisted we start all that fertility testing nonsense. Frankly, I didn't want triplets or a whole bunch at once unless it was preordained by Mother Nature."

"Okay," Kinsey said, frowning. "So, how did you and Irene end up together?"

"We were never *together*," he said defensively. "Irene had all sorts of problems. Strict, off-the-chart parents who, for God only knows why, approved of a boyfriend who thought he owned her. That creep dropped her off in the morning and waited for Irene in his souped-up piece of crap when she got off at night.

"Up until that point, she and I had made small talk, but one afternoon we left at the same time. Looking back, I probably should've kept my mouth shut, but I couldn't resist pointing out what a loser he was. I asked, 'What's with that guy? He sure has you on a leash.'"

Something sparked in her eyes, and I didn't give it much thought until later. The same night your mom gave me an ultimatum, saying she had more than enough money to support us both and *ordered* me to come home. I lost it and told her to stop using me as a stud."

Kinsey winced.

"You wanted to know. Mom hung up on me. I went to a bar near my office and started drinking."

"Irene was there?"

"No, but she came in later. She was already cute, to a man on his fourth or fifth whiskey, she was irresistible. She claimed she'd ended things with the loser, and it looked like Mom and I were headed for divorce. Irene and I started dancing, and one thing led to another."

He rose from the bed and moved to a chest of drawers. He picked up a picture of Gwyneth and him on their wedding day. "A lot of people thought I married your mom for her money. That couldn't be further from the truth. All I wanted was to make my own way in the world—without Grandpa's influence or his money.

"The next day, I went to Irene and told her what happened between us shouldn't have. Like I said, she was a nice young woman, and I wished her the best. Then I called your mom and came clean."

Kinsey joined her father at the dresser. "She forgave you?"

"At first. We'd been doing our best to work through it."

"What does *at first* mean?"

"I came home immediately to make everything right. I was so damn sorry it happened. But soon after, Irene called to tell me she was pregnant."

"Oh my God!" Kinsey backed away.

"Hear me out, Kins. Irene was also the one who called to tell me the baby had died."

More confused than ever, Kinsey stared at her dad. Irene had lost the baby? Then why had she come to Denver? Kinsey shouldn't feel such a loss over a child dead these many years, but that meant she'd lost a brother or sister.

She also understood now why her mother had never said a word. What woman wanted her daughter to know that her father had been unfaithful, sired a child, and nearly destroyed his marriage?

Kinsey wiped her eyes and hugged him. "Mom must've been so humiliated. No wonder she left the room. I'm sorry I barged in like that, but I had to know."

He brushed the hair out her eyes, the way he had when she was little. "I hope you can see now why I never told you. I'm not proud of what happened, and this is something I never wanted my children to know." He sighed and lifted his watch off the dresser. "No sense trying to sleep now. Our cab comes in two hours. What do you say we go give Mom a hug and take her up on that cup of coffee?"

"You're on."

On their way downstairs, Cordie bounded toward them. Kinsey laughed and scratched the dog behind her ears. "Oh, good. Mom let you out of your prison. C'mon, let's go find her."

But inside the kitchen, Kinsey and her father stopped short. The coffee pot was empty, and there was no sign of her mother. Perplexed, Kinsey followed her dad into the mudroom where they wordlessly stared at the single piece of luggage remaining.

"What the hell's going on?" he said, and opened the door to the garage. But no additional answers awaited them out there either. Kinsey stared at the bewildered man. But what could she say? *Gee, Dad, it appears Mom, her luggage, and her Lexus have left the building.*

Chapter Fourteen

KINSEY HAD RARELY asked for a substitute during her teaching career. Her students' education and well-being fell under her responsibility. But with her personal life in turmoil and her mother's odd disappearance, her father obviously hadn't taken off to the Aloha state on vacation alone.

He'd called Yasmine, waking her from a sound sleep. When she didn't have the foggiest clue where Gwyneth might be, Evan had driven to the art gallery.

Near ten a.m., Kinsey sat on the patio with her sister after filling her in on the excruciating event that had occurred before the Masters had children.

"Want another cup?" Lauren asked, pouring coffee into her own mug.

Kinsey shook her head. Her taste buds hadn't changed over time. She still hated the stuff. "Lauren, Mom hasn't called you? You're sure?"

Lauren handed Kinsey her iPhone. "See for yourself. Why do you think she took off like that?"

Kinsey buried her face in her hands. "Dad thinks my dredging up the past sent her over the edge. He's barely speaking to me."

"Should I call Jay?" Lauren asked.

"Probably. Maybe she took off to see him."

Phone in hand, Lauren pushed back her chair. The metal legs sliding over concrete grated on Kinsey's already battered nerves. "Wait," Lauren said. "What time is it in New Zealand?"

"They're a day ahead of us." Kinsey glanced at her watch. "Two a.m., I think."

When Lauren hesitated, Kinsey held out her hands. "What are you waiting for? *Call him.* This is an emergency."

"*Okay.*" Lauren stood and punched in a number. "Be right back, your highness."

Getting a clear signal close to the house was impossible. Lauren trooped toward the gazebo near the property line with Cordie on her heels.

From the west, snow-capped mountains rose in the distance. Early spring, the Masters's lawn had already turned a vibrant green, and Gwyneth's prized tulips poked multi-colored heads through the soil. Once again, Kinsey was struck by the beauty of her parents' property as well as the uncomfortable realization she might be tearing apart her family's world.

She sighed. Was her dad right? Had Kinsey, by demanding answers, driven her mother away? But why? Gwyneth Masters was the most self-confident, self-sufficient woman Kinsey knew.

As if summoned by her thoughts, her dad stepped outside onto the patio, dark circles shadowing his red-rimmed eyes. Dressed in a casual polo shirt and Dockers, he scanned the large, terraced backyard and settled on Lauren. "Who's she talking to?" Hope tinged his voice.

"Jay," Kinsey explained. Watching her father suffer hurt her heart and turned her insides. "I'm sorry, Daddy."

He waved her off. "How do I get hold of Nate?"

Kinsey swallowed over a lump in her throat. "He works at Major Crimes, District Six."

"Used to," her father shot back. "He's about to find himself out of a job."

"I'm sure he didn't know the whole story."

"Well, he's going to wish he'd checked out that half-truth with me first. As for you, young lady, what is it with you? Griff Colburn's about to be elected to Congress. He worships the ground you walk on. But, no, you prefer a man whose father's a no-good drunk and who sent his wife to an early grave. I think if Nate told you to go take a flying leap, you'd rent an airplane to do it."

Kinsey gripped the sides of her chair and strove to keep calm. "That's not fair. You can't judge Nate based on his dad. And FYI, I didn't approach Nate. He came to me. You're right, I handled it badly. But Nate doesn't deserve to have his career ended over this. We need to wait until we hear from Mom and stop overreacting."

Lauren and Cordie made their way up the walk.

"Anything?" her father asked.

"Nothing new, except that now Jay's all panicked. He's flying home."

Her father whirled from Lauren to glare at Kinsey. She'd taken all the guff she was going to. "Look, you're the married man who slept with another woman. Stop looking at me as though I'm the only culprit here."

Cordie whined and Lauren stepped forward. "Stop it. Both of you. I think it's time we called the police."

"Not necessary," their father growled. "I plan to pay them a visit."

"Not without me, you don't." Kinsey leapt to her feet. "I'm going with you."

HER HEADACHE down to a dull roar, Irene ate the last bite of her scrambled eggs and winced as a too-cheerful nurse in scrubs drew back the blinds.

"Beautiful day, Mrs. Turner. Your doctor's making the rounds. We had a houseful last night, but if all goes well, he'll discharge you this morning."

Irene opened her mouth to be polite, but evidently two people weren't required for this conversation. Going about her duties, the medical worker prattled on about everything and nothing in particular. When at last she took a breath, Irene said, "Thank you. If you're finished, I'd like some privacy." She'd waited all night to make her phone call, and she was going to do it.

"Of course." The nurse pointed to the call button. "If you need anything—"

"I'll page you," Irene said bluntly.

The nursed walked out, thankfully, without another word.

Irene picked up the phone, dialed the switchboard operator, and asked for an outside line. A few minutes later when Norma answered, Irene slumped in relief. "It's Irene," she said.

"Irene? Thank goodness. It's been days. What's going on? Did you meet Kinsey?"

"Sort of," Irene replied, banishing the image of Kinsey when she glimpsed the wild-eyed crazy woman wearing a sheet impersonating a hospital gown. "As far as what's going on, nothing good. My husband followed me to Colorado. He's dead, Norma. Murdered. In *my* car. And before you ask, no, I didn't do it."

It took Irene a good ten minutes to relay her visit to the police, her ill-fated decision to switch hotels, the fact that someone had attacked her in her hotel room, made off with the evidence Norma had provided, stolen her gun—possibly murdered Stephen with it—and finally, the details of her miserable hospital stay.

This time it was Irene who felt like the chatterbox nurse who'd recently left the room. But true to form, Norma listened intently.

"I need help," Irene said.

"I should say. I'll contact Lyle immediately. It's time the two of you met."

Irene hung up and rested her head back against the pillows. With the amount of faith Norma put in this Lyle person, he must be something else. Unfortunately, Lyle Wilkins, attorney at law, was licensed in Oklahoma. "That's very kind, but maybe Mr. Wilkins can refer me to a Colorado attorney."

"I'm on it," Norma said. "Hang tight."

I'm on it? Hang tight? Irene replaced the phone on the cradle. If it didn't hurt her head, she might have smiled. Her gung-ho eighty-year-old friend worked better than aspirin.

Chapter Fifteen

THE WORLD SHE knew falling apart, Gwyneth strode from the bank, cell phone in hand. To determine how much damage had been done, she'd needed to retrieve two long-hidden-away phone numbers from her safe deposit box. Yet, once she'd accessed them, she couldn't get a signal due to the close proximity of the vault and the thick walls surrounding the area.

Head down, scarf and glasses obscuring her face, she walked toward the car she'd left in the bank's underground parking garage. Although she might be hard to recognize on foot, to drive around in the city in her Lexus with plates that read MSTRPLN, she might as well have had a giant arrow pointing to her location.

No stranger to keeping cool under stress, Gwyneth evened her breathing, wiped her sweaty palms, and planned her next move. But while she could strategize what move to make next, she could only anticipate what others would do.

For a few minutes after Kinsey had barged into Evan's and her bedroom this morning, Gwyneth had stood by the door. After she'd gathered enough information to discover what had Kinsey in such a state, Gwyneth thanked the fates Evan had stored their suitcases by the garage door.

Her poor baby. What had gone wrong? Every precaution had been taken, every thread of blackmail reinforced to ensure the parties knew the lengthy prison sentences they'd undergo should they ever develop a conscience.

That left Evan. How much time did she have before he pieced together what she'd done all those years ago? Would he call the police? Team up with Nate Paxton who appeared to be Kinsey's contact in this fiasco? Evan had betrayed Gwyneth once. Would he think he had the wherewithal to bring her to justice now?

How dare he, when he'd forced her hand in the first place?

Inside her Lexus, she heaved air in and out, shucked off her sunglasses, and backed out of her parking spot. But as she looked over her shoulder and spotted another car, silver in color, and nearly identical to hers, she hit the brakes.

How fortuitous was this? She fixed her gaze on the plate's three letters and three numbers. Switching license plates with another Lexus might buy her some time. She pulled back into her space, left her car, and scanned the darkened garage for cameras. Finding none in her area, she popped the trunk.

Ever concerned for her safety, Evan had bought her an emergency roadside tool kit. Her throat clogged as she quashed a new bout of rage. She'd never asked for a tool kit or any of the gifts he'd showered on her. All she'd ever asked of the man was for him to be faithful.

She would *not* be the one who walked away with nothing. Kinsey. Lauren. Jay. Unlike Gwyneth, her children had never known what it was like to be ignored by their parents and raised by nannies. From the time she'd entered her teens, she'd vowed to be an outstanding mother.

For painstaking minutes, she worked in the dim to switch out the plates, once ducking from a white Corolla as the driver rounded the corner.

Heart thudding against her ribcage, Gwyneth tossed the tool kit into the trunk beside her luggage. The driver of the Lexus was in for a surprise the next time he was pulled over. If she were in a good mood, she might have laughed. But she couldn't laugh. She was desperate and in need of a shower. Gwyneth drove away, a new layer added to staying undiscovered.

Chapter Sixteen

DISTRICT SIX OF the Denver Police Department didn't have a complaint department. As such, Kinsey and her dad were escorted into a conference room where they waited.

Her father cracking his knuckles one moment and snapping his fingers the next had Kinsey ready to bolt from the room, or yell, "Stop that." But they'd already exchanged harsh words this morning, so she preferred not to use up any more of her allotment. Obviously, he wasn't nervous about a confrontation with Nate. In his commercial real estate business, he'd dealt with high-powered people as a matter of course. It was the fact his wife had vanished without explanation, and apparently of her own accord, that had to be driving him mad.

The door finally opened, but instead of Nate, a gray-haired Hispanic man entered the conference room. A newspaper tucked under his arm, he wore a blue shirt and dark blue tie, and by the badge on his breast pocket and the silver bars on his lapels, Kinsey suspected she was about to meet Nate's boss.

"Mr. Masters, Ms. Masters," he said, placing the paper on the table and shaking their hands. "I'm Lieutenant George Montoya, Supervisor, Major Crimes. I understand you have a problem with Detective Paxton?"

"We do," Kinsey's father said, annoying Kinsey that he chose to include her in his sentiment. "I don't know what kind of organization you're running around here, but I don't see how disrupting a young woman's life falls under the Denver Police Department's jurisdiction."

Kinsey crossed her arms and wondered what tack the lieutenant would take. Clearly, each of these men was used to getting his way. But, by the way her father had taken charge and stated his position, Kinsey had to give the first goal to him.

The lieutenant frowned. "When you put it that way, you make an excellent point. We do our best not to interfere. However, when a citizen comes to us with a complaint of a felonious nature, we have an obligation to check it out."

Kinsey massaged her stiff neck. There was probably no use in keeping score.

"You're talking about Irene Turner," said her dad.

"I am."

"And you believe this nonsense she's spouting about being my daughter's birth mother?"

"Quite frankly, I don't know what to believe. I've only heard her side. For someone not telling the truth, Mrs. Turner has had her share of unfortunate incidents since her arrival in Denver."

"I have no idea what you're talking about," Evan said.

The lieutenant slid the newspaper across the table. "Then let me help you out. Her hotel room was ransacked, personal property stolen, and last night, her husband was shot and killed."

Lightheaded, Kinsey leaned forward to peruse the article listed in the metro section. There on page 7A of *The Denver Post* were two pictures, one of the deceased Stephen W. Turner and one of Irene. Kinsey silenced a moan. This grainy photo was much more flattering than the mental image she'd been left with of the poor woman she'd seen last night at Lundgren Medical Center. The resemblance was also much more apparent. Kinsey hadn't even made it to the article before her dad pushed it out of her reach.

Someone knocked. The lieutenant said, "Enter," and Nate stepped inside.

"Sorry I'm late." He glanced around. "Mr. Masters. Kinsey." Nate chose a chair next to the lieutenant directly across the conference room table from Kinsey and her dad.

Dressed more professionally than yesterday, Nate's rolled-up cotton sleeves and unbuttoned collar hinted that he'd gotten an early start this morning. Kinsey tried not to focus on him any more than the other two people in the room. But hard as she tried, she was aware of him. His highly starched shirt enhanced rather than hid his broad shoulders and chest.

Her dad was right. She'd always had a thing for Nate. He was the man to whom she compared all others who entered her life.

So, how did she circumvent such an attraction, especially when he made it no secret he didn't return her feelings?

"I'm disappointed, Nate," her father began. "Frankly, I expected more from you."

Years ago, Evan Masters talking to the quiet and respectful Nate Paxton would have left the boy red-faced and stammering. The adult Nate Paxton appeared unfazed. He stared at her father, dark eyes intense and unshaken. "I've seen strong evidence indicating that years ago someone committed a crime. Now someone's murdered a man to cover his tracks, which gives that evidence credence.

"Just as an aside, Mr. Masters, I disappoint a lot of people—especially when I send them to prison. So why don't you tell us about your relationship with Irene Turner. Because I don't give a damn if I've disappointed you, and I don't scare easily."

Kinsey brought a hand to her chest. Her father leaned back in his chair. He opened his mouth, then all at once, came to his feet. "My lawyer will take it from here. Kinsey . . ."

She sat unmoving. "Sorry, Daddy. If you won't answer their questions, I will."

He bent close to her ear. "I've reconsidered, Kins. This is a private family matter. From here on out, we'll let our lawyers speak for us."

"I don't need anyone to speak for me," she said aloud. "*I've* done nothing wrong."

Never in her life had Kinsey challenged either of her parents over such a serious issue. She loved and respected them. But the situation had escalated. *Had* her dad done something wrong—past adultery? Did he know more than he'd admitted? Boldly, she followed Nate's example and returned her father's glare.

His gaze never softened, but slowly he returned to his chair. "What do you want to know?"

"The information Detective Paxton has already requested from you. Your connection to Irene Turner," Lieutenant Montoya said.

Thirty minutes later, her father had repeated the story he'd told Kinsey in the early morning hours.

Periodically Nate scribbled a note and made eye contact with her, but clearly, the person he was most interested in was her dad. Nate had never been overly demonstrative in high school, but at least he knew how to lighten up now and then. That wasn't happening now.

Wearing a sober expression, intensity radiated off of him. How much had he changed from the boy she once knew? He glanced up from his notes. "You hired a midwife to deliver Kinsey? Do you recall her name?"

Her father shook his head. "I don't. My wife hired her."

"I assume Mrs. Masters saw an OB/GYN as well?" Nate persisted.

"I assume so, too," her father said.

"You assume?" Nate frowned.

"I didn't keep track. It was twenty-eight years ago." Her dad gave an exasperated huff and turned toward the lieutenant. "Do you remember the names of your wife's health care providers?"

The lieutenant lifted a brow. "Can't say that I do."

"My point exactly," her father said. "Gwyneth was furious over my indiscretion. She threated to file for divorce. I wanted to try again. So, no, I don't know the names of her doctors or her midwife. We remained separated until she delivered."

Nate stopped writing. The lieutenant's eyes narrowed.

Kinsey struggled to breathe. "You and Mom didn't live together when she was pregnant with me?"

He raised his gaze to the ceiling then held out his hands. "As I told you last night, we were separated. But we saw each other—often. We spent time together, we went through marriage counseling. A woman can't hide these things. I assure you *she was pregnant.*"

Kinsey stared at her dad.

"Besides, you people are forgetting the pivotal flaw with what you're suggesting," he said, even though his face had turned a sickly shade of green.

"Irene called me. *She* told me she'd lost the baby *before* my wife delivered."

Bile rose in Kinsey's throat and tears threatened again. Staunchly, she ordered them back. She'd heard all this before, but that's when she'd thought the woman who'd raised her, whom Kinsey loved and admired, was downstairs making coffee.

Oh, God. Gwyneth Masters hadn't taken off because she was forced to relive her husband's affair. She'd taken off because she'd broken the law; she'd stolen Kinsey from Irene Turner!

Nate broke the stunned silence and asked the question that had to be utmost on everybody's mind. "Mr. Masters, how soon before your wife delivered did Irene place this call?"

Her father pitched forward. He placed his elbows on the table, lowered his head, and buried his face in his hands. A sob wrenched from his throat. "Three days."

Chapter Seventeen

IT WAS AFTER NOON by the time Evan Masters's complaint-turned-interview came to an end. Nate escorted Kinsey down the district steps, staring after her father, who'd left the conference room seconds before them and had already reached his car.

Nate shook his head. Maybe as Evan Masters drove away in his impressive BMW, he'd be a little less impressed with himself.

Yeah, this was personal; Nate didn't like the guy. He'd delved enough into his psych degree to conduct a candid self-analysis. Each time he came face to face with Masters, Nate felt seventeen again. A kid with an alcoholic father and a wonderful, but enabling mother, doing his best to create an identity apart from them—to be one hundred percent perfect—only one of the side effects of alcoholic children.

He'd been confident and admittedly cocky the night he'd picked up Kinsey for what he thought would be the first of many dates. Ultimately, Masters had put that notion out of Nate's head. He went home recognizing the truth. Kinsey was meant for bigger things in this world, and a middle-class boy from Denver, Colorado, wasn't fit to be part of it.

Still, he'd never wished Kinsey's father *this* kind of pain.

With Irene's help, Nate and Sammy, and a boss Nate hadn't given enough credit, were close to deciphering a crime nearly three decades old. They didn't know the ins or outs or the accomplices yet, but in his gut, Nate believed a woman set on revenge had instigated this sordid tragedy.

His chief concern was for Kinsey. She looked more beat up than after a soccer match. At the hair slipping from her ponytail, he tucked a loose strand behind her ear.

"I keep hoping to wake up from this nightmare," she said, standing on a step below Nate and glancing up at him. "Yesterday, I lived in a perfect world. Today I feel like someone took a wrecking ball to my life."

What could he say? She needed to talk, and he was more than willing to listen.

"I don't know whether to thank you or to deck you," she continued, negotiating the lower step. "You've just unraveled a family but given a mother and daughter a second chance."

"I'll be the first to lend you my boxing gloves," he replied, deadpan.

"Figure of speech, Nate." She whirled on him, exasperation in her voice. "I don't want to hit you. I want answers."

"And I want to get them for you, Kins."

"I know you do." Her hands balled into fists, and she closed her eyes. "Why would my mother do such a thing?" Without waiting for an answer, Kinsey rushed on. "Want to know what I'm thinking?"

"You have to ask?"

She inhaled and released a shaky breath. "When I was a girl, one of the neighborhood kids left her roller blades on the sidewalk. Lauren wanted a pair, and my mom, a real safety nut, wouldn't say yes and she wouldn't say no. So Lauren took the neighbor's. Soon she was skating around our driveway. Mom spotted her and asked Lauren where she'd gotten the blades.

"I'll never forget Lauren's punishment," Kinsey continued. "She was only six at the time, but my mom made her write out a detailed letter, admitting to the theft. Then she made my little thief-sister deliver the roller blades along with her confession back to their owner.

"The three of us kids learned a huge lesson about stealing that day. If you wanted to survive in our family, you *did not do it.*"

Kinsey's shoulders fell as she turned to Nate pleading, "Does that sound like a woman who would kidnap a *baby*?"

At the raw desperation that shone on her face, Nate had to force himself to think as a cop and not as her friend. "On the surface, no. But for Gwyneth to do something so reckless could be a sign of a deeper psychological problem."

"What if she has a logical explanation?"

"I'd love to hear it."

Kinsey's eyes darted as though working out a solution. "What if Irene and my mother made a deal? What if Irene, young, single, and saddled with an unwanted pregnancy made an agreement with my mother to raise me?"

"Actually, what you suggest is what should have happened," Nate countered. "But I'm not buying it. If they had an agreement, why did Irene come forward now? And even more telling, why did your mother run?"

Leaning against the precinct's support columns, he folded his arms. "If your version were true, Gwyneth could have simply explained her side of the story, and she and Irene could have hashed all this out in court. The penalties would have been far less severe."

The color drained from her face. Kinsey dropped to the top step, sat, and buried her face in her hands. "I'm grasping, aren't I?"

Wordlessly, he joined her on the step.

Kinsey raised her head and looked at Nate. "She did this, didn't she? Deliberately took me away from my biological mother?"

Part of the grief process was negotiation, reasoning, then coming to terms. In reality, Kinsey was coming to terms much faster than he thought possible. He wrapped an arm around her; she leaned into him and laid her head on his shoulder.

"What am I supposed to tell Lauren and Jay?" she whispered.

"You tell them what you know and take it from there. In my opinion, the actions your mother's exhibiting don't come from a rational woman. Did you ever see signs she was unstable?"

Kinsey lifted her head from his shoulder and scoffed. "Poised, polished, and driven Gwyneth Masters? Not in this lifetime. If we showed an interest in anything, she made us pursue it. She was the stitch that held our family together. I wanted to be just like her."

A faraway look possessed Kinsey and she hesitated. "Still, when I brought up the name Irene Turner, it was like a time bomb went off."

"Good analogy actually." Nate rested his elbows on his thighs and threaded his fingers. "Maybe that's what happened. You weren't the only one with a charmed life, Kins, so was Gwyneth's. As long as her crime went undiscovered, she was safe in her fantasy land."

"You don't think she'd do anything crazy?" Kinsey shifted to face him.

Felony kidnapping isn't crazy enough? "Like?" Nate asked cautiously.

She swallowed visibly. "Hurt herself?"

"I can't answer that."

Kinsey shot to her feet. She removed her cell phone and made a call. Seconds later, she shoved the phone back in her pocket and sighed. "Still no answer. I obviously can't hear her side of the story. How soon can I talk to Irene?"

"If you want to have a coherent conversation, I'd suggest you wait until tomorrow. Lieutenant Montoya had patrol pick her up from the hospital and return her to the Brown Palace."

"Tomorrow it is, then." Kinsey glanced at her watch. "What a *mess*. Today wouldn't work anyway. I promised Lauren I'd go with her to the airport to pick up Jay."

Nate stood from the steps. "Being with your brother and sister is a good thing. But you should let them know Lieutenant Montoya plans to contact the FBI."

Kinsey paled. "Why would he do that?"

"What Gwyneth committed is an interstate crime. There's no statute of limitation on kidnapping in Colorado."

Kinsey steepled her fingers against her lips.

"The Feds may tell us to go it alone, they may tell us they have bigger fish to fry, or they may want to assist. Either way, things would go better for Gwyneth if she comes forward on her own." Nate broke eye contact for a moment. "There's something else."

"More than the FBI may get involved and there's no statute of limitation?" Kinsey folded her arms. "Can't wait to hear it."

"Someone took a file from Irene's hotel room and murdered her husband. Gwyneth may have been out to dinner with your dad, which proves she was elsewhere. But she had means and motive, and that makes her a strong suspect. If you or anyone in your family hear from her, we need to know about it. Sooner rather than later."

Kinsey pressed her lips together. Nate knew the look. He'd seen it often enough when an opponent cornered her on the soccer field. She was thinking, *no way in hell.*

"Kinsey?"

"You want to talk motivation, Nate? Okay, I can see my mother's motivation for taking me. But to kill someone? Uh-uh. I can't believe that. You're also asking my brother and sister to turn on her. Good luck with that."

She removed her keys from her bag. "As for me, I feel terrible about what happened to Irene, and, of course, I want to know her. But I can't flip my emotions on and off like a light switch. I still love the woman who raised me." Kinsey's eyes flashed. "As for helping the police, I'll be siding with Lauren and Jay."

Jaw clenched, Nate stepped forward. "This can only end badly if your family doesn't cooperate."

Kinsey had no time to respond. A bronze Chevy Tahoe with tinted windows careened into the parking lot. Passersby whirled then scrambled out of its path to get behind parked cars. Guzmán never far from Nate's thoughts, he shoved Kinsey behind him and started to draw his weapon.

Some asshole illegally parked and exited the Tahoe. He rounded the vehicle, and Nate felt his adrenaline rush recede. He'd have to have been living under a rock not to recognize the former NFL great and congressional candidate whose radio and TV attack ads were annoying the hell out him.

"This isn't happening," she said with a groan.

"What *is* happening?" Nate asked.

"One more headache that I really don't need right now."

Colburn jogged up the district's stairs, sized Nate up with an inconsequential glance, and took Kinsey in his arms. "You all right, babe?"

Babe. So that's how things stood.

Nate moved aside to let the lovebirds talk. What had he been thinking? That time had stood still? No wonder Evan Masters had approached Nate with the same old hostility. Masters would have never told Griff Colburn to stay away from Kinsey. He was everything Masters could have dreamed of in a son-in-law.

"What are you doing here?" she asked tightly.

"Lauren called me. Thought you could use some moral support."

"That's nice, but I'm fine, and I can handle this." Kinsey lowered her head. "Griff Colburn, this is Detective Nate Paxton."

He acknowledged Nate with another *you're nobody look,* and said, "Paxton."

Kinsey pulled away from the big shot and turned to Nate. "I'll consider all we discussed. Are we done here?"

He reached for the police station's front door. "We are as far as I'm concerned. You're in an emergency lane, Colburn. Move it. Now."

Chapter Eighteen

TYPICALLY, WHEN Rodrigo attended Continental Miracles's board meetings, he remained focused, the consummate leader of an altruistic endeavor. Sleepless nights, however, had left him distracted, and now he'd received a text on his burn phone from Rafa, which read, 5-0 *outside on one-time turf.*

Rodrigo rose from the conference table. Surrounded by colleagues, he half-listened while interpreting Rafa's meaning. One of his marks was in plain sight at police headquarters.

Seated at the expansive mahogany table he'd imported from Brazil were the organization's physician/advisor, lawyer, treasurer, fundraising chair, and two board members at large.

Ordinarily in these meetings, Rodrigo forgot about drugs, gangs, and his contempt for the cartel. Here, he could hold his head high and be the man he'd once dreamed he would be.

Often, as in now, the conversation became heated. On the table were thirty-five grant petitions of critically ill, impoverished children. But no matter how committed, he and his board couldn't help them all.

He paused to look at the picture of Miguel on the wall opposite a window. He'd blown it up and had it restored from a torn snapshot, the only one he'd had before cancer weakened his brother. This was how Rodrigo chose to remember Miguel—happy, smiling—alive. As he would be, if only his family could have afforded proper medical care.

A second text chirped, and this time, members of the board stopped arguing long enough to face Rodrigo with quizzical expressions and raised eyebrows.

He ignored Rafa's message for the time being and motioned for Dr. Perez, to continue. The board had whittled down its decision to economics and statistics. Now his medical advisor would base his recommendation on which child had the likeliest chance to survive.

What insanity was this? In this room, he fought to save lives, while in another part of town he wanted two cops dead. Perhaps he should risk it. Order Rafa to take out the cop he could see now, leaving one down and one to go. But in doing so, the police would go after Rafa. His cousin would never surrender. Rafa would die in a bloodbath.

Rodrigo flinched. Had he sunk so low that he'd sacrifice a member of his family?

The board moved on to fundraising. Although the cartel kept Continental

Miracles in the black by laundering money to serve its immoral purposes, even a cartel couldn't compete with the myriad nonprofit agencies in the world clamoring for contributions.

The money part of the monthly meeting bored Rodrigo. He checked the text message, sighing in relief that he wouldn't order a drive by any time soon. Rafa's text read, *5-0 on turf with sum hoe*. Meaning the cop stood outside police headquarters with a woman. Rafa had attached a photo.

Diane Strickland, his fundraising chair, spoke next, enthralling the members interested in finance with a PowerPoint presentation. Another anonymous contribution for one hundred thousand dollars had found its way into Continental Miracles's coffers.

Applause and cheers trickled throughout the room.

Rodrigo turned his back on the group and closed his eyes. Oso and Sombra had struck again.

Rodrigo downloaded the photo. He stared at the close-up shot of the woman resting her head on Nate Paxton's shoulder. The woman at Griff Colburn's fundraiser? What was going on here?

He became aware of an awkward silence and that again people expected him to comment. Anxious to end the meeting so he could analyze the picture in private, Rodrigo said, "Excellent, Diane. What's next on the agenda?"

His fundraiser appeared crestfallen. Usually Rodrigo gushed after one of her reports, particularly one that reported an influx of money.

George Harlan, one of the board members at large, frowned. "Marketing and Publicity."

An assets drain as far as Rodrigo was concerned. The committee had discussed hiring a Hollywood elitist to be the organization's spokesperson. Harlan's action item had been to gather names and contact their agents.

The BMAL launched into his report spouting popular celebrities the group couldn't possibly afford. Even if the star agreed to work for free, the networks broadcasting the commercials would not. Rodrigo constantly reminded the group that its mission was not to spend money, but to get funds into the hands of sick children.

Vehemently opposed, and prepared to veto the entire idea, he returned to his seat at the table and waited for an opening in the discussion.

What was the beautiful Kinsey Masters doing with the traitorous Nate Paxton? Rodrigo surreptitiously studied Rafa's texted picture under the table. The couple's faces were serious, intense.

Just say the word, and she'll go to work for you. Confusion and paranoia twined like a creeping vine and wound their way through him. Why would Griff Colburn make such a random comment? Rodrigo's heart rate quickened. Was Colburn a spy for the police? Or had Kinsey Masters, knowing Rodrigo intended to attend the event that evening, planted the idea in the politician's head?

Paxton, the *cabrón*. Forcing evenness into breathing, Rodrigo poured a glass of water. He took a long swallow when what he wanted to do was hurl the glass against the window and watch it shatter into little pieces.

If Kinsey was in on the scheme to destroy him, he couldn't sit by and let it happen. Rodrigo's initial attraction to the beautiful athlete morphed into a thirst for revenge, then a goal he could use to his benefit, and one with domino effects.

The expression on Nate Paxton's face had been unmistakable. He cared for the woman beside him. Knowing of Paxton's feelings would also relieve Rafa of his constant surveillance. Rodrigo sent a text message to his henchman, dismissing him for the time being. The unguarded photo clearly proved that wherever Kinsey Masters went, Detective Nate Paxton would follow.

Rodrigo launched his new plan. "I've been opposed to this Hollywood nonsense from the beginning." He waved an arm over the grant requests left unfulfilled. "Do not forget our mission and that we are not The United Way." He tucked the phone in his pocket, stood, and circled the room. "If you're so intent on hiring a spokesman, at least use a celebrity close to home."

His statement was met with disappointed murmurs.

Harlan held up his hands for silence. "What the board initially agreed on is that we needed a household name. Someone to raise awareness," he added, clearly patronizing Rodrigo. "A local celebrity? How broad is his reach? Exactly who did you have in mind?"

"Did any of you follow the 2007 Women's World Cup?" Rodrigo asked.

As the board went from challenging to sudden interest, Rodrigo smiled. He would draw them into his web, the way he would Kinsey Masters.

"I know a woman who lives in Denver who will reach millions," Rodrigo said. "What's more, she's told me firsthand she admires our mission." He opened his laptop and googled her name. Seconds later, he transferred several action shots to the conference room screen.

Most of the board members had already come to their feet, but all were applauding. Undoubtedly, Rodrigo's next words weren't even necessary. He appraised his colleagues and smiled. "I propose we recruit Special K."

Chapter Nineteen

IRENE WASN'T SURE why administrators ordered beds for hospitals when, as far as she knew, no one slept. With a goose egg still bulging on the back of her head and accompanied by two of Denver's finest, she left Lundgren Medical Center.

She sat in the back of a squad car behind two silent police officers who promptly drove her to the Blue Star. There, they assisted her in gathering her belongings from her tossed hotel room. Naturally, she'd stopped at the front desk to collect her portrait of Danny.

Seven minutes later, they delivered her to the front steps of the historic Brown Palace. The passenger side officer who'd placed a call en route glanced over his shoulder. He handed her his cell phone and said, "For you."

Irene winced as she latched onto the phone. She had a strong inkling whom she was about to address.

"We've taken you to the hotel you should've never left in the first place," came Lieutenant Montoya's gruff voice. "If it's good enough for the Secret Service, it's good enough for you. There's been a development. Stay put."

Stay put? After all she'd been through, what did he think she could do, run a marathon? Her plans were simple for the day. Forget about that dreadful hospital gown, slip into comfortable pajamas, and recover from her head injury.

An efficient bellman met her at the revolving doors and commandeered her luggage. Tempted by the aroma wafting in from the adjoining coffee and pastry shop, she almost veered in that direction, but the bellman was already several feet ahead of her. She trudged past the shop with regret and made plans to stop by later.

Admiring the spit and polish of the granite and travertine floor, she was no less impressed with the Brown Palace than the first time she'd stayed here. While waiting to check in, she glanced about the voluminous lobby, focusing on the area set off by tables and chairs used daily for high tea.

Decades of craft must've gone into the rich paneling and stenciled wall paintings and interior design. Yawning upward, several floors of hotel rooms protected by decorative wrought iron led to a dramatic stained glass ceiling.

On her way to the elevators, her gaze traveled to a room off the lobby that read "Spa." Since the lieutenant had grounded her, so-to-speak, perhaps that's where she'd spend her time-out. She could only hope that the development he'd talked about didn't pertain to her. And if it did, that any new facts discovered cleared her one hundred percent of murder.

Inside her hotel room, she showered and dropped into bed. Her goal was to sleep a solid eight hours. But three hours later, her overtaxed brain and pounding heart shocked her awake.

She yanked the phone's receiver from its base on the nightstand. "Where will I find the business center?" she asked breathlessly.

She threw on her clothes and left the hotel room, careful to avoid the railing. A few feet beyond her fifth floor hotel room, she'd be able to look down into the lobby. She'd rather not. Heights had never been her thing.

First things first, she grabbed the coveted coffee she'd bypassed that morning and located the business center. Then, trying to hold on to what she recalled of the dream, she sat down at a vacant PC.

The dream had surrounded a man taking pictures of a little girl. Irene's mind latched onto that loose thread like a seamstress starving for work. She'd woken up remembering the name from the file: *Trevelle Detective Agency.*

Every search engine she checked gained her nothing, and Irene soon understood why. After a fire destroyed his agency, there was no sign that Trevelle had stayed in business. The little background she'd found on him said he'd run a successful agency up until June of 2001. He'd represented banks, corporations, and celebrity clients.

She sat back and folded her arms. So, how could she contact him?

Without the file she had no proof, the police had little impetus to pursue the private eye, and although Nate had seen the contents, his word now became hearsay. If Irene could find Trevelle, maybe she could find out why Dr. Mitchell, who'd publicly dedicated his life to helping unwed mothers, was a party to such a hideous crime.

An online search of the Denver *Yellow* and *White Pages* revealed zero. Finally, she approached the clerk running the hotel copy center. The employee handed her two cumbersome Denver telephone directories, and in no time at all, she located Trevelle's Littleton address.

She stepped out into the hallway and pulled out her cell phone.

A man answered on the first ring, his gravelly voice sounding an awful lot like the sourpuss lieutenant she'd met recently. She shook her head. Well, she'd trusted a lot of smooth talkers in her day. Perhaps it was time to rely on some bona fide grouches.

"I'm looking for Mr. Peter Trevelle," she said.

"Speaking."

Irene let out a breath and rushed on. "Mr. Trevelle, my name is Irene Turner. It's very important I see you. Unfortunately, I can't come to you." Her gaze wandered her four-star prison. "I'm prepared to pay handsomely for your time. If you'll meet with me, I'd be happy to buy you dinner."

"You're not from around here, are you?"

Damn accent. She lifted her eyes to the ceiling. "No. Will you meet with me or not?"

"No can do. Does your call have anything to do with your husband's murder, Mrs. Turner?"

Irene closed her eyes. "You read the paper?"

"Sure did. You kill him?"

"I did not."

"That's what I was thinking when I read *The Post*. I thought why would a trap shooting champion off her old man in Denver, when she could've easily disposed of him in her own state of Oklahoma?"

"The police hold your opinion, too, Mr. Trevelle," Irene said dryly. "But that's not the reason I'm calling."

"Oh? What is the reason you're calling?"

There was no way she was having this conversation over the phone. Up on the murder, he might not be somebody who was merely well read. He might be the scoundrel who had something to do with Stephen's death.

Irene cleared her throat. "As I said, I'd feel better if we had this conversation in person." *And in front of witnesses.*

"I repeat, 'no can do.' I'm in a wheelchair. Traveling's a problem for me."

Lord. "Would you meet with me if I came to you?"

"Are you still prepared to pay *handsomely*—and buy me dinner?"

"Are you still at the 869 Eagle Ridge address?"

"I am."

"Well, then, I'm on my way." Irene pushed end, gritting her teeth that her life had turned into one major pain in her backside.

The police had explained she should contact her insurance about her Mercedes, but what about Stephen's SUV? How long would it be off limits?

She shuddered as Lieutenant Montoya's warning of *Stay Put* went from nagging to screaming. She could call, explain what she wanted to do, but he'd nix her scheme in a Denver minute.

She rode the elevator back to her room, changed into a pair of capris and a light jacket. Then to cover the bags under her eyes, which probably equated to the size of the bump on her head, she dabbed on some makeup. Fifteen minutes later, Irene was back in the lobby.

She stopped at the front desk. "If anyone from the Denver Police Department calls or comes looking for me, and *only* the Denver PD," she said to the clerk, "I need you to do two things."

A fresh-faced young man, who reminded her of Danny, widened his gaze. "Yes ma'am?"

"You check his credentials, then you may give him my cell phone number."

"Yes, ma'am."

Irene sighed. She supposed she should face reality. She really did look like a ma'am. Outside, she spotted a waiting line of taxis and almost reconsidered meeting with Trevelle. Should she or shouldn't she?

You try to stay put when someone's kidnapped your daughter, murdered your husband, and tried to set you up with your own .38.

The *shoulds* won. Irene flagged a cab.

Chapter Twenty

AS A GIRL, GWYNETH would have never taken chances that compromised her parents' standing in the community. She had servants who did that type of thing for her. But this time, she was on her own, and after twenty-eight years, she knew how to do it.

She squeezed her Lexus into the single-car garage and dragged her suitcases into the musty living room. Then, unzipping her bag, she removed two water bottles and zipped it back up. With no furniture in the place, her largest piece of luggage would have to act as a chair. She slumped onto it and shuddered at the dirty walls and battered mini blinds.

Generally, she frowned on procrastination, but as she looked around the fixer-upper she'd purchased eight months ago, she melted in relief that procrastinate was what she'd done.

She'd bought it as a shelter, both for her taxes and for the starving artists the gallery sometimes housed when Masterpieces hosted their exhibits. Still, running a successful gallery took time and resources, so the tiny residence, located two blocks east of the family business, had sat empty and neglected the entire time.

It was also one of the many investments she'd acquired under her maiden name and kept from Evan. Miserable clod. He would soon learn how much he'd lost by betraying her.

The place had no water or electricity, but that was the least of her problems. She'd phone Yasmine after Gwyneth handled her urgent business and have her assistant call Xcel Energy to turn on the utilities. Of course, Yasmine knew about the property. She'd found it in the first place and had been in on the purchase from inspection to closing. Good luck to the police if they tried to pry her best friend for information. Yasmine was closer to Gwyneth than a sister.

Swallowing hard, Gwyneth tugged the paper she'd recovered from her safe deposit box out of her pocket along with her cell phone. She'd switched it off the second she'd left home, unable to bear the calls from her children that no doubt would follow.

She powered it on. As expected, numerous messages flooded the screen. Evan, Lauren, Yasmine, Jay. And finally the one message she desperately needed to see. *Kinsey.*

A very good sign that all would be well. Kinsey would never turn her back on her mother. Memories flooded Gwyneth of the infant who'd meant so much to her, the only child she'd thought she'd ever have, and the remarkable woman her daughter had become. Heart soaring, Gwyneth closed her eyes and prepared to push send. But at the last second, she moved her thumb away from the button.

Contacting any of her family right now would be a mistake. Before she could make things right with them, she had to find out what in the hell had gone wrong.

Gnawing her bottom lip, she keyed in the first number on the list she'd taken from the deposit box. Seconds ticked by until an ancient voice came on the line.

She placed her hand over her thudding heart. "Dr. Clifford Mitchell, please," Gwyneth said urgently.

"Who's calling?"

She rolled her eyes and scrambled to make up a name. "Sydney Myers. I'm a former employee of Dr. Mitchell's."

"Oh? When did you work for him?"

Who was this cretin with her twenty questions? "1992," Gwyneth replied, choosing an arbitrary date out of nowhere. Hearing suspicion in the old woman's voice, Gwyneth added another yarn to her lies. "I was a medical transcriptionist." There. The old crone couldn't possibly remember all the people who'd worked in the background. "I'm hoping Dr. Mitchell remembers me and will give me a reference." *Just put him on the phone.*

"I'm sorry, Ms. *Myers*, you said it was? Dr. Mitchell was my husband, but he passed away six weeks ago."

Oh God. No. "Really? He *died?*" Gwyneth nearly shouted. "Was it expected?"

Too late she realized how rude and hysterical she must've sounded.

"Good luck in your job search," the woman said. "If your attitude is any indication, I can understand why you're unemployed." The line went dead.

Dead. Gwyneth ran her fingers through her usually coiffed hair to find a tangled mass. Mitchell was old when she met him, so why did this bother her? Possibly because he'd had misgivings about giving her Kinsey until she and her checkbook convinced him otherwise. Had the fool made a deathbed confession?

Without ventilation, the empty house was stifling. Sweat beaded her forehead, back, and armpits. She shucked off her blazer then tried the next number on the list. Turner Industries. She huffed. Naturally, she would get voicemail. Stretching her neck and rolling her shoulders, she waited to be directed to a human being, cautioning herself not to blow it the way she had with Mrs. Mitchell.

Gwyneth needn't have worried. In the next instance, a message played, "Turner Industries is in transition following the tragic shooting of its president, Stephen W. Turner."

Shaking, she pushed end and stared at her iPhone. Something was very, very wrong. She'd bribed two men to get Kinsey, and within weeks of each other, both were dead.

Chapter Twenty-one

NATE DIDN'T STICK around to watch Kinsey fall into Griff Colburn's arms. Why add salt to a wound? A retired NFL player and future congressman, Colburn's fans would undoubtedly get him elected.

Good for Kins. They'd have little jet setting athletes running around and live happily ever after. Nate wasn't jealous—much.

Returning to the world he knew, he rounded a group of detectives' desks and found Sammy typing away. Nate's pony-tailed partner used his typical two-fingered approach to get the job done. When people ribbed Sam about this technique, his standard comeback was, "Why wear out the other eight?" Unorthodox maybe, but Nate had seen his partner turn in a report faster and with more accuracy than many others on the department.

Nate slumped in the chair facing his partner.

Without looking up, Sammy pecked away. "Kinsey and her dad on their way?"

"They're outta here. How goes the revision?"

"Got it down to the bare bones. I dare the judge to find one thing wrong with this thing of beauty."

Earlier, Sammy had presented a district court judge with a warrant to search Gwyneth Masters's residence and business for any and all evidence pertaining to Kinsey's kidnapping. The Honorable Lawrence Grossman had rejected it. He wanted the search whittled down to items pertaining to Stephen Turner's murder—specifically the file stolen from Irene's hotel room or evidence pointing to the people who'd broken in.

Not much to go on, but at least the warrant would get the police onto the properties.

Sammy stopped typing, and his desktop printer took over. After the sheets ran through the feeder, he picked up the reworded document. "*Vamanos?*"

Nate stood. "Yeah. Assuming Grossman clears the warrant, do you want to search the business or residence first?"

"I vote the gallery," Sammy said. "To keep the secrets Gwyneth did, she's not going to keep that kind of dirty laundry hanging around her *casa.*"

Nate walked with Sammy toward the stairs, relieved to be traveling in a different direction than Kinsey for the time being. With things already strained between them, he could just imagine her reaction when he and Sam showed up at her folks' home to go over the place.

Nate was betting that after Kinsey and Lauren picked up Jay at the airport, the trio would join their father at the house. He and Sammy would make it to the Masters's estate eventually, but Nate was more than happy to postpone that uncomfortable meet and greet.

Lieutenant Montoya caught up with them at the stairs.

Nate held open the stairwell door for him; the boss gave them the once-over before going forward. "You off to see the judge?"

He and Sammy replied in unison, "Yes, sir."

"Dot those i's and cross those t's. This investigation could kick up a firestorm."

"Any news on Irene?" Nate asked.

"No, and I like it that way," the lieutenant said. "Patrol dropped her off at the Brown Palace midmorning. My guess, with that bump on her head and up all night, she's sleeping it off." He hesitated. "But she has a tendency to wander, so I thought if I showed up and took her out to dinner outside the hotel, it'd serve two purposes."

Nate glanced at Sammy, who returned a not-going-there, vacant look. "What's that?" Nate asked.

"Keep her from feeling cooped up and see if anything's come to her about the Blue Star intruder."

When Nate and Sammy just stood there, the lieutenant cleared his throat. "Keep me in the loop." He headed upstairs.

Taking the flight in the opposite direction, Sammy said, "Think he realizes he has the hots for Irene?"

"Oh, yeah, he does." Nate reached into his pants pocket for his keys. "And it's scaring the shit out of him."

With last night's Interceptor farmed out to someone else, Nate and Sammy were stuck again with the department's *exploder*. The two rattled on in the ancient Crown Vic toward Gwyneth Masters's place of business and pulled into Masterpieces's parking lot thirty minutes later.

An elaborate set of chimes rang as they walked through the door. Sammy took one look around and whistled under his breath. "Swank digs."

"Art must pay well," Nate added, moving farther into the well-lit, high-ceiling gallery. He paused to look at a white curvy sculpture made out of limestone. Since it resembled nothing he could identify, he labeled it abstract and nearly hit the ground when he read the price tag. "They want fifteen thousand for this thing?"

But Sammy wasn't listening. He'd already crossed the room. By the way he was shaking his head, he was suffering sticker shock over some odd-shaped art form.

Nate joined him.

"Wonder what the rent is on a place like this?" Sammy said in a low voice.

"More than I keep in my piggy bank. Seems to me this location is recent. I don't remember the Masters operating out of such plush digs when I was a kid."

Sammy leaned forward to study something Nate thought looked like a cross between a whale and an overweight belly dancer. "Not only was Gwyneth's old man loaded," Sammy explained. "I read he contracted some weird disease in the hospital and died as a result. Gwyneth sued and won."

"Bucks heaped onto more bucks," Nate added.

A trim, attractive woman rounded the corner, her most noticeable feature her striking black hair. Generally, Nate estimated age well. Not with this lady. She could've been anywhere between thirty-five and fifty. Adorned with gold jewelry, she wore a white flowing dress with a red sequined belt, which matched the red of her traditional *bindi*.

"Welcome to Masterpieces," she said with a smile that seemed frozen in place. "How may I help you today?"

When Nate and Sammy held out their badges, she appeared to shrink. She'd obviously been notified of Gwyneth's disappearance. The question remained, by whom? A family member or Gwyneth herself?

Nate made the introductions and presented the court-ordered bad news. "We have a warrant to search the gallery, Ms. . . ."

"Takeri." She took the document, perused it, and frowned. "Yasmine Takeri. I'm Gwyneth Masters's assistant. It appears I have no choice. Where," she said stiffly, "would you like to begin?"

"Mrs. Masters's office," Sammy said.

Nodding, Yasmine escorted them through two sections of the gallery that led into a back hallway. On both sides of the walls hung various pictures of Kinsey, highlighting her soccer career. Nate slowed his pace while Sammy and Yasmine walked on ahead. Most every shot of the black and whites caught some level of Kinsey's skill, but there wasn't a shot that didn't capture her determination. Nate's heart felt a little stab. She'd been on fire back then. Still was.

He thought of Griff Colburn's showy exhibition in the police parking lot and his reference to Kinsey as *babe*. Nate put a lid on Memory Lane, caught up with his partner, and concentrated on the investigation.

Nate hadn't seen Gwyneth Masters in years, but nothing about her office surprised him. Her contemporarily furnished base was immaculate and efficient. Black and red art, complemented by silver chrome furniture and sculptures, carried the room. A clutter-free glass-topped desk lay over dove gray carpeting, and behind the desk, sat a matching dove gray executive chair. The other side of the room housed a glass-topped conference table and chrome accent chairs. This table held her laptop, legal pads, and portfolios, and was the place where Gwyneth apparently did most of her work.

Sammy donned gloves and approached the table while Nate studied the room and stifled a laugh. *Where the hell are the files?*

Gwyneth's assistant offered no help. She stood by the door, a confident smile on her face, arms folded.

Nate scanned the walls and found the false panel. Running his hand over the textured space, he saw no lever until he moved aside another one of her paintings. He pulled, the panel slid back, and four gun metal gray file cabinets appeared before him.

Finding them locked, he glanced over his shoulder and sent a challenging glare to Yasmine's defiant one. Her smile faded. She stepped forward and handed him a set of keys.

"Loyalty is admirable," he said softly, "but not in this case."

"Perhaps if you told me what you're looking for. I can assure you my employer has nothing to hide."

Sammy looked up from the conference table and perusing the legal pad. "How long have you worked for your *employer*?"

"A while," she replied.

"Try specifically," Sammy pressed.

She sighed. "Gwyneth and I met in boarding school in our teens. Honestly, I cannot fathom why you're here."

Detecting a fading Indian accent, Nate asked, "How long have you been in the States, Ms. Takeri?"

Her black eyes met his. "Nice try, Detective. I've been a naturalized US citizen since 1989."

"Ever heard of Stephen or Irene Turner?" Nate added.

"No," she replied.

"What about Gwyneth? You speak to her today?"

"Unfortunately not."

"We're going to be a while, Ms. Takeri." Sammy rose from the table and escorted her to the door. "We'll call if we need you. Don't let us keep you from your work."

In the doorway, she pivoted on her shiny red heels. "I'll be in my office right across the hall."

Once she was out of earshot, Sammy asked, "What do you think?"

"I think," Nate said, opening the top drawer of the file cabinet, "she's up to her *bindi* in everything."

Chapter Twenty-two

ON HER WAY TO Peter Trevelle's Littleton home, Irene directed the taxicab driver to stop at a deli she spotted en route. Climbing into the cab with her purchase of sandwiches, chips, and drinks, she smiled. Money wasn't a problem—yet. Still, she considered the amount she'd had to shell out a bargain. She'd been prepared to spend a great deal more at the hotel, wooing and coaxing information out of the handicapped detective.

In the backseat of the cab, she checked her cell phone for messages and drew a relieved breath when there were none. She switched off the phone and let it fall into the recesses of her handbag. The last thing she needed was three members of the Denver PD checking up on her.

As Denver transitioned into the suburbs, she barely noticed they'd left the Mile High City. Only the welcome signs the taxi passed indicated they'd gone through Englewood, followed by Littleton, arriving at last onto Cliff Swallow Drive, and Irene's ultimate destination.

No surprise, Trevelle lived in a yellow brick rancher. What she found astonishing were the seven steps leading to the front door, along with a freshly-mowed lawn. She asked the driver to wait as she studied her surroundings. Irene's gaze finally settled on the riding lawn mower and a handicap ramp, which led to a side door beside the garage.

Based on what she'd seen so far, she could only assume Peter Trevelle had been telling the truth.

She leaned forward and held out a hundred dollar bill. "I don't know the man I'm about to meet. It is my sincere hope that he's harmless. But you never know, do you? Wait here for ten minutes. If I show up at the front door and wave, you may assume I'm super-duper. If I don't show up in ten minutes, I'd really be obliged if you'd call the police."

The driver, who'd vigorously chewed a toothpick the entire trip, stopped chewing. He stared back at Irene, but at last took the money. "Okay, lady."

"If I do give you the all clear sign," Irene said, opening the door to the cab, "come back in one hour."

Arms loaded with a meal for a stranger, she made her way up the steps. She rang the bell, occasionally glancing over her shoulder. Trevelle lived in a modest area. A few of his neighbors were out and about, painting, mowing, and otherwise enjoying the mild April afternoon. But most importantly, the cabby sat waiting.

Facing the house, she rang the bell again and peered through the screen.

Much like the exterior, the interior seemed neat and orderly.

Soon, a gray-headed, mustachioed man wheeled himself into the living room. "Hold your horses," he said, rolling toward her. "Takes me a while to get where I'm going."

"Sorry," Irene replied. "I wasn't sure if you heard me the first time."

He opened the door and took the bags with the sandwiches. Irene carried the drinks to a cherry wood table in an adjoining dining room.

"Do we need silverware?" he asked gruffly.

"Nope, I brought sandwiches. Turkey on wheat and ham on rye."

He harrumphed. "The way you talked, I was expecting steak and lobster."

"That's when I thought you would come to me."

Frowning, Trevelle chose the ham on rye.

Behind her, Irene spotted *The Denver Post* on the buffet table beside a window. Clearly, the private detective had been telling the truth when he said he'd read the article about Stephen's murder.

When she sat unmoving, he said, "Aren't you going to dig in?"

"I will in a minute." She rose from the chair, crossed the room, and waved to the cab driver, then held her breath as he nodded and sped away.

She returned to the table, sat down, and unwrapped her sandwich.

Trevelle smirked. "Now that you're feeling safe, what did you want to see me about?"

She motioned to the nearby newspaper. "Anything in that article seem familiar to you?"

He continued chewing. "I don't know. Should it?"

Weren't detectives supposed to be curious? "How'd you end up in that chair?"

"Accident."

"Did it have anything to do with the fire that happened in 2001?"

"As a matter of fact, it did. You writing a book? What's on your mind, Mrs. Turner?"

She'd managed two measly bites of her sandwich. Irene ordered her protesting stomach to wait and set down her food. "Over the years, you took pictures of a little girl by the name of Kinsey Masters. The man who hired you was a man named Dr. Clifford Mitchell. I'm here to find out why he hired you."

Trevelle finished his sandwich. "Mitchell . . . Mitchell."

"You don't play coy very well, Mr. Trevelle, and, frankly, I'm sick and tired of being yanked around." She grabbed her purse and rose from the chair.

"Let me ask *you* something before *I* answer. Is Mitchell the reason you came to Denver?"

"He is."

"Why? What's he to you?"

Why was Trevelle being so evasive? As though she were playing chess with the man, she sat back down. "I answered your question. Answer mine first."

"Fair enough. Obviously I know who Kinsey Masters is, and, yes, I remember Clifford Mitchell. As to why he hired me, that's privileged information."

"Is it still privileged if he's dead?"

"Well, now that depends." Trevelle rubbed his hand over a jaw in need of a razor. "Does Mitchell's death have anything to do with your husband's demise?"

"Not in the least. According to Norma Mitchell, the doctor's wife, he died from Parkinson's. As for my husband, I have no clue who killed him, but I promise you, it wasn't me."

Irene went on to explain her contact with Norma and all of the un-fortunate events that had occurred since she'd come to Denver. She summed up her explanation with, "Finally, on the way to the hospital, the detectives I was with notified me that my husband had been found shot to death in my Mercedes with my gun, which is now missing." Irene held out her fingers an inch apart. "The police are this close to calling me a suspect. My goal is to lengthen the odds."

"That's quite a story." Trevelle watched her for a moment before wheeling over to the buffet. He tossed aside the *Denver Post* article. Beneath the newspaper lay a manila file.

Irene's heart stuttered. It didn't appear to be the stolen file from the safe, but what the hell difference did that make? She was to the point of changing her name to *Easy Target Turner*. She was paranoid with good cause. People *were* out to get her.

Trevelle grabbed the newspaper and file and rolled back to the table.

The open file revealed duplicate invoices and photographs of the originals given to her by Norma and later stolen from Irene's hotel room. Then Trevelle set the grainy photo of Irene from a trap shooting competition next to the last snapshot he'd taken of Kinsey during a high school soccer tournament.

"When you called, I got curious. So I did some research. You look a whole lot like Kinsey Masters, Mrs. Turner." His jaw turned to granite, and his gaze flashed with fury. "But you'll forgive me if I don't give you these papers so you can go bilk a young woman out of her hard-earned fortune.

"You see, Mitchell's whole purpose in having them taken was so the birth mother could observe how her daughter had grown throughout the years."

Irene sat back in open-mouthed astonishment. "Now you listen here. I couldn't care less about Kinsey's money. My only purpose in coming to see a numbskull like you is because I've been wronged, and I want a relationship with my daughter.

"Want to know why Kinsey looks like me? It's called genetics, Mr. Trevelle. Call me a good for nothing tramp, but I slept with Kinsey's father who happened to be married. I became pregnant. But here's the catch. When I delivered, that ethics-of-a-snake Dr. Mitchell told me my baby had died.

"My health records were in that file the doctor's wife gave me, along with the photocopy of a check for eight hundred thousand dollars, these pictures, and your invoices, which, by the way, is how I came up with your name. Evan and Gwyneth Masters had to have made a deal with Mitchell. I *am* the birth mother, and I can assure you that bastard never sent me so much as a sympathy card, much less my daughter's photographs."

The corners of Trevelle's mouth curved upward. Handicapped or not, Irene almost knocked him out of his chair.

"Pretty passionate speech, and after all that, I'm inclined to believe you. But before I dismiss the word of a respected doctor who's not here to defend himself, and take the word of a possible murder suspect, I'd be a fool not to ask for additional proof."

Irene hung her head. Short of attacking the man and stealing his information, all she could do was wait and order a DNA test as quickly as possible.

She yanked out her wallet. "Despite the fact I've wasted a trip, I promised to pay you. How much do I owe you?"

He shook his head. "This one's on me. Sorry I couldn't help you."

Irene was a fraction from returning her billfold to the purse when her wallet-size photos fell open. *Oh my God. I do have proof.* "Maybe my looks won't convince you, but hopefully my son's will. Irene slipped a photo of Danny out of its protective plastic. Gone these many months, the boy smiling back at her nearly split her heart in two. Irene swallowed over a painful lump. Then holding herself together, she laid it beside Kinsey's and gazed at the family taken away from her. "This is my son, Danny, Kinsey's half-brother. We lost him two years ago. He was fifteen."

Trevelle sat for a moment then picked up the photo. Studying it, the private eye gave nothing away. Irene forgot how to breathe. Damn this sinister world where evil made a mockery out of good.

"One-hundred-fifty-dollars a day, plus expenses." He rolled away from the table. "Come with me into my office. I want to go over with you the rest of the information I have on this case, so we don't duplicate facts we both know."

Her poor heart on a rollercoaster, Irene's knees wobbled when she stood. "You believe me?"

"I have eyes in my head, Mrs. Turner. I had little doubt in the first place."

Approaching stroke level, Irene lashed out, "Then why all this rigmarole to prove I was telling the truth?"

"Because twenty-eight years ago," Trevelle said. "I also believed Dr. Clifford Mitchell."

Chapter Twenty-three

KINSEY FLASHED Lauren a worried look and stared at her brother as Jay drained the last of his beer and ordered another. He'd traveled light after leaving New Zealand. A camera case and a carry-on duffle bag were all he'd arrived with at DIA.

Jay had been adamant about not going home. He wanted the complete story from Kinsey and Lauren before they talked with their dad. Not only could Evan Masters intimidate, he had a way of taking over. Right now, they wanted to talk *about* him, not *to* him.

They chose The Bull & Bush to have this conversation. Although the 40-year-old landmark would be booming in a couple of hours, on a weekday, and mid-afternoon, the place was fairly empty and absent any live music. What's more, the dim pub suited their moods.

Griff had disappeared to take one of his frequent phone calls, and at last Kinsey felt free to speak.

"It's not that I don't trust Griff," she said. "I do. But for right now, this is an intensely private family matter." She glanced at her sister. "I wish you wouldn't have said anything."

Lauren folded her arms and glared at Kinsey. "So, he was worried, Kins. Sue the man. Griff cares about you."

Jay set his beer on the table. "The last thing we need is for this to tear us apart." He slumped in his chair and ran both hands through his sun-bleached blond hair. "Dad had an affair? I'm never getting married. Of all the couples in the world who I thought had it together, it was Mom and Dad." Jay shook his head and looked directly at Kinsey. "And to learn Mom stole you as a baby. That's *crazy,* man."

"I'm having a hard time believing it myself," Kinsey said, spotting Griff coming toward their table again. "But apparently it's true. My question to both of you is, '*are we okay?*'"

Lauren reached across the table. "Quit being so melodramatic. We're fine. We're blood."

"Now just a little diluted," Jay said.

Kinsey sat back and sighed. But then catching her younger sister and brother's wink, she smiled in relief. She loved these two.

"Looks fun," Griff said cautiously. "Can I join this party?"

Lauren was right. He cared. For years before he'd shown romantic interest in Kinsey, he'd been her friend. And what had Kinsey done? Given him one and two word answers since he'd graciously offered to take them to the airport.

She motioned to a chair. "Here's what we know," she said. "Rather, what we think we know."

With every revelation, Griff grew paler. He glanced at Lauren. "This is a far cry from 'my mother's disappeared.' This is disastrous. Do any of you have a clue where she could be?"

Kinsey groaned. "You're thinking about the election?"

"Call me selfish, Kins, but, yeah, I am." Wherever he went, thanks to his dominating size, good looks, and his former Bronco status, Griff Colburn attracted a following. He looked both ways, before speaking. "My opponents get wind of this and they'll spin it until the public thinks *I* took you when you were a baby."

Kinsey held back reminding him that he was the one who'd done his best to link them romantically.

Jay held up a finger to a waiter, signaling for another beer.

"Take it easy, tiger," Kinsey said.

"Why? I'm not driving, and you're only my half-sister now, so that means you can only give half the orders."

"I can still take you to the turf, so watch out, you little pipsqueak, and ease up on the booze."

"So, this Irene Turner," Jay said, ignoring Kinsey's threat and advice, "according to the paper, she's a gun expert. Can't see how she's related to you, Kins."

"Got you there, Kins," Griff echoed. "You're pro-gun control."

Elbows on the table, Kinsey linked her fingers and rested her chin on her hands. "Maybe once I get to know her, I can bring her around to my way of thinking."

Lauren scoffed. "She's from *Ok-la-ho-ma.* They keep guns under their pillows, under their beds, and in every room in the house."

"Oh, they do not," Kinsey said, laughing. "And for that matter, so do a lot of people in Colorado."

"If she's your birth mother, what's she to us?" Jay asked.

"Lucky for her, nothing," Lauren said, rolling her eyes and elbowing her brother. "Why would you ask a question like that at a time like this?"

"Can't a guy be curious? When do we get to meet her?"

Griff's cell phone rang. Checking the number, he sighed. "I gotta take this."

He moved several feet away. Truthfully, Kinsey was glad to see him go. What she had to talk to her siblings about shouldn't involve a man running for congress.

"You'll meet Irene after I get to know her better." Watching Griff, Kinsey prayed he'd stayed put. "Mom's in trouble, guys. You remember Nate Paxton, don't you?"

"Ball player," Jay said.

"Smokin'," Lauren replied.

Kinsey went on to explain the FBI's possible involvement and that Gwyneth was now a suspect in Irene's husband's murder.

"There's more," Kinsey said dismally. "Nate wants us, if we hear from Mom, to encourage her to turn herself in."

That remark met with stunned silence. Her brother and sister didn't even blink.

Kinsey's shoulders fell. "Look. I can't tell you what to do, but I've been thinking about it. I think we should do what he says. I don't want to see her get hurt."

"I can't believe we're having this conversation," Lauren said. "This is our mother we're talking about. She's no kidnapper . . . murderer. That Irene Turner person, she's the gun expert. I'd rather help Mom acquire a false passport and get her out of the country than help the police send her to prison."

"I know a guy who knows a guy," Jay cut in.

"Then we all get into trouble," Kinsey argued, motioning her brother and sister to tone it down with her hands. "What good would that do? I'm no lawyer, and, of course, I want to talk to Irene. But if she's determined to see Mom prosecuted for kidnapping me as a baby, I don't know that I can change her mind." Kinsey hesitated. "Still, I'm with you, I can't see Mom killing *anyone*."

"So many secrets," Lauren said. "And Dad never knew?"

"Hey, don't give him a free pass," Jay said. "He started all this."

"If I can forgive a woman for stealing me from my birth mom, you can give Dad another chance," Kinsey shot back. "He's suffering, too, Jay, and he's worried sick about Mom." Kinsey stared at her brother and sister. "Where do you think she would go?"

Jay slapped his forehead. "I'm an idiot."

"You've just now figured that out?" Lauren took a swig of her beer.

"I know how to find her," he said.

"How?" Both Kinsey and Lauren cried in unison.

"An app on my phone. It's called *Find My Friends*. The last time I was home, Mom wanted to come with me to a photo shoot, but we needed to take separate cars. She was worried about losing me, so I loaded the app on her smart phone."

"Oh my gosh," Kinsey said. "Does she have to have it turned on?"

"Yeah, that's the problem. She does. If not, the app remains at her last activated location."

Lauren came to her feet. "Well, what are you waiting for? See if you find her."

Jay and his tech-savvy fingers went to work. Kinsey clutched her sister's arm. They waited.

He looked up from his phone. "Make that idiot past tense. You may now call me genius. Got her. Check this out."

Lauren peered over Jay's shoulder. "Wow, that's close to the gallery."

Griff ended his conversation and headed their way.

"He can't be a party to this." Kinsey lowered her voice. "I'll ask him to take us back to the police station, and we'll get my car."

"Then what?" Lauren asked.

"What do you think? We'll go find Mom."

PHONE IN HAND, Gwyneth rose from the suitcase and paced. *Think.* Who would've killed both Mitchell and Turner? Or could this simply be a huge coincidence that both men were dead? Who else had been involved? The midwife? That was a stretch. She was simply someone Dr. Mitchell had hired because he'd worked with her before, she'd keep her mouth shut, she lived in Denver, and she desperately needed money.

Irene Turner had to be the only logical explanation. Obviously, she'd found out about Kinsey and was out for revenge. Had the little adulteress killed the doctor, her husband, and now planned to get rid of Gwyneth?

In this closed-up house that doubled as an oven, sweat poured off her face and body. Her options running dangerously low, Gwyneth had no choice but to get out of the country. She couldn't help her children dead.

She grabbed her water bottle and ambled toward the kitchen. Opening the back door would cool off the house, but she didn't dare. The backyard was unfenced, the houses built close together, and she might attract a neighbor's attention. She pried open the window over the sink instead. A cool breeze drifted in. With no choice but to use the precious water, she soaked her scarf. Then, sponging off her décolletage and face, she wrapped the wet fabric around her neck.

Relieved for the time being, she shut the window and refastened the lock. She re-entered the living room and drew back the mini blinds. A quiet neighborhood, nothing but a stray dog in sight, Gwyneth sat back on her suitcase, relaxed, scrolled down to Yasmine's picture on her iPhone, and pushed send.

The call went straight to voice mail. *Yasmine. Answer. Please.*

Gwyneth pushed resend. This time Yasmine picked up, but her voice was so faint, Gwyneth could barely make out her words. "Why are you whispering?"

"The police. They're in your office. They have a warrant."

Gwyneth's gaze darted around the barren living room. "In that case, they're bound to find the deed to this property." With every second, the stakes rose higher. "All right. Don't talk. Listen. Find me a place out of the country. Some place without extradition, I don't care. You may have to leave the office to do it, just do so quietly. I'm turning off my phone." Her next words were trapped by a shuddering breath. "Thank you, Yaz, for everything. You've been my dear friend."

"Don't sound so defeated," Yasmine demanded. "This isn't like you."

Gwyneth gripped the phone. "This time, I'm afraid that's the case."

From outside, she heard frantic barking, followed by breaking glass. She jumped from the suitcase and onto her feet.

A hooded figure emerged from the kitchen holding a gun.

The heat she'd been draped in turned into ice cold dread. Her brain grappled to make out his identity behind the mask. But all she could focus on was the deadly barrel of the weapon. She'd outwitted every nemesis who'd ever crossed her. Not this time. He fired. As Gwyneth fell, she thought of her children. She even cried out for Evan.

SEQUESTERED IN Gwyneth Masters's private office, Nate took one file cabinet, Sammy the other. They would systematically remove stacks from the drawers, review them, and put them back again. The job was tedious, and, so far, had earned them no sign that Gwyneth Masters had abducted Kinsey as an infant.

Sammy dropped into Gwyneth's chrome back chair and opened the first file of a new pile. "I'll tell you one thing, if organization was a crime, this lady would get a life sentence."

"She pays attention to detail," Nate agreed. "She'd have to for her to carry out this kind of deceit. We'll drop off the laptop at IT, see what they can pull from the hard drive."

Sammy flipped another page and sighed. "Man. I'm in the wrong business. Even with the commission she charges, these dudes make money."

Nate grinned, but kept searching through data. "You'd give up all this to become an artist?"

"Hell, yeah. You saw what people pay for that weird shit out there. I made stuff just like it when I was two. Only hope Elena will let me borrow her Play Dough."

"Go for it. You'll live longer." Nate laughed, sobering when he stumbled upon the first useful piece of information he'd seen. "Check this out. Gwyneth recently closed on an investment property. It's in her name only."

Sammy's head shot up. He rose from his chair. He'd reached Nate's side, when from across the hall, Yasmine's cry of alarm, followed by, "Oh, my God!" carried from her office.

Nate and Sammy almost collided racing to the door.

Phone in hand, a wide-eyed Yasmine met them in the hall. "Gwyneth. I was on the phone with her. I heard a shot."

"Where is she?" Nate demanded.

"Two blocks away. Eight-ten Foxgrove Drive."

Nate yanked his gaze from Yasmine to Sammy. "Location of her recent closing."

Sammy nodded and was immediately on his phone. He notified Dispatch of the possible shooting, while Nate used his cell to request backup to secure the gallery due to the uncompleted search.

Patrol arrived less than four minutes later.

"Ms. Takeri," Nate said. "You're coming with us."

Yasmine grabbed her purse. "Not that I'm arguing. But why? Are you . . . arresting me?"

What were the chances guilt was eating her up in all this? "Should we arrest you?"

"Absolutely not."

He gripped her arm. "We're placing you in protective custody. Someone's either a vigilante or taking out witnesses."

Chapter Twenty-four

THE FIRST THING Irene planned to do when she arrived back at the Brown Palace was to lock away Trevelle's replacement file, the one with Kinsey's childhood photos and Dr. Mitchell's invoices, and then phone the police and turn the proof over to them.

Instead, the police were waiting for her. She came to an abrupt stop when she reached the corner near the front desk and saw the familiar profile.

Lieutenant Montoya stood listening to the young hotel clerk Irene had spoken to earlier. By the lieutenant's unsmiling countenance, the clerk had relayed Irene's message.

Throwing back her shoulders, she pasted on the most feigned smile of her existence and approached the front desk. "Hi, there. Looking for me?"

He was almost too calm when he acknowledged her. "Where have you been, Irene?"

"I had a small errand to run," she said quietly. "And you'll be happy to know, it didn't lead to one single altercation or murder."

When that statement failed to lift his spirits, she added, "Are you on duty?"

"I'm here, aren't I?"

Ouch. A part of her liked this brusque Hispanic man, and by his acts of kindness, she'd built it up in her head he liked her as well. To think he was just doing his duty bruised her already battered ego. "Then I suppose a drink is out of the question?"

He answered by way of a stare.

"I understand the hotel serves a grand high tea," she tried again. "Care to join me? I do have good news."

"I would love to," he said in a tone Irene found rather insincere.

She led him to a table and chairs off the lobby. They ordered their tea and sat facing each other like a couple of boxers ready to spar.

Irene decided that a detailed explanation of where she'd been just might bury her, so she handed the lieutenant the fruits of her very exhausting day.

A muscle in his jaw worked as he opened the file. "Where did you get this?"

Why did she get the feeling that no matter what she said she was doomed? Exasperated by his aloof manner, she took the offensive. "I truly meant to stay in the hotel. All I wanted to do was sleep. But I woke up. And when I did, I remembered the name of the detective who took pictures of Kinsey when she was a child." Irene went on to explain the considerable research she'd gone through to locate Peter Trevelle, how she'd worried about not following the lieutenant's orders, but when she learned the man was in a wheelchair, she had no choice but to go to him.

Her explanation didn't improve things between them. As a matter of fact, if he were a train and you set him on the tracks, with the amount of steam pent inside, he could probably fuel his way to Poughkeepsie.

He leaned forward, nailing her with his dark-eyed stare. "It never occurred to you to give *us* the name of the detective agency and let the police do the job the taxpayers hired us for?"

"It did," she said meekly. Then she thought to hell with this man who couldn't be placated and added some starch to her backbone. "But did it ever occur to you that it might be a little frustrating to be told to wait, to receive information third party when it's perfectly clear someone's doing their level best to frame me for murder?"

"And you never thought it might be this detective?" He thumped the file with his index finger.

"Sure, it crossed my mind. Just ask the cab driver."

"The who?"

"The cab driver," she repeated. "I paid him an additional one hundred dollars to stick around just in case I didn't come out when he expected."

Lieutenant Montoya glared at her. "I said *stay put.*"

"And I'm not a dog." Irene folded her arms. "I do not sit, and I'm not too good at fetching either. You said there'd been a development. What is it?"

He rested his strong brown arms on the table. "Gwyneth Masters disappeared early this morning."

"What?"

"You heard me. Apparently, Kinsey went to her folks and demanded answers."

"Oh, no," Irene said. "And no one knows where she is?"

"So far, no. Kinsey and her dad were waiting for me in the conference room this morning when I took time out of my busy day to have patrol deliver you here, and all I asked for in return was your cooperation."

"Well, quite frankly, Lieutenant, it's not that I'm not grateful for your assistance, but I'm glad I left. If Gwyneth's on the run and coming after me, I prefer not to be a sitting duck."

He shook his head.

She softened. "Is Kinsey okay?"

"Confused. But she'll be fine."

"How do you know?"

"Because she's stubborn and a survivor. She reminds me of another woman I know."

Focused on the lieutenant, Irene hadn't paid much attention to her surroundings. But a well-dressed man walking with a quad cane, caught her eye.

Irene dismissed him and returned her gaze to the lieutenant. "Do the Masters have any idea where Gwyneth might go?"

"Not at this time."

"I still think she had to have something to do with the break-in at the Blue Star and Stephen's death. Don't you?"

Lieutenant Montoya hadn't touched his tea. "She's a suspect."

"Meaning I am, too?"

"Your disappearing acts aren't helping you, Irene."

His cell phone rang.

Frustrated not to be able to finish defending herself, Irene sat back and planned her next argument.

The man with the cane was still at the front desk, talking with the clerk. The clerk pointed in Irene's direction, and the stranger glanced over his shoulder. Then, turning back to the hotel employee, he nodded. He and his cane sauntered her way.

"Paxton and Lucero left the gallery?" Lieutenant Montoya asked his caller. "All right. Make sure patrol secures the crime scene, and no one talks to the media but me." Expression dire, he slipped his phone back into his pants pocket.

Irene stiffened. "What happened? *What crime scene?*"

"That was Dispatch. Reportedly, Gwyneth Masters has been shot."

First Stephen, now Gwyneth? Irene grew lightheaded. She inhaled a shaky breath. "You have to know I didn't do this. My gun . . . it was stolen."

"So you claim. Let's go, Irene." The lieutenant stood.

She remained glued to the chair. "I was with Peter Trevelle the entire afternoon. Both he and the cab driver will vouch for me." She pointed to the file in his hand. "You're *holding* my proof."

"Maybe. It could also be part of the information you claimed was stolen from your hotel room. And it's clear I can't trust you not to take off."

Her brain told her to cooperate, but her arms and legs elected to disobey. She couldn't go through police apprehension a second time. She closed her eyes, hoping to escape this nightmare.

"I beg your pardon."

Hearing someone speak in a drawl that matched her own, Irene opened her eyes again. The man with the cane stood at their table. At his tailored three-piece suit, his grandfatherly good looks, and his confident swagger, not only was she curious, but grateful for the interruption.

"Who are you?" the lieutenant demanded.

"My name is Lyle A. Wilkins," he said, removing a card. "I'm an attorney with Wilkins, Armstrong and Cassidy in Oklahoma City. Mrs. Norma Mitchell hired me to represent Mrs. Turner." His gaze traveled from the lieutenant to Irene. "I'm so sorry, Irene. May I call you Irene? I would have been here a day earlier, but I had a court case yesterday, and those things are a dickens to reschedule."

"Your timing is both good and bad," Lieutenant Montoya said. "Mrs. Turner and I were just leaving."

"Oh?" Mr. Wilkins said.

Irene rose and shook his hand. "Mr. Wilkins, right now you're about as welcome as the cavalry. There's been a shooting, and the lieutenant here thinks I may have had something to do with it."

"Is that a fact? Are you placing my client under arrest, Lieutenant?"

The lieutenant's eyes narrowed and the same overworked muscle in his jaw jumped again. "No. She's not under arrest—yet."

"Well, then. Do let us know if you find hard and fast evidence against her," the lawyer said. "In the meantime, you have my card, and anything you have to say to Mrs. Turner will go through me."

Chapter Twenty-five

AS SIRENS SCREAMED in the background, Nate pressed the whining Crown Vic to its capacity. Sammy rode in the front, with Yasmine Takeri in back. Two police cruisers rode their tail. On scene, Sammy turned Yasmine over to a patrol officer while Nate raced for the door, crushing straw-like grass as he ran.

From the outside, Gwyneth's hideaway had fix and flip all over it.

The front door was locked when he got there. Sammy met Nate on the stoop. Nate glanced up and studied his options. They'd been through this a time or two. Sammy nodded for Nate to do the honors. Nate, the larger of the pair, had generally been the more successful.

He jumped. Grabbing onto the overhang, and praying the damn thing wouldn't collapse under his weight, he swung and kicked in the door. After turning the home's poor excuse for protection into toothpicks, he entered the house.

Next to a suitcase, Gwyneth lay sprawled on her back covered in blood.

Sammy drew his service weapon and disappeared into the rear of the house. Nate donned gloves and knelt beside her.

She lay unconscious, face ashen. Nate's gut felt like the door he'd just kicked in. This was Kinsey's mom, the woman who'd welcomed him into her home, who'd come to his games on occasion, and no matter what, she'd been loved.

He pressed two fingers against her neck.

Weapon still drawn, Sammy passed Nate in the living room. "Intruder came in through the back door. Glass everywhere." He entered a room off the living room.

Sweat beaded Nate's forehead, and he sagged at the irony. While Sammy searched for an intruder, Nate searched for a sign of life.

He breathed heavily. No pulse. Maybe he'd gotten too close to the jaw. He repositioned his fingers against her carotid artery and tried again.

There it was. *Weak but still beating.* He kept his hand there a second longer. A thready pulse was hard to pick up. He knew firsthand. One time he'd made the mistake of feeling his own.

Sammy dropped beside him. "All clear."

Nodding, Nate unbuttoned Gwyneth's shirt, overwhelmed by the blood soaking into her top, her bra, and the amount pooling beside her on the floor.

The smell of copper filled his nostrils. "Looks like the shooter missed her heart. Maybe hit her ribs." He eased the scarf free from her neck, alarmed when he found it wet. For a moment he thought she'd been shot more than once, but when he discovered no blood on the sheer blue fabric, he exhaled the air he'd been holding and wadded it up.

Pressing the material into the small hole, and careful not to bear down too hard, he said, "We could use a damn medic any day now."

As if on cue, footsteps pounded the outside landing, and the EMTs, a man and a woman, barged into the house.

The man, whose badge read Randall, squatted beside Nate. "Whatta we got?"

Numbly, Nate explained his observations and the little he'd done to keep Gwyneth alive.

"You did fine," Randall said. "We'll take it from here."

All too willing to relinquish control, Nate stood by his already upright partner.

The woman, whose badge identified her as Martinez, produced a stethoscope and a blood pressure cuff, while her partner spoke into a mic. "We have an unresponsive female, approximately fifty-five-years old, hemorrhaging from a gunshot wound to the chest." He removed a penlight and lifted her eyelid. "Pupils reactive, pulse thready."

"Blood pressure 80 over 50," Martinez said. "Looks like the bullet exited through her back."

Nate exchanged a glance with Sammy. Sammy was already on it, his gaze scouring the walls and the floor.

SQUEEZED INTO HER Audi with her brother and sister and taking street corners way too fast, Kinsey tried to combat Jay's "Hurry ups" to Lauren's "Slow the hell down."

"Would you two please shut up? I'm doing the best that I can." Kinsey mashed down on the accelerator, weaving in and out of Denver traffic, intermittently watching the road and following her GPS system's instructions.

"Up there on your left," Jay shouted. "Foxgrove Drive."

Kinsey swerved in that direction and immediately braked to a crawl as a policeman stood, diverting traffic.

"Oh, no." Lauren leaned forward, poking her head between the bucket seats. "That house down the street."

Kinsey had no need to voice her concern out loud. Everybody inside the Audi saw what was happening. Lights flashed on two cruisers and an ambulance was parked at the curb.

What were the chances they'd stumbled onto one huge coincidence and those emergency vehicles were for somebody other than their mother?

She rolled down the window to talk to the cop. "I'm Kinsey Masters. This is my brother Jay, and that's my sister Lauren in the backseat. If this has anything to do with Gwyneth Masters, you have to let us through. She's our mom."

The police officer nodded. "Drive slow, park where officers direct, and do not go beyond the yellow tape."

"Why? What's happened?" Jay croaked.

An unmarked unit with flashing lights drove up behind them and blurted two short raps from his siren. "You're blocking emergency vehicles," the cop said. "You'll have to move."

Kinsey drove to where the police directed then parked and got out of her car. With Jay and Lauren trailing her heels, the trio ran toward the house.

A patrol car's back door swung open and Yasmine stepped out. "Oh, my poor darlings, what are you doing here?"

Crossing in front of Kinsey, Lauren said, "What do you mean, what are we doing here? What are you doing here, and *what* is going on?"

Yasmine's face crumbled. "I was on the phone with your mother, and I heard a shot. You now know as much as I do."

Kinsey's cell phone blasted out the introduction to *Crazy Train*. Checking to see who was calling, she lowered her head. "It's Dad."

GWYNETH MOANED.

Nate stopped his search for the bullet in the wall and whirled toward the sound. He knelt beside her and his gaze turned toward the female paramedic. "Okay if I talk to her?"

Martinez nodded.

"Mrs. Masters. It's me, Nate Paxton. Do you remember me?"

"Nate," she rasped. "Hurt."

"I know. These people are here to help you."

"My . . . children—"

"—are fine. They send their love. Can you tell us who did this to you?"

Tears leaked from her eyes. Struggling for air, she gasped. "Couldn't . . . see. Stood by kitchen . . . fired . . . ran."

Envisioning how the scene went down, Nate frowned. He estimated fifteen feet separated Gwyneth from the kitchen. Even so, the way she'd landed, she had to have faced the shooter. "Was it a man or a woman?"

"Think . . . couldn't . . . tell." Her eyes fluttered shut.

"Mrs. Masters?" Nate smoothed the blonde hair from her face. "Mrs. Masters?" Damn. She'd lost consciousness again.

"That's about all you're going to get," Randall said, hooking up her IV. "I'm amazed you got that much."

Nate nodded and came to his feet. At least one thing was going right. Sammy had fished a bullet out of the wall and dropped it into a plastic evidence bag.

Raising the bag toward the light, he studied the slug. "Mutilated SOB. What are the chances we got us a .38?"

Nate didn't even want to think about what that meant.

A crime scene tech entered the living room from the back of the house. "Detectives."

Sammy handed the bag to the tech before he and Nate went with the analyst into the kitchen.

As another tech swept and bagged crushed glass, the one who'd requested their presence motioned them to the back door. "Intruder broke in through here. Notice most of the glass shattered inward. But we may have gotten lucky." He pointed his gloved hand to a half-inch jagged shard stuck in the wood. "See here? Shooter probably thought he'd cleared all the glass away, but when he reached in to unlock the deadbolt, this little sucker caught a portion of his sleeve."

The tech held up a bagged piece of navy blue fabric.

Nate took the baggy and studied it. "I love it when an asshole makes our job easier."

Tilting his head, Sammy said, "If it's one asshole."

Nate's head shot up. "What do you mean by that?"

"Last night we talked about an accomplice."

"What's on your mind?"

"Why'd he miss?"

"Bullet came close to her heart, Sam."

"Agreed. But this guy made a whole lot of mistakes. Last night when we went over Stephen Turner's crime scene, the killer didn't leave behind any trace evidence. What's more, he finished the job."

"Maybe because with Turner sitting in Irene's Mercedes, the killer was standing at point blank range," Nate argued. "This time he was standing farther away."

"So, why didn't he make sure Gwyneth was dead?"

"Panicked? Something scared him off."

"Could be," Sammy said, his tone doubtful. "Or this time, somebody else pulled the trigger."

Over the course of their partnership, Sammy's instincts had been right more often than not. But in this case, Nate couldn't be sure. These occurrences had happened in less than twenty-four hours. Unless their shooter was a professional or criminally insane, taking a life, and getting away with it, heaped major stress on a person's shoulders.

That's why most were apprehended. Stress in any occupation led to screw-ups. And maybe that's why their bad guy had gotten careless. Or as Sammy had suggested, they had two different shooters.

"You're right, Sam. We can't even guarantee these cases are connected or that he's using Irene's revolver," Nate said. "We'll compare slugs, see how they match up to last night, and hope something turns up in the NBIN database. All we have right now is speculation."

He stepped close to the back door and peered at the barely discernible sliver. "Let us know if you find blood or tissue in that area. In the meantime, if we can find this guy in the near future, he might have a scratch on his arm."

"Or glass embedded in his shoes," Sammy added. "That is, if he left the same way he came in."

Nate scanned the backyard as well as the adjoining properties. Patrolmen were already on foot talking with the neighbors. If anyone looked out his window, he'd have to have seen something.

Damn risky stunt to try in broad daylight.

"Good work," Nate said to the crime scene techs. "We'll be in touch."

Nate and Sammy returned to the living room where Randall and Martinez had loaded Gwyneth onto a stretcher and were finagling her out the demolished front door.

Before Nate could follow them outside, Sammy barred Nate's exit with his arm. "Your clothes, man."

Nate glanced down. Gwyneth's blood had seeped onto his shirt and his pants. It was SOP to keep a change of clothes in his Explorer. He gritted his teeth. "I miss my damn car."

"I got an extra shirt in the ambulance," Randall called over his shoulder.

"Thanks, man. I'll take what I can get." Nate stepped outside to follow, but Lieutenant Montoya made his way up the walk. As Nate and Sammy joined their commanding officer to give him an update, Nate scanned the crowd. An already bad day turned dismal. Along with the other onlookers who'd gathered, Kinsey stood behind the crime scene tape.

Chapter Twenty-six

KINSEY TWISTED HER mouth into a frown, stared at the phone with her father on the other end, and looked to her brother and sister for guidance. "What am I going to say to him?"

"The truth. I don't see that you have any choice, Kins. Better Dad finds out from us than from them," Jay said pointing.

She followed her brother's extended finger. Two news vans were inching their way past the police roadblock.

"Look," Lauren said. "They're coming out."

At the same time, the news vans came forward, emergency personnel exited the house, carrying not only the stretcher, but an IV hooked up to their patient.

Kinsey clapped a hand over her mouth. An IV meant good news, right? At least they weren't carrying their mother out in a body bag.

Screw this standing around. She handed her phone and her car keys to Lauren. "Here. Take these."

"Why? What are you going to do? And what about Dad?"

"I'm going to ride with Mom in the ambulance. As for Dad, tell him as much as we know and then tell him to meet us at the hospital." Kinsey started jogging.

"Which hospital?" Jay yelled behind her.

"The one you'll arrive at when you follow me in the ambulance," she hollered back. "Hurry up and go get my car. And, Lauren, let Jay drive so you don't lose us."

KINSEY RUSHED toward the emergency vehicle but slowed the closer she got. Oblivious to bystanders, two EMTs had started loading Gwyneth into the back.

"Hey," Kinsey said, breathlessly, drawing close. "I'm Kinsey Masters. I'm her daughter. How is she? Can I talk to her?"

The male EMT gave his partner a you-take-this-one nod and disappeared around the front of the ambulance.

The woman medical worker returned a sympathetic smile. "We're not doctors, Ms. Masters. Just know we're doing everything in our power to help her."

Kinsey moved close to her mom. She appeared dangerously pale, twined between an IV and chest tubes. "Mom?" She didn't respond. Kinsey's eyes welled. She looked to the paramedic. "Can she hear me?"

"Probably not. She's had a major trauma."

Kinsey swallowed. "Where are you taking her? Can I ride with you?"

"To Lundgren," the woman replied, then shook her head and motioned to the interior of the ambulance. "As you can see, it's a tight fit. I'm going to need all that space to monitor her vitals and to get to her if I need to."

The male EMT returned. "If you don't get carsick, you can ride up front with me."

"As long as you keep this thing on the ground, I'm good," Kinsey said. "I'd really appreciate it."

He helped his partner slide Gwyneth into the ambulance, then after shutting the vehicle's doors, motioned for Kinsey to meet him up front.

She rounded her side of the van, practically colliding with Nate who stood stripping off his shirt. Growing up around athletics and swim parties, she'd seen Nate shirtless before. One thing was for sure, he wasn't seventeen anymore.

Vowing to keep that image in her mind forever, Kinsey prepared to brush by him when she spotted the blood. "Oh, no. Nate. Were you hurt, too?"

He wadded up the bloody shirt and tugged on a replacement. "Not a scratch on me. Don't worry."

The paramedic leaned over the steering wheel. "Snug fit. Sorry about that, bro."

"I owe you a shirt, Randall."

"Unnecessary. You'd do the same for me."

As Kinsey slid into the passenger seat next to the driver, Nate called out to her, "I'm sorry about your mom."

She fastened her seatbelt. "Thanks. Will you come to the hospital?"

"Soon as I finish up here."

The ambulance's powerful engine roared to life, and Randall switched on the lights. As they sped toward Lundgren, Kinsey held on to an armrest and hollered over the sirens, "He's lying, isn't he? He's hurt."

The driver never took his eyes off the road. "Paxton arrived on the scene before we did. That wasn't his blood you saw. When we got there, he was working on your mom. Did a helluva job, too. Good guy."

Kinsey's heart swelled. Among sirens and the chaos of Denver traffic, she watched billboards, exit ramps, and buildings fly by. *Tell me something I don't know.* She'd summed up Nate Paxton from the moment she'd met him. "Yes, he is."

RANDALL'S SHIRT WAS like squeezing into a wet suit, but at least Nate wouldn't scare the neighbors. Tucking the shirt's hem into his pants, he watched as Lieutenant Montoya briefed the news teams. Doubtless tonight's headlines were already in production and station execs looked forward to ratings. The Masters made news around Denver.

Nate joined Sammy inside the house where the crime scene techs had finished up. The only break they'd caught was the piece of fabric trapped by a sliver of glass. All that could be done had been done.

The police officer assigned to guard Yasmine escorted her into the house.

"Ms. Takeri complained about the camera crews zooming in for close ups," the officer said. "Can't say that I blame her. She also said she wants to go to the hospital, but first she wanted to okay it with you."

"Fine," Nate said. "In fact, your appearance is timely." He motioned to the entrance. "To gain access, we had to kick in the front door. The intruder also broke out glass in the kitchen."

Yasmine pulled out her phone. "I'll call a repairman." She glanced around, caught sight of Gwyneth's blood on the worn carpeting and became teary-eyed. "What will you do with her suitcase?"

"It becomes evidence," Sammy replied. In his hand he held an iPhone and a piece a paper. "These, too."

"What's on the paper?" she asked.

"Phone numbers. One belonging to Dr. Clifford Mitchell, the other to Stephen Turner."

The color leached from Yasmine's face.

"After the officer takes you to the hospital, you're on your own," Nate said. "Might be a good time to come clean. We're good listeners."

Yasmine's dark eyes met his. "So is my lawyer. I will tell you this much. Before I heard the shot, Gwyneth cried out the name Evan."

Nate and Sammy exchanged looks.

"You think her husband shot her?" Sammy asked.

"I'm saying Gwyneth called out her husband's name."

"We'll check into it," Sammy said.

Montoya called from the demolished doorway. "Lucero, Paxton. Out here."

They met the boss outside.

He stood with an old man carrying a rubber trashcan. "This is Mr. Alfred Carmine," the lieutenant said. "He lives on the corner of Foxwood and Fillmore. Will you tell my detectives what you just told me?"

"No problem," he said. "I was out walking the missus's dog, and I see this car speeding up my street. Drives me insane, these cars tearing through the neighborhood. Anyways, as I was turning the corner toward my house, a car slams on its brakes.

"I squint, cuz I got cataracts, and my eyesight's not so good. But I know which one's my house, and this bozo gets out and dumps something in *my* trashcan.

"So, whatta I do? I run in and alert the missus. She's watching the news and tells me the cops is right here, one block away. So I decide I should bring it to you. Me and the missus, we watch a lot of CSI, and we know not to touch anything. So here I am."

"You get a good look at this *bozo?*" Sammy asked.

Carmine shook his head. "Darn cataracts make everything fuzzy, but he wore dark colors, that's for sure."

"How about the make and the color of the car?"

"White compact or maybe a mid-size." Carmine frowned. "Happened kind of fast."

"You look in the can, Mr. Carmine?" Nate asked.

"Well, yeah. But not on purpose. Whoever dumped it knocked off the lid. Lucky for you guys, the garbage company had already been by. I know from CSI how you people hate to go digging through trash."

"That we do." Nate smiled for the first time that day. "So, what's in the trash can?"

"See for yourself." Carmine held the can by its hand grips. "Like I said, I ain't touching nothin'."

Sammy loaned Nate a pair of fresh gloves.

He stretched into the bottom of the rubber container. Suddenly, Gwyneth's answer of *couldn't see* made all the sense in the world. Nate came away with a ski mask.

Chapter Twenty-seven

AFTER A HARROWING drive from the Foxglove crime scene, Kinsey, Lauren, and Jay met up at the entrance to Lundgren Medical Center to find their ghostly white father pacing. A hospital employee directed them to the Surgical floor, informing them that Gwyneth Masters had been prepped for surgery.

From that point, the entire clan was sent to wait in a small lounge off the elevators. Soon, Yasmine stepped off of the elevator, white dress smudged, her long black hair a tangled mass. The police department, she explained, had released her from her law enforcement shadow.

Kinsey studied her father and her mother's best friend surreptitiously. Dad pointedly ignored Yasmine. Instead, he joined Lauren and Jay in their quadrant of the lounge, while Yasmine went to the window on the opposite side of the waiting room and peered out.

Kinsey, already apprised of her father's one night stand and her mother's sordid need to kidnap a baby, chose a chair away from everyone. She wanted to confront Yasmine here and now, demand the truth, but with Gwyneth under the knife, the family was under enough stress and drama.

Still, Kinsey couldn't dismiss the thought that Yasmine had lied. She had to have taken part, or at least known, about her mother's fake pregnancy. Yasmine was never excluded from her mother's confidence.

An emotional wreck, Kinsey had been awake for a solid twenty-four hours. While Gwyneth underwent surgery, all Kinsey wanted to do was to sleep—and sleep hard, which she did.

SOMETIME LATER, she startled awake, stiff from the cramped hospital chair. Lauren dozed on a waiting room couch, while Jay, proving he had and could sleep anywhere, crashed on the floor, arms crossed, legs propped on his duffel bag.

Groggy and sick of the hospital's myriad smells, Kinsey checked her watch. What seemed like a few minutes had actually been two-and-a-half hours. She prepared to drift off again when dull voices stirred her awake. Through half-raised lids, she located her dad and Yasmine near the elevators, their body language broadcasting the contemptuous issues between them. At first, Yasmine stood folding her arms, but when Dad invaded her space, she held up a hand. He stepped back for the little good it did. He continued his verbal attack, his gesturing hands talking as much as he was.

Kinsey considered interrupting them, but based on what had happened this afternoon, this was likely one of many arguments to come. At least they were being quiet, so why delay the inevitable?

At last, they ended their conversation, each retiring to separate areas within the lounge.

Dad sat across from Kinsey, picked up a magazine, and impatiently thumbed through it. Yasmine sat closer to Lauren and Jay, took out her phone, and started to text.

Urging her mind to ignore it all, Kinsey crossed her arms, stretched her legs out in front of her, and prepared to sleep again. That was, until the elevator dinged, and to her immense relief, Nate walked onto the hospital floor.

She kept her lids lowered, watched him scour the room and walk toward her. He'd changed out of his blood-stained pants and Randall's constricting T-shirt, thank goodness. In their place, he carried a leather jacket over his shoulder and appeared the essence of GQ in a long-sleeved Henley shirt and jeans.

He sat beside her, and an unbidden smile came to her face. When his fingers wrapped around hers, she opened her eyes and whispered a protest, "I was sleeping, Nate Paxton."

"No, you weren't. You watched me all the way from the elevators."

And what a view. "How could you possibly know that?"

"People in a deep sleep don't flutter their eyelids, and most sleep with their mouths open wide enough to collect flies while they do it."

There was no denying that point. She'd been on enough trips with snoring, drooling, cavernous-mouthed soccer players to last her a lifetime.

Nate pulled out a bottled water from inside his jacket and handed it to her.

Kinsey smiled, twisted the cap and downed a few gulps. As she sealed the container again, she said, "Thank you. You think of everything."

"Been through this a time or two. How are you doing?"

"Okay." She sighed, suddenly aware of her father watching their every move behind his lowered magazine. "Where have you been?" she asked quietly.

"After we secured the crime scene, Sammy and I completed the search at your mother's gallery."

"And did you find what you were after?"

"Nothing pertaining to your kidnapping. How's your mom?"

"Been in surgery . . ." Kinsey glanced at the clock on her phone. ". . . three-and-a-half-hours now."

They sat quietly for a while until the doctor who'd taken Gwyneth into surgery appeared through the swinging double doors.

Dad stood and immediately nudged Jay and Lauren. Then along with everyone else, Kinsey and Nate surrounded the surgeon.

"Mrs. Masters did well," he said. "We performed a procedure known as a thoracotomy to repair a collapsed lung. Because the bullet exited her body, we merely dressed the wounds. They should heal on their own. At this time, her prognosis is very good."

Jay wrapped an arm around Lauren. Lauren reached for Dad's hand.

Touched by their show of unity, Kinsey felt her eyes well again and swallowed over the lump in her throat. "When can we see her, Doctor?"

"Not for a while," he said. "The main thing we're concerned about is pulmonary edema, so we're monitoring her closely. Opening up the chest cavity not only risks infection, but it's extremely painful and places a great deal of trauma on the patient. Mrs. Masters is on powerful antibiotics as well as a heavy dose of morphine.

"I know you all want to see her," the doctor continued. "But I'm going to deny visitors for a minimum of eight to possibly twelve hours."

"I'm her husband. Can't I at least sit with her?" Dad said.

"You heard the man," Yasmine added sharply. "He said *no* visitors."

Kinsey stiffened and held her breath. Before today, she'd never seen her father and Yasmine demonstrate such animosity toward each other.

"Mr. Masters," the surgeon explained, "I assure you your wife won't even know you're there. The best thing you can do for her right now is go home and rest up for when she does need you. And, yes, my instructions are 'no visitors.' Good night," he said walking away.

Nate followed. "Quick word, Doc?"

Cop and surgeon paused near the double doors.

Yawning, Kinsey stretched her arms overhead, linked her fingers, and addressed her overwrought family. "I don't know about the rest of you, but home sounds terrific to me."

"You could come to Mom and Dad's house," Lauren suggested. "That's where Jay and I'll be."

"No clothes." Kinsey held out her hands. "Frankly, I'm not up to a slumber party right now. See you tomorrow, okay?" She hugged them goodbye and waved as the group piled onto the elevator.

She grabbed her purse, but, Nate, still with the doctor, held up a finger and motioned for her to wait.

After parting ways with the man, Nate came toward her. "If you stick around a few minutes, I'll walk you to your car."

"You're staying?"

"Have to. We need to station an officer outside of Gwyneth's room, and one's en route."

Kinsey's shoulders slumped. "I guess when the doctor said her prognosis looked good, I forgot the small fact that somebody tried to kill her."

"Have a seat, Kins."

Nate sat across from her, a small coffee table between them. "We've been operating under the assumption that whoever tried to kill your mom was somehow connected to Stephen Turner's murder. We still believe that's the case."

"But?"

"We'd be foolish to overlook the possibility of someone using Turner's murder as an opportunity to kill your mom."

Kinsey narrowed her gaze. "I guess one conspiracy theory's as good as the next."

Nate lowered his head. "Yasmine claims that when the shot went off, Gwyneth called out a name."

Kinsey gasped. "Who?"

"Evan."

Now getting the full picture of what was going on between Yasmine and her father, Kinsey's stomach roiled. "You can't think my dad would hurt my mom. They've been married for thirty-two years."

"I don't *think* anything. I go by evidence and by what witnesses tell me, and then I go with my gut. I can't dismiss what Yasmine told us, Kins. Your dad's had the shock of his life. And he's certainly not hiding that he's angry. I have to check this out."

"I realize that." Kinsey massaged the back of her neck. "But I know my father. Yes, he thinks he rules the world and spouts off when he's mad, but to suggest that he might shoot my mother? He doesn't even own a gun. He hates them." Kinsey shuddered. "Runs in the family."

"One positive is that we've accounted for Evan's whereabouts during Stephen's murder. Hopefully, when Gwyneth wakes up, she'll tell us what happened." Nate folded his hands. "But one of the things I talked to the doctor about, and will reiterate to the officer when he gets here, is until we clear your father from suspicion, he's not to get close to her."

Kinsey dug her nails into her handbag's leather. If her dad hadn't paid a penance before, he would now. "Do you want me to tell him?"

"No. That's the Denver PD's responsibility. We also received a tip from one of the Foxglove neighbors that whoever shot your mom may have worn a mask."

Kinsey stopped the attack on her purse. She set it on the end table beside her. "Wow."

"Is there anyone you can think of who might want to see Gwyneth out of the picture, who hates her enough to kill her?"

"She runs a gallery. It's a competitive business. She turns people away all the time. Some of the artists feel they're more deserving. Frankly, you'd be better to have this conversation with Lauren or Yasmine. I coach soccer, teach school. *But . . .*" Kinsey hugged her middle and raised her free hand to her throat.

"What?"

"Yesterday when I arrived at Masterpieces, there were two men at the front desk. Artists. One guy by the name of Michael Whitney is the quiet type, but extremely bright. I've also heard he and Yasmine moved in together."

Nate removed a notebook from his coat pocket. "I'd rather have more facts than not enough."

"The next guy is named Ryan Stone." Kinsey scowled. "He's this redheaded prima dona who constantly asserts that my mom takes too much for her commission."

"What about Yasmine? How do she and your mother get along?"

"Close," Kinsey said. "Yasmine wouldn't hurt my mom. On the contrary . . ." Kinsey proceeded to tell Nate about Yasmine's cover up regarding Gwyneth's alleged pregnancy.

Just then, the elevator doors chimed, and a uniformed cop stepped onto the floor.

Nate stood, acknowledged the man, then turned back to Kinsey. "The doc said they'll be moving your mom to ICU. Let me talk to this officer, then we'll get you home."

We'll get you home? Kinsey allowed herself a small smile. She only wished Nate would take her home. She was still focused on her wishful thinking when the police officer re-entered the elevator and Nate returned.

He cocked his head. "Something funny?"

She linked her arm through his. "You are, Nate. You're just a scream. Walk me to my car, would you?"

Chapter Twenty-eight

WHEN KINSEY HAD arrived at Lundgren in the early evening via Randall's ambulance, the temperature had been in the low seventies. But typical of Colorado weather, somebody must've blinked. Now at ten-thirty at night, a cold front had swept in, and so had the wind and rain.

With Nate beside her, she rode the parking garage's elevator up to the hospital's top level, which as soon as the doors separated, opened to the elements. Peppered by howling gusts and freezing water, Kinsey's sweater hardly provided protection. And while Jay had conscientiously informed her what floor he'd parked her Audi on, her brother had neglected to tell Kinsey *which* space.

Huddling close to the wall, she used the elevator's frame to block out the cold, peeked out, and pressed her keys to sound the horn on her A4.

She jumped when a lightning bolt lit up the sky. "Great. Too many cars. I hear it, but don't see it."

Nate held out his hand. "Here. Give me your keys, wimp."

"Who are you calling wimp?" Even so, she flashed him her best be-a-dear smile. "Here ya go."

As Nate jogged out into the downpour, Kinsey alleviated her guilt somewhat by telling herself that at least *he* had a jacket. Soon, he and her Audi drove up a row of parked cars. Maneuvering her sporty little car like he'd driven it forever, he veered sharply and screeched to a stop near the elevator.

He flipped his collar and rounded the driver's side. "Your chariot, *wimp*."

Leather jacket or not, he was soaked to the skin. Laughing, Kinsey pressed the hold button and pulled him into the elevator. She brushed the wet hair out of his eyes. "You're something else, Nate Paxton." Then studying his rain-drenched face, she felt seventeen all over again, and she sobered. "But you've always known how I feel about you, haven't you?"

His gaze veered toward the flooding parking lot. "Really? Couldn't we talk about this someplace other than an elevator?"

Leaning into him, she steeled herself for his rejection and implored him with her eyes. "What happened, Nate? If we'd had a fight, I could understand. But for me, it was one of the best nights of my life. What did I do wrong?"

"Nothing." He averted his gaze and adamantly shook his head. "It was me. All me." Then, to her surprise, he bent his head and pressed his lips against hers.

Kinsey's heart leapt. Years of memories and expectations pooled together like the puddles at their feet. She hadn't made him up. Her festering emotions were more powerful than this Colorado storm.

Nate drew her tighter and deepened their kiss.

Like always when it came to Nate Paxton, Kinsey followed her heart. She wrapped her arms around him and responded.

Lightning flashed again, followed by a quick clap of thunder, and the pewter sky unleashed more torrents.

He broke away and grasped her arms. "This is crazy. Go home. Before you catch cold."

"Come with me."

"I'm working a case that involves you. I *can't*."

Where was her pride? Why couldn't she walk away? She'd done it before. "You can't? Or you won't? If we don't talk about this, Nate, I'll make it my number one goal to forget you—permanently. And that'll be too damn bad, because no way did that kiss feel platonic."

He hardened his jaw and scoured their surroundings as though fighting an invisible war. Then, growling the words, he pulled her close again. "I should arrest you for blackmail. I've never had a platonic thought about you in my life. Give me your address. I'll meet you there."

HIS SOAKED LEATHER jacket hanging on Kinsey's dining room chair, Nate refused to sit on her couch for obvious reasons. One, his shirt was still damp, and, two, she'd be sitting there soon.

Unlike him, she'd changed out of her soggy clothes. Wearing a T-shirt and jeans, she'd padded barefoot into the kitchen.

"How about some hot chocolate?" she asked.

Staring into the orange and blue flames of a gas-lit fireplace, Nate held out his hands to get warm. "Sounds good."

Why had he kissed her? She was more off limits now than she'd been when they were kids. Regardless of her ultimatum, he should make his excuses and go. But his feet didn't seem capable of budging, even though staying spelled disaster.

Her townhouse wasn't what he'd anticipated. He liked that she'd bought one on the third floor, but it was smaller in square footage than he'd expected from a Masters. She'd furnished her place in leather and oak, and naturally, her walls displayed a few art pieces from her mother's gallery. What he really found strange was the lack of pictures promoting her athletic career. No more than two pictures of the USA Team sat on the mantle reflecting her life as an Olympic athlete.

A sliding glass door facing west led out to a balcony. In the daytime, if there weren't too many obstructions, she'd be able to see the Rocky Mountains. The terrace contained a few potted plants, a lounge chair, and a grill.

That single chair pleased Nate. Maybe it meant she didn't entertain much.

Or, he thought, frowning, it only signaled she wasn't home much to entertain.

Her lack of window coverings didn't make him happy. If Guzmán's goons had followed Nate, it was improbable they could see as far as the third floor. Still, ever cautious, he moved away from the window, just in case.

Kinsey entered the living room with two cups of cocoa. She handed Nate his and moved to the sofa with hers.

He motioned to her sliding glass door. "Bet your neighbors love the show."

Kinsey sipped her cocoa. "What neighbor's? All that's behind me is wide open space—so far. No roads, no traffic. It's one of the reasons I bought the place." Patting the sofa beside her, she smiled. "You're probably dry now. Wouldn't you like to sit down? Or maybe the way you've been looking out my window, you've been thinking about jumping."

"Maybe. How far down is it?" Reluctantly Nate joined her on the couch.

"Far. And you'd land in scrub oak." She wrinkled her nose. "Painful."

Nate smiled. "I hate pain. Guess you're stuck with me."

Kinsey's smile faded as she stared into her chocolate. "You're probably wondering why this is so important to me after all these years."

The long hours were catching up with him. Once again he questioned the soundness of coming here. He wasn't proud of the way he'd treated Kinsey all those years ago, far from it. But as badly as he'd handled the situation, he'd done it for her. "And if I don't have an excuse?"

She set the cup on the table. "Why is this so hard for you? Why can't you tell me what happened?"

"Did it ever occur to you that I was a punk kid with the maturity of a fish egg? We were seventeen. You had opportunities I could only dream of, and the way you talked when we went out to Chatfield, you were ready to put them on hold—for me."

"You didn't seem to mind when we were lying on that blanket and looking up at the stars," Kinsey argued.

Nate couldn't help himself. He moved closer. He hated distorting a night that had meant everything to him. "What guy in his right mind wouldn't love lying next to you? It was later, when I got home, that I panicked. I was hung up on a girl who was making national news on a weekly basis."

"Hung up? You had a funny way of showing it. You were my friend. One of my best friends."

"And that's what I was comfortable being. And then . . ."

She sighed and tucked her legs under her. "I asked you out. It was Sadie Hawkins day. I thought if I showed you how I felt about you, you'd finally reciprocate."

Nate closed his eyes. "I was there, Kins. No need for the play by play."

"You came this close to making love to me." She held her fingers an inch apart. "Perfect setting, big yellow moon." Her voice grew soft, and her eyes shimmered. "And then you stopped, like someone had pushed the pause button. I thought it was because you liked me, respected me. Until the next day when I saw you all over Jennifer Spinner."

Her verbal punch landed below the belt. Nate swallowed hard. "What can I say? I thought if there was someone else, you'd do what you were supposed to do."

"And what's that?" Kinsey set her cup down and lurched from the sofa. She walked to the fireplace, turned, and folded her arms.

"Hate me. Figure out what I already knew, that I wasn't good enough."

"Sorry, that excuse doesn't work. There was no one more secure than you, Nate Paxton, and you know it." Kinsey shook her head. "Anyway, for a long time it worked. Until you showed up two days ago, I did hate you."

Nate rose from the couch. "On behalf of that teenage jerk, I officially apologize."

Kinsey searched his face. "Why do I think there's more to this story than you're telling me?"

Damn, could he feel any more awkward about having this conversation? He couldn't tell her. She was already at odds with her father. For Nate to tell her the truth threatened to destroy a family already in despair.

"Honestly, there's no more to tell." He took her in his arms. "Just know I paid a price, too. Besides the fact I have a job from hell, my memories of you interfered with my other relationships." Against every chastening thought warning him not to, he kissed her. Kissing and tasting and making up for all the years and the heartbreak that had separated them. Finally, his rational thoughts battled back, and he came up for air.

He placed his forehead against hers. "I'm a cop, working a case. You're going through a major identity crisis. We can't take this further. Not now. And it's not that I don't want you, and that's no line. Besides, we haven't even broached the topic of why Griff Colburn calls you *babe*."

Kinsey smiled and stroked Nate's cheek. "Would you believe he wants my vote?"

"Among other things." Nate shook his head.

"He's a friend," Kinsey said, her face flushed and beautiful. "You're still not off the hook, Paxton, but at least I feel better."

He crossed the room to his jacket.

"You're leaving?"

"Got to. It's safer that way." He headed to the door.

She called after him, "Coward."

In the doorway, he pointed to her alarm. "Set this thing. And for God's sake, buy some damn drapes."

She rolled her eyes, but before he closed the door behind him, Kinsey rushed forward. "In light of all that's happened, I suspect you're about to get busy."

An understatement, Nate thought, and he nodded.

"Tomorrow morning, with or without you, I'm going to see my mom."

He shrugged. "Okay."

"My birth mom," Kinsey replied. "I can't put it off any longer. Tomorrow morning, I'm going to talk to Irene."

Chapter Twenty-nine

FOR AS LONG AS Irene could recall, every morning when she awoke, she did one hundred sit-ups and fifty pushups in that order—except, of course, when she'd been pregnant with Danny. She rose from her hotel room floor, drew back the drapes, and greeted the Wells Fargo Building in front of her with a scowl. "Why can't you look like a mountain?"

Her hotel phone rang, and she jumped. She'd never heard it before. She rounded the corner of a raised-platform bed and answered, "Hello?"

"Irene, Lyle Wilkins," came his OK City drawl. "How are you this fine morning?"

How am I? "I guess I'm better than a hangover or a heart attack. How are you, Mr. Wilkins?"

"Lyle, please. I discovered something. I like to eat every mornin'. Care to join me for breakfast?"

Her growling stomach accepted before she did. "I believe I would."

"Good. Meet me at Ellyngton's in, say, thirty minutes?"

"See you then."

She hung up, drained the glass of water by her bed, then picked up her cell phone. Not that she'd expected any, but checking for messages had become a compulsion. She flipped the device shut, sat on the bed, and pressed a hand to her cheek. Not a word from her surly lieutenant, nothing from the wheelchair-bound Trevelle, and what she had really hoped for, was something from Kinsey.

Irene felt as out of the loop as if they'd buried her six foot under. Perhaps her daughter didn't give a hoot that she'd been stolen at birth. Maybe she loved her life so much she wanted Irene and the whole ugly mess to go away.

She gazed at the portrait of Danny she could no longer keep locked away in a safe. She'd retrieved the picture last night from the hotel manager and set it upon the desk. "If that's the case, son, you may look alike, but she's nothing like you."

She stripped and stepped into the shower.

A short time later, she towel dried her hair and checked her cell again. No change. That's when she saw the red light blinking on the hotel's landline. She retrieved voice mail and nearly dropped the phone as she played back the caller's words.

Irene sat on the bed, trembling. She glanced at the portrait. "That was Kinsey, Danny. Your sister's on her way."

"PAXTON! LUCERO!" Lieutenant Montoya bellowed from his office door and across the detective division.

Sammy yanked his gaze from the monitor. Nate hung up the phone. Both jumped to their feet.

Heading their boss's way, Nate said, "We've been here a total of ten minutes. What's he got stuck up his ass this time?"

"Maybe he wants to know what time you got home last night, lover boy."

Hell, Nate hoped not. His collar threatened to strangle him. Had the lieutenant found out about Nate's late night visit at Kinsey's?

Sammy on his heels, Nate entered Montoya's office.

"Take a seat," Montoya said. "Nice job on the search warrants. What are you working on today?"

Rather than tug at his collar, Nate crossed his arms.

"District Four sent over the crime scene video of Stephen Turner's murder," Sammy explained. "So far, no recognizable faces in the crowd."

The lieutenant made a note on his electronic tablet. "What about you?" he barked in Nate's direction.

"Got the ballistics back on the slug at Gwyneth Masters's crime scene." Montoya raised his head. "And?"

"Sammy was right. Forensics confirmed it's a .38." In police work a .22 or a .45 were readily identifiable. Not so for a .38, 9mm, or .40 once they'd impacted something.

"Meaning," Montoya added, "it could've come from Irene's gun and used in Stephen Turner's murder. You compare them to any unsolved shootings we have on file?"

Nate shook his head. "No match in the database. With Irene's gun missing, we're thinking the shooter may be using hers."

The lieutenant sighed. "You check out her alibi?"

Nodding, Nate pulled out his pocketbook. "Taxi dropped her off a little after noon and picked her up at Peter Trevelle's address an hour later."

"Did you talk to Trevelle?" Montoya asked.

"Yes, sir. Irene's story checks out."

"What do we know about this Peter Trevelle?" the lieutenant asked.

"Legit. Retired," Nate said. "But occasionally takes on cases. He's in a wheelchair."

"So Irene mentioned." Lieutenant Montoya lowered his head and went back to typing on his tablet. "What's Gwyneth Masters's status?"

"Spoke to the hospital this morning," Sammy said. "She'll live. Her surgeon, and now her primary care physician, still are denying visitors."

Montoya stiffened in his chair, jabbed a finger first at Nate, then Sammy. "I want both of you over at Lundgren as soon as she's cleared. No lollygagging. No one goes in before we get our interview."

Nate rose, but Sammy was already to the door.

"Paxton."

"Sir?"

"Irene's got a new guard dog looking out for her, an Oklahoma City lawyer by the name of Wilkins." The lieutenant handed Nate a card. "Get me all you can on this guy."

"Something wrong with him?" Nate asked.

Montoya returned to his tablet and grumbled, "I don't know yet."

Back at his desk, Nate sat down and studied the card. "You think Montoya wants Wilkins checked out because he's helping Irene?"

The sides of Sammy's mouth lifted. "I think the lieutenant wants Wilkins checked out because he's a man." Seconds later, though, Sammy wasn't smiling. "Nate, check this out."

Nate rounded the desk to look over his partner's shoulder.

Sammy held up the eraser tip of a pencil to the monitor. "Look at the little turd we got scoping out Turner's murder."

"Zoom in a little."

Sammy moved his hand over the mouse and adjusted the screen.

"Well, if it isn't our old murdering buddy, Rafa Lopez," Nate said.

"Gabbing on his phone." Sammy indicated with the pencil. "Now who do you suppose he's talking to?"

"Guzmán." For an instant, the silence hung heavy between them. "If that's the case, Guzmán knows we work together. He also knows what we look like outside of Vice."

Sammy tapped his palm with the pencil. "So, if Guzmán's been tracking our every move—"

"Why are we standing upright and having this conversation?"

Chapter Thirty

"HELLO, MS. MASTERS," said a smiling hotel clerk as she pointed across the lobby. "Mrs. Turner asked that you join her in Ellyngton's."

Kinsey thanked her, but in truth had no need of directions. When her grandparents were alive, the family often celebrated holidays at the Brown Palace.

The restaurant, with its tantalizing aromas, was sparsely populated at eight-forty-five in the morning. Kinsey spotted Irene immediately seated with an impeccably dressed older man. Assuming she'd be meeting with Irene alone, Kinsey hesitated, but Irene stood and waved her over.

Winding her way around tables covered with starched white linen and precisely placed silverware, she took hold of Irene's outstretched hands.

"I'm so glad you could come."

"Me, too." Kinsey scoffed at the suddenly tongue-tied moment. Where was the woman whose teammates had elected her team captain? Still, what did you say to the woman who gave you birth, but whom you'd never officially met? "You're . . . looking better than the first time I saw you." She bit her lip. "I'm sorry I walked away like that."

"Don't give it another thought. I'm sure I've been nothing but a shock to your system."

The man with Irene had risen when Kinsey reached their table and had remained standing.

"Kinsey, this is Lyle Wilkins. He's an attorney from Oklahoma." Irene pursed her lips into an ironic twist. "He's been sent here by my friend Norma to save me."

"You're very kind," he said to Irene. "But I assure you there's nothing to save." Acknowledging Kinsey, he said, "Your . . . Mrs. Turner has done nothing wrong."

The trio sat down, and in addition to speechless, Kinsey found she couldn't take her eyes off of Irene. The emotions churning through her were a virtual storm. She loved looking at this woman who resembled her so closely, and her accent, Kinsey adored it. She was filled with an irrevocable sense of loss over the years that had been stolen from them.

Still, as much as she wanted to accept Irene into her life without hesitation, that couldn't happen yet. Someone had put her *adopted* mother in the hospital, and Irene Turner hadn't been cleared of all charges.

Lyle drained the rest of his coffee. "I'll be on my way to take care of the rest of our business. Kinsey, I find it interesting that even though I didn't know you until this moment, I followed your career."

Soccer she could talk about. "Thank you, Mr. Wilkins. Are you a soccer fan?"

"Of women's," he said, his Oklahoma drawl every bit as strong as Irene's. "So full of fire and spirit, I could watch the women's team for hours. I rarely watch the men anymore. A bunch of crybabies. They get injured running onto the field."

Lifting an eyebrow, Kinsey laughed and glanced at Irene. "I like him."

Lyle picked up the check and motioned to a waitress. "I'll be in touch. An honor, Ms. Masters."

"Good luck," Irene said.

"Not needed." He ambled off with the aid of a cane.

Kinsey stared after him for a moment then focused on Irene. "Good luck?"

"Lyle practices law in Oklahoma, which means if I get into trouble, which I seem to be excelling at these days, I'll need someone local. He's interviewing Denver lawyers today for that very reason." Irene smiled and reached out to touch Kinsey's hand. Then, as if she thought better of it, she drew back and picked up her cup of coffee. "It's lovely to meet you, Kinsey. I heard about Gwyneth yesterday from Lieutenant Montoya. How is she?"

Unsure how to behave, Kinsey folded her hands and placed them on the table. "She'll survive physically. Emotionally and mentally, I'm not so sure." A waitress came by with a coffee carafe. Kinsey declined and asked for orange juice.

"Lyle is right. I should have handled this differently," Irene said. "I should have contacted you through the court system. I truly was trying to protect you and keep all this quiet. I'm so very sorry."

Kinsey sighed. "I don't know what I would have done. I guess the best we can do is deal. Look. I hate what my mother . . ." Kinsey shook her head. "I don't even know what to call her anymore—what *Gwyneth* did to you. But like it or not, she, my dad, my sister, and brother are a huge part of my life. I need them as much as they need me. I hope you can understand."

"I admire your loyalty." Irene lowered her gaze. "You say 'what Gwyneth did.' You don't hold your father responsible as well?"

Frowning, Kinsey told Irene about the night she confronted her parents, her dad's explanation, followed by her mother's odd disappearance. "He claims he didn't know. When Dad and I opened the door to the garage and found Mom gone, he was as shocked as I was.

"You knew him once upon a time," Kinsey said. "What do you think?"

"Sadly, your father didn't exaggerate about our relationship. We knew each other in passing and met at a time when each of us was vulnerable. But he was always kind and, don't forget, handsome. When I called to tell him I was pregnant, he was shocked, of course. But he didn't shirk his responsibility, not for an instant. I started receiving financial support immediately.

"So, yes," Irene continued. "The idea that he would bribe a doctor and kidnap you without telling me, when he said he wanted visitation rights, is hard to imagine."

Crazy Train sounded on Kinsey's cell phone; Irene blinked and sat back.

"It's my sister. Excuse me for a minute." Kinsey shifted in her chair. "Hey. What's up?"

Lauren gave Kinsey an update that said things at the hospital remained status quo, then asked what Kinsey's plans were for the morning. By the sound of her voice, Lauren wanted her big sister with her.

Torn, Kinsey wanted to get to know Irene. "I have errands to run. Keep me posted." Kinsey pushed end and flushed under Irene's candid gaze.

"I'm an errand?" She smiled.

"For now you are, Irene. Sorry."

"I'll take what I can get."

Tapping her fingernail against her glass, Kinsey studied the rim. Things had been going well so far—might as well get the first mother/daughter conflict underway. "Did you have anything to do with what happened to your husband or my mother?"

Irene's gaze never left Kinsey's. "I did not. I want to know who's behind this as much as you do."

"I had to ask."

"Of course you did."

All at once, the walls seemed to close in on her. Kinsey glanced around the old restaurant and asked, "Are you tired of being cooped up in this place?"

"It is nice, but if I don't see the outside world soon, I just might go bald."

Smiling, Kinsey tucked her chin in her hand. "That look wouldn't do a thing for you."

Irene made a pathetic face. "I know."

"What do you say we get out of here?" Kinsey came to her feet. "I know somewhere we can walk and talk and turn back the clock."

Irene laughed. "And where's that, my little poet?"

Despite her best efforts to keep the moment light, Kinsey had to work to swallow. "A place I should have visited with my real mom a long time ago. What do you say we visit the zoo?"

NATE WAS UNDER the impression that most ICUs became madhouses only at night. That impression was widely corrected when he and Sammy entered Lundgren's critical care unit the next morning.

Ahead of them, doctors and nurses focused on one area in particular, and when they wheeled in a crash cart, Nate's stomach plummeted. Fortunately, no cop stood nearby, and it wasn't the room given to them by the admission's clerk, so Nate and his partner kept walking.

Several doors down from the tragedy, a uniformed officer stood outside, indicating a shift change had occurred. He wasn't the same cop Nate had briefed last night.

Nate introduced himself and his partner. "Any problems?"

A man, whose badge read MacNair, replied "All quiet. Of course, I'm out here." He glanced over his shoulder. "Nurses and techs have been in and out of there all night."

Speaking of nurses, one approached. Instead of introductions, this time, Nate and Sammy produced their badges.

"Five minutes," she said. "Mrs. Masters has had a very rough night. Besides the substantial pain, I don't know that she'll be able to tell you anything. She's still coming off the effects of the anesthesia."

"We'll take our chances," Sammy said.

The unhappy nurse stalked off. They entered a room too bright in Nate's mind for sleeping. Even so, by the rise and fall of her chest, and the help of a morphine drip, Gwyneth didn't share the same opinion. Hooked up to an EKG monitor, an oxygen-read on her finger, and an IV inserted into her left arm, she looked small and fragile tucked into a bed between side rails.

But not innocent, Nate reminded himself. He steeled himself for the job he had to do.

Not fond of the antiseptic smells, he nevertheless dealt. He took out a small pocket recorder and nodded at Sammy who'd circled the opposite side of the bed.

"Mrs. Masters, I'm Detective Sammy Lucero, Denver Police Department."

She gave no response, and the EKG machine maintained a steady pace.

Nate motioned for Sammy to let him have a go. "Mrs. Masters, it's Nate Paxton. Are you with me? We need to talk to you."

Gradually, the activity on the monitor increased. Gwyneth's eyes fluttered, but didn't quite open. "Nate?" she said, groggily.

"Yes, ma'am."

"Where am I?" she slurred.

"You're at Lundgren Memorial," he said softly, subsequently studying her face and then the monitor. "You gave us a scare yesterday. Do you remember?"

She winced. "I . . . hurt."

"That's because somebody shot you. We need your help to find out who did this to you."

Her face became a billboard of pain. She groaned as the EKG markers steadily advanced.

"Your entire family was here last night," Nate continued, watching the screen. "They wanted to stay, but your doctor told them to go home. Kinsey, Lauren, Jay, Yasmine, and Evan, they all send their love."

Beeps and lines, though progressing, showed no noticeable increase during the mention of one specific family member's name.

"Mrs. Masters. This is important. We have to know what happened," Nate said.

When she didn't reply after several seconds, he sighed and stood upright. The nurse was right. An interview this early was getting them nowhere. They'd have to wait to get answers.

Then in a gravelly voice, she said, "Talking . . . Yas . . . Smash. Turned . . ." The eyelids she'd been struggling to open relaxed altogether.

Nate glanced at Sammy. On the other side of the hospital bed, he stood like a frustrated marionette ready to yank on the strings.

"Stay with me," Nate said.

A tear streamed from her left eye.

He brushed it away. "You heard a smash, is that right? Then you turned. Did you see anything?"

"Someone . . ."

Sammy gripped the safety rail. "Could you tell if it was a man or a woman?"

"Mask." She moaned. "Happened . . . so . . . fast."

Sammy gave a thumb's up, his signal to Nate to make sure he caught the connection. Her account corroborated that the neighbor Carmine, with his limited vision, had witnessed the shooter. The police had finished canvasing the neighborhood, and so far no one with better eyesight had come forward. Nate made a mental note to ask the lieutenant for media support to enlist the community.

"Could you see what your assailant wore?" Sammy asked.

"Dark . . ."

"Did you hear anything?" Sammy prodded. "A voice maybe?"

"Just . . . fired." She moved slightly and gritted her teeth.

The nurse came into the room and tapped her wrist watch.

Nate nodded impatiently at the woman. "We're almost done. Mrs. Masters, Yasmine recalls that at the end of your phone call you said something. Do you remember what it was?"

The nurse stood glaring as precious time ticked by. Gwyneth seemed paralyzed until a sob tore from her throat.

Nate and Sammy bent close, hoping to capture her words.

Nate had deliberately not mentioned Evan. Sammy had gone too far asking about a voice, particularly with it being recorded. To ask anything specific and leading, with Gwyneth under the influence of some potent medication, she could get confused. This was the stuff defense attorneys loved and would use later to acquit his client or have a case thrown out. They needed Gwyneth to corroborate Yasmine's statement on her own.

"His fault," she said, one gasp after another. "But . . . couldn't . . . didn't want . . ."

The beeps and bleeps on the EKG screen increased and the nurse stepped forward.

"To die . . ." She moaned deeply, then began arching and twisting.

The monitor sped up, the nurse ran to Gwyneth's bedside, muscling Nate out of the way. She jabbed a get lost thumb at Sammy. "That's it, you two. Interview's over."

Nate followed Sammy out of the room, while a woman in scrubs ran past them.

"That went well," Sammy said. "*Not*. We came out with what we went in with. *Nada*."

"Evan Masters is still on the *do not admit* list," Nate told the guard at the door.

"Got it," the cop said.

Outside the hospital, Sammy put on his sunglasses and perused his surroundings more than he had in the last two days. "Do we know where Evan was at the time of the shooting?"

"Claims he was at home the whole time. Alone." Nate scanned the area as well, including the rooftops. "If we're being followed, I'm not seeing it."

"That makes two of us. Why would Guzmán call off his dogs?"

"Manpower shortage?"

"You're killin' me, Nate."

Approaching the car, he tossed the keys to Sammy. "You're edgy. You drive."

Sammy slid the keys into the ignition. "You know that old saying, just because you're paranoid doesn't mean nobody's after you. I hate being spineless for no reason. What do you say, since Guzmán's made us, we pay the slimeball a visit?"

"Walk into Continental Miracles and just say hey?" Nate asked.

"Might save our scrawny necks and the taxpayers' money."

"You mean when the LT finds us harassing a suspect and fires our asses?"

"No. When Mr. Upstanding and his little pocket saint sees us coming, has a heart attack, and does our job for us."

"Shows initiative. I like it," Nate said. "Let's do it. Swing by."

Actually, Sammy's brainstorm couldn't be better. If they did have a tail, their arrival at Continental Miracles would force Rafa or whatever flunkey had been assigned to them to notify his boss. No way would the gangster allow two cops to walk into Guzmán's office unannounced. Should he make that mistake, undoubtedly the flunkey would disappear.

If Guzmán were notified by the tail, then his tremendous ego would tip his hand. In front of his staff and donors, he'd smile and welcome Nate and Sammy as if they were old friends. If he appeared startled and angered upon their entrance, that meant that Guzmán had figured some other way to take them out and no longer was having them followed.

Sammy swerved off Bannock, traveled west on 8th Street, then veered onto Downing when road construction blocked his way. Finally, they arrived on Lafayette and the two-story complex that housed Continental Miracles.

"We're not being followed," Nate said, eyes still peeled to the side mirror.

"I think you're right." Sammy pulled to the curb. "Let's go make Guzmán's day."

Nate opened the passenger side door when Sammy's cell phone rang.

His partner glared at the device. "I'm telling you, that guy has eyes in the back of his head." Sammy answered after two more rings. "Lucero . . . Where are we, sir?" He lifted his gaze to the vehicle's ceiling and shook his head. "Sorry, Lieutenant. You broke up for a minute. Just left the hospital. No change in status. Gwyneth didn't confirm Yasmine's statement but did confirm that the shooter wore a mask.

"What are we doing now?" Sammy looked to Nate and held out an open palm in exasperation. "Waiting for instructions from you, sir, of course." He listened, then closed his eyes. "Yes, sir. We're on our way."

"How do you do that?" Nate asked.

"What?"

"Go from kickass to bootlicker in nothing flat."

"It's a learned behavior," Sammy said. "Started the first day of the police academy."

"No reunion?" Nate asked.

"No fun for us today." Sammy pulled away from the curb and mashed down on the gas. "Forensics found hairs in the ski mask."

IN HIS CORNER office, Rodrigo controlled his anticipation as Griff Colburn sat in the chair across from him. "I hated to pull you off the campaign trail, Mr. Colburn. But Ms. Masters's number is unlisted, she no longer employs an agent, and so far she's been impossible to reach."

"Please, call me Griff. I would have given you the information over the phone," he replied. "Frankly, I was glad for the detour. I'm delighted you thought of her. With all that Kins is going through right now, Continental Miracles may be just what she needs."

"She's exactly what we need," Rodrigo said. *The perfect bait to draw out a couple of snitches.* Rodrigo removed his little pocket icon of St. Gemma, patron saint of the poor. "Terrible news about her mother. I read the account in *The Post.* I hope they find who did it. And that whoever it was doesn't try again and succeed."

The politician nodded. "The entire Masters family is walking a tightrope."

Rodrigo placed the little icon back into his pocket and folded his hands on the desk. "What I'm about to ask may be imperfect timing. I also insist that you keep this confidential. Continental Miracles has a number of celebrities that we're contacting, people whose egos can't tolerate being considered *second best.* Personally, Kinsey's image is what I want to represent my organization. Still, with everything she has going on in her life, I'm hesitant to call her—*and have it traced to me*—when she might not be easily persuaded. You mentioned you're engaged."

Griff Colburn lowered his head. "I misspoke when I made that statement."

"A politician misspeaking?" Rodrigo lifted a brow.

"It happens." A flush appeared on his face. "The truth is, I've decided to give Kinsey some space. I pay the people running my campaign a lot of money for their advice, and because of Gwyneth's attack, they recommend I cool things with Kinsey until after the election. I've been dreading telling her."

"I see." Rodrigo unfolded his hands. "Then it appears I've wasted both our time. If Ms. Masters accepted my proposal, I was prepared to make another sizable contribution to your campaign."

Colburn's sky blue eyes widened, and in that instant, Rodrigo saw the color of greed. "I think your advisors are looking at the situation incorrectly. Naturally, I don't know the entire story, but it appears Ms. Masters is the victim here. If you stand by her, that only endears you to your constituents, not hurts you." Rodrigo used the most judgmental tone he could muster. "If you reject her for a situation beyond her control, well, I can't support—"

"You're absolutely right," the all-but-salivating man said. "In this case, I've been ill advised."

"What a relief." Rodrigo breathed deeply. "My faith has not been misplaced."

"What do you want me to do?" Colburn said.

"Tell her of my proposal and how much I think of her. Then schedule a meeting where I can meet with her in person. I'd like to pick her up, give her a tour of some of our local affiliations."

"I can do that."

"And, please, stress the confidential nature of my request. I won't be happy, but if she turns me down, I will have to consider others."

"You have my word," Colburn said. "I'll make sure Kins understands the situation, too. I can't promise she'll say yes, but I can't see any harm in her hearing you out."

Rodrigo smiled. "No harm whatsoever. Thanks for stopping by, Griff."

Chapter Thirty-one

AT THE DIRECTION of their lieutenant, Nate and Sammy stopped in at the Denver Police Department's forensic lab. Three technicians sat at windowless workstations poring over material. Nate advised the closest analyst what they'd come for.

She glanced up from a microscope. "That'd be Johnny's area."

Johnny turned out to be a pale analyst who looked like he'd never spent a day in the sun. Rummaging through his files, he said for the fourth time, "This is so interesting," until he found what he wanted and opened it up. Several hairs were stored in plastic bags marked *Evidence*. "Your perpetrator's a redhead," he explained.

Nate blinked, his mind immediately turning to his conversation with Kinsey. *He's a redheaded prima dona who constantly asserts that my mom takes too much for her commission.*

Sammy bent to examine the hairs and shrugged. "Could those be dyed?"

"Could be. But they're not," Johnny said.

"What about sex? Can you tell if they belong to a man or a woman?"

"Sure," the tech said. "But that'll take weeks and DNA testing."

"Send them for analysis," Sammy said. "By then maybe we'll have a suspect and only need them for corroboration."

Johnny nodded and filled out a form.

Outside the lab, Nate referred to his notes. "According to Kinsey, one of the artists who works at Masterpieces has red hair. Guy by the name of Ryan Stone whose specialty is stained glass. Most importantly, he's not happy with Gwyneth."

"Yasmine open the gallery today?" Sammy asked.

"No reason not to. But we can't be sure Stone will be there. I'll make a call to Yasmine and see if he's in today."

"While you're doing that, I'll check with Dispatch and get his street address."

RYAN STONE LIVED on the fringes of downtown Denver in a warehouse that had been converted to condos. At one time, the area might have been an up and coming place to live, but as Nate pulled off onto a side street, boarded up windows and a beer bottle landscape said things had gone downhill.

He turned off the sputtering Crown Victoria and glanced Sammy's way.

"If we don't notice a tail by the end of the day, I'm ready to take my chances with my Explorer."

Sammy nodded. "I hear ya. Same goes for the roommate situation. No offense, partner."

"I'll try not to be crushed."

With Sammy to his right, Nate moved up the sidewalk and surveyed their entire surroundings.

"Which one do you suppose is Stone's?" Sammy asked.

Nate pointed to the condo in the middle. "Easy, check out the stained glass window."

They entered a foyer of sorts, which in past years must have been state of the art. Today, however, over the intercom system, someone had posted a cardboard *out of order* notice. The door to the building's inner sanctum had been propped open by a rock. Grafitti-enhanced mailbox units along the wall identified Stone's apartment as 5C.

Even from the entrance, the pot smell was strong.

"Well, if you didn't smoke it before, you do now," Sammy said.

They climbed the metal stairs to Stone's apartment. For a building full of dope smokers, the place was relatively quiet. The only music Nate heard emanated from inside Stone's residence.

He knocked.

A disembodied voice from the other side of the door said, "Jerome, what part of *working* do you not understand?" Stone yanked open the door. He straightened, his expression going from furious to pleasantly surprised in a fraction of a second. "Well, hello."

Sammy held out his badge. "Ryan Stone?"

"Shoot. I knew you were too good to be true. Whatever it is, I didn't do it. And if it was Jerome, not that I'm speaking to him at the moment, he didn't either."

"May we come in, Mr. Stone?" Nate said.

Ryan Stone motioned with a hand. "With two brutes like you, who's here to stop you?" He said to Sammy, "Anyone ever tell you that you have a gorgeous skin tone?"

"Knock it off, Stone," Sammy said. "We're here because of Gwyneth Masters's shooting yesterday. Where were you between the hours of ten and two?"

"I never left my studio. I was here the entire day. *Poor Gwyneth.*" Stone rolled his eyes. "Who'd want to kill *her?*"

"Did you know about the house on Foxglove?" Sammy asked.

"Worst kept secret ever. Yasmine told Michael and Michael told *moi.*"

"Michael Whitney?" Nate asked.

"Yes, genius," Stone replied, making no secret he was giving Nate the once over.

Immaculate was the first word that came to mind as Nate circled Stone's great room. That, or if he didn't make it as an artist, with all the stained glass in this place, he'd be a natural as a church window supplier.

Stone obviously couldn't work *stoned.* On the west wall, a ventilation unit did a fair job of blocking out the marijuana from the other apartments.

He'd divided the room into two—living and work. Overhead skylights saturated the room with natural lighting, and diffused light bounced from the stained glass window Nate and Sammy had seen from the sidewalk.

As for Stone's workspace, everything about it said he was as precise as the angles and edges of his work. Soldering irons in one space; shears, scissors, and needle nose pliers lying beside them; a hand broom, bins full of glass, and spools full of copper and lead sat on a wooden work table.

"You like?" Stone asked.

"I like," Nate said, glancing at the copper spools, a meth addict's dream, and the distance to Ryan Stone's front door. Fortunately, the door was metal with two good-sized deadbolt locks, but Stone was still a prime candidate for burglary or robbery. "I take it you didn't care for Mrs. Masters?"

"Who? Gwyneth? Only that on top of being a bitch, she's the devil. She makes a fortune off of the artists she commissions, feeds on their desperation with iron-clad contracts, then she owns us." He laughed sardonically. "But it wasn't me. I abhor violence. Why on earth would I be a suspect?"

"Reports say you don't like her, and we found hair strands at the crime scene," Nate said, deliberately leaving out that the shooter had worn a mask.

"Ah, and I take it they were red?"

"Yeah, Stone, like yours," Sammy said.

"Along with ten million other people," he replied, lifting an exaggerated gaze toward the skylights. "Just for the record, mine's real."

"We could clear this up real fast and be out of your authentic red hair, if you'd supply us a sample," Sammy said.

"I don't know," Stone hedged. "Maybe I should call a lawyer."

"Decision's yours," Nate said. "We can get a warrant. But that's going to take time neither of us has. Looking at this place, something tells me you're one dude that doesn't like people handling your stuff. Hard as we try, we sometimes make messes."

Stone's freckled skin blanched. "Oh, all right." He strode into another room and came back with a hair brush. "Keep it. I have more, and I'm not your *dude.*"

Prepared, Nate opened a sealable bag given to him by Johnny, the Denver PD's analyst.

Stone placed the brush inside.

"Nice of you to cooperate," Nate said.

"I only hope I'm not sorry I did." Stone hesitated. "I'm not the only one who hates her, you know."

"Really? Who else should we be talking to?" Nate asked.

"Michael Whitney. He's smitten with Yasmine, you know. He says she's the real genius behind Masterpieces, but Gwyneth treats her like an indentured servant."

"We didn't see that," Sammy said. "From what we gathered, they're close."

Stone laughed. "To the outsider, maybe. Work with them and you learn all their dirty little secrets. By the way, Yasmine is starting to listen to Michael. Gwyneth is all about family. She's given her children joint ownership of Masterpieces."

"And Yasmine and Michael find that unreasonable?" Nate asked.

"Maybe not for Lauren and Jay, who are actually artists. But the real insult is that Kinsey doesn't want anything to do with the business. And now we're hearing that *Special K* isn't even Gwyneth's biological child."

"Who'd you hear that from?" Sammy asked.

"Yasmine told Michael, and Michael told *moi*."

"Got it. If you think of anything else, Mr. Stone." Nate handed the artist a generic Denver PD business card with scribbled contact information. Vice cops didn't carry stationery, and Nate and Sammy, too new on the job, hadn't ordered any yet. "You've been very helpful."

"Make it up to me by telling people about my work," Stone said, showing them to the door.

Back in the Crown Vic, Nate asked his partner, "What do you think?"

Sammy fastened his seatbelt. "He's not the shooter. Way too anal. He would have finished the job. That is, if he didn't *abhor* violence."

"And his comments about Yasmine and Michael Whitney?"

"Wouldn't be the first time an employee sucked up to an employer but wanted him dead. Situation bears watching." Sammy pulled down the passenger side visor and studied his reflection in the mirror. "I do have nice skin tone, don't I?"

Nate dropped Stone's bagged hairbrush in the console. "You know, up until Stone mentioned it, I never noticed. I was always distracted by the size of your nose. Let's run this by the lab before reporting in."

Sammy leaned closer to the mirror. "You think my nose is big?"

UPON THEIR reappearance in Forensics, the crime scene analyst didn't appear overly excited that they'd brought him a sample so quickly. Elbows on his desk, Johnny shook his head. "I blew it, Detectives. No excuse, but the workload sometimes makes us sloppy. I can already predict the hairs from this brush are not going to match the crime scene."

"What tipped you off?" asked Sammy.

"You did actually." Johnny reached for a folder, and this time located it immediately. "When you told me to send the hairs for DNA analysis, I was all set to do that. DNA can be extracted in two ways, mitochondrial DNA from the hair shaft and nuclear DNA, which comes from the bulb. That's when it hit me, I couldn't find any follicular material, e.g., the bulb in any of the hairs we obtained from the ski mask."

"And that's unusual?" Sammy frowned.

"Extremely so. I would expect to find a few broken-off follicles, but all of them? That's when it became clear these hairs had been cut, not yanked, which made me look again. That's when I saw my blunder."

"Which is what?" Nate asked.

"I found traces of glue on these hairs."

"What does that mean?" Nate felt like a hamster on an exercise wheel. "Are these strands red hair, and are they from a human being?"

"These strands are human all right, and they're virgin red hair at that, meaning it hasn't been treated. But even though they're all close in color, size and texture, they're not from the same human head."

"We got a bunch of redheads wearing one ski mask?"

"In a matter of speaking, yes. Have a look under my Unitron and tell me what you see."

Nate and Sammy both took turns at the microscope.

"Looks like crusty hair to me," Sammy said.

"Good description," Johnny said. "That *crust* you're describing is glue."

Johnny removed Stone's brush from the bag. "I'll compare the samples I get from this hairbrush to the samples we've collected here. But don't get your hopes up. I'm 99.9 percent sure the hairs from our ski mask came from a wig."

Chapter Thirty-two

KINSEY'S IDEA TO visit the Denver zoo with Irene was a resounding success. Determined for this to be the first of many of their times together, she dropped Irene back at the Brown Palace just as she received a return call from an employee of Lundgren Hospital. Her mother was able to receive visitors, sans one—her father.

Bluetooth in her ear, Kinsey groaned and gripped the Audi's steering wheel. Her voice mail wasn't full from his tirades, so she called Lauren to find out how he'd taken the awful news.

"Not well," she said. "But he's okay. He mentioned he's behind at work and left for the office."

"That may be the best place for him right now." Kinsey merged onto Speer Boulevard.

"All I can tell you is that Dad's crushed, and I don't know how to help him, Kins."

"I do. Let's take him out to dinner tonight, just you, me, and Jay."

"He would love that," Lauren replied. "We'll even let him pick the place."

Kinsey hung up, smiling. She would hold her family together if it was the last thing she did.

A dutiful daughter would head straight for the hospital. Yet real or imagined, the smell of zoo animals permeated her hair and clothes. Before someone agreed and told her she smelled rank, Kinsey stopped off at home to clean up.

FORTY MINUTES later, she stepped beyond the rain-glass shower out into her steam-filled bathroom, no longer able to see the mirrors. Thirsty and dressed only in a towel, she left the bathroom and headed for the kitchen. But as her gaze traveled to the sliding glass doors, for the first time ever, she felt self-conscious.

Nate's comment to buy window coverings had obviously done the requisite damage. For crying out loud, she was three floors up, backing up to miles and miles of Rocky Mountain terrain, vegetation, and isolation.

Much like her toughest opponent on the soccer field, Nate Paxton had gotten inside her head.

Kinsey groaned. She ran back into her bedroom and tossed the towel. Rifling through the drawers, she tugged on the first pair of shorts and tank top she could find. Then, pivoting, she came face to face with her laptop lying in the same spot she'd left it, unused, for the last two days. At the very least, she should send the substitute teacher a lesson plan.

Ignoring the traitorous items in her house turning against her, Kinsey made herself a peanut butter sandwich and poured a glass of almond milk. Back in her bedroom, she sat against the headboard. Legs stretched in front of her, she rested the laptop on her thighs and logged on to Lamar Bryant High School's web site.

She answered three emails from students and assigned her junior English students to finish reading *MacBeth*. Then, rather than let them believe they were on vacation, she tasked them with writing a paper on *Why Shakespeare Wrote MacBeth*.

Satisfied she hadn't shirked her duties, she rose from the bed and had moved on to scrounging for something appropriate to wear to the hospital when the doorbell rang. With damp hair resembling Medusa's, she crossed the living room and peered through the peephole.

She opened the door to Nate, surprised to see him so soon, particularly after last night's heart-to-heart. "Decide you can't live without me?"

He kissed her cheek as he entered her townhome. "How'd you know?"

"In the summer, I work part-time as a mind reader."

"Whoa. Don't go there." He stopped at the fireplace. "No blinds yet?"

"I don't think they make 14-hour window coverings."

"How'd your visit with Irene go?"

"Great." Kinsey grinned and shoved her hands in her pockets. "She's really something, Nate. Funny. Wise."

He moved toward her, his dark eyes shining with interest. "Something like you."

"You think?"

"I know." Nate took her in his arms and kissed her again.

Kinsey returned his kiss and ran her hands through his hair then eased away, breathless to look at him.

Whatever Nate wore, he stood out. That was the benefit of standing six-three with good genes and the determination to keep it that way. But today, dressed in a gray button-down shirt and tailored black pants, he appeared particularly striking.

"Not that I'm complaining," she said, doing her best to act as though men entered her living room and kissed her every day. "But what brings you by, and what was that for?"

He smiled and ran a finger over her cheek. "I came by because I need a favor, and the kiss, well, it's because you started it."

"By opening the door?"

"Last night in the elevator."

"I guess I did." She closed one eye and gave him a sheepish expression. "Mad at me?"

"Furious." He kissed her again, until she was close to dragging him into the bedroom. Evidently, there was more than one mind reader in the room because he abruptly released her. "About that favor . . ."

Still reeling from kissing him, she said, "Name it."

"Let me be in the room when you talk to Gwyneth."

That killed the mood, and she put distance between them. "I should have qualified my agreement with anything but that."

"It's important, Kins. Your mother told us very little that we didn't already know this morning. I'll wager she's aching to talk to you, to make sure everything's all right between you two. We're hoping she'll let down her guard."

"I don't know, Nate." Kinsey shook her head. "It's so personal. I'll be honest, I want some alone time with her to understand what was going through her mind all those years ago."

"I understand that. But I want you to understand something, too. I'm not out to bust her for an age-old kidnapping. I'm out to catch a killer."

"Make a deal with you?"

"I'm listening."

"Let me talk to her first, and I'll ask her to talk to you."

"If that's the best you can do."

"It is. I'm sorry. She'll hold back if you're there."

"I had to try. We want to catch this guy."

"Guy?" Kinsey asked. "Meaning you don't think it's Irene?"

"Figure of speech." Nate walked to the sliding glass doors, looked up, and shook his head. "We don't know." He turned to face her. "And that's dangerous. It means we don't know who or what to look for when the suspect tries again."

Chapter Thirty-three

"AND THEN KINSEY brought me back here," Irene said, holding the phone to her ear to give Norma an overdue update. Staring out her hotel window, she noticed the gods hadn't followed her instructions. The Wells Fargo Tower still stood where she'd specifically ordered a mountain.

"A trip to the zoo. How fun," Norma said. "Is Kinsey everything you thought she would be?"

"Oh, Norma, she's more. Such a good heart and head on her shoulders." Irene traced her fingers over Danny's handsome face and caught her sappy smile in the mirror. Rolling her eyes, she grinned wider. She'd given birth to such beautiful children. "Are you doing okay?"

"I'm fine," Norma replied. "I'm invested in a good book, and Cliff's daughter has spared me her vitriolic presence for several days."

"No doubt she's devastated to learn of her father's actions," Irene said.

"That's just it. She doesn't believe a word Lyle or I say. Lyle's been the Mitchell family lawyer for years, and now Sabrina's threatening a slander suit against both of us."

That wiped away Irene's smile. She despised what the crystal ball of tomorrow predicted—a civil lawsuit against the Mitchell estate, a criminal trial for Gwyneth Masters. But now that Irene had shaken the hornet's nest, there was very little she could do to outrun the sting.

"There's no way I'm going to let you suffer for coming forward with the truth. Once I'm officially cleared of Stephen's murder, I'll have his estate. I'm not going to be hurting financially. Please tell your stepdaughter I want justice, not money."

"That's just it, Irene. I'm rather enjoying this. I know having a stepmother enter the picture is never pleasant, but I bent over backwards for that girl. But she's snubbed me every step of the way. I say let her fret for a while."

Irene disconnected after promising to keep in touch more. She'd talk to Lyle and possibly Peter Trevelle to see what could be done about appeasing Ms. Sabrina Mitchell.

The swelling in her head was much less today, but Irene still looked forward to a nap. She'd closed her eyes for all of sixty seconds when the bedside phone rang.

"Mrs. Turner, this is Claire at the front desk. You have a visitor, a Mr. Evan Masters."

THE ONLY THING Irene did to prepare for meeting the man she'd slept with twenty-eight years ago was to brush her teeth and dab on lip gloss. She rode the elevator to the lobby and exited for what could only be a dismal reunion.

Dashing came to mind as she watched Evan approach; he blended in with the Brown Palace décor as though he owned the place. He dressed a lot like Stephen, undoubtedly wearing some designer's signature collection. He'd added a few extra pounds, but then who hadn't? He also looked like a man who'd recently lost a whole lot of sleep.

His extended hand held no interest to her. Until she was absolutely convinced he had nothing to do with Kinsey's kidnapping, she'd just as soon string him up than make nice.

He arched a brow as though registering surprise, or maybe it was the awkwardness of the moment. "No wonder Kinsey's convinced. I see her every day, but I'd forgotten . . . I read the paper. For a woman who survived an attack, you're looking remarkably well."

Standing this close to Gwyneth's husband, ice cold fury ripped through Irene. *How could he not have known?*

He glanced about the lobby. "I don't blame you for not making this easy on me. But is there a place we can talk, privately?"

She chose the same restaurant where hours earlier she'd sat with Kinsey.

Evan sat across from her, and when the waiter came, he ordered a glass of red wine. "You, Irene?"

"Rum and coke, please." She'd almost ordered iced tea, but seeing him again, and wondering *why* she was seeing him again, she decided on something stronger. "What do you want, Evan?"

He picked up a fork and studied it as though unsure of its purpose. "I don't know where to start. I thought you'd lost the baby. You even called to say so. I had no idea my wife was capable of such—"

"A crime?"

Frowning, he nodded. "All right. Yes."

The waiter served their drinks and stood by until Irene said, "We won't be having anything to eat." Then, as he walked away, she said to Kinsey's father, "If I call you an idiot, I suppose I deserve the same title. Stephen duped me as badly as you say Gwyneth fooled you." Irene sat forward. "But in your heart of hearts, when you looked at Kinsey, you never suspected?"

"I give you my word." Evan held out his hands. "I was as blindsided by all this as you were. Why would I question my wife about giving birth? It's not like you were around, or that I saw you regularly."

She stared back at the man. "All right. I'm willing to concede you didn't know. I'm also not sure I'm at the apology stage, but I am willing to form a truce for the sake of our daughter."

"Our daughter." An involuntary muscle ticked above his left eye, and for an instant, she saw the temper behind the façade. Just as quickly, though, he smiled, and the powerful CEO regained control. "Again, I'm sorry this happened, but it's a long time ago, and what's done is done."

Irene sat back in her chair, unsure whether to laugh or cry. She'd actually believed he'd come on his wife's behalf to bargain to keep Gwyneth out of prison—not that Irene had any say at this point. Suddenly, her entire countenance lightened, and she knew. The man with whom she shared a table was pathetic, remarkably like Stephen, and she had a perfectly good rum and coke in front of her.

"I assume you aim to have a relationship with Kinsey?"

Irene sipped her drink. "You assume correctly."

He sighed. "I thought as much. Whether you like it or not, Kinsey's the person she is today because of the environment Gwyn and I provided. Right now, she's devastated . . . confused. Remember, I'm familiar with your background. The truth is you have nothing in common. If the two of you pursue this, you'll both realize it."

Holding her sardonic laughter in check was nearly impossible. "It doesn't disturb you that Kinsey and I have nothing in common because your wife arranged to steal Kinsey the minute she was born?"

He had the grace to look guilty. "Of course it does. But up until now I never knew of my wife's mental issues. I've already been in contact with the best doctors available. After she's released from Lundgren, she'll be psychologically evaluated, admitted for treatment, if necessary."

Oh, it's necessary. "That should fix everything." Irene sipped her cocktail.

He seemed to grasp that she was laughing at him, and his eye muscle jumped again. "Do you think this is a joke? I'm fighting for my family. Kinsey's very close to her brother and sister, and, believe me, they'll never accept you. Don't make her choose. Please. Stay out of her life."

"No."

His golf-course tanned face blossomed into red. He put down his glass and tapped a finger on the table. "This isn't even like a couple divorcing. Be reasonable. We had a one-night stand."

"Which is precisely why I'm ready to go on the lecture circuit and warn young women not to do it." Irene took out a ten from her wallet and tossed it on the table, for the first time grateful for dormant emotions. Evan seemed only capable of seeing his side of the picture. "If Kinsey wants me out of her life, all she has to do is say so." She stood. "Thanks for the drink, but I'll buy my own."

He grabbed her wrist as she passed his chair. "What's the matter with you? I don't remember you being so cold. At least consider recanting on this Pandora's box you've opened. At least say you and Gwyneth at one time discussed *adopting* Kinsey."

Irene tried to pull away, but his manacle-like grip prevented her from leaving. At this time of day, the restaurant wasn't busy, but a few nearby diners were staring. She bent close to his ear and deliberately increased her drawl.

"Perhaps when Gwyneth sees those incredible doctors you mentioned, you should go, too. Back home in the trailer park, with two of us going, we'd ask for a discount." She clenched her teeth together. "Now you let go of my arm."

He did; Irene picked up her rum and coke and drained the glass. Empty, she set it back down on the table. "Well, look at that, I've finished my drink." Moving toward him, she tipped over his glass. "I think you should finish yours."

A gush of red wine spread over the table and into Evan's lap. A waiter rushed forward. Irene walked out of Ellyngton's without a look back.

Chapter Thirty-four

TWELVE MINUTES after Kinsey entered Gwyneth's hospital room, she came out, shaking her head.

Nate glanced up from the chair where he'd sat between counting the minutes and staring at his thumbs. He stood. "Nothing?"

"Nothing that made sense." Kinsey wiped away a tear.

The nurse who'd been a thorn in his side earlier that morning was still on duty. Hands on her ample hips and still thorny, she said, "Mrs. Masters doesn't have the flu or a headache. She's been shot in the chest, and she's in pain. She requires time to heal to even remember what happened. Come back tomorrow, if you must. Better yet, give her a full day's rest and come back on Saturday."

"I'd love to give her all the time in the world," Nate said. "But I doubt the person who tried to kill Mrs. Masters is on our same timeline. We'll be back as often as it takes."

Narrowing her gaze, the nurse harrumphed and took off like the last time their professions had gotten in the way of each other.

Kinsey stared after the Nurse Ratched clone. "I wouldn't want to meet her in a dark alley."

"The only thing she's guilty of is being good at her job." Nate brought his attention back to Kinsey. "Your mother didn't say anything?"

"She mumbled something about never meaning to hurt me, then passed out holding my hand. She's hooked up to so many tubes and machines. I think the nurse is right. Mom's not going to be able to tell us anything for a while."

"We don't have a while." He paused to talk to the replacement officer by Gwyneth's door. "Orders still stand."

Nate walked Kinsey to her car, enjoying having her near. Being with her was far too comfortable, though, too much like the old days, and the insecure kid from his past warned him not to get used to it.

"Hate to admit it, but the nurse is probably right about tomorrow. If we set something up for Saturday, what time can you be here?" Nate asked.

She propped her butt against her Audi, checked her iPhone and raised a brow.

"Conflict?"

"No. Just a surprising text from Griff. How about I meet you here at nine?"

"Nine it is." Nate knew better than to ask. Kins wearing an off the shoulder blouse and a long gypsy-type skirt and stylish boots wasn't dressed for kickin' it around the house. "Plans with the reckless driver tonight?"

"No. Griff apologized about his driving, by the way. Said he was worried about me, that's all. Jay, Lauren, and I are taking Dad out to dinner." She peered at her phone again. "Speaking of which, I gotta go. The natives are getting restless. See ya." Kinsey blew Nate a kiss and slid behind the wheel of her car.

DAD CHOSE *Cucina Colore* for dinner, an Italian restaurant and a family favorite. But as Kinsey sat talking with Lauren and Jay, their distraught father had yet to make an appearance.

She watched her brother and sister's faces as she told them about her morning spent with Irene. When they showed little reaction, Kinsey said, "This is weird, isn't it?"

Lauren, never one to mince words, spoke first. "What's weird is Mom kidnapping you and you keeping secrets from us. You wanting to have a relationship with your birth mother—call me crazy—seems perfectly normal. I can handle it." Lauren turned to Jay. "What about you, squirt?"

Jay, long immune to Lauren's taunts, bobbed his head up and down, then hesitated. "I think I'm cool with it. But I'd like to at least meet this enigmatic, semi-relative before I'm forced to lay the hammer of approval down on her. Maybe there should be some kind of test."

"Would you like multiple choice or essay?" Kinsey waggled her eyebrows. "What a goof."

"You tell anyone I said this, I'll deny it, but Jay makes a good point," Lauren said. "Here we are talking about *us* accepting Irene. What if Irene couldn't care less about Jay and me and only wants a relationship with you?"

"I never thought of that. It hasn't come up yet. I just assumed." Reaching across the table, Kinsey squeezed both their hands. "But who wouldn't want a relationship with the two of you?"

I know," Lauren said, exuding her typical confidence. "We're amazing. But this is a new concept to all of us and should be addressed. Then, we'll move on to how the parents, all three of them, will adapt to this. I think Mom and Dad will have the most trouble. We've always been this *Stepford* family."

"And don't forget that Mom might end up in jail." For the first time, Jay brought up what had yet to be addressed.

"If she even gets that far," Lauren said. "Don't forget someone's trying to kill her."

For a moment, all three sat with their chins in their hands.

Kinsey dropped hers first and straightened. "If you had to name a suspect right here, right now, who's the first person that comes to mind?"

"Yasmine," Jay said.

"The man coming toward our table," Lauren replied.

Kinsey glanced up to see their father. She caught the worry on her siblings' faces and joined in their concern. "Oh, God."

NATE RETURNED TO his desk and caught up on paperwork. With that completed, he took the opportunity to run a background check on Lyle Wilkins, the Oklahoma attorney who'd shown up on Wednesday to rescue Irene. After that, Nate's plans for the night were simple—to drive his own car and sleep in his own bed. Fortunately, there were several articles on Lyle A. Wilkins and the law firm of Wilkins, Armstrong & Cassidy had a tricked-out website. Nate printed various articles, and ten minutes later, he'd compiled a 15-page *curriculum vitae* on the lawyer.

The lieutenant's door was open, so Nate ambled that way.

Rapping twice, he realized too late that his boss was on the phone. Nate prepared to wait outside until Lieutenant Montoya waved him inside.

"Thanks for the heads up," he said to the other party. "If there's any damage, let me know." Ending the call, he glanced Nate's way. "What's up?"

He slid Wilkins's report across the lieutenant's desk. "Information you wanted on Irene's lawyer. Had some drama in his personal life, but he's the muscle of the organization and looks legit."

Drumming his fingers, Montoya stared back at Nate. "How so in his personal life?"

"He's on wife number three."

"Figured as much. He's too smooth for my blood. He's still married?"

Nate nodded.

The lieutenant set the report on his desk and skimmed pages. "You don't find it the least bit strange that Irene's friend asks a senior partner, earning five-hundred-dollars-an-hour, to become an errand boy?"

Nate cocked his head and mulled it over. "I assumed Norma Mitchell was an important client he wanted to keep happy. Want me to keep digging?"

"No. I'm satisfied . . . I think." Montoya stood. "Irene spilled wine on Evan Masters's lap today."

Nate shoved his hands in his pockets. "On purpose?"

Montoya returned a not-funny glare.

"When?"

"This afternoon at Ellyngton's. That was the manager. I asked the hotel staff to keep an eye on her. Tempers flared . . . obviously."

"Obviously. What was Masters doing there?" Nate asked.

"That's what I'd like to know."

"Want me to find out what set her off?"

"Yeah. And do it out of earshot of her attack lawyer. Remind her that we may have cleared her, but Masters is still a suspect." The lieutenant reached for his sports coat, which hung on a tree rack beside his credenza. "Speaking of the Masters, did you get anything from Gwyneth Masters today?"

Nate shook his head. "She's hooked up to a morphine drip and in considerable pain. Getting her to talk about the shooting, much less confess to a kidnapping, is going to be tough, Lieutenant."

Montoya rubbed his jaw. "I know, I know. Just keep your recorder on, and let's see where the conversation goes. And whatever you do, *don't* arrest her in the hospital."

"Gotcha." Nate blew out a breath. He'd had some close calls on Vice. He and Sammy had been forced numerous times to hospitalize suspects. To arrest them while they were admitted proved costly to law enforcement. The patient's insurance—if he had insurance—and the responsibility for payment then transferred to the City of Denver and the Denver Police Department. And God forbid, if the patient relapsed or died. Then the family members along with *their* lawyers were coming out of the broom closet.

"We'll work on an arrest after Gwyneth is home. Once we leave the hospital, Sam and I will talk with Yasmine Takeri and Michael Whitney."

"Good job. You boys have hit the ground running."

Good job? Was that a compliment Nate heard? From the moment he and Sam had entered Major Crimes, they'd been told the lieutenant's praise was as infrequent as pay raises. And here Nate sat with his recorder turned off. Sammy would be pissed to have missed the high praise. Then Nate relaxed. No, he wouldn't. Sammy wouldn't believe it.

AFTER MAKING A scene with Evan, Irene returned to her room. She'd paced for a good ten minutes, needing an outlet for her hurt and anger. This was the man, whom over the years, she'd built up in her head as perfect?

Age might be hard on the eyes, but time and distance had a way of clarifying things. Evan might be Kinsey's father, but that was all he was anymore. As for his devotion to Gwyneth, well, those two deserved one another.

Irene didn't have a punching bag or any particular place to go, but she did have access to a spa downstairs.

An hour-and-a-half later, dressed in the hotel's robe, she left her therapy room, less agitated. Inhaling the lingering scents of orange and peppermint, she changed into jeans and a sweater then smiled as her therapist met her at the door with a glass of water. Irene accompanied her to the cashier behind the counter.

"Feeling better?" the therapist asked.

Irene reached into her wallet to withdraw cash for the tip. "I think you had to order out to find all of those knots and kinks."

"Oh, no, they were all yours, I promise you, Mrs. Turner. Drink lots of water tonight, stay away from rum and sugary drinks, and come back and see me."

"It's a date."

She left the spa determined to do something about her wilting hair when she saw Lyle at the front desk. With his luggage beside him, evidently he was checking out.

"There you are," he said. "I should have known you'd be enjoying the hotel's amenities. I left you a message. Actually, it's more like a novel." He turned toward the hotel employee. "The material I left for Mrs. Turner, do you have it handy?"

The clerk handed him a manila envelope.

Lyle guided Irene away from the counter and lowered his voice. "In my professional opinion, the police have nothing conclusive to link you to either your husband's murder or Mrs. Masters's shooting. Your missing revolver, and the fact the killer may be using it to commit these crimes is problematic, of course. It's also circumstantial. Nonetheless, you must be able to account for your whereabouts at all times.

"On this envelope, I've included the resumes of two lawyers who are more than qualified to represent you. The one with three stars, I obviously like best, but people sometimes don't share my good taste, so the two-star lawyer can also get the job done."

Irene hugged him. "Thank you, Lyle, for everything. And be sure to give Norma one of those from me when you see her next time."

"Will do." He narrowed his gaze. "Coming home soon?"

"There's only one thing keeping me here." Irene stared off wistfully. "It all depends on Kinsey."

A lump settled in her larynx when Lyle, his cane, and the bellman, wandered off toward the revolving doors. But her melancholy didn't last long. From across the lobby, she saw a man lower his newspaper.

Irene shook her head and lifted her hand in a subtle wave. She sure hoped the manager wasn't paying attention to the number of male visitors who called on her. He might question her occupation and ask her to leave. A visit this afternoon from Evan, a note from Lyle upon his checkout, and now Detective Paxton headed her way. Suddenly, it was raining men.

Chapter Thirty-five

WHEN THE ALARM clock rang Saturday morning, Kinsey did what she did everyday—hit the snooze button and closed her eyes again. She and mornings didn't get along. Especially when she'd tossed and turned all night, consumed with Lauren and Jay's bizarre speculations about who might have shot their mother.

Neither of their theories appealed to her. Certainly not her father, which Lauren had to be out of her mind to suggest in the first place. And definitely not Yasmine, who'd been closer to the Masters children than any biological aunt.

Then, of course, Irene was still under scrutiny.

Shifting onto her stomach, Kinsey wrapped her arms around the pillow she held tightly to the back of her neck.

When the alarm went off again, she tossed the pillow and hit the off button once and for all. A half hour later, dressed in a T-shirt, jeans, and sneakers, she grabbed a protein bar and drove toward Lundgren. She entered the ICU at 8:45 a.m. Nate hadn't arrived yet, which suited her fine. She wanted to speak with her mother first about Lauren's and Jay's suspicions.

Kinsey gave her name to the police officer guarding her mother's room. He located her on the approved list and allowed her inside. Someone had drawn the heavy hospital drapes, cloaking Gwyneth's room in the shadows.

Throat clogged, her heart breaking, Kinsey sat in the bedside chair and watched the woman who'd raised her sleep. *What were you thinking when you kidnapped me? Did you love me? Hate me? Was I simply a tool, a mean-spirited joke to get back at Dad? Or the ultimate revenge to hurt the woman who'd slept with him? What I really want to know is how did you get away with it?*

Gwyneth moaned, and her EKG machine bleeped faster.

"Mom?" Kinsey wrapped her hand around a spoke in the safety rail. "It's Kinsey. Can you hear me?"

Slowly, Gwyneth turned her head and opened her eyes. "Kinsey?"

"Hi." She smiled and reached for her mom's hand. "How are you feeling?"

She gasped. "What day is this?"

"It's Saturday. We've been worried about you. Do you remember what happened?"

Gwyneth licked her cracked lips and struggled to speak.

Kinsey's heart wrenched. She located a small pitcher next to a glass and a straw on her tray table. "Are you thirsty?"

At Gwyneth's slow nod, Kinsey stood and held it to her mother's lips.

Gwyneth squeezed Kinsey's hand. "You know, don't you? Everything."

"No. I know some things. Why, Mom? Why'd you do it?"

Gwyneth's face contorted in pain. "Unfair. *I* . . . wanted you. Tried so hard. Month after month, year after year. And Irene Morrison got pregnant after one . . . measly . . . try."

Morrison. Until that moment, Kinsey didn't even know her biological mother's maiden name. She staved off her furious tears. "How did you come up with the idea?"

"Yas," Gwyneth said. "We talked about it . . . for weeks. Angry talk at first."

Kinsey studied the EKG monitor and prayed for her mother to stay calm. So far, so good.

"Then, the idea took hold. She . . . Irene . . . didn't deserve to have my hus . . . band's baby." Tears ran like rivulets down Gwyneth's face. "Yas went to Okla . . . homa to learn everything.

"Soon . . . we knew. About her doctor, her fiancé . . . her trailer trash home." Gwyneth gritted her teeth. "This was where . . . she wanted to . . . raise you?"

Kinsey winced as the EKG monitor took off. A young nurse entered the room. Still holding Gwyneth's hand, Kinsey asked, "Mom, do you want me to go?"

Adamantly, Gwyneth shook her head back and forth. "No. No. No. Need . . . to explain."

Frowning, the nurse hesitated but eventually backed out of the room.

Gwyneth wheezed, coughed, and summoned more air. "I did it for you, baby. If I didn't take you, we would be . . . connected to her . . . forever. Your father, might . . . leave me for her. So, I went there to . . . talk to her."

"You talked to Irene?"

"No," Gwyneth rasped. "Found her fiancé instead. He was angry . . . too."

Kinsey felt her gut twist. She yanked her hand free. What was she, a pawn in a soap opera? Gwyneth had stolen a baby out of fear that her husband would leave her?

Gwyneth's monitor sped up, no doubt due to the angst of her confession, but also by Kinsey's reaction. But now that Kinsey had learned this much, she wasn't about to give up. "Dr. Mitchell, Mom. How was he a part of this?"

"Offered him my . . . trust fund. That's . . . how much I wanted you. Pleaded, convinced him . . . you'd be better off . . . with me."

Gwyneth raised her hand, met Kinsey's gaze, and tried to touch her tear-soaked face. She never got that far. Her hand dropped, she closed her eyes and faded.

Numb, Kinsey watched the rise and fall of her mother's chest. Right or wrong, she understood Gwyneth's motivation. Had she done things through appropriate channels, she might have adopted Kinsey and had the same outcome.

But she hadn't. Her mother had stolen Kinsey with the sole purpose of punishing Irene Turner and excluding her from Kinsey's life. Kinsey always knew her mom was ambitious. What she'd never guessed was that Gwyneth Masters was vengeful enough to mastermind such a diabolical plot.

Kinsey rose from the chair and left the room. The woman who'd raised her had just lost the title of mother.

NATE PACED BACK and forth, glancing periodically at the clock, then turned to eye Gwyneth Masters's hospital room while waiting for Kinsey to make an appearance. She'd done exactly what she said she would do—talked to Gwyneth alone. As far as the police were concerned, that was a mistake. If Kinsey learned anything crucial, and it incriminated someone she loved, how likely would she be to tell Nate? Worse, would she recognize that what she'd heard might identify a killer? The door remained closed, and he continued to pace.

His cell phone rang. His caller screen read S. Lucero. "Paxton," Nate said. "She still in there?"

Nate checked the clock. "Ten minutes now. What's new on your end?"

"The Blue Star Hotel's security firm answered the warrant. Last night I picked up the digital footage and dropped the evidence off at the IT Department. Get this. We got a guy who'll work Saturdays. Running over there now."

"I'll meet you there after I finish up here. Then we'll tag team an interview with Yasmine Takeri."

The door to Gwyneth's room opened and Kinsey exited, head bowed and frowning. She pressed one hand to the small of her back and ran her free hand through her hair.

Nate's gut clenched. "Kinsey came out. Let me talk to her before her relatives arrive, and then I'll meet you at IT."

Nate crossed the waiting room lobby and gently took hold of her arm. "How about we talk downstairs?"

She fairly wilted as she nodded.

Nine-thirty on a Saturday morning, the cafeteria was a mass of hospital personnel in white coats and scrubs. Ignoring the smell of bacon and rising bread, he grabbed a coffee for himself and a sports drink for Kinsey.

Choosing a table away from the fray, he questioned Kinsey until he felt he'd gotten the gist of everything Gwyneth had told her. The subject of the shooter hadn't come up, and the topic of Evan Masters had been addressed only in passing. And although Yasmine may have known and traveled to Oklahoma to research Irene's background, there wasn't a thing on the books that made snooping a criminal offense.

Elbows on the table, Kinsey massaged her temples. "In my mind I knew what must have happened. But to hear her admit everything she and Yasmine did to Irene . . . I've always admired these women."

Kinsey didn't need any input from him. Nate drank his coffee and listened. Finally when the morning was slipping away, he said, "I gotta meet Sam. You going to be okay?"

"Who me?" She peeled the label from her sports drink. "Never better. After I return a phone call, I plan to swing by my parents' house, pick up our dog, and go for the longest run of my life."

Chapter Thirty-six

PETER TREVELLE had Irene's attention at "I've got . . ." By the time the private detective said information, she'd already reached for a pad and a pen. He couldn't release what he'd learned without sustenance, however. So, repeating the same scenario, Irene instructed the cab driver to stop at the family delicatessen she had before and picked up lunch.

She paid the cab driver his fare, asking him to return in an hour. This time she didn't loiter on Trevelle's doorstep waiting for the man. He sat at his dining room table perusing paperwork.

Leaning in close to the open screen door, she let out a sarcastic, "Yoo-hoo."

He put down his files and wheeled her way. "What kind of sandwich did you bring me?"

"A Reuben. Hope you like Thousand Island and sauerkraut."

"It'll do."

Irene joined him at the table. He proceeded to drive her mad when instead of explaining what he'd found, he began to chow down. To pass the time, she entered his kitchen, found a glass in one of his low-hanging cabinets, and filled it with tap water.

A few bites into his sandwich, he set it down and wiped his mouth. "When I had my agency downtown, I kept duplicate records. My wife at the time called me obsessive, but I can't tell you how many times having a backup saved my butt in those days. Especially after the fire in my agency. Problem was, I kept everything on a zip drive. Know how hard it is to find a place that will transfer files off of old technology? Anyway, don't worry, Irene, I'll be adding it to your fee."

She lifted an eyebrow and stared at the man. What she wouldn't give for her .38 about now. She'd point it at Trevelle and demand he get to the point.

"I went back to the time that Mitchell contacted me. Now I'd like to think my sterling reputation stretched as far as Oklahoma City," Trevelle yammered on. "But the truth was, the doctor had visited Denver quite a few times."

"Why was that?"

"His first wife moved here after their divorce. Apparently, she wanted to live closer to their daughter."

"Dr. Mitchell's daughter lives here? Does he have more than one?"

"No. One daughter, and she *used* to live in Colorado. She attended Colorado College, a private liberal arts school in Colorado Springs. But the mother chose to live in Denver after the split."

"Does the former Mrs. Mitchell still live in Colorado?" Irene asked.

"She does. Goes by the name of Collette Lipton now."

Irene was ready to bolt from the chair. "When can we talk to her?"

"What's this 'we' business? You hired me, and I already have."

"You have? When?"

"Yesterday afternoon."

Irene shook her head. "No offense, but we should do this in person—"

"I am offended. I did talk to her in person. She lives in Highlands Ranch."

"But you said you don't go out because of your wheelchair."

"Wrong. I said I don't go to the Brown Palace in downtown Denver in my van and hunt for a parking place. County Line Road and I get along fine."

"All right," Irene said, exasperated. "You found her, you went there, and you saw her. What did she *say?*"

He started to pick up his sandwich again, but Irene narrowed her gaze. She picked up the plastic knife provided by the deli and shook it at him.

Trevelle grinned and held up his hands as though acquiescing. "She said twenty-five years of marriage was twenty-five years too many. She was married to a workaholic and a mama's boy besides. Dr. Mitchell was raised by a single mother, and when she became terminally ill, the doctor established the Victoria Mitchell Home for Girls in her honor.

"He also transferred a lot of personal income out of the clinic he'd started to keep the girls' home afloat. That made Collette furious. So, when she filed for divorce, her lawyers instructed the doctor to either buy her out or sell the institution."

"The eight hundred thousand dollars," Irene said.

"Can't pull anything over on you. Guess whose trust fund coincidentally was emptied, and who miraculously came up with enough funds to stay solvent when the Mitchell's divorce was final?"

"You found a connection between Dr. Mitchell and Gwyneth."

"I did."

Irene set the knife down. "Finish your sandwich."

"Thanks, I believe I will."

She rose from the chair, faced the front door, placing her hands on her hips, and pivoted. "You didn't happen to ask Collette Lipton where she was during the time Stephen was murdered or when Gwyneth was shot, did you?"

"Not straight out. I can't move very fast in this chair, and I figured I should leave something for the police to do."

"What about Collette's daughter? According to Dr. Mitchell's second wife, the daughter lives in Oklahoma."

"Sabrina," he said.

"What?"

"Daughter's name is Sabrina. She has an interesting job, by the way."

Irene crossed her arms. "Are you enjoying that sandwich, Trevelle?"

"Very much."

"If you want to finish eating it and not wear it, you will answer my question."

"You're no fun, Irene." Peter Trevelle shook his head. "Turns out Sabrina Mitchell's a chip off the old block. When her dad died, she took over as administrator for the Victoria Mitchell Home for Girls."

Irene picked up her handbag.

"Where are you going?" Trevelle asked.

"To give the police something to do."

Chapter Thirty-seven

NATE ENTERED THE Denver PD's IT Department to find Sammy and a computer technician already gathered around a computer monitor reviewing the surveillance footage from the Blue Star.

Nate approached, keeping silent, while a tech named Will Fisher explained what they were seeing. "The Blue Star may have wanted its guests to feel secure, but anyone who understands the guts of this system knows the hotel purchased its protection on a shoestring.

"For example," he continued, "there's no audio that correlates to the digital feed, and the hotel management only has one camera per floor. They're each installed over the emergency exits above the stairwells. No one monitors the video feed. The camera downloads into a hard drive, and they only pull the footage if there's a problem."

"Nate and I believe whoever broke into the Blue Star and killed Stephen Turner didn't make many mistakes. Hope you can prove us wrong," Sammy said.

"This may change your mind." Will pulled out a DVD. "The warrant narrowed the surveillance down to April 16th from noon to five p.m. on the sixth floor." He inserted a disk into a drive. Soon, an empty hallway appeared on the screen. "As you can see, there's not much activity there. Guests occasionally come and go."

The footage cycled through a series of cameras, each one showing a near identical hallway, sometimes empty, sometimes with people passing by, with a time code and location identifier.

Will fast forwarded until it read *Blue Star, Sixth Floor, April 16, 2013, 12:32 p.m.* and showed a woman exiting her hotel room.

"That's Irene." Sammy pointed to the monitor. "In the same outfit she wore when we got the call, along with that monster handbag."

Five days had passed since Irene was attacked and she'd landed in the hospital. She was well on her way to recovering. Even so, Nate felt like he'd taken a blow to his solar plexus. The footage had to reveal what happened.

Will kept scrolling. "Near three p.m. is when we get our first clue." Will froze that particular section. "Notice at three, the hallway is visible. Camera surveillance is on target." He fast forwarded. "But look what happens at 3:02."

"The hallway disappears." Nate bent forward, placing his foot on an absent co-worker's chair. "Someone's screwing with the camera, doing something to cover the lens."

"Uh-huh. Now watch what happens at 3:03. The party removes the block and everything's back to normal. Nothing happens for the next few minutes until 3:44." Will forwarded to that time code.

Nate squinted. The door opened, and a grainy image of a man carrying the safe appeared. But no sooner had he stepped into the hallway than his partner near the emergency stairs covered the lens again.

"Our safe bandit had an accomplice," Sammy said.

"Not a very good one." Nate removed his foot from the chair, his gaze glued to the passing footage. "Somebody should have told these guys to use a jammer. His help is too slow."

Less than one minute later, according to the digital clock, the accomplice removed whatever distraction he was using, and the hallway came back into view.

"All right. Got it." Nate folded his arms. "The first block was to let him in, the second to let him out. But what was the sidekick using to cover the lens, and how did he get it up there? Those are eight-foot ceilings. Surely, the guests or staff would have noticed a person carrying a ladder, and he sure didn't jump up there."

His hands clutching the back of Will's chair, Sammy frowned. "Maybe he used a broom or a mop from housekeeping."

Will reversed the footage until the time of the blocked out lens. "I'm not sure, but I think I can make out a shadow beneath whatever's hindering the lens."

"We could use everything you've got," Sammy told Will.

"No problem. Now, watch this." He fast forwarded to 3:54. "The lookout does his thing, covers the lens for a few seconds, removes it, and here comes our hallway."

"Giving our boy time to get back in the room," Nate said.

"Right." Will fast forwarded to 4:31 p.m. when Irene returned.

Every muscle in Nate's body tensed. Knowing the outcome didn't help. At 4:31 he had been at Lamar Bryant High School with Kinsey, broaching the subject of her birth mother.

Shopping bags in hand, Irene fumbled for her pass card. She entered her hotel room.

Nate closed his eyes. "The bad guy's lying in wait."

At 4:37, the door opened again. A man walked out, hands in his pockets, head down. Once again the slow-responding accomplice covered the security camera's lens.

"Seven minutes." Sammy wore a look of disbelief. "He knocks her out, ransacks her room, and takes her .38."

"Back that up again," Nate ordered.

Will backed up the video and froze it on the suspect exiting the hotel room a split-second before the man ducked his head.

"Damn it," Nate growled. "It's one big blur."

"Give me a sec. We use a forensic plug-in for Adobe Photoshop," Will's fingers danced over the keyboard. "Let me see if I can enhance the image." Then, his right hand on the mouse, the computer tech ran the tool over the grainy image several times. With each click, the picture came more and more into focus. Until at last, the suspect's face sharpened into view.

Sammy's gaze never left the screen. Jaw tight, his hands left the back of Will's chair. "Well, we know who attacked Irene. Good old dead Stephen Turner."

Nate shook his head. "Irene leaves her husband. He tracks her to get the evidence she has against him. When he can't open the safe, he simply takes it. That's why he tosses the room to see if she has anything else she can use against him. Then, whether out for revenge or whether he intended to kill her, he delivers one helluva wallop."

Sammy straightened. "You think whoever was covering the lens turned around and killed Stephen Turner?"

"I'd say it's in the high probabilities. Turner damn sure didn't kill himself. All we know for sure is that Karma took care of the bastard."

Chapter Thirty-eight

"SIT, CORDIE. SIT." Leash in hand, Kinsey worked to collar the excited black lab that pushed on her legs, nearly knocking her over. "I said sit!"

Jay strolled by laughing. "Good girl, Cord. Be a good dog and take Kinsey for a walk."

She finally got control and forced the dog into a sitting position. "You are a good girl," she cooed. "Now let's make Uncle Jay run with us. What do you think? Ten miles?"

Jay performed a human caricature of eyes bulging out of their sockets. He backed up a few steps, a twenty-one-year-old contradiction. He carried a coffee cup in his hand, wore glasses on his nose and flip flops on his feet. All he was missing was the gray hair and wrinkles to look like a senior citizen. "I'd love to kick your ass, but I've got a photo shoot this afternoon."

"Slacker," Kinsey called as Cordie dragged her to the door. "Anyone ever take this dog to obedience school? See you later at the hospital?"

"I'll be there around three," Jay called from a room off the foyer.

"Okay, I'll be there by three then, too."

Kinsey left the house, grateful she'd missed her father. Just like Nate, Dad would have asked her to repeat everything that Gwyneth had said. And what Kinsey could tell him, he wouldn't like. Gwyneth had said nothing about seeing him, and so far he was still barred from entering her room.

Cordie loping beside her, Kinsey jogged down the house steps and ran into Griff exiting his Tahoe with a vase containing a spring bouquet. She smiled at him. "The campaign get so bad you decide to sell flowers?"

"They're for you and to apologize for whatever I've done that you aren't returning my calls."

With her life in shambles, Kinsey refused to feel guilty. She was also clearly a stop-off point for the aspiring politician. Dressed in trousers and a pinstriped cotton shirt, his sleeves rolled up, he was undoubtedly off to shake hands with people who could get him elected.

"I'd ask you to go run with me, but I can see that you're busy. And I did return your calls . . . well, at least one. I told you I'd get back to you as soon as I could." She took the flowers, inhaled their sweet fragrance, then kissed him much as she had Nate yesterday afternoon. Unfortunately, she felt the difference.

At Griff's narrowed gaze, she wondered if he had, too.

Cordie whined.

"Here, hold her a minute. Let me put these in the house." Sighing, Kinsey ran into the entryway and placed the flowers on a sideboard next to a silk arrangement.

She jogged down the steps and regained her hold on Cordie. "They're beautiful, thank you. I'll be over at Kent if you change your mind." She moved to sidestep him, but Griff caught her arm. "Can you slow down for two seconds?"

Kinsey blew out a breath. Cordie and her powerful black body strained at the leash. "You're on the clock."

"You may actually thank me after I tell you what I've been up to. Do you remember last week at the Hyatt when I introduced you to Rodrigo Guzmán?"

"Sure."

"He took you at your word when you said you'd go to work for him. He went to Continental Miracles's board. This is hush-hush, so I need you to promise you won't say a word, okay?"

Unable to hide her irritation, she folded her arms. "*Okay.*"

"Continental Miracles wants you to be its international spokesperson. They want to know if you would be willing to do TV and radio spots to promote the organization."

Suddenly, poor Cordie and Kinsey's run could wait. "Oh, wow. What an honor."

"Rodrigo asked if you'd be willing to meet with him privately to discuss the matter. And, again, he stressed confidentiality."

"Okay, but why the big secret?"

"Because he's the head guy, and it's his prerogative. They have other candidates, and he doesn't want to offend those waiting in the wings. We didn't talk money. But you could probably demand top dollar. That's how anxious he is for you to be his representative."

Kinsey squatted to pat Cordie who was being unbelievably patient. The black lab licked her squarely in the face. "I would love to, Griff, honestly." Smiling, she rose and wiped her mouth with the back of her hand. "But with everything going on right now, I have to say no."

"An opportunity like this doesn't come around every day."

"I know, and it's killing me to decline. But I have a job, and I coach. Plus, I have a mother in the hospital who will likely go to prison, and a birth mother to get to know. So as much as I'm flattered—"

"He's a campaign contributor, Kins. I'd consider it a personal favor if you'd do this for me."

"Okay, here we go. Was this all your idea? Did you push me off on him?"

Griff held up his hands. "I swear I didn't. He contacted me about *you*. So what do you say?"

She pressed the button on the Audi's remote. "If he still wants me in a month or so, I'll consider it. If he wants my decision right now, it's an absolute no. How's that?"

"That's all I can ask."

Griff pulled her against him and kissed her.

She grinned. "I really am thrilled. I hope it works out. Thanks for the flowers."

Chapter Thirty-nine

THEIR SESSION AT the IT Department complete, Nate and Sammy traveled to Cherry Creek, the next stop on their agenda—Masterpieces. It was time for a discussion with Yasmine Takeri and her significant other, Michael Whitney. Ryan Stone, in all his redheaded, don't-touch-my-stuff glory, had suggested strongly that Yasmine wasn't the loyal confidant to Gwyneth that police had assumed.

Nate eased the Explorer east onto Sixth Avenue while Sammy ended a call with their lieutenant. He'd called to give the boss an update on the security footage, the good news for cops, the lousy news for Irene that her husband, with the assistance of another, had lain in wait inside her Blue Star hotel room.

"What'd he say?" Nate asked, referring to their lieutenant and skating around more road construction and growing traffic.

"The usual," Sammy said. "Growled and said he'd be the one to tell her."

"Better him than us." Nate veered around cars by rote. Had Irene suspected Stephen had been the one to attack her? Had she any idea how cunning and desperate her husband was? Or was she in for an additional shock and heartbreak?

He glanced over at Sammy who had a growing attachment to his smart phone.

"Why can't things be simple?" he asked, thumbing through messages. "Gwyneth talks through all the pain and the drugs, fesses up, lays it out on a silver platter what happened all those years ago, and we figure how the past fits into the present."

"Because easy would bore the hell out of you."

"There's that." Sammy leaned over the console and showed Nate a picture of his little girl playing with her grandpa in El Paso.

"Cute," Nate said.

"All this then-and-now stuff is hurting my head," Sammy continued.

"I agree this case isn't your typical whodunit. Especially when two of the co-conspirators, the doctor and Stephen Turner, are dead."

"So who's left?" Sammy counted on his fingers. "During the LT's and your session with Kinsey and her dad, Evan claimed that Irene called him three days before *el bebe* arrived in the Masters' home. Correct?"

"Right. Irene calls Evan to tell him he's off the hook in the support department—she's delivered a stillborn. And by doing so, she unwittingly sets up the works to get Kinsey to Gwyneth in Denver."

"Okay. But Kinsey didn't crawl to Denver. So, who carried her over state lines? And how did a supposedly smart corporate guy like Evan Masters buy into the fake delivery scenario?" Sammy tossed Nate a suspicious glance. "Unless Evan knew the whole time, and he had something to do with it?"

"If he did, he's one helluva an actor." Nate felt his scowl deepening as he negotiated traffic. "Thought he was going to puke his guts out when we pinned him down with all the facts. My money's on Gwyneth and Yasmine. Stone knew too much to be guessing. Yasmine helps Gwyneth kidnap a baby. Years later, it leads to resentment. Gwyneth's giving the gallery to her kids ticks Yasmine off when she doesn't get the payoff she thinks she deserves."

Sammy nodded. "Don't stop now. You're on a roll."

"Gwyneth plays the stricken wife. She keeps Evan at arm's length after she tells him she's pregnant. Then, using her I-hate-hospitals-after-her-father-dies-in-one scenario, she somehow bribes a midwife."

"Gwyneth bribes, or was it Yasmine?" Sammy countered. "Remember, Gwyneth admitted to Kinsey that Yasmine did all the legwork. When we get to the gallery that should be our focus. I expect these people to lawyer up at any time."

"Got it." Nate pulled into the Masterpieces's parking lot and switched off the engine. "Headache better?"

"No." Sammy opened the passenger's side door. "Why?"

"Because, partner, we gotta find the midwife."

INSIDE MASTERPIECES, Nate greeted an unfamiliar woman holding court in the reception area. The honey blonde, with dreadlocks and wearing a colorful moo-moo, gave them a welcoming smile. Until Sam and Nate produced their badges. Then she stepped back, and her beaming face soured.

"We're here to see Yasmine Takeri and Michael Whitney," Sammy said.

She lifted a heavily pierced eyebrow. "Lucky for them, they're not here."

"What time do you expect them?" Sammy circled the desk and invaded her space.

"I don't know." She widened her vibrant green gaze and sat down in a chair. "They haven't called in."

"That unusual?" Nate rested his arms on the counter.

"Extremely." She took her eyes off Sammy for a moment and fixed them on Nate. "Gwyneth, when she's not in the hospital, that is, comes and goes. She doesn't necessarily tell us her whereabouts. But Yasmine always gives us her itinerary and her contact number." The blonde glanced at her watch. "Well, I guess, until today. She hasn't called in at all, and here it is almost noon."

"What about Michael Whitney?" Nate asked. "Any word from him?"

"No, but that's not unexpected. If it's not Michael's day to man the desk, he works in his studio."

"You have contact info on these two?"

The receptionist huffed, logged onto her computer, and scribbled the information.

Nate took her proffered information and handed her his card. "If you hear from either of them, we'd appreciate a phone call."

She took it with two fingers.

Outside the gallery, Sammy placed a call to Yasmine's cell, while Nate phoned Michael. When neither party answered, Nate called in a welfare check on Yasmine's downtown condo. When officers confirmed her place appeared empty, Nate and Sammy opted to hit Whitney's suburban address. They arrived in Arvada a half-hour later.

Sammy went around back, while Nate scoured the front for signs of movement in any of the upstairs windows. *Nobody home.*

"See anything inside?" Nate asked as Sammy strolled to the front yard.

"All the windows I could reach had coverings. No warrant. Want to ask Arvada PD for assistance."

"I do. Let's pay them a visit."

As they made their way back to the Explorer, a woman pulled into the drive next door. She left her car, tugging on two cloth grocery bags and eyed them suspiciously. "Can I help you?"

Nate met her half-way. "We're with the Denver Police Department. I'm Detective Paxton, and this is my partner Detective Lucero."

She closed her eyes and seemed to grip the bags tighter. "Please, don't give me bad news. I just saw them this morning."

"Them?" Sammy asked.

"Michael and Yasmine. They got married last night in a private ceremony. They left on their honeymoon this morning. Michael's been my neighbor for years."

"Honeymoon?" Nate's stomach dropped as he slid Sammy a look. Married couples couldn't be compelled to testify against each other. "Did they say where they were going?"

"Or when they'd be *back*?" Sammy cut in.

"They didn't. All I know is they were flying. As for their return, they won't be gone long. Those two live for their jobs."

Not so, if one or both were afraid of prison. Nate wrote down the neighbor's contact information and gave her the same informational song and dance he'd given the mumu woman. "If you hear from either of them—"

"I'll contact you right away." She and her cloth bags sauntered away.

On their way back to Denver, Sammy ran a hand over his soul patch. "Yasmine Takeri has international connections. What are the chances they stayed in the States?"

Nate veered in and out of traffic. "About zero to one. What the hell else can go wrong?"

Chapter Forty

RODRIGO SLAMMED down the phone. One month? In a month, Oso and Sombra would have Rodrigo's head on a spit and leave his body for the maggots and scorpions. He'd barely been civil to Colburn as the idiot tried to sound as though he'd given Rodrigo the best news ever.

Kinsey Masters had time to run with an animal, but she didn't have time for him? In order to learn her whereabouts, Rodrigo had feigned interest in running. The trail behind Kent Denver Day School was where Colburn mentioned she ran. The decision point had come when none of his machinations had worked. Rodrigo had no choice but to up the risks. He picked up the phone.

"Yes, *primo*," Rafa said.

"I have a job for you. Take three of your men. None of your new recruits. Use only those you trust with your life. Then, listen to me carefully and do exactly as I say."

Chapter Forty-one

THERE WERE numerous reasons Kinsey stayed in Denver: family, familiarity, a young population. But chief in her consideration were the numerous parks and trails. A section of the High Land Canal ran behind Kent Denver. Close to her parents' house, she could be in and out of the area in less than an hour, if necessary. In addition to the canal, a huge greenbelt grew in this area and made up some spectacular scenery.

As for Cordie, the dog loved the place. She took to the greenbelt and the water like an old friend coming home.

In the summer, the area was packed. Today, however, it was cold and rainy, and Kinsey shivered as she encountered an empty parking lot. She preferred to see people around. Still, she carried mace in her fanny pack, and, although Cordie would lick an attacker to death, many gave the three-year old lab a wide berth.

Kinsey started off at a good pace. Her muscles groaned at first, but as they loosened up and endorphins kicked in, she let Cordie set the pace. With her coat gleaming black, she was young, muscular, and full of stamina, and Kinsey loved that she had to work to keep up. The dog whined when she spotted the pond, and Kinsey felt guilty. Often, if no one was around, she let the lab off her leash to swim. But she was already wet, the dog had no qualms about going after a squirrel, and the madhouse events in her life had to trump Cordie's outing. To appease her best friend, Kinsey reached into her pocket for a doggie treat. She knelt to stroke the lab's neck and promised, "Next time, girlie."

A few minutes later, as she jogged toward the parking lot, another runner passed by. "Hey, Special K. Looking good."

She smiled and waved. "You, too."

Cordie preferred to leave the house rather than return, and getting the dog into the Audi was often a process. As they approached the parking lot, Cordie literally strained at her leash and sat back on her haunches. Kinsey cursed the fact she'd given the dog her last doggie treat. "You, my friend, are *going to obedience school.*"

As a matter of course when she took the lab, Kinsey covered the backseat with a sheet. She opened the car's rear door and ordered the dog inside. But Cordie's whines had transitioned into a growl.

"Inside, Cord, now," Kinsey said, frustrated and a little freaked out. She'd only seen one other runner, and Cordie rarely growled.

Kinsey had never come across a predatory animal, but occasionally a mountain lion or bear moseyed into the area. She wasn't anxious to encounter either creature, and Cordie obviously sensed something—her soft black fur stood on end. To be on the safe side, Kinsey removed her mace from her fanny pack. Then with all of her strength, she hefted the dog inside and slammed the door. That's when the dog threw herself against the window, bared her teeth, and started a relentless barking.

Mace in hand, heart jolting, Kinsey whirled. A small Hispanic man, navy bandana over his nose and mouth, arms riddled with tattoos, stepped out from behind the underbrush. With Cordie going crazy inside the car, Kinsey's first impulse was to back away from him, round the sports car, and get to the driver-side door. Yet, the moment she turned, another man, his face also hidden, blocked her escape from the other side.

Damn it! Where had they come from, and what did they want?

She held up her keys. "You want the car? Here ya go. Just let me get my dog."

They made no move to accept her keys, and the malice that shone in their eyes said this was more than a hijacking.

Kinsey narrowed her gaze. Her breathing turned frenetic. Ice-cold fear combined with fury invaded her bloodstream. She raised her mace, aimed for the second creep's eyes. But he ducked, knocking the canister from her grasp, while the one behind Kinsey grabbed her arms. Nearly pulling her shoulders out of their sockets, he imprisoned her from behind.

She screamed at the top of her lungs, slammed her foot down on his instep, and elbowed him squarely in the face.

He cried out, let go, and clutched his nose.

Kinsey's brain ordered her to run. Run!

But a white van tore into the parking lot and stopped inches away from her. The side panel slid open. Another masked man jumped from the van and dragged her inside. Terror engulfed her when he forced her face-down on the floorboard.

"You *cabrónes*," he shouted, in a hoarse Hispanic accent. "You almost let her get away. Give me that needle."

Kinsey thought her heart would burst when she felt a prick in her bicep. She tasted salty tears on her face. The door slammed shut, and Cordie's barks faded. The vehicle pitched forward. It started to roll. As the van sped away, her fingers and toes tingled, and her muscles numbed. She slipped into semi-consciousness and past caring.

Chapter Forty-two

IRENE THANKED THE chubby, angel-faced detective who escorted her to the lieutenant's door, smiling as he walked away. Then, considering the man she'd come to see, her smile vanished, and she readied for war.

George Montoya looked up, clearly annoyed at being distracted, but at Irene's still-poised-to-knock fist, his dark gaze softened. "Mrs. Turner," he said.

"Lieutenant Montoya." She remained outside his door. "I wonder if I might have a moment of your time."

He glanced from side to side. "Does your lawyer know where you are?"

"My lawyer says I don't need him. He left town, gave me a couple of legal beagles to consult with, and told me to have a nice life. I'm here because I have some information I'd like to discuss with you."

Montoya stood and met her at the door. "Then by all means, come in. Actually, I'd planned to call you. I have something to go over with you, too."

She chose the nearest of the two chairs opposite his desk, still amazed at the size of that trout on his wall. That sucker must've been the neighborhood bully when it swam through the water.

She refocused on the man she'd come to see, startled that he loosened his collar when he returned to his seat.

Her insides quivered. "*I* tug at my collar around *you*, not the other way around. What's wrong?"

He pinched the bridge of his nose. "In this job, everything. Why don't you go first."

She narrowed her gaze but took him at his word. A man in his position undoubtedly bore the weight of command. "You recall I hired a private investigator named Peter Trevelle."

"You have to remind me?"

Irene pitched forward in her chair. "Trevelle was familiar with my past. I needed someone on my side, even if he did shuck me like an ear of corn before agreeing to help."

"Mistrust is ingrained, *Irene*. Peter Trevelle was a cop before hanging out his shingle."

"I know that, *George*. But I'm here to tell you I'm as honest as they come." She leaned back and crossed her legs. She was dressed in a sweater and capris a nun would feel modest in, still he followed her movements with interest. Unsure if she should be pleased or irritated, she shook off the distraction and added, "I've never committed a crime in my life, and after being a prisoner, even in a luxury hotel, I'm not about to start."

"You're in that hotel so no one sets you up for murder or makes sure you end up on a slab. Tell me about Trevelle and what the two of you came up with."

Irene related her second visit with the wheelchair-bound detective, and his discovery that the doctor's first wife lived in Highlands Ranch. "What's more, the daughter moved back to Oklahoma after attending school in Colorado, and today I learned she heads up her father's nonprofit."

"And you think . . ."

"I don't think anything per se, but I *know* that when Norma went to Lyle Wilkins and ordered the lawyer to correct her husband's wrongdoing, the daughter gave her stepmother fits. Not only does the daughter stand to lose her inheritance, if I brought the doctor's treachery in front of a jury, she stands to lose her family's legacy."

"All right. I'll have my detectives look into Mitchell's daughter and wife number one."

"That's all I ask. One more thing." Irene made a slashing motion over her eyebrows. "I've had it up to here not being mobile and hiring cabs. I realize my Mercedes is out of the question, but why can't I drive Stephen's SUV?"

The lieutenant leaned back in his chair and sighed. "Until the DA releases the SUV, it stays in Impound. That generally doesn't happen until after a case is closed. May be time to contact your insurance agent, buy another car, or hire a rental."

Irene let out a huff and held up her hands. "And watch my rates go through the roof when I do it."

He shook his head sympathetically. A moment later, he rounded his desk and sat in the chair next to her. "Can't do anything about your insurance premiums, but we have discovered who attacked you."

Montoya watched her as though he thought she might dissolve into a puddle.

"I take it I know this person?"

"Detectives Paxton and Lucero went over the surveillance tapes at the Blue Star Hotel." Montoya lowered his head, taking his own sweet time before meeting her gaze.

"Damn it. I'm not a porcelain doll. Tell me."

"Your husband attacked you, Irene. Planned and calculated, and with the help of another, he stole the safe with your file, hid in your hotel room, tore the place apart, and waited until you came back to ambush you."

She stood, grasping the straps of her purse with both hands. "Is this the part where I fall apart and say, 'woe is me?' What did you think when your men found his SUV in my parking spot? That he was just in the neighborhood?"

"Frankly, with a woman like you, I thought he might have come to win you back," the lieutenant muttered.

"Oh, I think Stephen got past the reconciliation stage when Lyle sent him the divorce papers the day I left town. That's also about the time he started worrying about prison. My husband aided a woman in kidnapping my baby, told me the child died, and hid it from me for twenty-eight years. I assume Gwyneth made it worth his while. I recall him saying he'd received an inheritance, and me, excelling in gullible, believed him."

"You're not upset?"

"That I was a dolt? I'm furious. My only consolation is that I'm still here and I'm reunited with my daughter, who by the way, seems to be a terrific young woman, despite being related to me."

He smiled. Not a full one, but the little curve that had a sexy appeal. "You're all right?" He rose from the chair.

"I'm fine, Lieutenant."

"What happened to calling me George?"

"Possibly after all this is settled. Right now, those gold bars on your lapel . . ." She shaded her eyes as though avoiding the sun. "Well, they're a little hard to get past. Gotta run. Gustav's waiting."

"Who the hell's Gustav?"

"Someone with a severe meter fetish," Irene said dryly. "Thanks again for your time. I know how busy you are."

"I am. Busy. In any case, I'll see you out. I'd like to have a look at this Gustav."

Chapter Forty-three

FORGET SIT DOWN meals, fast food was becoming a luxury. Nate wolfed down a burger with Sammy then dropped him at police headquarters. The cloud covered sky and rainy weather fit his mood. Now that Yasmine Takeri and Michael Whitney had flown to parts unknown, Sammy needed the use of police resources to check flight passenger logs. And if they'd left the country, that led to all kinds of snafus. Since the couple was merely wanted for questioning, the chances that either Homeland Security or the State Department would assist without warrants was nonexistent. Extradition was hard enough when a person was actually charged with a crime.

Nate's cell rang the moment he pulled out of the police parking lot. He identified the caller, immediately missing Sammy, who generally buffered these calls. He inserted his Bluetooth. "Paxton."

"You off to Lundgren?" Montoya said.

"Yes, sir."

"After you finish at the hospital, head over to Highlands Ranch."

"What's in Highlands Ranch?"

"A lead."

"Sir?"

"From Irene."

Nate winced. "She left the hotel again?"

"Sure did. Went straight to Peter Trevelle, the PI she hired, and asked him to do yours and Lucero's job. As a matter of fact, Trevelle's doing such a bang-up job, I'm thinking of splitting yours and Lucero's paycheck with him."

Nate ground his teeth. "What's the lead, Lieutenant?"

"Dr. Mitchell's first wife. Woman by the name of Collette Lipton. Trevelle discovered she lives in *Colorado* of all places."

At the rain flooding his windshield, Nate switched on his wipers and muttered, "Shit."

"My sentiments exactly. Find out how the doctor's ex and her daughter, Sabrina Mitchell, play into all this," Montoya said sharply. "I've texted you the address and notified Mrs. Lipton to expect you." The lieutenant disconnected.

Nate hit the gas. Might be a new record around Major Crimes. Less than twenty-four hours to fall out of the boss's good graces.

He parked in Lundgren's visitor's center, raised his collar against the cold and wet, and pulled out his phone to call Kinsey. But just as fast, he returned the cell to his pocket. He'd see her inside.

Nate looked for Kinsey when he strode from the elevator, but the only two people in the waiting room were Lauren and Evan.

Lauren bounded from her chair the second she saw him. Grasping Nate's arm, she dragged him toward the elevator. "You have to do something. Every other sentence from my dad is when will they let me see your mom?"

Nate stared over her shoulder. He couldn't stand the guy, but Masters looked pathetic pacing in front of the hospital's picture window. Even so, Gwyneth had yet to clear him as the person who'd shot her.

"I'll see what I can do. Where is everybody?"

"Kinsey went for a run. Jay had a photo shoot." Lauren sighed. "Since you're learning so much about my off-the-wall family, here's another fact you should know. No one ever does what they say they'll do or sticks to a schedule."

Nate returned a sympathetic smile and wandered over to the officer standing guard. Removing his pocket recorder, he entered Gwyneth's room, mentally giving the ill-tempered ICU nurse kudos. Forty-eight hours *had* made a difference. Either that, or Gwyneth's pain medication was highly effective. Although she was still hooked up to her machines and IV, she sat upright, her hair brushed, her face void of color.

He moved farther into the room. A muted television broadcasted a game of professional golf. "Who's leading?" He turned on the recorder and placed it on the rolling tray table that fit over her bed.

Her gaze fell to the recorder, and she turned off the TV. "Fowler, Mickelson, who cares?" Her words came out a gruff whisper. "You're here to make me face my moment of truth?"

"Comes with the job." Nate walked to a ledge that jutted from the wall. Several flower arrangements lined the shelf, among them a dozen long-stemmed red roses.

"Did Evan send these? He's waiting outside, you know. Anxious to see you, anxious to help."

She played with the threads of her dressing gown. "How's Kinsey?"

So much for Evan. "She's devastated, Mrs. Masters."

Lifting her gaze, she met Nate's. "She told you what we discussed this morning?"

"Her version, yeah." *And all hearsay.* "Might go a long way toward healing your relationship, might even help your case if we heard the account straight from you."

She shrugged. "I've lived with these secrets a lot of years."

Gwyneth Masters was an interesting study. She didn't want to lose Kinsey. But even now, disgraced, shot, and recovering from a painful surgery, she showed no remorse, just steely determination.

Nate pushed off from the wall. "Let's give it a try anyway. Why don't we start with the day of the shooting. Yasmine reported that before you were shot, you said something. Do you remember?"

"An old habit, I guess." She sounded like she'd swallowed rocks. "All these years, I've been so angry . . . so *betrayed*. But my children came first. I hid my feelings for their sake. In public, or when Evan and I took trips, I got lost in the adventure. All right, in him." She picked up a cup and sipped water through a straw. "I'm good at charades. But I never forgot."

"You're not afraid of Evan?"

She rolled her eyes. "Oh, please."

"It wasn't him who broke into your property and shot you?"

"Evan's a big man. The person who shot me was . . . smaller. What about Irene Turner? Does she have an alibi?"

A good one. If she wanted you dead, you wouldn't be here. "Mrs. Turner can account for her whereabouts during your shooting."

"*Mrs. Turner,*" Gwyneth spat. A series of coughs attacked her. After she hacked into her elbow and finally stopped, she pointed a finger. "Don't underestimate the trollop. If Irene didn't shoot me, she hired somebody. She's not Snow White. She *slept* with my *husband*."

Many years had passed since Nate had studied a DSM-IV manual, a diagnostic and statistical book of mental disorders. As a cop, it wasn't his place to make an assessment. That didn't mean he couldn't form an opinion—Gwyneth's vitriol bordered on antisocial personality.

"Can you describe your assailant? You say he was smaller than Evan. Do you remember any distinguishable marks?"

"You're obviously not hearing me," she snapped. "Whoever it was wore dark clothes, gloves, and a mask." She hesitated. "But the eyes . . . There was something about the eyes."

"What about them?"

Her brows drew together, and her entire body went still. "Dark, I think. More importantly, they were furious. This was personal."

Furious eyes? Were her drugs affecting her ability to think? Furious was an emotion, not a physical trait. Nate raised a brow.

Despite the recorder, he took out his notebook to jot his impressions. "Can you think of anyone at the gallery, friends or family, who might hold a grudge against you?"

"My family? Never. But I am a business owner. I don't win popularity contests."

"Do you trust Yasmine?"

"With my life."

"What about Michael Whitney?"

"Talented. Not much of a people person."

"You've never had a falling out?"

"With Yasmine? No. With Michael? Not that I'm aware of."

"What would you say if I told you Yasmine and Michael Whitney got married last night and left town this morning?"

Gwyneth's smile held the warmth of a Canadian winter. "I'd say, 'He's not what I'd want in a spouse, but he'll never cheat on her.'"

To combine Gwyneth's personality and that raspy voice was like interviewing a female Marlon Brando playing the Godfather. "It doesn't bother you that your assistant left the gallery unsupervised?"

"Who do you think told her to get out if she had to?"

"You?"

She raised her right hand.

"Why did she leave? Does Yasmine have something to hide?"

"Nothing but being my friend." Gwyneth attempted to smile. "As for a falling out, Yas and I pretended there was tension between us. The malcontents around the gallery bought it. Allowed us to find out which artists we should invest in and which ones to get rid of."

"Which list was Ryan Stone on, the stay or let go?"

She held a hand to her throat and winced when she swallowed. "As long as the clients loved his work, he was on the stay list."

"I understand you left the business to your children, excluding Yasmine."

"Yasmine's not hurting for money. I gave her bonuses in addition to her salary."

Is Irene the only one who can make you snap? Nate tapped the pen to his notebook. "I admire your loyalty. Good to know you've taken care of her. But then Yasmine's taken care of you, too, hasn't she? When you found out about your husband's infidelity, she went to Oklahoma. She researched and helped you plan this entire scheme, didn't she?"

Gwyneth sighed and changed positions.

"Who contacted Dr. Mitchell and Stephen Turner? Who picked up the baby and brought Kinsey across state lines?" Nate kept his voice conversational. "You couldn't have done it. You were in Colorado, allegedly about to deliver. People would have noticed if you disappeared three days before you went into labor. So, who helped you with Kinsey's kidnapping?"

"I negotiated the deals with both Mitchell and Turner," Gwyneth insisted. "Remember, I had months to contact them. And instead of calling me a kidnapper, I think people—especially you, Nate Paxton—should be thanking me."

"Why's that?"

"You've been in love with Kinsey since the day you laid eyes on her. Really something. So cute and respectful. Now look at you. Quite a man, *Detective*." She flashed him an admiring glance. "Kinsey wouldn't be the young woman she is today if not for me. You'd have never met her."

"Maybe not, but she'd know her mother."

A look of disdain replaced Gwyneth's self-satisfied smirk. Nate checked the recorder capturing every word. His superiors and the DA would hear this. Couldn't be helped.

"How about I tell Kinsey how well you cooperated, so she'll still consider a relationship with you? Back to my second question, since there wasn't an actual baby to deliver, who'd you hire as a midwife?"

"A woman. I don't recall."

"You don't remember her name?"

"Think she gave me a real one?"

Nate moved to her bedside and kept his voice low. "All right. I don't care about the midwife anyway. Let's stick with Yasmine. She brought Kinsey from Oklahoma to Colorado, didn't she?"

Gwyneth reached for her IV pump and pressed a button. "I know what it's like to be betrayed Nate. Don't ask it of me."

He stared between the IV bag and the IV needle in her arm and felt his heart take off. How much time did he have before she succumbed to her pain meds and made this interview useless? "I'll take that as a yes."

"It's killing you not to know, isn't it? Poor Nate." She raised her hand as though taking an oath. "I swear to you, Yasmine was by my side the whole time. She did *not* deliver Kinsey to Colorado."

Nate wanted to get in Gwyneth's face, he was so frustrated. But her monitors were worse than Internal Affairs. "Why would she run if she didn't have something to hide?"

"Bye-bye, Nate," Gwyneth said in a sing-song voice. "I'm tired." Settling back in her pillows, she lowered her eyelids.

He had to break this ice queen. Gritting his teeth, he circled the bed. "Don't go yet. We're just getting started. So, loyalty means everything to you, right? Because you've always been so fiercely loyal to those you love, haven't you? You mentioned the word *betrayed*." He bent over the safety rail and whispered. "You're a fraud, Gwyneth. Kinsey worshipped the ground you walked on. How do you think she feels? You betrayed the one you said you loved most."

Throughout his verbal attack, she showed no reaction. He watched the rise and fall of her chest, and after several moments, had to accept that he'd failed. He prepared to switch off the recorder, when a sob tore from her throat. He pulled back his hand and left the recorder playing.

Through closed eyes, tears streamed down her face. "The midwife brought Kinsey to Denver, not Yasmine."

Nate's heart went into double time, and he straightened.

Gwyneth's entire body shook as she forced out the next words. "I can only guess Yasmine ran because she hired the midwife."

NATE STAYED WITH Gwyneth until she succumbed to the morphine and drifted off. Then he re-entered the waiting room. Evan came to his feet, his face a mask of anxiety. Lauren stood, gripping her father's arm.

"She's sleeping," Nate said to Evan. "But she cleared you of any involvement."

"Thank God," the older man shot back. "I hope you're satisfied. My family's in crisis because of your meddling."

Nate took the high road in lieu of a response and strode toward the elevators. At times, human nature was utterly inexplicable. Why was it when the police got involved, it became their fault and not the guilty party's? He rode the elevator down to the first floor and texted Kinsey.

Leaving hospital. Where r u?

He headed for the Explorer. Next stop. Highlands Ranch.

Chapter Forty-four

DR. MITCHELL'S ex-wife lived on a street called Wintersong Way. One look at the three-story home with rock, stucco siding, and gable roofing, and Nate whistled under his breath. Either Collette Lipton did well in her first divorce or lucked out the second time around.

A workman's truck sat in the driveway.

Nate walked past the dented, rusty Chevy, noting the gardening tools, ladder, paint buckets, and myriad other supplies stacked in the bed. He approached the ornate front entrance, almost missing the old man in a smeared T-shirt and painter's pants who'd blended in among the hedges.

He lowered his sheers and frowned. "Can I help ya?"

Nate flashed his badge, and the workman's wariness lessened. Definitely an irony, for years as a vice cop he'd kept his credentials hidden. Now he used them to get people to open up. He was coming to like this new job.

"Is Mrs. Lipton at home?"

The old timer scrubbed his gray bristles. "Oh, sure. She told me to be on the lookout. Just keep ringing if she doesn't answer. She's a little hard of hearing."

Nate thanked him and kept ringing per the old man's instructions. A thin-faced woman opened the door. Dressed in a black pantsuit, a wrist full of bangles, and two matching rhinestone combs in her silver hair, she inspected him from head to toe. "Detective Paxton?"

"Yes, ma'am."

"Your lieutenant told me you'd be by. Come in."

He entered the foyer, pivoting when she remained at the door. She poked her head out and lowered her glasses. Turning to Nate, she huffed. "Good, the old goat's still working. Let's sit in here, Detective."

Nate switched on the recorder resting in his sports coat pocket. Recording an interview was legal, but wasn't always appreciated.

The marbled entryway, with a central chandelier, was beyond stately. Two rounded staircases connected at an upstairs hallway. Collette Lipton led him into an old-fashioned parlor off the foyer. A gas fireplace, a grandfather clock, and a Yamaha baby grand piano complemented a loveseat and two wingback chairs. Between the chairs stood an end table with claw feet, its top holding a crystal vase filled with chrysanthemums.

Collette motioned for him to sit in the chair, while she chose the loveseat. In addition to several antiques, a framed picture of a young brunette in a

Grecian-style debutante gown rested prominently on the baby grand.

"Your daughter?"

"That's right."

"Pretty," he said. Thirty years had passed since Sabrina Mitchell had poised for that picture. Nate tried to envision her appearance with the passage of time.

"What can I do for you, Detective?" Collette held his gaze with the same piercing blue eyes as her daughter's. "I answered the other detective's questions. Don't you people talk to each other?"

"Mr. Trevelle is a private investigator, ma'am." Nate flipped to a new page in his notebook. He wrote down her name, the date, and asked her to recite what she'd talked about with Trevelle.

She complied in a matter of fact manner.

Nate explained his reasons for coming. He spoke of the doctor's second wife, her discovery of the file, and that she'd presented it to Irene Turner. From there, Mrs. Turner had traveled to Denver and unleashed a past that someone wanted undiscovered.

Throughout Nate's explanation, Collette remained unmoved and offered little input.

"You don't seem surprised by this information."

"When that man in the wheelchair told me as much, I was shocked. Now that I've had time to mull it over, I can only gather Cliff must've been desperate. At the time, I had no idea how he could afford to buy me out." She tugged at an earring. "The truth was, I didn't want to crush him. But I didn't work outside our home, and I didn't want to be penniless, either. Then, out of the blue, he had money?"

"You never asked how or where he got it?"

"I left that to my attorney. We thought he'd been hiding funds. Cliff claimed he'd received money from an anonymous contributor. He'd always had donors and benefactors, but nothing this extraordinary. So his life's work wouldn't be destroyed, and Sabrina and I wouldn't be destitute, I let the matter drop."

"You say his life's work. Did Dr. Mitchell seem obsessed? Do you think he might have done this more than once?"

She sat quietly, hands folded. "That's a very interesting question. Why don't we get to the point? Do I think my ex-husband was in the stolen baby business? I can't swear he wasn't. But I can tell you I believe in my heart, this was out of character for Cliff.

"My ex-husband beamed when he brought babies into the world. He fretted over these young women—spent more time with them than at home, which, frankly, was our problem. For your information, I wanted the divorce, he didn't." Collette closed her eyes and rubbed her forehead. "When Mr. Trevelle came yesterday, I was so upset I called Sabrina. She already knew what her father had been accused of, but hadn't wanted to worry me."

"How did she know?"

"Norma Mitchell, Cliff's second wife," Collette explained. "After Cliff's marriage to Norma, he changed his will. Everything goes to Norma except for a trust set aside for my daughter. It's been terribly hard for Sabrina to accept that her father could be so . . . taken in. And now it appears Norma Mitchell has no problem disparaging my ex-husband's good name."

Nate scribbled the words *motivation* and *bitter* followed by a question mark in his notebook. "You moved to Colorado after the divorce?"

"After Sabrina went to college. I met my second husband here and decided to stay."

Nate scanned the elaborate furnishings, Venetian paint, and intricate crown molding. "Mr. Lipton's been successful?"

"He was an investment banker before he retired. Yes, he's done well. Honestly, Detective, I'm stunned to learn that Cliff was a party to this woman's tragedy. But I'm in no way responsible, if that's what you and that private detective are implying. Cliff and I were divorced by the time this event happened."

"I'm not suggesting anything." He glanced at the portrait. "You say your ex-husband set up a trust fund for your daughter, but now she runs his nonprofit? In my mind, a trust is set up for control reasons. To turn over the administration of his business, implies faith. Am I wrong?"

"Cliff never put Sabrina in charge. Norma is executor of the estate. Divorce is hard on children, Detective. Sabrina . . ." Collette stared at her daughter's picture. ". . . took a long time to discover what she wanted to do with her life. But, eventually, she did. Perhaps Norma felt Sabrina was ready."

"Sounds like a generous stepmother," Nate said.

"Or maybe, like me, she didn't want to be shackled to the girls' home Cliff set up in honor of his mother. Times have changed, Detective. Unwed mothers aren't scorned as they once were. Although there *is* the clinic Cliff started. That continues to thrive. Sabrina receives no proceeds from it, though Norma sits on the board of directors."

Nate nodded and drew three lines under motivation.

"What did Sabrina do before heading up the home for girls?"

"After college, she had aspirations of being a performer. Later, she became more serious about making a living. She worked for accountants and in hospital administration. Perhaps that's why Norma set her up to oversee The Victoria Mitchell Home for Girls."

Nate glanced at the piano. "Yours?"

Collette glanced at her watch. "Now it is. Originally, we bought it for Sabrina."

"Do you see her often?"

"Not often enough. Why all these questions about my daughter, Detective Paxton?"

"Loose threads, ma'am," Nate said easily. "How long has it been since she's been in Colorado?"

"Last year. Easter, I think. Are we almost through? If I don't leave immediately, I'll be late for a doctor's appointment."

"I won't keep you." He stood and handed her a card. "You've been very helpful."

At the door, she said, "I trust two interviews are sufficient?"

Probably not. "I appreciate your cooperation, Mrs. Lipton."

Nate left the house, drove the Explorer down the dead-end street and waited. True to her word, the garage door opened, and Collette Lipton drove away in a black Chrysler 300.

Disappointed at learning nothing conclusive, Nate started the car. As he drove past the Lipton residence, he spotted the man who'd been pruning Collette's hedges and parked at the curb.

He approached the gardner on foot. "Hey, sir? Do you have a card? My wife's been after me to hire a handyman, and I keep forgetting."

The man, who was hauling a ladder from a lowered tailgate, grinned. "Like to help you, but I'm not a handyman."

Nate glanced from the man to his truck. "Oh?"

"I'm Cecil Lipton. I live here."

A genuine flush spread up Nate's neck, and he grinned back. "Sorry, Mr. Lipton. I don't see many homeowners so well prepared."

Cecil nodded to his truck. "Bought this old beauty when I retired. I'm president of the homeowner's association. I do odd jobs around our church. I like to keep busy. Collette gets aggravated—claims I put our stuff last." Lipton glanced around. "This place look unkempt to you?"

"Looks like a show home to me. Don't be too hard on her. Mrs. Lipton raved about you."

His eyebrows nearly reached his hairline. "You sure you talked to my wife?"

Nate laughed. "If she's the woman who answered the door, yes, sir. Beautiful piano inside. Do you play?"

"I can't tell a white key from the black. Belongs to my stepdaughter."

"Right. Right." Nate screwed up his face as though pondering. "Your wife mentioned she came for a visit last week."

"That's right."

"Was it short? Extended?"

"In and out of here in less than two days."

"Did she fly?"

"Flew in to Denver," Cecil said, frowning. "Cancelled her return flight and drove a rental car home to . . . Oklahoma."

"Did she say what she did during her visit?"

Cecil squinted. "You didn't really come back to ask if I was a handyman, did you? What's going on?"

Nate met the man's gaze with a directness of his own. "I'm investigating a murder that occurred on April 16th, and a shooting the day after."

"And you think my stepdaughter's somehow involved? If I keep talking, you might be investigating mine."

"She's not a suspect, but we feel the shooter may have asked her to hold on to a key piece of evidence during her stay. She may not even recognize it was important. Did she stay with you when she came for her visit?"

Cecil nodded.

"Mind if I look in her room?"

"Make that *will be* investigating my murder. Yes, I do mind."

"Either way, Mr. Lipton," Nate said sympathetically. "I'll be back with a warrant."

Cecil set the ladder on the ground then looked both ways. "I've been in her room since she left. There's nothing in there. Might as well clear this up here and now. C'mon. Before Collette gets home."

Rarely did cops catch a break like this. Nate tamped down his excitement and followed Cecil into the house. They wound their way up one of the staircases to the upstairs hallway. The homeowner opened the second door on the right.

Nate entered a large room with a bay window that faced the front yard. Like the parlor downstairs, this room, accented in peach and blue, was filled with antiques. That wasn't what drew Nate's interest, though. His gaze fixed on a vanity dresser with overhead lights next to a canopied bed. The table held two Styrofoam busts for wigs, one brunette, the other platinum blonde. Naturally, a red-haired wig used by Gwyneth's assailant would be too much to ask for.

While Cecil hovered in the doorway, Nate examined every picture of Sabrina on the wall. Her mother hadn't exaggerated—Sabrina Mitchell was a performer. Each photograph showed her singing, dancing, or acting on stage.

Nate searched the dresser and under the bed. Coming up empty, he moved toward the closet. The double doors swang outward, blocking his view of the nervous homeowner. A number of gowns and costumes hung neatly on the rack. Several shoe boxes had been placed on the top shelf with equal precision.

"Nothing, right?" Hope inflected in Cecil's voice.

"Not that I can tell. I think our lead got it wrong." Nate backed up from the closet doors to catch the man's gaze. "I notice Sabrina likes to wear wigs. Are these the only two she owns?"

Cecil shook his head. "I wouldn't know. Those hair pieces have been on that dresser forever. Much as I'd like to clean up the place, Collette can't seem to part with her daughter's stuff. Sabrina's forty-seven years old, Detective. She gave up making acting a career a long time ago."

Nate nodded and began opening shoe boxes. Unfortunately, he found nothing but shoes obviously meant for the stage. Whoever had shot Gwyneth had tried to dump the ski mask upon leaving the scene. The shooter disposed of evidence—didn't hang on to it. He opened the last box, his hope fading. A pair of girl's Mary Jane tap dance shoes lay inside.

He slid the box back into place and stared at the floor. This search was nothing but circumstantial.

That's when he noticed something shimmering in the closet's carpeting. Kneeling for a closer look, Nate discovered small glass fragments trapped in the carpet's fibers.

If we can find this guy in the near future, he might have a scratch on his arm. Or glass embedded in his shoes, Sammy had said.

"You almost done in there?" Cecil called from the doorway.

"Just tying my shoe lace," Nate stalled. He hadn't driven to the Lipton's home intent on performing a search. And no way did he want to tip his hand to the homeowner. But to convince Lieutenant Montoya he was onto something, Nate needed to show him this glass. Even so, how was he supposed to get it out of here? Closing his eyes, he shook his head and opened his wallet. Talk about improvising.

He tore open a condom wrapper, stuffed the rubber in his pocket, and scooped up the glass into the aluminum foil container. Then, adding it to his pants pocket, Nate came to his feet. "You're right, Mr. Lipton. This place is clean as a whistle."

Color returned to the old man's face. "Told you so. That's why I let you in. Now, I've done my best to cooperate, but you best be on your way."

"I'll let myself out."

Sending Mr. Lipton a brief salute from the Explorer, Nate quickly inserted his Bluetooth and swung away from the curb. He replied to a missed call from Sammy, told his partner about today's successful interviews, what he'd found in the Lipton's closet, and the lengths he'd gone to secure it.

"You used a condom wrapper?" Sammy's laughter echoed through Nate's earpiece.

"When in Rome," he replied. "What's happening on your end?"

"Continental Airline reports Yasmine Takeri and Michael Whitney's final destination was Rio de Janeiro's Galeao International Airport. The Brazilian police aren't interested in expending their resources on an age-old kidnapping where nobody was hurt. They're gone, partner."

"Nailed down by more bureaucratic red tape." Win some, lose some had never worked for Nate, and he pounded the steering wheel. "We gotta have something we can use. What do you think? Can we compare glass from the Lipton's home and the Foxglove crime scene?"

"Possibly. Old home, definitely not built to the same standards as current ones. Also, the lab might find paint fragments, dust, and what not. Still, you didn't get a search waiver from the homeowner. Judge'll block a warrant, Nate."

He rolled his eyes. "Those wigs on her dresser don't wave a red flag?"

"To me and you they do. Just saying, if Sabrina Mitchell's our gal, we need to come up with another way to catch her."

She's our gal, all right. And we just might have a couple of eye witnesses to help us prove it. Nate presented his idea to Sammy, then asked his partner to meet him at Lundren Medical Center.

With rush hour traffic in full swing, and stuck at the I-25 North exit, Nate scrolled through the rest of his messages. He'd hoped to find a return message from Kinsey. Not that she'd promised to keep in touch. But since her mother's shooting, she'd been phoning or texting on a regular basis.

It'd been more than an hour since he'd sent the text, and she hadn't replied. A sense of foreboding churned in Nate's gut, and his mother's voice slipped into his thoughts. At times like this, Janet Paxton would have said, "Listen closely, the universe is speaking."

Memories of his mom flooded his consciousness as he returned the phone to the console. Much as he'd loved his mom, she'd been a card-carrying member of the free spirits. Nate reminded himself that the universe had never brought down a suspect. He ordered his logical side to get a grip and drove toward Denver.

Chapter Forty-five

WITH THE CASE opening up and luck going his way, Nate considered buying a lottery ticket. That idea was quickly nixed when he and Sammy returned to Lundgren and approached Gwyneth's closed door. Evan stepped out of her hospital room, accompanied by a man who looked like he'd just walked off the golf course.

Satisfaction oozed from Evan as he introduced the lawyer he'd hired to represent Gwyneth. As for the Rolex-outfitted attorney, he studied Nate and Sammy like a hero coming to deal with a couple of schoolyard bullies.

"We've had enough of your tactics," Evan said. "She has nothing left to say to you."

"That's too bad." Sammy slapped an eight-by-eleven manila envelope against his palm. "We thought you might be interested in catching the person who tried to kill your wife."

Evan opened his mouth to speak, but the lawyer touched his arm. "We're listening."

Seconds later, Nate and Sammy were admitted to Gwyneth's room. While Nate was en route to the hospital, Sam had run off photocopies of a young Sabrina Mitchell from various Internet sites.

Evan stayed close to Gwyneth's bed as she studied the images. "Take your time, sweetheart."

She shot him a glare then focused on the pictures again. "There's no need. That's her. Who is she, and how did you find her?"

Nate explained that since Sabrina had lived in Colorado at the time of Kinsey's kidnapping, her father had asked his actress-daughter to portray the midwife.

Gwyneth slumped against her pillows. "Mitchell said he'd take care of the midwife, so I never asked. I assumed he'd bribed someone within the profession. I never even knew he had a daughter. And you think she's the person who wore a ski mask and shot me?"

"All evidence is pointing to it," Nate said. "But, your cooperation brings us one step closer to ensuring she doesn't get another chance."

OUTSIDE IN THE hospital parking lot, Nate walked with his partner toward their vehicles. This Saturday had been a long one, but at least it had stopped raining. With only a couple more hours of daylight remaining, and all leads followed for the time being, Sammy suggested a beer.

Nothing sounded better to Nate, and he agreed, which was probably a mistake. The next thing he knew, his cell phone rang. Murder investigations didn't keep business hours, nor did they take time off on weekends. The caller was the IT tech they'd met with earlier that morning.

Nate talked to the man and disconnected. "That was Will Fisher."

Sammy rubbed the back of his neck. "He wants a beer, too?"

"Says he can make out the image of what Turner's accessory used to block out the security camera. I don't think beer's in our future, Sam. He wants us to stop by."

Chapter Forty-six

IRENE RETURNED TO the Brown Palace, bemused over George Montoya's talk with Gustav and her awakening feelings for a police lieutenant clearly off limits. Interesting, though, her taxi driver hadn't charged her a dime extra for waiting at the police station for thirty minutes. Also, when Gustav returned her to the hotel, not only had he gotten out, he held open the cab door and very nearly escorted her through the revolving doors.

She was drawing a bath and still smiling when the hotel phone rang. She ran into the bedroom to answer. "Hello?"

"Mrs. Turner?" came a young woman's voice.

"Speaking." Irene clutched the folds of her bathrobe.

A pause, followed by, "My name's Lauren Masters. Please don't hang up. I'd like to talk to you."

Irene sat on the bed. "I don't plan to hang up, Lauren. You sound upset. What can I do for you?"

"Is Kinsey with you, by any chance?"

Irene's heart clenched. "No, Lauren, she's not. Should she be?"

"No, just checking. She hasn't answered a text or her phone all day. I know she's upset, so I gave her some space. The last time we heard from her she was going for a run behind Kent Denver. I asked Jay—that's our brother—to go over there, but he's tied up at a photo shoot. He thinks I'm nuts. Our black lab is with her, and Cordie would never let anything happen to Kinsey."

"You're at the hospital?"

"Yes, ma'am."

"Is Kinsey always on time?"

"No," Lauren admitted. "But if I can't reach her by phone, I can always get her by text. It's probably nothing. I'm sorry I alarmed you. I'm just trying to figure out where she is."

Lauren's agitation was contagious. Irene fought not to panic. She reached for a pen and the hotel's scratch pad. "This place where Kinsey runs, where is it?"

Irene scribbled an Englewood address. "I'll call a friend of mine at the police department and see what he suggests. Meanwhile, I'm going to make a trip over there."

"I'll meet you there."

Irene hung up the hotel phone and grabbed her cell. She keyed in Kinsey's number, and as Lauren indicated, received Kinsey's cheery voice mail of: *I'm not available right now. You know the drill. Do your thing, and I'll call you back.* Irene left a message and dialed the lieutenant.

He answered on the first ring.

"I hate to bother you, and I'm hoping this is nothing but a false alarm." Irene repeated the conversation she'd had with Lauren then said, "I wonder if you might send someone to check on my daughter."

Chapter Forty-seven

RODRIGO LOVED rich people, especially when they willed him their estates. He affected his most gracious smile to the childless elderly couple sitting across from him. They'd narrowed their search to three nonprofits, one of which was Continental Miracles.

Trapped in a sales pitch, the cell phone he held might as well have burned a hole in his hand. But to let millions of potential dollars slip through his fingers distressed him more.

"Our organization is made up of committed professionals who watch every dime," he stressed. "We're still small enough not to get bogged down in the administration. We get the money to the people who need it the most, poor, critically ill children who will not survive without us."

The man and woman shared an approving glance with one another. Rodrigo opened his computer and pointed to the screen on the wall. "Perhaps you'd like to see some of our success stories."

As the two became engrossed in the video, Rodrigo seized an opportunity to check for Rafa's update. Rodrigo opened his burn phone and read, *Hooked up.*

He inhaled deeply, and his smile graduated from insincere to authentic. Two short words that meant Rafa and his men had followed Rodrigo's instructions to kidnap Kinsey Masters and delivered her to a vacated auto dealership now owned by the cartel.

He texted back. *Don't make a move without me.*

"How very impressive, Mr. Guzmán." The woman in clunky black shoes and thick stockings fiddled with the latch on her purse, which rested primly on her lap. "But I hope you understand. We have to be sure, and we do have a few more questions." She pulled out a list.

Rodrigo shuddered and glanced at the clock. "Ask away."

Chapter Forty-eight

NATE FOUND IT odd how fatigue vanished when cops closed in on a killer. He and Sam stood on either side of Will Fisher as the tech pulled up a file labeled *Blue Star* and the case number assigned. The white image that Stephen Turner's accomplice had used to block the camera lens once more filled the screen.

"I put the recording from the security camera through three automatic processes," Will explained, displaying each level on individual frames on his laptop. "First, autofocus, meaning the main object is now much closer to the camera. Second, an auto-white balance that helps if there's a sudden change in lighting. And, third, an auto-aperture adjustment in case the light intensity changes.

"From here I took a screen shot to see if I could pick out any details of the image." Will swiveled his chair, zoomed in with his mouse, and pointed to a larger monitor beside the smaller computer. "Notice the material contains woven threads. This tells me your accomplice covered the lens with a cloth.

"But if I adjust the intensity," Will said, clicking the mouse, "you can see patterns forming *beneath* the cloth." He picked up a pencil. "There appears to be four support points four inches apart from each other."

"What the heck is that?" Sammy asked. "We were thinking the guy stood on a ladder or propped the cloth with a broom."

"It's definitely not a broom." Will zoomed in on one of the support points, and the faint shadowing increased in contrast.

Sammy narrowed his gaze, while Nate leaned closer to the monitor.

"Each support is circular, about one-inch in diameter," Will said. "Each appears to have a pattern of concentric circles on it. In my opinion, these support patterns are more in line with a rubber boot, you know, what you might find on a crutch."

"Our guy was on crutches?" Sammy frowned.

"Not crutches," Nate said. "A crutch has one rubber sole. The dimensions on that image have four. They're a quad design." He straightened and backed away. "Holy cow. Will, print me off a few copies of that?"

"Sure thing." From over his shoulder, the analyst looked curiously at Nate then placed his hand back on the mouse.

"What's going on?" Sammy asked.

Nate moved to the printer and willed the pages to appear faster. "We've always said Turner's killer couldn't have acted alone. I'm thinking the person who's been helping Sabrina Mitchell used a cane."

HAPPY HOUR forgotten, Nate and Sammy sped back to District Six, betting their lieutenant hadn't gone home. Once again, the odds proved in their favor. Montoya's door was ajar, although, typically, another detective was in his office.

Before someone took cuts, Sam folded his arms and propped a hip on a nearby desk, while Nate wore a hole in the carpet outside the LT's office.

Lyle Wilkins had teamed up with the doctor's daughter? Nate thought of the background check he'd run on the lawyer. Wilkins was in his sixties, and, from what Nate had read, fit the stereotypical male in mid-life crisis. Each time he'd remarried, he'd traded up, tying the knot with someone younger or more beautiful.

Had Wilkins let himself get dragged into a murder scheme with Sabrina Mitchell because she'd been slated to become wife number four? Supposition, of course, but Nate couldn't wait to run their financials. How much had all of his failed nuptials cost him? And had Norma Mitchell, by giving Irene Turner the file on Kinsey, unwittingly set up the death sentence of one and the attempted murder of another?

A grim-faced Major Crimes detective nodded as he left the boss's office. Montoya waved them in.

Sammy and Nate remained standing. Seated behind his desk, their commanding officer asked for an update, surprising Nate at the little emotion he showed over IT's discovery that Turner's accomplice had used a cane.

"We think it's Lyle Wilkins, LT," Sammy said as if the lieutenant was slow in understanding their explanation.

"I suspected as much. High priced suit like that doesn't give up billable hours or a day at the club. He sends a first-year associate." Montoya narrowed his gaze. "Either of you hear from Kinsey Masters today?"

Nate's heart took off like a horse at the starting gate. "This morning, why?"

"Irene called, said Kinsey's sister's concerned. Kinsey hasn't checked in since her run."

Nate turned toward the door. "I'll check it out."

"No need," the lieutenant called after him. "Englewood Patrol's on their way."

Pulse skittering, Nate paused in the doorway, further startled when the phone rang.

Montoya answered and replied with a simple, "All right." He dropped the receiver onto its base, and any pretense at calm faded. "Kinsey Masters's car was found at Kent Denver. Patrol reported her dog's in the car, no sign of Masters. Get over there."

Chapter Forty-nine

WHEN NATE REACHED the parking lot adjacent to the Kent Denver property, he slowed his vehicle but kept his police lights flashing. In addition to the Englewood Police and Fire Department, a crowd had gathered—the obvious standouts: Irene, Kinsey's kid sister and brother. Nate couldn't have spit if he wanted to. Anguish settled low in his belly.

"Well, hell, the gang's all here," Sammy said.

They exited the vehicle in time to hear Kinsey's alarm go off in her Audi. Obviously, fire personnel had been working to open the door. A hefty black lab leapt from the car, and soon Kinsey's siblings were all over it, opening containers of water.

A nearby police officer instructed the Masters to give the emergency personnel space so they could do their job.

Lauren grabbed the dog by the collar and led her to the north side of the lot.

Irene, on the other hand, wasn't nearly as accommodating. She approached Nate the moment she saw him. "Where is she, Nate?"

"We're doing our best to find out. Do me a favor? Wait over there with Lauren and Jay." Trying to display a calm veneer over his jack-hammering heart was nearly impossible.

"Find her, Nate. You *find her.*" Irene stalked off in the Masters' direction.

He took a deep breath, gathered his wits and joined Sammy already in discussion with the Englewood Police.

A black patrolman with a shiny shaved head pointed to an orange marker twelve feet away. "We found a container of mace over there. Lauren Masters says her sister never runs without it.

Close to the Audi's trunk," the officer continued, "we found skid marks, indicating they could've slammed on the brakes and took her by surprise when they grabbed her." He glanced out at the canal, the pond that fed from it, and frowned. "That is, *if* they took her."

Nate grew lightheaded. If Kins were in the water, they were too late. If they waited for divers and she wasn't, they were wasting precious time.

A vehicle sped into the lot, and Nate rolled his eyes. But it wasn't Griff Colburn's Chevy Tahoe that had him wanting to punch a fist through the aspiring politician's windshield, it was the news van that followed.

Colburn left his own set of skid marks as he stopped and jumped from the Tahoe. "Where is she?" he demanded, jogging toward Lauren and Jay.

Sammy headed in Colburn's direction, and Nate decided to get to the guy before Sammy shot him. But a female reporter solved Nate's problem. As Sammy neared Colburn, so did she and her camera crew. Sammy did an about-face. Vice had left a permanent mark. He would forever have an issue with microphones or cameras being shoved in his face.

Colburn, however, was in his element. He said something to the press, spotted Nate, and strode his way. "Paxton, right? What's going on? What's happened here?"

"We're trying to find out. Any way you can call off your media hounds until we do?"

"I'll see what I can do." Colburn headed toward the crew.

Whatever the politician said had no effect on the on-scene reporter. Even from where Nate stood, and in spite of Colburn's gesturing hands, it was clear she'd instructed the video guy to keep filming. She was still shoving a microphone back and forth and firing her questions when Nate stalked toward them. He was a fraction away from tossing their equipment in the pond when Colburn evidently got through to her. He handed the reporter a card. Seconds later, she and her cameraman loaded their gear into the van and sped away.

"Done," he said jogging over. "Although I had to promise them an exclusive to get them to leave." He pressed a hand to his forehead. "I can't believe this. I just spoke to her this morning."

Nate waved toward Kinsey's Audi. "There's her car. The officers have bagged her mace, which means she might have fought back. Can you think of anyone who would go after Kinsey?"

"No one." Griff closed his eyes. "She doesn't have any enemies."

"Has she ever complained of a stalker? Anyone taking an unusual interest in her?"

Griff shook his head. "No. Everybody . . ."

"Everybody . . ." Nate narrowed his gaze. "Something crossed your mind. What is it?"

Griff's mouth formed a thin line. "Never mind. It has no connection—"

Nate stood close enough to do a chest bump. "Do you want to find Kinsey or not?"

"You're out of line."

"Take it up with my boss after we find her. Something occurred to you. What the hell is it?"

"I'm telling you it has no bearing. A nonprofit has expressed interest in making Kinsey its spokesman, that's all. The CEO asked that I keep the information confidential, which is why I hesitated."

Nate wanted to throttle the jackass. He'd take every unrelated straw he could get. "CEO's name and organization."

Colburn glowered at Nate and stiffened the broad shoulders that had landed in many an end zone. His receiver hands curled into fists, and Nate prepared for his assault. Evidently, though, Colburn remembered he was running for office. He lowered his hands. "Rodrigo Guzmán. He heads up an organization known as Continental Miracles."

Nate stopped cold. Guzmán? Why would Guzmán go after Kinsey, who'd been out of the limelight for the past six years? Point in fact, he wouldn't. Suddenly, Nate grasped why Guzmán had called off the tails.

Nate pivoted from Colburn and honed in on his partner talking with the Englewood police officers. As he sprinted toward the Explorer, Nate shouted, "Sam, let's go!"

"It's Guzmán," Nate growled when Sammy came within hearing distance. "I'll kill the son of a bitch."

Chapter Fifty

BEHIND THE WHEEL of his Explorer, Nate tore up University Boulevard the way he wanted to tear into Guzmán's hide. He'd throw the philanthropist fraud into the pond next to Colburn where both scum would feel right at home.

"Nate, chill. Sammy reached for his phone and tossed Nate a look. "Why do you think Guzmán took her?"

"Because he ended the tails. Neither of us understood why, but think about it. He didn't have to track us anymore." Nate choked on his next words. "He found . . . my weakness."

Sammy shook his head. "I figured as much. The minute Montoya brought up her name, you went screwy on me. All right. That would mean Rafa, or whichever *pendejos* were watching us, saw you and Kinsey together."

"I got stupid." Nate pressed down on the gas. "Forgot who I was. Went to Kinsey's school, walked her to her car, even let her blackmail me until I dropped by her house—"

"What the hell? You've practically been dating the girl."

"You can call me every name in the book some other time. Just help me find her."

"How about I call you human? As for getting her back, if someone grabbed my family, I wouldn't have to ask."

The Explorer couldn't move fast enough. If it wouldn't take too much time, he'd pull over and puke. The idea that Rodrigo Guzmán or his filthy gangsters had put their paws on Kinsey . . .

"Paxton!" Sammy shouted. "Slow the hell down. Those are crosswalks we're nearing."

Nate bit back bile and eased up on the gas. He couldn't help Kinsey by falling apart. He focused on his driving and how to get her out of the godforsaken mess he'd gotten her into.

"When we get back to headquarters," Sammy said, "we'll contact her cell phone provider, apply for a trace on her GPS, and track her that way."

"Headquarters? Are you out of your mind?" Once past the school zone, Nate floored the accelerator. "I'm going to separate Guzmán's head from his body."

"Nate." Sammy braced his arm against the dash. "Slow this thing down and pull over."

"No way, Sam."

"He'll kill her, is that what you want? Pull this thing over and let's think this thing through."

It was the hardest thing Nate ever did in his life to take his foot off the gas.

Chapter Fifty-one

KINSEY FOUGHT TO lift her head while the room danced in and out of focus around her. She tried to rub her eyes, but her arms were too heavy, too disconnected to locate her face. *Stand up,* she ordered her body. Instead, her head dropped backward onto the hard, sour cushion beneath her.

Voices came from above and below, from everywhere and nowhere, followed by men's deep cackles and laughter. Her tongue felt thick, her lips numb. *So thirsty.* She sucked in air and let her body drift.

Chapter Fifty-two

NATE DIDN'T GIVE a damn that the boss's door was closed, or that every detective working late had lifted his head. With Sammy on his heels, he barged inside the lieutenant's office.

Montoya sat with a man at an oval table, and both straightened, stopping short at the interruption. Neither were as stunned as Nate, however. He recognized DEA Supervisory Agent Gerald Zelinski immediately. He'd worked closely with the DEA boss on numerous drug busts and stakeouts.

He looked from Zelinski to the lieutenant and said breathlessly, "No sign of Kinsey when we checked out her car. We think Rodriogo Guzmán's behind her abduction."

Sammy cut in, "Griff Colburn indicated Guzmán had taken an interest in her. That's not a likely coincidence, LT."

The lieutenant glanced at Zelinski who in return lifted a brow.

"Not a coincidence at all," the agent said. "Pull up a chair, Detectives."

"I'll stand," Nate said. "What's going on?"

"I have two of my agents with Rodrigo Guzmán right now. The Masters's kidnapping was . . . unexpected."

Nate advanced on the agent. Zelinski and the lieutenant shot from their chairs. Neither their startled reactions nor Sam's python-like grip on Nate's arms could hold him back as he grabbed the Fed by his collar. "Sorry if she interrupted your little sting operation, but if you have people in his office, arrest the murdering thug, and let's save an innocent woman!"

"Detective Paxton," the lieutenant roared.

Zelinski held up a hand, Nate let go of his collar, and Sammy loosened his slack on Nate's arms—but not entirely.

Sidestepping Nate, the agent adjusted his collar. "While that might make all the sense in the world to you, it'll do Ms. Masters little good. Three members of Guzmán's gang fell off our radar this morning."

Sammy croaked, "Rafa Lopez?"

"Rafa Lopez." The agent sighed.

A thick lump lodged in Nate's throat. He'd never witnessed Rafa's perverted exploits, but he'd had to endure the punk brag. As the reality of what they were up against sunk in, the four stared at each other.

A knock came from the door. "Lieutenant," a uniformed officer said. "The desk sergeant informed me your conference light was on and told me to interrupt. There are two women downstairs. They're demanding to see you. An

Irene Turner and Lauren Masters. They claim it's urgent."

Nate bowed his head and squeezed his hands into fists.

The lieutenant's face turned purple. He turned to the officer at the door. "For God's sake, put them in the community room and tell them I'll be right down. Agent Zelinski, brief the detectives on what we talked about while I put a tent over this circus."

UPON THE OFFICER'S return, he escorted Irene and Lauren into a large room off the lobby, and there they continued to wait. Since meeting Lauren face to face at the High Line Canal, Irene had given Lauren plenty of space. Five years younger than Kinsey, the young woman looked all of sixteen. Blonde, pretty, and petite, she'd been polite to Irene, but then Kinsey's abduction had taken front and center. Panic had ended any need for civility.

Then, when Nate and Sammy had driven off without a word, Lauren had instructed her brother to take care of their dog and volunteered to drive Irene to police headquarters.

Now, she wrung her hands, sighed deeply every few minutes, and paced. Irene would grant these kids one thing, they weren't criers. They were proactive, troubleshooters, a trait she deeply admired. Their love for each other and for Kinsey blazed bright and foremost. If she had to give Evan—and, yes, Gwyneth—credit for anything, it was that these kids had an unfailing devotion to family.

In this particular case, Irene could offer few words of comfort. Still, the silence was deafening, so she had to try. "I hope your dog's okay. Stuck in that car for three hours."

Lauren paused in her pacing and seemed to remember Irene was in the room. "Kinsey must've put her inside while she was wet. Cordie smelled pretty rank. Thank God, it wasn't hot outside. She could've been in real trouble." Lauren shook her head and pulled out the phone she'd been frequently studying.

"Are you looking for a text?"

She shook her head. "The day my mother was shot, my brother showed me an app. It's called *Find My Friends*. You have to have the person's permission, of course, but the app lets you keep track of them so you can meet up and hang out. Kins and I have had a lot of time on our hands in that waiting room, so we downloaded it to our phones."

Irene's breath stalled. "You can trace Kinsey's phone?"

Lauren sighed and closed her eyes. "Technically. But her phone isn't on."

Like most people her age, Kinsey was glued to her phone. The fact Lauren couldn't locate her with the app, and that her sister hadn't answered for hours, meant only one thing. Someone had taken the phone from Kinsey and powered it down.

"Keep checking," Irene said.

The door opened, and Lieutenant Montoya entered the room. He strode to Irene and wrapped her in a fierce embrace. "I know you're upset," he said when they pulled apart. "But this isn't where you should be right now."

"It's the only place I . . ." Irene glanced at Lauren who stared between them intently. "*We* can be right now. You have to let us in on what's happening."

"We have a lead. We're looking into it, and that's all I know at this point." The lieutenant focused on Lauren. "We'll get her back, Ms. Masters."

"Lauren," Irene said. "Show Lieutenant Montoya the app you just showed me."

She held out her phone and repeated her explanation of the *Find My Friends* feature.

"May I borrow this?" he asked.

"Sure," Lauren said. "But just so you know, Kinsey's phone is turned off."

"That's just it. We can put someone on it to watch it nonstop. If she turns it on, we'll know the second she does."

The desk sergeant stuck his head in the door. "Lieutenant, we got another Masters out here. Says his name is Jay."

Despite her worry, Irene had to smile at the lieutenant's exasperation and this tight-knit family.

"I'm counting on you, Irene," he whispered. "You want a long-term relationship with Kinsey, you'll do whatever you can to keep these two busy. And you will stay out of this investigation."

Irene gritted her teeth. "And I'm counting on you, George. Against my better judgment, I'll do what you say. But only if you'll do one thing for me."

"What's that?"

"Don't you dare let anything happen to my daughter and promise you'll find the bastard who took her."

Chapter Fifty-three

NATE HAD SAT in on numerous sting operations. He'd also participated in inter- and intra-agency briefings. None that he'd attended, however, had been of the critical nature, held as much urgency, or had been as personal as this one. Kinsey was in the hands of slimebags known for murdering and raping just for the fun of it. These a-holes, who had long ago lost any notion of right or wrong, reported to a cartel—a cartel that would stop at nothing to send Nate and his partner a message—preferably written in blood.

Thirty minutes had passed since Nate and Sammy had arrived at the Major Crimes, and the conversation that had begun in his lieutenant's office had transitioned into the largest conference room within Denver Police Department's District Six. The LT's office simply wasn't big enough to accommodate them all: The Chief of Police, the tactical lead commander of SWAT, and, of course, the supervisory DEA agent in charge.

No word yet on Kinsey's whereabouts, but the bosses suspected, and Nate agreed, it was only a matter of time. One of Guzmán's henchmen would phone and demand an exchange—Kinsey Masters for Nate Paxton and Sammy Lucero.

Nate would go willingly. Problem was, even though Sammy had volunteered, he had a family to think about. Not that Nate's supervisors would approve such a negotiation in the first place. The Department's goal, and arguably the proverbial longshot, was to get Kinsey out without giving in to her abductor's demands.

Nate glanced over at Sammy. He stood against the wall like a wind-up toy ready to perform. Nate could have been his twin.

"Rodrigo Guzmán hasn't left Continental Miracles in hours," the DEA supervisor provided. "Nor has he made or received any phone calls since Ms. Masters was taken."

"How do you know that?" Nate asked.

Zelinski offered a half-smile. "We have our ways."

Nate bit his tongue. Typical DEA, their agency played *I've got a secret*, but expected the police department's full cooperation. *Whatever.* All Nate wanted to know was that Guzmán was covered.

"He could send a text," Sammy said.

"True." The DEA agent shrugged.

Nate's heart refused to slow to a normal rate. He wrapped his fingers around the burn phone he'd used while on Vice. Sammy had one, too. Guzmán had both numbers. Why hadn't he called?

Lieutenant Montoya rose from the table, expression grave. "We estimate that Kinsey was taken from the Englewood area of the High Line Canal between noon and one. The only witness that has come forward is a runner in the area. He claims he saw Masters and her dog jogging toward the parking lot at the time he set off on his run—11:45. He said she was in good spirits and under no sign of duress." Montoya pressed a button on a laptop computer on the conference room table. Four mug shots of Guzmán's cutthroats filled the screen.

"Let me tell you what we know about these charmers. Each have sheets so long you won't remember, so take notes."

No amount of deep breathing helped. Nate's eyes locked with Sam's. They didn't have to reach for a pen. They'd lived deep undercover with these gangbangers.

Since Nate's meltdown at the canal, his partner had gauged Nate's every move. In front of their superiors, Sam continuously shot "be cool" looks.

Nate swallowed his rage. How cool could he be? He knew what these bastards were capable of. And he was going out of his mind knowing the who, what, when, and why, but not a clue *where*.

Chapter Fifty-four

KINSEY LICKED her lips. The room weaved in and out, and the world was a haze. She tried to push up from a sandpaper-like couch, but whatever they'd injected her with had sapped her strength, and her arms felt like Jello. She closed her eyes and snorted a laugh. Oh, Kins. *Arms aren't made out of Jello.*

She opened her eyes again and got down to business. Find something to drink. She'd seen this place before. Desk, chair, wastebasket. *Office?*

She slid from the sofa onto the wood floor. C'mon, Jello arms, do your stuff.

Chapter Fifty-five

CONVINCING THE Masters *children* to leave the station wasn't the easiest thing Irene had ever done. Lauren and Jay were adults, with strong personalities and minds of their own. Further, she was the *other woman*, the one who'd ripped apart their ordinary world. Now Lieutenant Montoya had said *keep them busy?* Exactly how should she go about doing that? *Hey, ya'll, let's hang out* didn't quite work in this scenario. She was forty-six years old, these kids were in their twenties. Furthermore, neither Lauren, Jay, nor Irene seemed in the mood to go clubbing.

She settled by stepping out of character and becoming a chatterbox. She asked them all kinds of questions about their backgrounds. They eventually, albeit reluctantly, opened up. And despite their worry for Kinsey, the two artists offered to show Irene some of their work.

Jay rode in the backseat, and Irene sat on the passenger side of Lauren's Passat as the girl drew her car into a narrow alley. Tucked between the backside of Masterpieces Art Gallery and a warehouse across from it, the only things Irene could make out for sure in the narrow passageway were the dumpsters. It was dark now, the wind had picked up, and the temperature had dropped again. Combining the chance of more rain and the creepy location, she felt about as secure as if she'd entered a scene out of Whitechapel.

Lauren shrugged and smiled awkwardly. "Here we are. This is my lair."

Irene glanced around. "Lair, huh? Good word for it." Shivering, she left the car, holding her middle tight, and entered the warehouse. Immediately she was drawn to the trestle and the long flight of stairs upward.

As though Lauren and Jay climbed to the top of that towering monster on a regular basis, they jogged up the clamoring steps and stood on the metal grating a short time later.

Lauren held out her arms. "So what do you think of him?"

Irene grew dizzy craning her neck to look up. "Him?"

"Abernathy," Lauren said. "He's my dragon."

The scrap metal she'd welded had indeed taken shape, complete with fierce-looking wings. As if the evening hadn't been suspenseful enough, Irene pictured the dragon looming then swooping down to devour her.

"He's . . . something, Lauren. Exactly what are we going to do with Abernathy?"

"He's been commissioned for a children's museum. My helpers and I have about six more hours of cutting and sandblasting. After that we'll paint him and off he goes."

"By crane, I hope." Irene smiled up at the girl so clearly passionate about her art. "I hope he won't fly out of here."

Lauren waggled her eyebrows. "You never know. Come on up, Irene. You can really see what he looks like from where we're standing."

"Oh, honey, I'd love to, but, what's that old saying, 'three's a crowd?'"

Jay and Lauren glanced at each other.

"She's just like Kins," Jay said.

"How so?" Irene's heart threatened to flip at the reminder of her daughter.

"She hates heights. I can get her up here, maybe on a dare. But only for a minute or so, then she wants her feet on the ground."

Speaking of Kinsey, the mood turned somber. Jay and Lauren descended the platform and once again met Irene on the floor.

"Jay, what about you?" Irene asked. "Show me your work."

He walked to the far side of the warehouse. "Over here I have a dark room. Next to it, I use computers when I download digital. My finished work is in the gallery, though."

Irene clasped her hands, bribed him with a hopeful grin, and rocked back on her heels. "Love to see it."

"Okay. I guess so." But once again, he looked at his phone.

Irene followed the two out of the warehouse, crossed the alley, and entered the gallery. Jay silenced the alarm and flipped a switch. The museum flooded with light, exposing paintings, sculptures, and myriad glass patterned arrangements.

With Lauren leading the way, Irene entered a large hall dedicated to Jay Masters's photography. Images in black and white and in color completed the area—indigenous people, hunters on safaris, wildlife on every continent, mountains, oceans, and other nature shots comprised his collection. But what captured Irene's heart and soul were the two walls, all black and white photos, dedicated to Kinsey and her soccer career.

Irene's knees nearly buckled.

Lauren touched her elbow. "She'll be fine," Lauren whispered. "The lieutenant promised, remember?"

"You're turn," Jay said, eyes shimmering with concern. "Show us what you do."

That comment caught Irene off guard. "What I do?"

"We could go to a shooting club," Jay said.

Irene stifled a cough. "We could, but, unfortunately, I don't have my shotgun with me."

"They'd probably loan you one," Lauren offered.

"Oh, they might. But I prefer to use my own." Irene cleared her throat. She was already in enough trouble with Evan. She was damn proud of her right to bear arms, but she had no idea how he felt about guns. The last thing she needed was him to accuse her of corrupting his children. "Some other time, okay?"

Lauren studied the floor.
Jay went back to checking his phone.
The night dragged on.

Chapter Fifty-six

FORTY-FIVE MINUTES after the elderly Mrs. Lachlan had pulled out her infernal list of questions, Rodrigo escorted the couple from Continental Miracles's lobby.

Returning to his office, cell phone in hand, he breathed his relief and slumped into his executive chair. The questions the couple had asked had been good ones, and unexpected from senior citizens. Ordinarily, the video produced for his nonprofit had people in tears and completing the paperwork on the spot.

Mission accomplished, Rodrigo wiped away the sweat that had collected around his neck. Due to the time lapse, he started to forego his own strict policy—to never phone Rafa or his men from his office. He was desperate now for a status report. He started to phone, then hesitated. *Not a time to turn stupid.* Using his burn phone, he texted for an update.

Rafa returned, *Jacked up. Upstairs. Eses want payment.*

Rodrigo bit down on the inside of his cheek. Meaning the gang wanted to take turns with Kinsey Masters. He should allow it, send Paxton the ultimate lesson. Although, after tonight, Detective Nate Paxton would never know Kinsey had been brutalized. Still, the former athlete's admiration of Rodrigo counted for something. *You're a legend, Mr. Guzmán. I don't know many who could start an organization at seventeen.*

Rodrigo texted back, *No time. Ese's payment in cash. Set plan into motion.*

Chapter Fifty-seven

IN THE DISTRICT'S conference room, Nate went from leaning against the wall to pacing. The chief had said his goodbyes, demanding to be kept informed. The SWAT leader, too, had gone back to his regular duties. Now all that remained were the DEA supervisor, the lieutenant, and Sammy. With fewer personnel, the conference room should have circulated more air. Nate struggled to breathe.

Lauren Masters's phone sat in the middle of the conference room table, an ever-present reminder that Kinsey was beyond his reach. The app's GPS signal remained off.

The DEA supervisor's phone received a series of knocks, his version of a ring. "Zelinski," he answered.

He listened, then replied, "All right. Stay with him."

Zelinski disconnected. "Guzmán's crafty. I had operatives in his office for a good two hours, and they planted a bug. Agents claimed he was as smooth as an Oriental silk tie. They've been gone for fifteen minutes, and he hasn't made a sound. If he did order Kinsey Masters's abduction, he's playing it very smart—and safe."

"I'll be in my office," Lieutenant Montoya said, as though admitting defeat.

Nate forced out a long breath. "I say we bring him in for questioning."

"He'll lawyer up." Sammy moved away from the wall. "He's done it before. The only thing that'll accomplish is a charge against you for police harassment, and with his vendetta against you, you still won't have Kinsey."

Nate white-knuckled the back of a chair. "We can't just stand here with our thumbs up our ass. Let's do *something*."

Hands on his hips, Zelinski blinked as he stared down at Lauren Masters's phone. "It appears your wish is our command, Paxton. We'll haul Guzmán in, and soon. Check this out, we got a signal."

Chapter Fifty-eight

BECAUSE IRENE simply didn't know what else to do, she suggested to Lauren and Jay that they find a coffee shop close to the police station and await the lieutenant's phone call. Not the most ingenious of solutions, but then, bowling or laser tag seemed out of the question.

In addition to coffee and light meals and desserts, this particular shop provided board games. To pass the time, Jay and Lauren played backgammon, while Irene, down to her last nerve, ordered her stomach not to roil and her head to quit pounding from the myriad coffee and food smells.

Lauren took a call from Evan, deliberately evasive when he must have wanted to know why his children hadn't shown up at the hospital. "We just needed a break tonight, Dad." Before disconnecting, she said, "We'll see you tomorrow. Love you guys."

Leaving her second cup of coffee to get cold, Irene rose from the table and massaged her aching lower back. She was staring outside the coffee house into the Denver darkness when Lauren stood, too, and joined her.

"The good news is, so far the media hasn't released anything about Kinsey's abduction. The last thing we need is my parents freaking out."

Irene nodded.

"I'm sorry this is so weird for you. I can't imagine what you're going through. If it's any consolation, my sister has a huge heart, and she wants us all to be part of each other's lives."

"Does she?" Irene glanced at Lauren, surprised.

"She does. And we're not all bad once you get to know us," Lauren said, hinting at a smile. She turned toward her brother who sat with his chin in his hand, staring at his smart phone. "Well, I can't speak for Jay."

Irene laughed. "From what I've seen of you two, I think Kinsey's the luckiest woman on earth. I'm proud to know you both."

A natural beauty, Lauren's cheeks flushed a pretty pink. She folded her arms and sighed. "How much longer?"

Jay looked up from his phone. "Hey, get over here. Signal's back on."

After receiving the signal, it took everything Irene had to persuade Lauren and Jay to wait at the coffee shop until the lieutenant returned her call. She'd phoned him ten minutes ago and still had received no response.

Jay had quickly identified Kinsey's whereabouts, and brother and sister wanted to drive straight to the locale, something Irene sensed could get them all killed.

A new round of customers entered the premises. Anytime, she expected the manager to accuse them of loitering and ask them to leave. To prevent that from happening, Irene bought her third cup of coffee.

All right, George. You told me to keep them busy, and I did. So call already.

So much for a psychic connection. Her phone remained silent.

She stared at the Masters's sullen faces and realized she'd run out of time. "All right, he hasn't called back. Let's go back to the station."

In a matter of seconds, Lauren and Jay were out of their chairs and through the door.

Naturally, Irene's phone rang the moment she'd attempted to follow. She paused in the coffee shop's entrance and breathed, "George?"

"Irene? What's going on?" His voice was clipped, distracted.

"We received Kinsey's signal. Have you seen it?"

"Yes. We're in the critical stages now. I know this is hard, but try not to worry."

"You really are coming up short in the half-brain department. Tell me my daughter's safe, *then* I won't worry."

"Nate and Sammy are on their way to her now. You have to trust me on this. *Hell.* Just a second. I have another call coming in."

Irene stared at the phone in her hand. Had he really put her on hold?

Lauren honked the horn, Jay waved a frantic 'let's go', and Irene squeezed her eyes closed.

The lieutenant came back on the line. "Irene. You say Jay Masters is with you? Maybe there is something you can do."

Irene's coffee slipped from her hand as she listened.

Chapter Fifty-nine

THE COMPLETE tactical team reunited, Nate stood among them, all eyes on the conference room table, in particular, Lauren Masters's smart phone and the signal emanating from it. His first reaction was to burst from the station, follow the GPS, charge in to wherever the map ended, and locate Kins.

Fortunately, his brain overrode his hell-bent emotions. A signal this late into her disappearance and no calls or texts received very likely meant Kinsey hadn't been the one to turn on the phone. This setup had a trap smell all over it.

"Address is the intersection of South Platte River and Santa Fe Drive," a uniformed officer announced brusquely upon entering. "Empty building formerly owned by Truitt's Classic Automotive."

Seated at the far end of the table, Sammy, who'd been resting his head in his hands, looked up. He met Nate's gaze at the same time Nate made the connection.

"Good old Jeffrey Truitt." Nate grimaced. "Truitt's was a reputable auction house until 2008, when Arthur Truitt died and left the business to his freeloading son. After Jeffrey took over, he drove the place into the ground."

"He got into bed with a chop-shop ring and ran drugs on the side," Sammy added. "Last time we checked, Truitt had sold the building and was in Cañon City doing time."

Nate resumed pacing. "Bet you anything the new owner is a shell company for the cartel."

Montoya had left the office to take a phone call. He re-entered and said, "We'll need blueprints of the building. Aerial photos from the police chopper."

"We'll use long range lenses," the SWAT commander cut in.

Nate whirled. Any other time, he'd be all over roof surveillance and protocol. But with Kinsey at risk, the scenario left him icy with fear. "If Guzmán's gangsters hear a chopper—"

"Besides it's unnecessary," Sammy said. "Nate and I have been in the building numerous times." He went to the whiteboard and began sketching a layout of the building.

Across the conference room, Zelinski spoke on the phone. A satisfied smile came to his face as he said to the party on the other end, "All right. Do it."

All eyes in the room locked on the DEA Supervisor in Charge.

"Warrant came through. I've authorized my team to search Continental Miracles and detain Rodrigo Guzmán for questioning."

Nate didn't know whether to clock Colburn the next time he saw him or pound him on the back. His statement about Guzmán's interest in Kinsey had obviously satisfied a district court judge. Nate glanced at the watch and tamped down his panic. Going on 2100—Kinsey had been gone eight hours.

Chapter Sixty

NEAR EIGHT-THIRTY, doors locked, security system armed, and the lights turned off, the small staff of Continental Miracles had long gone home. Rodrigo sat alone in the dark of his second-floor office, clutching his pocket saint and waiting for a text from Rafa saying he'd followed through on Rodrigo's orders.

Rafa rarely violated Rodrigo's commands. Even so, the gangster had never had a woman as tempting as Kinsey Masters under his power before.

Grinding his teeth, Rodrigo sprang from the desk and willed the burn phone to ping with Rafa's texted response. If the men went against his will, Rodrigo would personally turn them over to Oso and Sombra and watch the cartel tear them apart.

His body singing with nervous energy, Rodrigo could no longer stand by. He sent a text to Rafa, *What is happening?*

Rafa returned, *Out of building. Box in position.*

Rodrigo exhaled in relief. He glanced at his watch. Kinsey's phone had been turned on for ten minutes now. Surely, Nate Paxton and Sammy Lucero had seen the signal and were well on their way.

But what if they weren't?

Rodrigo texted back, *Call targets. Tell them where to find package.*

He'd just pressed "send" when through his office window came an explosion of blue lights, the security system went off, and a crash sounded downstairs. A maddening cacophony of sirens combined with shouts of "Police!" echoed from the first floor corridor.

Thundering footfalls raced up the steps.

Sweat poured off of Rodrigo as he tucked the burn phone into a slit between the arm and the seat of his leather chair. Then, crouched under his desk, he strained to reach for his Sig Sauer in the top drawer. In the dark, however, he fumbled. The gun fell with a loud thump to the floor.

"Federal Agents, US Drug Enforcement Administration," voices shouted from beyond the door, then his office door flew open. Two hulking figures in night goggles and raid gear crashed into the room. "Put your hands up!"

"I'm unarmed," Rodrigo croaked. "What is the meaning of this?"

He stood, hands up, but not before seeing the outline of his gun from the window's illumination. Gingerly, he kicked it farther under his desk. "What's going on? Why are you here?"

"Rodrigo Guzmán, we have a warrant to search your premises."

Somebody hit the lights.

Blinking against the sudden brightness, acid rose in his throat. "On what charge?"

"Drug running and kidnapping."

"The drug charges again? These allegations are insane. And *kidnapping*? I save lives, I do not take them."

The larger agent, a man with a thick mustache, threw off his goggles. He moved toward Rodrigo, grabbed his arms, pinned them behind his back, and withdrew his handcuffs. "If we've made a mistake, we'll apologize later."

OUTSIDE, IN THE cool night air, the mustachioed man dragged Rodrigo to an unmarked car and placed him inside. And there he waited. His head spun, trying to pinpoint where he'd gone wrong. His gaze traveled to Continental Miracles, the organization he'd built from the ground up when he was just a teen. Every light in the old Victorian was on as a team of agents ransacked the building.

A television van pulled up on the scene.

Imprisoned in the squad car's cage, Rodrigo turned his head in the opposite direction and swallowed hard. Provided the agents didn't find his burn phone, his lawyer would have him out by midnight. His files were deeply encrypted. They had nothing on him.

On the other side of the street, the agent who'd handcuffed him stood in conversation with the couple who'd earlier left his office—the Lachlans.

Rodrigo's stomach sank. "Those people beneath the street light," he said to the man behind the wheel. "Who are they?"

The driver peered in the direction Rodrigo had indicated. "Looks like a couple of civic-minded citizens to me."

Chapter Sixty-one

BY 21:30, THE CONFERENCE room was filled to capacity as more off-duty SWAT members trickled in. Further, the former classic car dealership known as Truitt's was now under the scrutiny of Vice. Assisting the operation, Vice would move in to get a view of what was going on outside the building while doing its best to get infrared images of the inside.

Early in their careers, Nate and Sammy had participated in SWAT. Nate had only been called twice to participate in his seven years on the force. Now, in particular, he was glad he had.

Aerial surveillance had been secured from a long-range telephoto lens, which the SWAT commander spread over the table. "Here," he said, circling a grainy image and the roof's access point, "is where the team will go in. You'll note from Detective Lucero's whiteboard sketch, this entrance will drop us right into the center of the auto body shop. From there, you should be able to see the stairs that lead to the manager's office. It's in this section of the building where the detectives believe Ms. Masters is being held."

The commander dragged out a new set of schematics. "Detective Paxton, you will brief us on the area's exterior surroundings."

Nate narrowed his gaze. "Sir, I don't want to go cowboy on you, but what do you mean 'us'? My partner and I know Truitt's. We also know the area. The whole reason Ms. Masters is in this predicament is because of Sammy and me. I'll be happy to brief *you* for backup. But Sammy and I should be the ones to go in."

The SWAT commander glared. "Negative. I'm familiar with your backgrounds, Detectives, so don't take this personally. You're qualified. But my men are more so. They have a better chance of getting Ms. Masters out alive." He frowned. "Provided she *is* alive."

"I have to agree with my partner," Sammy said, far more tactfully than Nate had. "We've disgraced a cartel. You're right to expect a trap. But this could be a major shoot out. These *pendejos* carry assault rifles the way a baby carries a pacifier. Nate and I have been working a case. Rafa Lopez kidnapped Kinsey Masters so that we'd come after her."

"And you know this how?" the commander shot back. "Have the kidnappers contacted you? Made any demands?" He glanced around the room. The group's earlier murmurs had whittled down to silence as all eyes focused on the confrontation taking place.

Nate felt for the phone that he'd used as a vice cop. Why the hell hadn't it rung? Had he and Sammy guessed wrong? Had Rafa and his cutthroats killed Kinsey and left her body to send him a lesson? Nate couldn't believe that. No way, after their betrayal, would Guzmán let Nate or Sammy live.

"Shall we try this again?" The SWAT commander said. "Detective Paxton, brief the team."

Reluctantly, he moved to the whiteboard and picked up a marker. "A wholesale mattress store abuts Truitt's to the south. I'd say these stores are no more than ten meters apart. About fifty meters to the north of Truitt's is a medical marijuana dispensary. If I know Rafa Lopez, he'll have a man stationed in this vicinity watching for cops."

"Right," Sammy added. "He won't stand out in a pot shop. He'll have watchers everywhere, on the sides and in the back, too. It's the gang's standard MO to cover the entire building."

The conference door opened, and either a vice cop walked in, or a homeless person had made his way off the streets of Denver and into the station.

"Lobo?" Sammy grinned. "Almost didn't recognize you under all that grime."

Lobo clasped Sammy's right hand.

Nate blew out a breath. He'd worked with Greg "Lobo" Myers a number of times on the streets.

"Detective Myers, status," the commander said.

"One man positioned on the western perimeter behind the building, which backs up to the Platte River. Probably one stationed out front. Lots of activity coming from Simply Pure, the pot store next door. But we got something on infrared. Two heat images coming from the upstairs office."

Two? The idea that someone was upstairs with Kinsey made Nate's gut sink.

"Thank you, Myers." The commander shot Nate and Sammy a you're-wrong-and-I'm-right-kind of look. "Hmm. One guard, possibly two. You indicated the entire perimeter would be covered. The positive is that one of those heat images could be from Kinsey Masters. She may still be alive."

The phone in Nate's pocket vibrated. He snatched it up and put it on speaker before raising it to his ear. "Paxton."

"*Paxton?*" Rafa said. "That's not right. I thought it was Gilcrest, you miserable piece of shit."

"Save the sweet talk, Lopez. You got something I want. So what's the deal? How do I get her back?"

"Simple. You and that motherfucking *Eduardo* come and get her."

"Just like that?" Nate glanced at Sammy.

Sammy stood, hands on his hips, jaw set. *Ready.*

"Just like that. Oh, and because I really want to liven things up, if we see anybody besides you two *putos* around Truitt's, we put a bullet in *Special K's* brain."

The line went dead.

One second later, Lobo's phone buzzed. "My partner's still over there, Commander. Mind if I take this?"

The SWAT commander nodded.

"Lobo," he said. He listened for a few minutes and disconnected. "Now it looks like there's one heat image generating from the upstairs, and no sign of *anyone* guarding the building."

Lieutenant Montoya rose from his chair. "All right, Commander, let's get over second-guessing what these lowlifes will do and get on with it. A young woman's life is at stake. As you can see, my detectives are more than willing to put their necks on the block. I think Paxton had the right idea in the first place. He and Lucero go in, and SWAT assumes backup. You got a problem with this, let's you and I go upstairs and talk to the chief."

Chapter Sixty-two

IN LESS THAN seven minutes a plan was in motion to hoodwink Rafa Lopez into thinking Nate and Sammy would sacrifice themselves to save Kinsey.

Attired in Kevlar vests and bomb squad gear, Nate strode with four SWAT members toward a police van camouflaged to look like a floral delivery service, while Sammy and another SWAT member resembling Nate would follow in Nate's Explorer.

The sound of someone running behind them, however, slowed their paces.

"Detectives!"

Nate pivoted, and Zelinski came toward them. "We got him," the out of breath DEA supervisor said. "We nailed Guzmán."

"Fantastic," Nate replied. "But you'll have to fill us in la—"

"I'll brief you *now.*" Zelnski held out a disposable glove-covered hand. In it, he held a tiny black phone.

Sammy's eyes widened. "Guzmán's?"

"We have him in interrogation. Waiting for his lawyer, of course, but we've placed him officially under arrest. I knew he had to have a burn phone someplace. He'd never conduct business over his regular line. Almost missed this little beauty."

Nate glanced toward the van. "Where'd you find it?"

"In the arm of his chair. And a Sig Sauer .45 under his desk. Saint Rodrigo should consider changing his name to Lucifer—that or dumbass. The real clencher that sealed his guilt was when I stood outside of interrogation before confronting him. I'd taken his Continental Miracles's business card with his legit cell phone number and called it with his burn phone." Zelinski grinned. "He answered."

"Idiot," Sammy said. "Probably didn't recognize his own burn phone's number on his Caller ID."

Nate started walking. "Thanks. We get Kinsey out of this, I'm buying drinks."

"If you're still around," Zelinkski countered. "You boys are anticipating bullets. We believe Guzmán's cronies have planted a bomb."

Chapter Sixty-three

ON THE EAST SIDE of Santa Fe Drive, opposite the chaos taking place at the shopping center and near the river, Nate sat on the passenger's side of a van marked Ertha's Flowers. Next to the van, Sammy had parked Nate's Explorer. Then, entering the utility vehicle, Sammy joined SWAT members who sat on parallel benches facing each other, waiting for the go-ahead.

Santa Fe Drive was a major thoroughfare in Denver and the surrounding suburbs. It connected with I-25 and other arteries. Commuters loved to take this route during major traffic snarls.

Fortunately for commuters, and unlucky for cops, at 2400 the rush hour was long over. In between the blur of vehicles traveling north and south, Nate studied their quarry through binoculars.

A too-far distance and not an ideal location for cops, but the best they could manage given Rafa Lopez's threat to kill Kinsey if law enforcement showed a presence.

Sammy knelt on the floorboard with SWAT to finalize the operation. Nate and a team member would go in via the roof, while Sammy and the Nate look-alike would drive Nate's Explorer to the front of Truitt's as though they intended to follow through with Rafa's demands.

Already, police had enlisted the cooperation of the management of Oldenburg's Mattress Warehouse next door. From there, law enforcement would utilize Oldenburg's rooftop and extend an extension ladder to Truitt's. An easy enough plan, as long as the rescue attempt went unseen. A too-risky plan if Lobo's contact had missed an additional watcher.

Lobo and his partner had resumed their homeless personas and now stumbled alongside the Platte River, which ran behind Truitt's. The vice partners would come up the river route, searching for anyone standing guard. They also would perform another infrared scan of the building.

During times of stress, sweat was a regular occurrence. Tonight, the stench in the small occupied van was palpable. Nate lowered his window and stared at Lauren Masters's phone on the dash, emanating Kinsey's signal.

In any other case, this operation would already be deemed a success. With Rodrigo Guzmán in custody and substantial evidence against him, he might be persuaded to turn state's evidence and give up the names of the cartel. A lot of negotiation and protection guarantees stood behind the word *might*.

A case once so vital to Nate meant nothing anymore. Until he held Kinsey in his arms and begged her forgiveness for getting her into this god-awful mess, his focus could be on only one thing. Kinsey.

If he got her out—*when* he got her out—he'd make things right. He'd do what her father had told Nate to do in the first place. Stay the hell away from her—let Kins live out the life she was meant to live. Safe—without him.

His cell phone rang. Nate lowered his lenses. "Paxton," he said.

"Lobo here. Truitt's exterior is clean. Good thing Zelinski stumbled onto those texts. Makes sense why everybody scrammed. We got one heat image coming from the upstairs office."

"Kinsey," Nate said.

"Hope so, bro. Heat means she's alive. Here's the deal," Lobo continued. "Somebody's gotta be watching the place. Most likely over at Simply Pure. The owners lock up the pharmacy, but on Saturday night, the retail section stays open until two a.m."

Nate rolled his eyes. "Pot paraphernalia and tattoos. We're in the wrong business, Lobo."

"Got that right. Listen up. I may have caught us a break. Two weeks ago we got a lead that a cartel had bought a large shipment of C-4 explosives. That's the first thing I thought of when you told me about Zelinski and Guzmán's texts.

"We got nothing to go on but snitches," Lobo continued. "And at this late juncture, no time to x-ray the building. What do you think?"

Nate twisted to look over his shoulder into the rear of the van. "Sam, you ever see any signs that Guzmán dealt with explosives?"

Sammy shook his head. "Strictly drug deals. The bomb stuff's new and different."

Nate returned to the phone. "Gotta go with your gut, Lobo. In every situation I've been in with Guzmán, his people stand guard. That's why I think you're right. The building's loaded. Unless you're a suicide bomber and want to go out that way, C4 can be detonated away from the site. That's why there's only one person inside. Someone's waiting for Sam and me to make an appearance. Bad guy either has a detonator or makes a phone call to a cell phone left in the building." Acid churned in Nate's gut. "Once we walk through the doors, the business formerly known as Truitt's goes into orbit."

"Let's *hope* it's only Truitt's," Lobo said. "Got one more problem. I've been kicked out of Simply Pure. Get this. Manager said *I'm* bad for business. I'll head that way now and hope the dude has the night off."

"Thanks, Lobo. I'll let the team know what's happening. And do some hopin' they really do plan to blow the C4 with an off-site detonator. If they've hidden a timing device in the building, and it goes off before I get Kinsey out, she and I will never know the difference." A beep signaled Nate that he had an incoming call. "Watch your back." He waited for the new call to ring through and said, "Paxton."

"Nate. Montoya. I've come up with something. Before you say a word, hear me out."

At the conclusion of his boss's phone call, Nate jumped from the van. He put his hands on his knees and tried to control his breathing. When that didn't help, he tried kicking the tires.

Sammy, who'd left the van's side door by the time Nate attacked tire number two, listened while Nate recounted their lieutenant's whacked-out idea. "Well, can you think of something better? The guy's a pro, Nate. I say we run with this."

The entire unit gathered in the back of the van. Sammy laid out the new strategy. Five minutes later, Nate closed his eyes, and he nodded.

"Let's move," Sammy said.

Chapter Sixty-four

"WHAT DO YOU mean you've been inside Simply Pure?" Lauren demanded, glancing over her shoulder at her younger brother while pressing down on the Passat's gas pedal. "You need a prescription to go in that place."

Irene braced her hand against the vehicle's dashboard and tried not to look at the speedometer.

"Not to walk in the door. They have other stuff besides weed." Jay peered between the bucket seats. "Sweet, Lauren, you're going eighty."

Lauren lifted her gaze to the ceiling and eased up on the accelerator. "All right. Irene, let's go over this one more time."

"Gladly. All the lieutenant wants is for Jay to go into Simply Pure and get pictures of the people inside with your phone. Your specialty, Jay. They're looking for someone who seems distracted, someone who's more interested on the outside than what's going on inside."

"Someone who's watching Truitt's Classic Automotive," Jay added.

"Exactly," Irene said.

"Okay, but why don't the police just arrest this creep?" Lauren asked, merging onto Santa Fe Drive. "Wouldn't that be the safest thing to do? My brother's not smart enough to be afraid."

Jay actually grinned.

Irene ran her fingers through her hair then, lowering her hands, felt compelled to go against the lieutenant's advice. These two deserved to know the danger involved. "I need to tell you something. Jay, you cannot approach anyone in Simply Pure under any circumstances. The man the police are after may be carrying some type of detonating device. The lieutenant says it may look like a phone or a push button switch."

Lauren swerved and shouted, "Oh my God. Why would he do that?"

Irene swallowed hard. "Eyes on the road, *please*. It's a trap for the two detectives who want to get Kinsey out of there. Kinsey's captors plan to blow up the building."

"With Kins in it?" Jay croaked.

"And the detectives. But not if we can help it," Irene said, her throat threatening to close.

"This is all Nate's fault," Lauren raged. "If anything happens to my sister, I'll never forgive him."

Chapter Sixty-five

EARLY IN HIS CAREER, Nate had run in a Kevlar vest. Making his way behind a commercial strip to reach Oldenburg's, the mattress warehouse next to Truitt's, he wished he'd kept up the routine. Unlike the SWAT team member jogging beside him, Nate found running in night vision glasses and hauling around an extra seventy pounds of gear grueling. Guess he should count his blessings; some of the people with him tonight were rigged in all-out bomb gear.

Panting from the half-mile jaunt and sweating his ass off, the Platte River roaring in the background, Nate arrived at the rear of Oldenburg's in under twelve minutes.

Per their arrangement with Oldenburg's manager, the back door had been left unlocked, and the place appeared evacuated. Nate and his SWAT partner took the stairs, entered the attic, and made their way to the building's flat roof.

Nate shook his head. Oldenburg's manager deserved a commendation; a commercial extension ladder lay beside the store's ventilation units on the roof's graveled surface.

Nate spoke into a mic. "Team Leader One in position."

Sammy said, "Team Leader Two, waiting for your go-ahead."

Nate and his black-geared associate moved to the roof's edge and peered over a two-foot protective barrier. From this vantage point, they could look into a darkened bathroom window, a room adjacent to where they believed Kinsey was being held prisoner.

Closer now, Nate's heart threatened to pound out of his chest. A rooftop away from Kinsey. But with explosives in the building, he might as well have been in another galaxy. If it were just about him, he'd take the risk, enter through the bathroom. Still, Kins should have a say in this, and she might prefer caution.

"Team Leader Three, status," Nate said.

"All clear, Team Leader One," replied Lobo. "Heading to new objective."

Nate closed his eyes and tamped down his impatience. No watchers around the building. He *hoped* someone was controlling the detonator off-site. If Lobo couldn't get inside, it was up to Jay Masters. *Get us those pictures, Jay. Rigged building, cell phone, detonator, or something else? Tell us what we're up against.*

Nate returned his focus to the bathroom window. *Hang on, Kins, I'm coming.*

Chapter Sixty-six

"HERE GOES NOTHING." From the backseat of the Passat, Jay held up his phone and reached for the door handle.

"Be careful, Jay," Lauren said. "You're finding this all too exciting."

"I'm trying to help my sister," Jay retorted. "Sorry if I'm not going along with your usual quivering."

"Stop it, you two," Irene said, her maternal voice taking over. "In and out, Jay. No talking, just look around. If you can get pictures without raising suspicion, do it. If you can't, get back to this car."

Lauren switched off the ignition. "Irene, will you hand me my purse in the backseat?"

Irene grabbed Lauren's handbag and gave it to her. Lauren removed an unopened tube of lipstick and ripped through the protective plastic. She applied red to her lips and cheeks.

Irene folded her arms and tried to ignore the girl. Lauren hadn't struck Irene as overly concerned about her appearance. But, honestly, what a time to primp. She tried instead to focus inside Simply Pure and to follow Jay's movements, but already he'd disappeared within the store's aisles.

After the makeup session, Lauren started with the hair. Plumping the blonde tresses, she changed her conservative hairstyle to something a Playboy bunny might wear to impress Hugh Hefner. When she tugged off her shirt, Irene could no longer keep her mouth shut. "Lauren, honey, what are you doing?"

The girl, wearing nothing but a spaghetti strap tank top and jeans, said, "I do *not* quiver. Jay can't handle this by himself. He needs a distraction." Despite Irene's protests, Lauren stepped out of the car.

Irene blinked. What had just happened? What she wouldn't give for her gun. She opened the glove box and came up with nothing but a pen flashlight. Hardly a substitute. She texted the lieutenant. *Things out of control. At Simply Pure. Send help now.*

She almost tossed the light back into to the glove box, but at the last second, stuck it inside her pants pocket. Then, Irene grabbed Lauren's keys out of the ignition and went in after the fearless pair.

With the exception of the piped-in trance music, Simply Pure might have been an old-fashioned mom and pop shop. Truly eclectic, the store had bongs, pipes, and reefer wrappers, of course. But it also had candles, lamps, mood music, and machines for generating white noise. Magazines, cookbooks, and

213

literature about the breakthroughs in medical marijuana, the store also kept a supply of history books on the subject. Also, like any neighborhood grocery, the store had a collection of snacks and a refrigerated section for beverages.

At first glance, no more than five people occupied the store. On a second pass, Irene saw a few more studying the various items on the shelves. People as diverse as the store's contents—an older Asian couple, a middle-aged white man and his much younger arm piece, two African American women, and four Hispanic males. And if that didn't make the ensemble complete, a homeless man wandered the premises. The poor guy reeked of alcohol and seemed to stare longingly between the snacks and the cold drinks.

Irene couldn't help herself. She pulled a ten-dollar bill out and slipped it into his hand. He smiled, exposing dingy, rotten teeth. Shuddering, Irene walked off, hoping she hadn't made his problem worse.

Ambling down aisle after aisle, she turned often toward the front door. No one appeared to be watching Truitt's. *No one.* Could George have been wrong about what he suspected?

She got as far as the pharmacy portion of the business, an area barricaded by a metal cage, and released a breath when at last she saw Jay. Calmly holding the phone to his ear, he paused to make small talk with every person he passed. *So much for following instructions.* The kid could have worked here. At one point, he held up the white noise machine on display and touted its benefits to the Asian couple Irene had passed earlier. The couple actually picked up a boxed unit and sidled toward the cashier.

From the row over, Irene tried to make eye contact, but Jay had moved on. She rounded the corner where she ran straight into Lauren. Oh, for crying out loud. Kinsey's sister stood, a hand on her hip, flirting dangerously with the four Hispanic males.

What was she doing? These men with their bandanas, low-riding jeans, and tattoos on every visible part of their bodies devoured Lauren with their eyes. One with a large diamond in his left ear appeared to be the most intrigued. Displaying a lecherous smile, he grasped the tips of Lauren's hair and ran them between his fingers. The other three circled her from behind, their intent certainly not *Ring around the Rosie.* Then the fourth sauntered off toward the entrance studying his cell phone.

Prepared to put an end to this perverted business, Irene hesitated. Jay stood off to her right getting every shot. Oh geez, she was too old for this. Irene gulped painfully and followed the fourth man to see what she could see.

Chapter Sixty-seven

A LIFETIME ELAPSED before the first texts with Jay Masters's photos came through to Nate. In all actuality, ten minutes had passed. Still in position to get from Oldenburg's to Truitt's rooftop as soon as he had the all clear, Nate forwarded the texts to Sammy. Nate had worked as Guzmán's bodyguard. Sammy had been in the trenches with these goons. Nate could recognize them by face. Sammy could identify them by name.

The SWAT member kneeling beside Nate stared through the scope of a Remington bolt action precision rifle. Ready. A man trained to wait and good at his job.

Sammy texted back. *Gaspar, Marco, and Poke with Lauren. Rafa the man walking off.*

Nate spoke into his mic. "Team Leader Two, initiate second phase."

For the first time since he'd set foot on the roof, Nate took his gaze off the bathroom window. Any second now, Sammy and the cop acting in Nate's place, would drive Nate's Explorer past Simply Pure and into the front of Truitt's Classic Automotive.

Nate watched them drive into the lot slowly. Parked in a section that formerly housed luxury cars. Then, Sammy and Nate's stand-in climbed out and walked toward the building's glass doors.

Chapter Sixty-eight

AFRAID TO GET too near the man holding the phone, Irene picked up a magazine from a nearby rack. Rolling up an issue of *Cannabis Weekly*, she tapped it against her palm, pretending to be looking for something specific among the shelves.

The clerk at the cash register obviously wasn't the owner and had no problem with this. He hadn't moved from his spot since she'd entered. Or maybe he thought the anti-theft mirrors behind the counter and near the front entrance deterred shoplifters.

At least the mirrors allowed Irene to see other parts of the store. Even so, she had to get closer.

She ambled along the aisle, turned the far corner and came up several feet behind the lone Hispanic. He glanced over his shoulder and eyed her warily. But by this time, Irene had developed a fascination with the purple striped bongs.

Her subject stopped and faced Irene. Then, ignoring her completely, he returned his fascination to his phone.

She risked turning her head to study him fully. Watching his baggy-panted backside in the security mirror, she could also see he appeared to be watching a movie. It was then that she saw he carried an additional phone.

He strode into a different section. Irene followed. What kind of creep watches a movie after he kidnaps a woman? And then it occurred to her, maybe he was spying on Kinsey. Despite the risk, Irene trailed him down yet another aisle to stop short and almost let out an eek of surprise. Lauren was really putting on a show. Wrapped in the embrace of one of these losers, she stroked his face, while the other two looked on as if in a trance.

The man with two phones paused, said something to his people in Spanish, and they laughed.

That gave Irene an opportunity to inch closer, and with the advantage of height, she could see what was on his screen.

She swallowed a gasp. No wonder he hadn't stood by the door all night. He wasn't staring at Kinsey. Irene watched in horror as the phone's display showed Nate's Explorer pull into the lot. Nate and Sammy got out and approached the front doors.

The gang member moved on from Lauren's spectacle. He lowered the smart phone in his right hand and flipped open the device in his left. Light bulbs went off in Irene's brain. Once Sammy and Nate were inside that old dealership, Two Phones would detonate the bomb.

Out of time, she felt for the small-diameter flashlight in her pocket. She held her breath, took a couple of strides, and jabbed the poor excuse for a weapon into his back. "Call out to your friends," she murmured, "and it'll be the last sound you make. I'll take that phone."

He stiffened. "You a cop, bitch?"

Grinding her back teeth together, she said, "You wish. I'm the mother of the woman you've kidnapped, and I'm ready to kill you right here and now."

"Go away, Mommy," he said in thick accented Spanish. He shifted his thumb toward a button.

Irene pressed harder. "Know what a .38 feels like when delivered point-blank range to the kidney. I repeat, asshole. Give me that phone."

He hesitated, as though he might fight. And if he did, she was dead. Kinsey was dead. To her absolute shock, he reached over his left shoulder and handed her the phone.

Praying her bladder wouldn't release and spoil the effect, Irene took it and kept the flashlight in position. "Now you and I are going to walk out that door."

Their departure from Simply Pure never happened. Along with Jay, the homeless man she'd given money rounded the corner, an actual weapon raised. "Get your hands up, Rafa," he whispered and spoke into a phone. "Team Leader Three. All systems go. *Now.*"

The SWAT team invaded the store.

Chapter Sixty-nine

NATE'S PLAN TO enter through Truitt's window never happened. At 0130, Nate received the *all clear* signal. Rafa Lopez and his gang of cutthroats were under arrest, Lopez's phone detonator in police custody. Leaving his SWAT partner on his own, Nate scrambled from Oldenburg's rooftop to enter the jumbled confusion of police cars, emergency vehicles, and people milling about on the ground.

He didn't stick around to figure out what had gone right. Tunnel vision had him entering Truitt's abandoned warehouse. He sprinted past the heavily geared bomb squad techs on the first floor and took the stairs.

The office was locked. He kicked in the door. Sprawled on her stomach, Kinsey lay unmoving. He dropped beside her, pressed two fingers to her carotid artery, and pleaded with the universe.

Slow, slow, slow . . . too damn slow.

"Kins, baby, can you hear me?" He risked turning her over to face him. She stank of sweat and urine, and her breathing was raspy and shallow. He guided his fingers over the fresh track marks in her arm. A junkie look-alike— but alive. *Thank God, alive.*

Nate gathered her in his arms, pressed his face against her clammy, smooth cheek. Then, eyes welling, he carried her downstairs. The bomb techs scouring the ground floor looked up. Nate crossed the warehouse, in his arms the most precious cargo he'd ever hold. A tech near the Truitt's entrance rushed to open the door. And on the verge of collapsing in despair, Nate got her the hell away from this nightmare.

"Detective Paxton, over here," someone shouted.

The paramedics he'd met at the Foxglove crime scene rushed toward him. The sight of Randall and Martinez pushing a gurney in Nate's direction was too much. He'd seen what these lifesavers could do. Their presence added hope to his overburdened emotions and the dam in Nate broke. With tears streaming down his face, he said, "Help her."

Randall hefted Kinsey from Nate's trembling embrace. "You got it, man."

Spotlights and light bars had made the Denver parking lot as bright as a gloomy day. It matched Nate's mood. Uniformed officers had set up crime scene tape and formed a barricade. Too worried about Kins to form a rational sentence, Nate placed his ringing phone on vibrate and hovered outside the ambulance.

While Randall intubated Kinsey, Martinez hooked up an IV and spoke on a portable phone. Still, Kinsey had yet to move. Nate violated his own rules of noninterference and strode too near the rear of the vehicle. "Anything?"

From inside the ambulance Randall gritted his teeth. "Don't make me call a cop, Paxton. We're working in here."

Martinez never even looked Nate's way as she flicked a hypodermic syringe. "You be cool, man. We'll know when we know."

Randall's reprimand provided a shock-absorbing jolt to Nate's system. He stepped away. And, eventually, when Kinsey moaned, he'd never heard such a beautiful sound.

Randall shouted out from the rig. "Vitals are improving; she's coming around."

From that point, Nate backed off. Way off.

Randall jumped from the rear of the vehicle and slammed the double doors. "You know the drill. Gotta run. Don't forget you owe me a shirt."

"Shirt?" Nate released one of the most relieved sighs of his life. "One dozen Verducci's on their way."

"All right!" The paramedic rounded the ambulance.

As Randall, using lights and sirens, hauled ass from Truitt's, Nate grasped his knees. He breathed in and out several times until he thought he could function again. Then, he took out his phone to find Sammy.

Chapter Seventy

AT FOUR A.M. ON Sunday morning, Irene slipped out of Lundgren's ER. She hadn't had time to form an opinion about Griff Colburn—other than the fact the big guy sure was in love with himself and liked to talk. From everything he said to the throng of reporters outside Lundgren's Medical Center, one would think *he'd* single-handedly rescued Kinsey.

Even so, Irene smiled, and her heart swelled. From what she'd learned in these early morning hours, a gang polluting society with their toxic drugs, indoctrinating others, and performing unspeakable acts wouldn't do so again for a long, long time.

She'd stayed simply to get the doctor's evaluation of Kinsey's prognosis. He'd indicated she'd been shot up twice with an awful drug rearing its ugly head around junior highs and high schools. Black tar heroin made cartels rich and young people addicts. Bad enough for a junkie the doctor had said. For a young woman who'd never touched drugs, these injections could have caused respiratory failure and even death.

Following the doctor's pronouncement, an assistant DA, who'd aligned himself with Evan, had added attempted murder to the charges against the gang who'd kidnapped Kinsey.

Still, the gist of everything Irene heard was that Kinsey was enormously strong and healthy and would recover fully in less than a day or so.

Evan had even managed to say thank you to Irene. Never mind he murmured the words like he'd swallowed a bucket of horned frogs, but perhaps there was hope for Kinsey's father in the humanity department yet. She'd tolerate the man; he had wonderful children.

She strode toward her waiting cab, her plan to catch up with Kinsey tomorrow. In no mood to socialize, Irene was done here.

"Leaving the party so soon?"

In spite of her fatigue, hearing the lieutenant's voice elevated her spirits. He'd been so busy with Evan, the kids, the staff, the press, he'd barely acknowledged her earlier.

She paused to find him walking toward her with Sammy Lucero.

"Afraid so," she replied. "You folks in Colorado take excitement to a whole new level."

"You did good tonight, Mrs. Turner," Nate's partner said. "Didn't have a chance to thank you at the scene or in the ER. You got guts, lady."

"Thank you, Detective. And it's Irene, remember?" She released an exhausted sigh. "I don't know about guts. Personally, I find fear highly motivating."

Both men returned her smile.

"Is Nate okay?" With the sun yet to rise, Irene glanced around the hospital's dimly lit perimeter. "I didn't see him inside."

"He dropped by for a while to talk to the docs and the paramedics," the lieutenant explained.

"Awkward situation for Nate," Sammy added. "He and Kinsey have been friends a long time. He cares about her and feels responsible for what happened. He'll probably make himself scarce around her from here on out."

"Especially if Evan Masters has anything to say about it," the lieutenant growled. "I'm sure we haven't heard the last of him."

"Perhaps, instead of everyone assuming guilt and assigning blame, we should ask Kinsey how she feels," Irene said. Thinking of Kinsey on Griff Colburn's arm turned her stomach. Still, Irene figured she should take her own advice and remember Kinsey didn't need any interference from her. But she'd watched Nate's reaction at the High Line Canal when Kinsey went missing. Friendship had nothing to do with how he felt. That boy had love written all over him.

The lieutenant invaded her thoughts. "Thought you'd like to know Rafa Lopez, the man you relieved of the cell phone detonator, told his lawyer he knew you didn't have a gun."

"Oh, really?"

"Seems he'd been having second thoughts the whole time. You simply gave him the opportunity not to obey Guzmán's orders."

Sammy laughed. "Trust me, if that slimebag could have pushed that button, he would have done so. It's a matter of misguided honor with his type. He hated being taken down by a woman, that's all."

"I get that a lot," Irene said.

"Seriously, you, Lauren, and Jay Masters saved the day." The lieutenant shook his head. "These jokers hadn't a clue what they were fiddling with. Bomb squad said there was enough C4 in Truitt's to take out that building, Oldenburgs, *and* Simply Pure. We were very, very lucky, and the citizens of Denver are in your debt."

"Stop. You're making me blush." Her back and feet were killing her. She changed her stance and repositioned her handbag over a stiff shoulder. "I seem to have my days and nights mixed up around your fair city. I'm packing it in." She'd almost turned completely around when she hesitated. "About my case?"

"We're close, "Sammy said. "Any day now."

"Good. Assuming *close* has nothing to do with me, is there a problem if I return to Oklahoma in the next couple of days?"

The lieutenant lifted a brow. "You're no longer even a blip on our radar. You're free to go. Still, I thought you might stick around and get to know your daughter."

Irene smiled at what she thought might be a hidden message in his meaning. "I want that more than anything. But Kinsey needs to recuperate. She also needs a break from the pressure I've put her through since my arrival. She'll let me know if she wants to pursue a relationship. Besides, I have bills to pay and a decision to make about my house." Irene faced the crosswalk again and her waiting cab. "Goodnight, you two. I'll be in touch."

Chapter Seventy-one

AROUND NOON ON Monday, Kinsey opened her eyes, and they stayed open. For twelve hours, she'd been a victim of heroin-induced nodding, and although yesterday she'd been held for observation, she'd slept away most of the day. She turned her head. No dark, empty office surrounded her, and no slimy gang member walked in and out of the room to leer. Glorious sunlight streamed through the window revealing a crystal blue day. She lay in her own bed in her own beautiful house.

Overwhelmed by gratitude—and hunger—she threw back the covers and left her bedroom.

Asleep on her living room floor, Jay lay flat on his back, one of her sofa pillows supporting his head. Kinsey's heart squeezed. Her baby brother, her protector, had brought her home from the hospital last night and refused to leave her side.

She tiptoed around him.

"What's for breakfast?" he said through closed lids.

A grin spread over her face. "What would you like? I have cereal, peanut butter on toast, and apples."

"All of the above." Jay slowly climbed to his feet and followed her into the kitchen. "Here. Let me. You've been through hell."

A point she couldn't argue. The early Sunday morning hours screamed back at her. She'd awoken in the back of an ambulance to find paramedics working over her and one EMT yelling something at Nate.

Kinsey flattened her palms on her kitchen counter. *Nate.* He'd been there, and he'd been worried. His lieutenant had explained that Nate had carried her out of the building, but she couldn't recall that.

"Kins?"

She met her brother's wide-eyed gaze, and she hugged him. "I'm okay, Jay." And she was. Though drained, Kinsey felt almost normal.

Jay didn't exaggerate about eating her out of house and home. He prepared everything she had on her shelves and in her refrigerator. Devouring their meals, they sat on the floor at Kinsey's coffee table, legs crossed, their backs propped against her sofa.

Jay told Kinsey how he, Lauren, and Irene had spent Saturday night and part of the previous day. Explaining that the *Find My Friends* feature had assisted the cops, that Jay had *killed* Lauren at Backgammon, and finally about their invasion of a pot shop to bring down a gang.

In between being awestruck and wiping her tearing eyes, Kinsey put down her spoon. "You three are amazing. How on earth did you hook up with Irene?"

"Lauren thought you might be with her, so she called." Through a mouthful of toast, Jay added, "Irene's a good lady. If she doesn't go back to Oklahoma, I think we should keep her."

Kinsey laughed. "Why would she go back to Oklahoma? And does Lauren feel the same that *we should keep her?*"

"Yeah, she does. As for Oklahoma, Irene was chill during your abduction. But afterward, we could tell it took a lot out of her."

Kinsey stared at what was left of her apple core. "You're right. She always seems so . . . controlled. But I keep forgetting she lost her husband recently, and now this happened to me. I'll talk to her."

"Now all we need is to get Mom and Dad to accept her, and we're set."

Yeah, and Colorado might fall into the ocean.

Kinsey's frown deepened. Gwyneth Masters faced prison and the uphill battle of her life. A nuclear family ripped apart, the Masters weren't set by a long shot. But it was good to know that Kinsey had her brother and sister's approval as far as her birth mother, because no matter what her parents said, Kinsey planned to make Irene Turner a central part of her life.

"Thanks, Jay," Kinsey said.

The downstairs bell rang. Before Kinsey could blink, Jay was up and pressing the intercom.

"Floral delivery," came a disembodied voice though the speaker.

Jay glanced at Kinsey from over his shoulder. "Be right back." He returned carrying a vase filled with a dozen yellow roses.

She opened the card and read: *Kinsey, I can't tell you how sorry I am that I let this happen to you. Wishing you only great things and happiness in the future ~ Nate Paxton*

Kinsey reread the card and nearly tore it up in frustration. She stared out her sliding glass door, minus its window coverings, and pictured using the pathetic, obtuse, and stubborn Nate Paxton as a punching bag.

"Jay, where's my car?"

"Dad had it towed to the house."

"After I grab a shower, will you take me there? I have people to thank and a few heads to set straight."

Chapter Seventy-two

PANICKED OVER Kinsey's abduction, Nate thought the last two days were the worst days of his life. It turned out Monday wanted to compete. Due to the hostile reception he'd received in the ER from Kinsey's family, Lieutenant Montoya had ordered Nate to act as the silent partner for the remainder of the investigation.

At seventeen, he'd lost Evan Masters's approval, simply by not being good enough for his daughter. This time, he'd put Kinsey in harm's way. Now he was particularly *persona non grata*, and rightfully so. The Masters weren't the only ones furious at Nate. Every time he looked in the mirror, he'd see the face that had exposed her to unbelievable danger.

But if the lieutenant thought Nate having a less active role would slow the Masters's antagonism for the rest of the police department, he was wrong. Gwyneth was scheduled to be released that morning, and the moment she was wheeled out of the hospital, Sammy, accompanied by police officers, would be waiting to place her under arrest for kidnapping and conspiracy.

Nate had every intention of following his lieutenant's orders, but no way could he not apologize to Kinsey. He'd ordered a dozen yellow roses sent to her townhouse, when he'd preferred to send red. But red would send the wrong message. He was through pretending there could ever be something between them. Yellow meant friendship. Nothing could've been closer to the truth. No matter how she felt about him, he'd always remain her friend. Even now, thinking what might have happened to her, Nate's throat threatened to strangle him.

If he went looking for a positive in this situation worthy of nightmares, he'd never have to convince her they weren't right for each other again. After her drug-induced ordeal as Rafa's prisoner, she undoubtedly was over her fixation with Nate for good.

So, why did he feel emptier than the first time he walked away from her?

Nate did his best to shake off the doldrums and got back to work—just what he needed—documenting the events of last weekend. Based on Kinsey's kidnapping and the grave risk to the Denver population, it was not a prediction there would be lawsuits in the Denver Police Department's future, it was a guaranteed fact. Montoya wanted to be well ahead of the litigators when they subpoenaed his department records.

Nate also spent Monday morning at his desk conferring with his counterparts in the Oklahoma City Police Department and emailing PDFs of the substantial evidence they had against prominent citizens, Sabrina Mitchell and Lyle Wilkins.

In addition to Gwyneth Masters's eye-witness verification placing Sabrina as the midwife twenty-eight years previously, IT had provided its extensive digital footage of the deceased Stephen Turner leaving his wife's hotel room with the safe, the appearance and reappearance of the Blue Stars' sixth floor hallway, all of which appeared to be blocked out with the aid of a quad cane—matching one owned by Lyle Wilkins.

In a heralding case of efficiency, Forensics had also come through. Taking the glass from the Foxglove crime scene and comparing it to the glass Nate bagged into his condom foil, the analysis showed both sets of glass fragments to be of the same grade and consistency.

Finally, Nate used Monday to verify the dates that Sabrina and Lyle were in Denver. On Tuesday, April 16th, the day Turner was found murdered in Irene's Mercedes, each had arrived on separate flights via Denver International Airport. Both were in the Mile High city the next day when Gwyneth Masters was shot, and both left two days later—Lyle Wilkins by plane, Sabrina Mitchell, canceling her flight and driving the white Corolla she'd rented during her stay back to Oklahoma.

Nate suspected Mitchell chose that particular option because she'd been afraid to either get rid of the wig, the murder weapon, or both. To check the gun into her luggage during a flight would have led to her immediate arrest and discovery.

Nate drummed his fingers and studied the monitor. He and Sammy had built this case to the best of their ability. Now all they needed was for the Oklahoma City Police Department to agree that their evidence stood up.

His attempt to concentrate was slowed by an extraordinary case of déjà vu. Thirteen days earlier, the lieutenant had escorted a woman through Major Crimes. She'd looked a helluva lot like this one. But Lieutenant Montoya wasn't walking with Irene Turner, he was walking with Kinsey.

Nate rolled back his chair and grabbed his jacket, but a detective two desks over hollered, "Paxton, Lucero's on line three."

Nate clenched his jaw, rolled his chair forward, and picked up the phone. As Sammy's enthusiastic voice came over the line, he informed Nate that the arrest had been uneventful; that Gwyneth's new mouthpiece had more than earned his retainer; and that she'd made bail after an emergency arraignment, but not without the DA's insistence and the judge's concurrence that she be fitted with an ankle monitoring device.

Nate listened impatiently, never taking his eyes off the lieutenant's closed door. Then when it opened, and Montoya headed straight for Nate, the déjà vu came at him faster than a gangbanger's bullet. "Great, Sam, call you back." He hung up the phone.

Montoya slid into Sammy's vacant chair. "Use my office. She wants to talk to you."

Reluctantly, Nate rose from the chair. Swallowing hard, he told himself that whatever Kinsey had to say to him, he'd take it like a man. Aware he held every detective's attention in the division, he crossed the room.

He sucked in a breath, knocked once, and entered Montoya's office. And when he did, physical pain invaded his chest. Thanks to him, this woman had been kidnapped, drugged, and had come close to dying. And what was she doing? Meeting his gaze and smiling back at him.

He shut the door behind him. "Kinsey, I . . ."

"Thanks for the roses." She walked his way, fixing him with the beautiful brown eyes he'd fallen in love with and thought he might never see again. "Next time you send them, just so you know, I prefer red."

His uncooperative heart continued to hammer. "Kinsey, there won't be a next time. I'm surprised you're even speaking to me. Your family certainly understands what I put you through."

She tilted her head. "*You* kidnapped me and threw me into that van?"

"I might as well have. Don't you understand? Guzmán took you to punish me."

"Now, there you got me." She lifted an eyebrow. "Knowing you and Guzmán were enemies might have been helpful. But, no, Nate, I don't hold you responsible. How can I, when I owe you my life?"

"You owe Irene your life. *She* brought down Rafa Lopez."

"Semantics. I'm grateful to everyone who was at Truitt's on my behalf." Close enough to touch him now, Kinsey shocked him by raising a palm to his cheek. "Your note was so tragically pathetic. Why do you do this?"

He lowered her hand from his face but couldn't force himself to let go. "Why do I do what?"

"Cop out on me . . . on us."

"Kinsey." He squeezed his eyes closed. "There is no *us*. This isn't a high school crush where I'm worried you might give up your dream. We're talking about your life here. Rodrigo Guzmán and the sewer rats he employs are just a *few* of the bad guys I've put away—"

"My *dream*?"

Ah, hell. Nate let go of her hand. If he backed up any farther, he'd fall over Montoya's coffee table. He needed space from this woman who could see right through him. He maneuvered around her, stopped at the lieutenant's desk, and pivoted to face her. "The night I took you home from Sadie Hawkins, your dad met me outside. He already wasn't crazy that we'd been out on a date. But that was beside the point. He asked if I was really your friend."

"He didn't." Kinsey's hands balled into fists.

"Yeah, he did. But hear me out. He had his reasons. Stanford's head coach had called while you and I were away. He told your dad that out of all the recruits, they'd narrowed it down, and you were number one on their list."

Kinsey uncurled her fists, studied the floor, and raised her hands to her temples.

"Your dad said that night that you'd wanted to attend Stanford since you were a little girl."

Dropping her hands, she looked at Nate. "It was all I ever talked about."

His throat tightened. "Do you remember what *we* talked about that night?"

"As if it were yesterday."

"I'd finally got it through my head that you cared about me. You'd decided to attend college in-state so we could be together. When I took you home later, I wasn't thinking about college, I was trying to figure out what I could hock to buy you an engagement ring."

Tears in her eyes, she walked toward him. "I wanted to go to Stanford, but I wanted you more. If things would have worked out between us, I would have gladly stayed in Colorado."

"And given up what you'd wanted your whole life?" Nate's voice broke. "Don't be mad at your dad for telling me the truth. Every word he said got through to me. I *was* your friend, and we were too damn young. He wanted you to go as far as you could, and after I stopped feeling sorry for myself, I wanted that for you, too."

Kinsey blinked away tears. "That's why you gave me that unbelievable cold shoulder?"

Nate nodded. Averting his gaze didn't help. He'd hated hurting Kinsey. But maybe this time she'd finally understand.

"And you're doing it again?"

"What?"

"Turning all selfless and taking away my choices." Kinsey moved even closer, then seemed to reconsider and stopped. "If I know what I'm up against, Nate, I can face any opponent."

"This isn't a game—"

"I'm not talking about a game anymore, I'm talking about life. I may not like the risks you take, but you still choose to be a cop. For your information, I would *never* try to control you."

Nate couldn't speak. All he could picture was her drugged body in Truitt's, accompanied by the overwhelming fear that he'd lost her.

She dropped her hands at her side. "You have nothing to say to me?"

"If anything ever happened to you—"

Her entire body went rigid. "You just don't get it. *Nobody* makes my decisions. Not my father, my family, not Griff Colburn, and especially not you! If you can't accept me on my terms, then you're right. We have no future together."

"Kinsey, I'm sorry."

She grabbed her purse from the lieutenant's chair and strode to the door. Yanking it open, she turned in the doorway. "You know what, Nate? You'll never go for the gold. You're too big a coward."

Overcome, Nate stayed in his lieutenant's office for nearly five minutes.

He walked out into the division to twenty occupied desks and chairs, curious glances, and absolute silence. His boss stood across the room talking with a group of detectives.

Ready to blow this place, Nate grabbed his coat from his chair. But as he slipped it on, his desk phone rang. He all but growled his name as he answered, "Paxton," then slowly returned to his seat. His caller was the lead detective from the Oklahoma City Police Department.

Chapter Seventy-three

"HELLO?" HOPPING on one foot, Irene winced. She'd tripped over her suitcase to reach the hotel's guest phone on the nightstand and stubbed her toe.

"Mrs. Turner? Good afternoon, it's Claire at the front desk. Ms. Kinsey Masters is here to see you."

Irene glanced around her hotel room. After Sunday morning's episode at Truitt's and Simply Pure, she'd escaped the memory by sleeping in. Then, on Monday, she'd had to pack, and as a result, she'd foregone maid service. Hopefully, Kinsey wouldn't consider Irene too much of a slob. "Could you send her up, please?"

"My pleasure, miss," Claire replied.

Miss. Irene hung up, wondering if there was any way she could stow Claire away in her luggage.

Rather than try to repair the disaster of a room, Irene brushed her hair and added some color to her face. Turned out to be the wiser choice as an instant later Kinsey knocked on the door.

Smiling, Irene favored her toe as she opened it. "Hi, Kinsey."

"Hi, Irene."

Never had a hug felt so wonderful. Holding Kinsey in her outstretched arms, Irene studied her daughter from head to toe before releasing her. "Well, one look at you and you'd never know you'd been through such an . . . ordeal."

"The paramedics gave me a drug called naloxone," Kinsey said, walking farther into the room. She pressed a hand to her heart. "They said I'd be fine, and, thank God, they weren't lying."

"You're sure you're all right?" Irene said, closing the door.

"I'm still a little shaky, but the truth is I don't remember much of anything after the kidnapping. I was too out of it to be afraid. Hard to believe people do this to themselves on purpose."

"Frightening, isn't it? Please, excuse my mess."

Eying the open suitcase on the floor, Kinsey stepped over it. "So, it's true. Jay said you were leaving." She turned to face Irene. "May I ask why?"

"Sit down, Kinsey."

Much to Irene's embarrassment, Kinsey kicked off her flip flops and chose the middle of the unmade bed. In any event, her daughter appeared oblivious. She sat akimbo and gazed back at Irene expectantly. And to Irene's amazement with open admiration.

"I came to say thank you and to tell you you're the most amazing woman I've ever met."

Irene laughed. "Why? Because I conned a gang member and made him think your sister's penlight was a gun?"

"That, and because you made my brother and sister fall in love with you in less than twenty-four hours. With all the obstacles we're facing with my parents, I was planning on significantly longer."

Leaning against a dresser, Irene folded her arms. "It's easy to put differences aside when someone you love is in danger. Lauren and Jay helped me as much as I helped them." Irene couldn't contain her smile as she sat close to Kinsey on the bed. "You would have been so proud of them, Kinsey. Although I must say, they took a few years off my life."

"Jay thinks you're leaving because of everything you've been through. I'd hoped you'd stay for a while."

Irene smoothed a hand over the hotel's thick white comforter. "Jay's right in a way. The past two weeks, and especially this past weekend, have been hard. But I'm mainly leaving because you're fine, and I have personal matters to take care of."

"What kind of personal matters?"

"For one thing, my husband's body," Irene explained. "Apparently the Denver Medical Examiner's Office objects to his no-good corpse taking up their space. Not that I feel particularly obligated, but I suppose I should bury him."

"Oooh, I hadn't thought of that."

"Then I need to get home, pay some bills, and decide if I want to sell my house."

"It's a buyer's market in Denver." Kinsey grinned. "Just say the word—"

"That's definitely a possibility, but later." Irene rose from the bed and walked to the dresser where she'd lovingly rewrapped Danny's picture with Norma's bubble wrap packaging. "I hope you're up to hearing this, Kinsey. There's another reason this weekend was so hard for me."

Kinsey's gaze fell to the item in Irene's hands. "Trust me, Irene. I'm just beginning to find out how strong I am. What is it?"

She unwrapped Danny's portrait and rested it on the bed. Kinsey reached for the framed picture and drew it to her lap. Her voice cracked. "Who is he?"

"His name was Danny Turner. He's your half-brother and my son. He passed away when he was fifteen years old."

Kinsey traced her fingers over his image and a pose she'd no doubt made hundreds of times in her athletic career. In the portrait, Danny knelt on one knee, the other raised, a ball in front of him, smiling for the camera.

"He played soccer," Kinsey breathed.

"He did," Irene replied. "That's one of the reasons when Norma contacted me with the file containing information on you that I knew immediately you were my daughter. You look so much like him, and he loved soccer, too."

Kinsey's eyes flooded. "When did he die?"

"Two years ago in June. Doing what he loved. He was coming home from a soccer match, and his bus crashed."

Kinsey opened her arms to Irene who held onto her. "I would have given anything, and I mean anything, to have known him."

"And he would have adored you." Irene squeezed back and swallowed over the lump in her throat. "Losing a child is unbearable. And now that Stephen's no longer alive, I'm reluctant to give up my son's childhood home. But I am amenable to traveling back and forth, and I hope you'll come see me."

"I have three months off this summer. Try and stop me." Kinsey sat back and stared at Danny's likeness a while longer. "Remember earlier when I said you were amazing?"

Irene flushed and nodded.

"Multiply that by one thousand. I'm so grateful you came into my life."

"Oh, sweetheart, the feeling's mutual."

"When will you leave?"

"Tomorrow morning. So, as you can see, I have to pack."

"Think you could put it off long enough to have an early dinner with your daughter?"

"I'd love to."

DOWNSTAIRS IN THE hotel's Ships Tavern, she'd been talking with Irene for more than two hours—the fastest two hours of Kinsey's life. Irene Turner had a wicked sense of humor, and Kinsey could have listened to her charming Oklahoma drawl forever.

Irene assured Kinsey she wouldn't be alone when she went home. Irene had lifelong friends who had sustained her after Danny's death.

Nevertheless, Kinsey didn't want her to go. Kinsey wanted to know everything about her birth mother, and so far, she'd just touched the surface. Pushing away her dessert, Kinsey peeled away one more layer. "I understand you're a marksman."

"That's right."

"I think that's the one thing you and I will never have in common. I don't like guns. I never have."

"And I'll never try to influence you otherwise," Irene said. "But like soccer, trap shooting is a sport, and I promise those clay pigeons I decimate never feel a thing. I'll also make another thing perfectly clear. The night Rafa Lopez held a detonator in his hand, you'll never know how much I wanted a gun in mine."

"You did fine without one." Kinsey smiled.

"Tell that to my gray hairs," Irene said, smiling in return. "So, are we ever going to talk about the men in your life?"

Frowning, Kinsey sat back in the booth. "Sorry to disappoint you, but they're nonexistent."

"Really? The way Griff Colburn talked yesterday morning, I think he might argue the point."

"Griff's . . ." Kinsey tilted her head and seemed to search for words. "Griff. He'll always be number one in his life. I'm looking for someone who'll give me equal time."

Irene smiled and stared into her coffee cup.

"No comment?"

"You're twenty-eight years old. I already broke one promise by asking. How about I keep the second one and keep my advice to myself."

Kinsey wilted and pressed a hand to her heart. "Please, please advise me."

"About the nonexistent men in your life?"

"There's someone." Kinsey sighed. "And you've met him."

"Wouldn't be Detective Nate Paxton, would it?"

"I'm that obvious?"

"No. He is. I saw his reaction when he carried you out of Truitt's. Now nobody's ever accused me of being Einstein, but I can add two and two."

Kinsey placed her chin in her hand. "Your math is good. But he's still off limits, I'm afraid, at least as far as Nate's concerned." Kinsey related the details about their long-time relationship and their conversation inside the lieutenant's office.

Her elbows on the table, her hands clasped, Irene listened intently. "George actually gave up his office? That old softie."

"George?" Kinsey lifted an eyebrow.

"Lieutenant Montoya, I mean." Irene cleared her throat and stretched her hand across the table. Folding it over Kinsey's, she said, "You're a grown woman, and you've done fine without me up until this point, and you're more than capable of making your own decisions.

"I also believe Nate is wrong to be so overprotective. But know if I'd had my druthers, I'd choose a man who worried about my safety over one who tried to own me."

"I see your point. But how about I hold out for a man who does neither? Are you sure you want to leave?" Kinsey said wistfully.

Irene wasn't listening. Kinsey turned to see what or who had consumed her attention.

Lieutenant Montoya meandered their way.

"Ladies," he said upon reaching them. "Irene, I need a word. It's about your case."

"Kinsey and I have no secrets, Lieutenant. Won't you join us?"

He hesitated then slid into a booth beside Irene. "We believe we've uncovered your husband's accomplice at the Blue Star. We think it's Lyle Wilkins."

Irene gripped the handle of her coffee cup. "George, are you sure? It can't be Lyle."

At her mother's distress, Kinsey felt a knot of panic. "Irene? Are you all right?"

She nodded.

"We can't be *one-hundred percent* certain. But the evidence we have against him is daunting. It disturbed me that such a high-powered attorney would drop everything to do Norma Mitchell's bidding. He had to have more than a client's best interest at heart.

"We subpoenaed your husband's phone records. Wilkins and the deceased Stephen Turner spoke several times from April 14th, the day you left for Denver, until April 16th, the day your hotel room was broken into. Wilkins is Sabrina Mitchell's lawyer as well."

Astounded by this revelation, Kinsey couldn't keep silent. "And how does my . . . Gwyneth play into all this?"

"We wondered the same thing," the lieutenant said. "The moment Norma Mitchell gave Irene that file, we suspect her stepdaughter became intent on getting rid of any connections to the past. For reasons unknown for now, Wilkins agreed to help her.

"This investigation's not over, of course. But we found it impossible in the timeframe allotted for one person to travel to a shopping center across town, kill your husband, and return Stephen's SUV to the Blue Star. We believe one person rode with Stephen in your Mercedes, lured Stephen to the abandoned center, while the other lay in wait. He . . . or . . . she killed him and took the safe containing the file."

Kinsey blew out a breath. "All right. But how did either of these two know about my mother's house on Foxgrove when none of us did?"

"My detectives have been busy. Records show Sabrina rented a white Toyota Corolla. When we impounded Gwyneth Masters's Lexus, we found a bank parking stub two hours before she was shot. We interviewed the parking attendant on duty at that time. She remembers a white Corolla following Gwyneth out of the lot, and specifically that the driver had red hair."

"Pretty good memory," Irene said. "That was six days ago."

"You two are good at this," Montoya said. "The reason the witness re-members her so well is when Gwyneth drove away, the redhead in the Corolla became agitated. She tossed a twenty at the attendant and said, 'Keep it,' and sped after the Lexus."

"Wow, that's weird," Kinsey said.

"It gets weirder," he said. "That same day, after Gwyneth was rushed to the hospital, a homeowner came forward with a trashcan, claiming he'd seen someone in a white vehicle drop something inside. That something turned out to be a ski mask, which we later discovered contained red-haired fibers from a human wig."

"You've really done your homework." Irene wore a stricken look. "I can understand Sabrina's involvement, but Lyle? Poor Norma. This will destroy her. I've never seen a woman put so much faith in a man."

"If you'd stayed at the Blue Star and away from police scrutiny, quite frankly, I don't believe you'd be alive to be having this conversation. Lyle Wilkins played it brilliantly. He almost got away with it.

"Which brings me to my reason for coming this evening. You can't tell her, Irene. To do so, puts Mrs. Mitchell in mortal danger. I'd also like you to do one more thing for me."

"As long as it doesn't include sticking up a man with a detonator, I'm all ears."

"Detectives Paxton and Lucero are booking a flight to Oklahoma City later tonight. They'll be working with OK City police to garner confessions in an attempt to extradite the two suspects back to Colorado. I'd consider it a personal favor if you'd stay in Denver until that conclusion."

Kinsey hid a smile behind her hand.

"As nice as this place is, I've been looking forward to not living in a hotel."

"It's just for a little while, and you can forget about staying in a hotel." Kinsey reached for her hand. "You'll be staying with me, *Mom*."

Irene glanced between the two and gave each a wide grin. "In that case, Lieutenant, how can I refuse?"

Chapter Seventy-four

AS CARA CARMICHAEL passed the ball to a teammate playing forward, Kinsey smiled from the sidelines. Carmichael had apparently learned cooperation after all. Kinsey's team had willingly increased their practice sessions to make up for their coach's absence.

Three days had passed since the lieutenant visited her mother at the Brown Palace, and just this morning, Kinsey had put Irene on a plane for Oklahoma. Although Kinsey would miss Irene terribly, she loved the sensation of normalcy and being with her girls.

Kinsey cupped her hands over her mouth and hollered, "Nice pass, Carmichael."

The blonde grinned over at the sideline and ran after the ball.

Kinsey glanced up at the hill overlooking the soccer field. The boys were back, unfortunately. Still, she felt too darned good to shoo them away at present.

One lone figure stood out among the mix, and Kinsey's heart skipped. Nate, Sammy, and a group of Oklahoma detectives had made national news after taking into custody a prominent nonprofit administrator and her longtime attorney.

Unfortunately, Nate and Sammy hadn't been very successful in keeping a low profile during the breaking news. The networks were going wild over the story and enjoying the ratings. Kinsey suspected their undercover days were over.

As for Kinsey, she had no problem staying out of the limelight. She'd turned off the TV, had no comment when contacted by numerous media outlets, and certainly had no wish to relive her kidnapping in a made-for-TV movie.

She passed off her clipboard to her assistant and climbed the hill. The high school boys immediately scattered. But the solidly built man Kinsey had seen from the soccer field stood his ground. In his hand he carried a cellophane-wrapped bouquet of red roses.

Kinsey's heart swelled with every trudge up the incline. Taking the flowers, she walked into his embrace. "Now that's more like it. Are you all right?"

"I am now."

"What's with the red roses?"

He looked out toward the field, his expression grim. "Bad judgment, maybe?"

Sighing, Kinsey stepped back. "Don't blow this, Nate. Talk to me."

"All right." He blew out a breath, removed his mirrored sunglasses, and at last looked at her. "A woman I care about more than anything set the record straight about yellow.

"I've put you through hell and back, and still you wouldn't give up on me. You mentioned in my boss's office that you'd never ask me to quit being a cop. I'd always thought I was selfless, but when you said that, I realized you put me to shame." Nate held out his hands. "If you want me to quit, Kins, say the word. I'm through pushing you away, and I'll submit my resignation tomorrow."

Kinsey's eyes flooded, and she shook her head. The poor guy just didn't get it.

"There's one thing I can't change," he rambled on. "I do want to go for the gold, but I'll always want to protect you. It's who I am." Staring down at her, he swallowed hard.

"I'm sorry." She held the roses to her heart and swiped at a tear. "I can't agree to your terms."

Nate nodded and lowered his head.

She tilted her head to capture his gaze. "What would say to you keeping your job and our protecting each other?"

He all but slumped in relief. "I'd say you drive a hard bargain."

She couldn't contain her smile as she lowered the roses to her side and stepped into his embrace.

Holding her tight, Nate whispered against her temple. "I love you, Kinsey Masters—always have."

"*Finally.*" Kinsey's heart soaring, she raised her lips to meet his.

Epilogue

Oklahoma City

ON A SWELTERING, humid day in July, Irene assumed a position near Station number one. In her arms, she nestled her prized 12-gauge shotgun, and because she was feeling particularly ornery today, winked at the man beside her.

Webb Jenkins threw back his head and nearly split his big old gut laughing. "I suppose I had that coming, didn't I, little lady?"

Irene shook her head. "Good to see you, Webb."

"I see you brought your own cheering section," her old friend said. "Who'd you leave in Colorado?"

"I think one or two people stayed behind." Irene smiled. She adjusted her amber shooting glasses, and from over her shoulder, she waved to the crowd.

Kinsey, Nate, Lauren, and Norma Mitchell sat on the top row, the entire group waving and whistling, and, generally, causing a commotion.

Near the range operators, Irene located Jay. Along with a sophisticated-looking Nikon camera around his neck, he stood ready to capture the event.

What had really astonished Irene was that Lieutenant George Montoya had flown in for the event as well. Unlike the rowdy group on the top row of the bleachers, George appeared hesitant and out of his comfort zone. Arms crossed, he stood with other spectators on the sidelines.

"You know," Webb said, "When it comes to guts and overcoming challenges, there's not a woman I admire more. That's why it's so hard on me to have to beat you today."

"Why thank you, Webb," Irene returned his taunt. "But I have to ask. Don't you ever get tired of hauling around all that hot air?"

He smiled and repositioned his trap gun on his hip.

Irene made an elaborate gesture of covering her ears with her noise muffs. But already adrenaline had flooded her body. She'd been practicing on the range for this event for several weeks now. Many years ago, she'd picked up her husband's shotgun at the suggestion of a friend to ward off the empty hours. With each fire, she gained accuracy and became more confident. No way did she plan to lose to this good-natured blowhard again.

Suffer enough betrayal in your life and you become as skittish as a newborn colt. Yet, reunited with her daughter and people who loved her, she'd somehow found the courage to survive.

Irene snapped the gun to her shoulder and hollered, "Pull!"

Acknowledgements

I called upon so many people to help with BETRAYED, who without them, this book would never have been written. Rather than put them in alphabetical order, I tried to call upon my memory in a chapter by chapter scenario.

My thanks go to Ben Larson, Four-time Junior All American Team American Trap Association, (ATA), Carla Roth-Lindley and David Hartzell, Capt. Marcie Freund Walton, USAF, Sylvia Rochester, Keri Curnow, Orb Writer, Laura Hayden, Dr. Fred Collins, Melanie Jane Addison-Bell, R.N., Joe Collins, Annette Dashofy, Colleen Collins, Shaun Kaufman, Edward Gleason, Kris Oppermann Stern, and Debra Faulkner, tour guide and historian of the Brown Palace Hotel.

For the crime scenes in this book I depended hugely upon Wally Lind, Sr. Crime Scene Analyst/Police Officer (retired), Chief Wesley Harris, (retired), US Drug Enforcement Administration's Special Agent, RT Lawton (retired), and Col. Jimmie H. Butler, USAF (retired).

Last but not least, to my critique group, Rose Colored Ink, and my online mystery critique group, you made this book, and me, a better writer. To Lois Winston and Pat Van Wie, I can't thank you enough for working with me up until the book's final stages. And to my family, I couldn't do what I do without your support. To my husband Les, you've amazed me. Thanks for making the coffee every morning.

—*Donnell Ann Bell*

About Donnell Ann Bell

Donnell Ann Bell has put her first two novels on ebook bestseller lists, including her sophomore release, which hit #1 on Amazon Kindle's best sellers' list. *Betrayed* is her third novel. She lives with her family in Colorado. You can visit her website at www.donnellannbell.com.